GLENDA YOUNG

The Miner's Lass

HEADLINE

First published in 2021 by
HEADLINE PUBLISHING GROUP

First published in paperback in 2021 by
HEADLINE PUBLISHING GROUP

1

Cataloguing in Publication Data is available from the British Library

ISBN 978 1 4722 6860 0

Typeset in Stempel Garamond by Avon DataSet Ltd,
Arden Court, Alcester, Warwickshire

Printed and bound in Great Britain by Clays Ltd, Elcograf S.p.A.

Headline's policy is to use papers that are natural, renewable and
recyclable products and made from wood grown in well-managed
forests and other controlled sources. The logging and manufacturing
processes are expected to conform to the environmental
regulations of the country of origin.

HEADLINE PUBLISHING GROUP
An Hachette UK Company
Carmelite House
50 Victoria Embankment
London EC4Y 0DZ

www.headline.co.uk
www.hachette.co.uk

Hello there!

Thank you from the bottom of my heart for choosing my novel, *The Miner's Lass*.

I grew up in the northeast coalmining village of Ryhope, where the story is set, and I continue to love writing about the village close to my heart.

The Miner's Lass is set around the life of a young woman called Ruby Dinsdale, who is perhaps my most innocent heroine yet.

Ruby is from a mining family – her dad and brother are coalminers and there's danger to be faced in this book. It's fair to say that I don't give Ruby an easy time in this novel, but as with all of my heroines, she learns to become resilient and strong. There's also a lot of love between the Dinsdale family members, and I hope you will enjoy being drawn into the drama of their difficult lives.

Once again, I hope that I've done justice to Ryhope and its coalmining history in bringing this story alive.

Thank you again for choosing *The Miner's Lass* and I hope you really enjoy the book.

Glenda Young

Praise for Glenda Young:

'Real sagas with female characters right at the heart'
Jane Garvey, *Woman's Hour*

'The feel of the story is totally authentic . . . Her heroine
in the grand Cookson tradition . . . Inspirationally delightful'
Peterborough Evening Telegraph

'In the world of historical saga writers, there's a brand new
voice – welcome, Glenda Young, who brings a freshness
to the genre' *My Weekly*

'Will resonate with saga readers everywhere . . .
a wonderful, uplifting story' Nancy Revell

'I really enjoyed . . . It's well researched and well written and
I found myself caring about her characters' Rosie Goodwin

'Glenda has an exceptionally keen eye for domestic detail
which brings this local community to vivid, colourful life and
Meg is a likeable, loving heroine for whom the reader roots
from start to finish' Jenny Holmes

'I found it difficult to believe that this was a debut novel, as
"brilliant" was the word in my mind when I reached the end.
I enjoyed it enormously, being totally absorbed from the first page.
I found it extremely well written, and having always loved sagas,
one of the best I've read' Margaret Kaine

'All the ingredients for a perfect saga' Emma Hornby

'Her descriptions of both character and setting are wonderful . . .
there is a warmth and humour in bucket loads' *Frost Magazine*

'A gripping saga' *People's Friend*

By Glenda Young

Saga Novels
Belle of the Back Streets
The Tuppenny Child
Pearl of Pit Lane
The Girl with the Scarlet Ribbon
The Paper Mill Girl
The Miner's Lass

Helen Dexter Cosy Crime Mysteries
Murder at the Seaview Hotel
Curtain Call at the Seaview Hotel

For Mam and Dad

Acknowledgements

My thanks go to my friend Paul Lanagan for sharing resources to help research this book; Sharon Vincent for her knowledge of women's social history in Sunderland; David Powell, archive manager at D. C. Thomson Ltd, for information on *The Red Letter* magazine; my cousin Sonia Martin-Reed for her knowledge of the history of the Queen's Head pub; Ryhope Heritage Society; Tony Kerr; Beverley Ann Hopper; John Wilson and staff at Fulwell Post Office; Hayley and the team at Sunderland Waterstones; Dr Rob Shepherd for information on Ryhope asylum and the Toll Bar hotel; Sunderland Antiquarian Society for research on the Blood Pit. To my editor, Kate Byrne, at Headline for her patience and expert guidance; and to my agent, Caroline Sheldon, for helping to bring magic alive. And to Barry, for the love, support and endless cups of tea when I lock myself away to write.

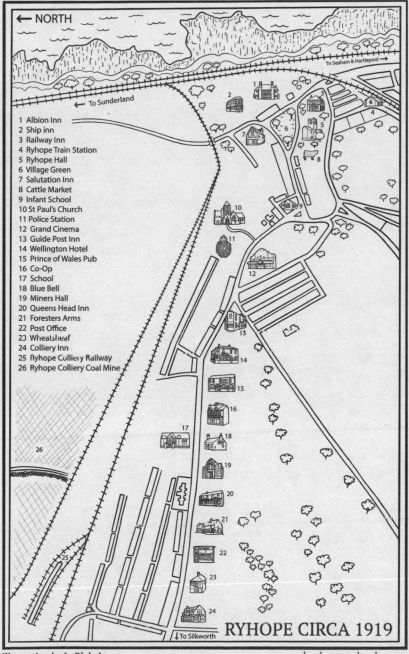

← NORTH

To Seaham & Hartlepool →

To Sunderland

1 Albion Inn
2 Ship inn
3 Railway Inn
4 Ryhope Train Station
5 Ryhope Hall
6 Village Green
7 Salutation Inn
8 Cattle Market
9 Infant School
10 St Paul's Church
11 Police Station
12 Grand Cinema
13 Guide Post Inn
14 Wellington Hotel
15 Prince of Wales Pub
16 Co-Op
17 School
18 Blue Bell
19 Miners Hall
20 Queens Head Inn
21 Foresters Arms
22 Post Office
23 Wheatsheaf
24 Colliery Inn
25 Ryhope Colliery Railway
26 Ryhope Colliery Coal Mine

↓ To Silkworth

RYHOPE CIRCA 1919

Illustration by Jo Blakeley

www.glendayoungbooks.com

Chapter One

July 1919

Ruby ran her finger down the Jobs Vacant column in the *Sunderland Echo*. 'What about this one, Mam? It says "Girl wanted for housework. Must have good character."'

'Where's it at?' Mary replied.

'One of the big houses in the village,' Ruby said excitedly. Her voice sank as she read on. 'But I'm not old enough. It says girls who apply should be aged at least eighteen.'

'You will be in three months,' Mary said.

'But you haven't got a good character,' Michael piped up.

Ruby ignored her brother's taunt and carried on with her search. Michael returned to the adventure comic he was reading, and it caught Mary's eye.

'Where did you get the money to buy that?' she asked.

Michael pulled the comic up to shield himself from his mam's question.

'Michael?' Mary demanded. 'If I find out you've been

wasting money when we barely have enough to buy food, I'll give you what for.'

'I got it off Bobby at work. He gives it to me once he's read it.'

Mary knew she shouldn't deny her bairns pleasure, even if it was just a comic, but the truth was that her family needed every penny they could get.

'Here's a good one, Mam,' Ruby said. ' "General serving girl wanted. Cleaning and cooking for small family. Wages eight pounds per week." '

'Eight pounds a week?' Mary cried. 'Why, that's a small fortune!'

Ruby held the paper up and Mary peered at the ad.

'The job's at Ryhope Hall,' she read. 'But there's a problem, as you know only too well. Cooking, Ruby? The amount of times I've tried to teach you to cook and bake, you should be able to do it by now.'

Nothing Ruby cooked came out right, no matter how hard she tried. She might have inherited her mam's fair skin and bright eyes, but she'd missed out on her ability in the kitchen. Even under Mary's expert guidance, when Ruby baked bread it came out of the oven unrisen. Her pastry was too hard and she didn't think her mam would ever forgive her when she boiled a pan of potatoes dry.

'She's bloody useless, our Ruby,' Michael quipped.

'We'll have less of your swearing, thank you very much,' Mary said. She whipped a cloth from the kitchen table and flicked it towards Michael's head.

'Ow!' he yelled.

'What are you shouting for? It never touched you.'

Michael put his hand to his brow and swooned in an

2

overly theatrical fashion. 'I'm dying, Mam. You've killed me!'

'You daft lump. I will flamin' kill you if you don't get off your backside and go and fetch water for your dad's bath. He'll be home from the pit soon. And bring the bath in from the yard.'

Michael's bottom lip shot out. 'It's not my turn to fetch the water, it's our Ruby's. I did it at dinner time. Ah, Mam, it's my day off today. I shouldn't have to do her work for her on my day off. It's not fair.'

'Our Ruby's busy looking for a job.'

'She shouldn't have got herself sacked from the Albion Inn.'

'It wasn't my fault,' Ruby said defensively.

'You gave the customer the wrong change, Ruby. Whose fault was it?'

'For a little lad, you've got a big mouth.'

Michael puffed out his chest. 'I might be little, but at least I've got a job, working on the pit top. And when I turn fourteen in November, I'll be earning even more underground.'

'Michael, there's no need for that kind of talk yet,' Mary said sternly. She dreaded the day when her son would join her husband hewing coal. It was dangerous, heavy work.

'At least me and Dad are bringing money in,' Michael said. 'We're not skiving like our Ruby.'

'She's never skived in her life, Michael. Don't say that about your sister. None of us Dinsdales could ever be accused of skiving. And she didn't give the customer the wrong change, so don't go blaming her, you hear?'

'It was the barmaid's dilemma,' Ruby said.

'Which barmaid?' Michael asked.

She shook her head. 'It's not a person. It's what they call the old four-shilling coin. A fella in the Albion Inn passed it off as five shillings. It's hard to tell the difference between the two coins, and because I was new in the job, I didn't know. So I gave him change from five shillings instead of four, and Jack Burdon sacked me when he found the coin in the till at the end of the day.'

'He's a hard fella, that Jack,' Mary tutted.

'Hetty, his wife, defended me. Said she'd fallen for the trick herself years ago. But Jack wouldn't budge and I was out on my ear.'

'And now you have to find yourself another job. Get your nose stuck back in those ads, Ruby. Michael? What you waiting for, son? The bath's not going to bring itself in.'

Michael did as he was told while Ruby returned her attention to the paper. Surely there must be a suitable job? As she read the ads, her bobbed brown hair fell over her face and she pushed it back behind her ears.

'"House parlourmaid wanted, second week of July only",' she read.

Mary raised her eyebrows. 'Just one week's work? Keep on looking and we'll come back to that one if you can't find anything else.'

'"Nursemaid wanted immediately to care for two children. Must have experience."'

Mary shook her head. 'No, lass. There are some things we know you've got experience in, like cleaning and washing and sewing. But looking after bairns? No. I can't let you pretend you know how to do that, it'd be wrong. You've never done that sort of work. What else is there?'

'"Strong, useful girl wanted for bar work. Apply the Queen's Head, Ryhope."'

Just then the tin bath appeared, with Michael walking behind it. He set it down on the kitchen floor in front of the roaring coal fire, for although it was a warm summer day, the fire was lit, as always. It was the heart of the Dinsdales' small cottage in Tunstall Street. The kitchen was where the family spent most of their time. The room was small, filled with sticks of furniture: a rickety table with four chairs, and a battered old sideboard. Home-made rugs covered the floor. Upstairs were two bedrooms, one large one for Mary and Arthur and a smaller one that Ruby and Michael shared. Keeping them all safe, fed and warm was the coal fire. They depended on it wholly. One of Ruby's many chores was to black-lead and clean the grate, while Michael's was to bring in buckets of coal and keep the fire stoked. Mary made bread dough that rose on the hearth, and she and Ruby hung clothes to dry there on washing day if it was raining outside. Arthur liked to sit by the fire on an evening smoking his pipe with his feet on the fender, while Mary sat opposite sewing or knitting.

'Strong and useful? Our Ruby?' Michael laughed.

'Michael, stop teasing your sister,' Mary said. 'Ruby, carry on reading the ad. It sounds perfect so far.'

Ruby shrugged. 'That's all it says.'

'No mention of the wages they're paying?'

Ruby shook her head.

'Nothing about the hours or days of the week you're to work?'

Ruby glanced again at the ad in case she'd missed something. 'No,' she said.

'Well then, you'd best get yourself up to the Queen's Head before any other strong and useful lasses in Ryhope get there before you.'

Ruby leapt to her feet. 'What'll I wear, Mam?'

'You're asking as if you've got a choice,' Mary laughed. 'Ever the optimist, our Ruby. Come here, turn around. Let's have a look at you.'

Ruby stood in front of her mother, ready to be inspected. Mary looked deep into her eyes, seeing the girl she'd once been reflected in her daughter's open face. Mary's own face was lined now and her body thin; she was barely more than skin and bone and her clothes hung from her limbs. She'd not been feeling too good lately. It was too early yet to talk to Ruby and Michael about what she feared was wrong. Besides, she wouldn't breathe a word to anyone until she'd spoken to Arthur, and she planned to tell him when he came home from work. A shiver ran down her back.

'You all right, Mam?' Ruby asked.

'Think a ghost walked over my grave.' Mary smiled as she pulled herself together. 'Before you go, brush your hair and wash your face, and wear your grandma's brooch for luck. When you get there, stand up straight and smile, don't speak until you're spoken to, and if they ask where you've worked before, tell them you worked for Hetty at the Albion Inn.'

'I'll not mention Jack,' Ruby said.

'Best not to, love. If the Queen's Head need a character reference for you, tell them to ask Hetty. And whatever you do, don't tell them about the carry-on with that coin, the barmaid's wotsit.'

'Dilemma.'

'Well, whatever it was called, keep your mouth shu and don't be cheeky.'

'I'm never cheeky, Mam,' Ruby said. 'You're getting me confused with our Michael.'

Mary put her hands on her daughter's shoulders. 'Now listen, there'll probably be a lot of cleaning to do, not just serving at the bar. And if they're asking for a strong lass, there'll be beer barrels need moving. Tell whoever you talk to there that no task is too tough. You're a Dinsdale lass, after all.'

Ruby pulled a brush through her hair, then ran up to the bedroom she and Michael shared. Under her bed was a cardboard box where she kept her special things. There wasn't much in it. Just a couple of hairpins, a length of scarlet ribbon, and her precious copy of *The Red Letter* magazine. She'd found the magazine months ago lying on the colliery bank where someone had dropped it. It was full of fiction, love stories that gave her an insight into the adult world she was on the brink of. Under the magazine was her grandma's brooch. It was worthless to anyone but Ruby. Just a tiny piece of red sea glass wrapped with a twist of metal that Mary's dad had turned into a brooch for his wife. And when she died, it was passed to Ruby.

Once she'd pinned the brooch on, she headed into the yard to wash her face at the tap. Michael followed with the bucket in his hand, ready to fill it for their dad's bath.

'Good luck, Ruby,' he said. 'Knock 'em dead at the Queen's Head.'

'Oh, you're a poet now, are you?' Ruby laughed.

'Seriously, I hope you get it. That job's got your name all over it.'

'Just because I'm useful and strong?' she said.

7

ise you're pretty. The older lads at work
going in pubs. They say they like a good-
maid – it's the only reason some of them

Ruby looked at her brother, at his brown eyes and
cheeky grin. They could fight like cat and dog some days,
but she knew she wouldn't trade him for the world.

'Keep your eyes peeled, onion face!' she called. It was
their standard parting shot to each other, to which Michael
replied as he'd done since they were small.

'If I see you first, you're the worst!'

Ruby walked along the back lane of Tunstall Street. The
ground was uneven and rutted with mud. The cottages
squashed in rows had been built by the Ryhope Coal
Company for the families of miners who worked at the
pit. They were lime-washed dwellings, with small upstairs
windows looking out to the lane. On Mondays, washing
day, clothes were strung across the lane from each yard.
Dresses and shirts blew in the wind and dried in the
sunshine. Bloomers and drawers were hung up to dry
for everyone to see and pass comment on. The men's
pit clothes – their trousers and shirts, jackets and waist-
coats – had the coal dust beaten from them before being
scrubbed and pegged up. But today the back lane was
empty, for washing day was still a few days away.

Ruby was keen to reach the Queen's Head quickly,
bearing in mind her mam's words that another lass might
be on her way to apply. She walked as fast as she could,
all the while remembering to smile and not speak until she
was spoken to and all the other things her mam had told
her to do. She kept her head down, watching where she

put her feet on the uneven ground, avoiding the horse muck from the carts that used the back lane for deliveries. There was the Co-op grocery man with his horse, Meg the rag-and-bone girl with hers, the fish man, the meat man, the man who brought the eggs . . . They all used the back lane to deliver to the miners' wives.

'Where you off to, lass?' a man's voice called.

Ruby looked up and a smile spread wide when she saw her dad walking towards her. She recognised the stooped way he walked, as if he was carrying the woes of the world. He looked crumpled, small, as he always did when he came home from work. After he'd had his bath and his tea, though, he relaxed a little, uncurled, seemed to grow back into the strong, dependable dad she loved with all her heart. Every exposed inch of his skin was black. His eyes, ears and nose were thick with coal dust. His whole face and his hands were covered. No matter how much he bathed, or how much her mam scrubbed him clean after a hard day at work, coal remained etched in his skin. He smiled at Ruby and the lines around his blue eyes creased greasy and black.

'There's a job going at the Queen's Head, Dad.'

'Good luck. And if I were you, I'd keep quiet about that coin, the barmaid's problem.'

'Dilemma,' Ruby laughed. 'I know, Dad, I'll try not to mention it.'

And with that, Arthur headed home, exhausted after working a long shift in a waterlogged seam of coal, while Ruby turned the corner and headed across Ryhope Street, towards the Queen's Head.

Chapter Two

The Queen's Head wasn't the biggest pub in Ryhope, nor the grandest. It was a two-storey building situated on the gentle slope of the colliery bank, easy to miss if you didn't know it was there, as it was tucked into a terrace of shops. Mining was thirsty work, and with over two thousand men and boys working at the pit, Ryhope pubs did a roaring trade.

The entrance sat between bay windows, two on either side. A dark open passageway separated the pub from its neighbour and was where horses were led to stables at the back. The upstairs had four plain windows above the downstairs bays. Ruby saw curtains hanging and wondered who lived up there. Well, there was only one way to find out. She waited for one of the store's delivery carts to trundle by, and as it did so, she recognised the driver.

'Bert!' she called.

Bert Collins was an old friend of her dad's, a good-looking man with dark hair and a chiselled chin, a winning smile and muscled arms. He was a good man, a nice man, everyone said so. He was also something of an enigma. He was one of the oldest unmarried men in Ryhope, still a bachelor although he was in his mid forties. It was an age by which most men were married and settled down, but not Bert. He'd somehow managed to avoid falling into wedlock, though many local single women were attracted by his good looks and the polite way he had about him.

'Morning, Ruby! You all right, pet? How's your dad?'

But before Ruby could reply, Bert and his big black horse Lucky Star had already moved on. Across the road, Ruby caught sight of Elsie Hutton, one of two spinster sisters who had lived together since their parents passed away. Rumours flew around Ryhope that the women were worth a small fortune from money left to them by their father, who'd been a manager at the coal pit. Whatever the truth of the matter, they obviously had enough to live on comfortably, with no need for either to go out to work. They were often hard to tell apart, as they both had thick hair that was as black as coal and they always dressed in black. They both walked with a slight stoop, and if anyone saw them together, they were reminded of two crows pecking back and forth.

The two women were regular visitors to the Dinsdales' house, and Elsie was Mary's best friend. Ruby enjoyed listening in to their conversations when she got the chance. There was always a mischievous glint in Elsie's eyes and a pink flush to her round, pretty face. Ruby guessed that she was in her late thirties, with her sister, Ann, a few years older. Ann always looked the more stern of the two, her lips pursed and her eyes darting from side to side in case she missed anything that might be going on.

Ruby waved to Elsie, but the woman's mind was

elsewhere, watching Bert Collins pass by. And was Ruby mistaken, or did Bert just blow Elsie a kiss? In broad daylight, too!

Ruby crossed the road, straightened her back and knocked hard at the door of the pub. Then she took a step back, stuck a smile on her face, as her mam had told her to do, and touched her sea-glass brooch for luck. She knocked again, harder this time. Still nothing, so she knocked a third time, this time so hard her knuckles hurt. She waited. She smiled wider, so wide that her face started aching. 'Come on, you lazy lot, open up,' she muttered. As she glared up at the windows, her smile finally slipped from her face. And that was when the pub door was flung open.

'Oh!' she cried.

In front of her was a man not much older than her dad. He wore a dark shirt buttoned to his neck with an even darker waistcoat on top. A pipe hung from one side of his mouth. He was clean-shaven, with a long, thin, pale face. His shirtsleeves were rolled to his elbows. He looked friendly enough, but still Ruby's heart jumped in her chest.

'Aye? What?' The man's pipe jiggled in his mouth as he spoke. Ruby was transfixed by it; she was waiting for it to fall, yet it just seemed to hang from his lip. She quickly found her smile, and remembered her mam's instructions.

'I've come about the job.'

The man eyed her keenly. 'Aye?' he said, and again the pipe wobbled. He made no attempt to take it from his mouth.

'The job for a strong, useful girl that was in the

Sunderland Echo,' Ruby continued. She pushed her feet forwards in her worn, tattered boots. 'That's me. I'm just like it said in the paper.'

'You'd best come in and talk to the wife. It's her pub.'

This time the man took the pipe out of his mouth and used it to point upwards, to the name above the door. Ruby looked up and read: *Licence Holder: Dorothy Hutchinson.*

She followed him into a passageway that split into two. On the right it led to a snug, a small, cosy room, and to the left was a larger bar.

'Sit in the bar, I'll fetch her,' he said.

It was the smell that hit Ruby first. The stench of beer and tobacco that was soaked into the soul of the place. She looked around the room but wasn't too keen on what she saw. The pub didn't have the friendly feel of the Albion Inn, where she'd worked last. The tables and chairs had seen much better days, and the paintwork on the walls and woodwork was chipped. But the place was clean, she'd give it that. She sat in silence, taking it all in. She recognised familiar brand names on the bottles behind the bar and saw pumps from local breweries Vaux and Castle Eden. They'd had the same ones at the Albion Inn. The bar till didn't look too different from the one she'd used at the Albion either. The familiarity of it all eased her mind and calmed her racing heart.

'Come about the job, have you?' a woman's voice barked.

Ruby leapt from her seat. Her mam's voice roared in her head. *Smile! Smile!* She tried, she really did, but she was so terrified that she ended up grimacing. The stout woman in front of her had a generous bosom that strained against a white blouse. Her long brown hair was swept up in a bun at the back of her head, and wisps fell around her plump face. A pair of deep brown eyes glared at Ruby.

'Cat got your tongue?'

Ruby shook her head as the woman continued.

'I'm Polly Hutchinson. I run this place with my husband Jim and son Stan. I understand you've just met Jim. He says you saw the ad in the paper, is that right? You can read?'

Ruby swallowed hard. 'Yes,' she said.

'Yes what?'

'Yes . . .' She paused. 'Mrs Hutchinson.'

'Call me Polly, everyone does.'

Ruby saw the tiniest smile flicker on the woman's face. The name above the pub door had been Dorothy, and Ruby was heartened to be given permission to use the landlady's less formal name. The mention of Polly's son Stan rang bells in the back of her mind, which disappeared as Polly gestured for her to sit down then sank into a battered wooden chair opposite. Ruby sat with her hands in her lap, feet firmly on the floor.

'Worked in a pub before?' Polly demanded.

'At the Albion.'

'With Jack and Hetty?'

'I worked with Hetty mainly,' Ruby said with as much authority as she could muster. 'She said you can ask her for a character reference if you need one.' She hoped the conversation wouldn't turn to why she'd left. But she knew that in a village as tight-knit as Ryhope, where gossip was rife, it could hardly remain a secret.

'Why aren't you working there now?' Polly asked.

Silence.

'Come on, spit it out. You know what Ryhope's like. If you don't tell me, all I have to do is go out there and find someone who will.'

'I was sacked, but it wasn't my fault,' Ruby said quickly.

'Then whose fault was it?'

She locked eyes with Polly. There was no point in being anything but honest. If Polly didn't like what she heard, then so be it. There must be other jobs Ruby could find in the paper. Well, as long as they didn't involve cooking.

'I was sacked over a barmaid's dilemma.'

Polly slapped her thigh, then rocked her head back and let out a loud and raucous yell. 'You daft bugger,' she said when she'd calmed down. 'You didn't fall for that old trick, did you? I can't believe it's still being passed around. I thought they'd all gone out of circulation. Well I never. And you, little Miss . . .' She stared at Ruby. 'What did you say your name was?'

Ruby knew she hadn't been asked her name, but she also knew now was not the time to mention that. From Polly's manner so far, it struck Ruby that the landlady of the Queen's Head was a woman not to be messed with.

'Ruby Dinsdale.'

'Well, little Miss Ruby. If I take you on here, you won't fall for that trick again, will you?'

'I swear I'll check every coin I get given. Twice.'

Polly sank back in her chair and eyed her keenly. Ruby knew she was being appraised. What she did or said in the next few minutes would determine whether she was given the job. She stayed still and quiet, but under her cotton dress her heart was going nineteen to the dozen.

'So you've got experience working in a pub, we've ascertained that,' Polly said. 'And there'll be cleaning to do, heavy lifting; that's why I need someone strong.'

'I'm strong,' Ruby said. 'And I can clean. I can do anything that's needed.'

'Can you cook?'

Her heart skipped a beat.

'Course you can cook, every lass can,' Polly said without waiting for a reply.

Ruby bit her tongue. She hadn't had to lie. But just to be safe, she crossed her fingers to ward off bad luck.

Polly folded her arms. 'It's rough, this pub,' she said sternly. 'It's got a bit of a reputation. You need to know that if you're to work here. When a fight breaks out, my husband and son will see to it. You don't get involved; stay out of it and you won't get hurt. Does that scare you?'

'No,' Ruby said defiantly.

And the truth was, she wasn't scared. She'd seen fights in the Albion Inn, men going at each other after too much ale. She'd kept out of the way there and she'd do the same in her new job. She knew her place was to serve beer and do what was needed behind the scenes. At the first sign of a fight she'd slip away to a snug or the yard and leave the pub hosts to sort things out.

'Good,' Polly said. 'Because we've got the Peace Parade next week and it'll be all hands to the pumps. We're open all day from early morning until we run out of beer.'

Like everyone else in Ryhope, Ruby had been looking forward to the Peace Parade. And now here she was being given a role at the heart of the celebrations. She couldn't have been happier. She locked eyes with Polly and straightened in her chair.

'You're a bonny lass, Ruby,' Polly said. 'The fellas we get in here are going to like that. A pretty face behind the bar could see our takings rocket. A good barmaid is an asset to a pub.' She stuck her hand out. 'I'll speak to Hetty about your character. All being well, can you start tomorrow night?'

'Yes,' said Ruby.

The two women shook hands.

'Then welcome to the Queen's Head.'

Chapter Three

Ruby returned home with a spring in her step and a warm glow in her heart. As she walked, she hummed a tune she remembered from school. She couldn't wait to tell her mam about her new job. She knew the money she'd bring in was much needed for food, for the pantry shelves were bare. She hoped her news would cheer her mam up; she'd seemed distant lately, as if she had something on her mind that she couldn't find the words to express.

Ruby knew how much her parents worried about paying the bills. Money had always been tight in the Dinsdale house, but recently things seemed to have been getting worse. She had watched them on an evening totting up figures in a notepad, trying to figure out how to make ends meet. There were her dad's wages coming in, and the little Michael was paid, but it was never enough. How Mary put food on the table, conjuring meals out of thin air as far as Ruby could tell, was a mystery and nothing short of a miracle. She knew she'd willingly hand over every penny she earned.

When she walked into the yard, there was a space on the wall where the tin bath usually hung. That was her cue to go no further, for it meant her dad was still having his bath. Only after he was washed, dried and dressed and the tin bath carried out, its black water chucked into the lane, could she enter the kitchen. Their house was poky, and privacy was hard to come by.

She wandered back into the lane and peered left and right. At one end three children were playing catch, squealing and yelling each time they were caught. At the other end two women were talking, arms crossed, heads together, passing on gossip. Ruby wondered who they might be talking about. Did they know, she wondered, about Elsie Hutton being blown a kiss by Bert Collins? She wouldn't have believed it herself if she hadn't seen it with her own eyes.

Across the lane was a pile of stones. She walked over, picked up the largest one she could carry, dusted the muck off the top and took it to her back gate. There she placed it carefully in the mud and sat down on her own little throne. At least it would stop her dress getting dirty. She didn't want to do anything to upset her mam, especially as she'd been so wistful lately. The sun was high in the sky and she turned her face to it, letting it warm her. She thought of Polly and Jim, her new employers, and wondered about their son, Stan. She mulled his name over. Stanley Hutchinson. She'd known a lad by that name when she was at school. He'd been quiet, kept himself to himself, a tall, gangly lad with freckles and a shy smile. She wondered if it was the same boy. She hadn't known him well enough to find out if his parents ran a pub. Well, she'd meet him soon enough.

Lost in her thoughts, she closed her eyes and enjoyed the warmth of the sun on her skin. Despite the noise from the mine – the winding gears, the trains taking coal from the pit or bringing goods in – sitting there on her stone, Ruby felt at peace. With her eyes closed, she didn't see the black dog that skulked along the lane. She had no idea it was there until she felt something nudge her hand. She pulled away in shock, opened her eyes and was stunned to see the animal staring right back at her. Was it about to attack? It wasn't barking or jumping, just standing there gazing into Ruby's eyes. It was a big dog, entirely black, and its ribs showed through its skinny frame. It nudged her hand again. This time she stroked its head, gingerly at first, cautious in case it decided to bite. But it just laid its head in her lap, its eyes flicking up at hers and then quickly away.

She'd never seen the dog before, she was sure. Some of the miners kept dogs in the pit lanes, whippets for racing. Ruby wasn't keen on whippets; they were too small, too skinny and they didn't seem friendly. The dog in front of her was bigger, sturdier, less nervous than any whippet she'd seen. She didn't know what breed it was, or who it belonged to. It had no collar around its neck, not even a piece of string. She looked into its eyes and stroked its velvet nose.

'You hungry?' she said. The dog nudged her hand.

Behind her came the sounds of talking and footsteps. She swung around to see her parents walking from the kitchen, struggling with the bath between them.

'Shift, Ruby,' her dad called.

'I got the job!' Ruby said excitedly.

'Not now, lass,' Arthur said.

Ruby was confused. Why weren't her parents congratulating her on her new job? She moved from her spot while her dad chucked the water in the lane. Once the bath was empty, he hung it back on the wall.

'Ruby, get yourself indoors,' her mam said. 'Me and your dad want a word with you and Michael.'

Ruby's mind raced as she thought desperately about what she'd been up to that might warrant a telling-off, for that was what it sounded like. But try as she might, she couldn't think of anything she'd done wrong. Maybe Michael was the one about to be scolded? But then why did she need to be included? She was puzzled as she headed into the house. The black dog remained sprawled in the lane and laid its head on the stone where Ruby had been sitting. She cast it one last glance. She didn't expect to see it again.

Inside, she was shocked by the formal scene that greeted her. Her mam was sitting in her chair by the fire – there was nothing unusual there. But her dad was standing at his wife's side with his hand firmly on her shoulder. He was wearing his stern face, the one he used when he was giving Ruby and Michael a silent warning to behave.

Michael came clattering down the stairs. 'Is tea ready yet?' he yelled as he hurtled into the kitchen. He stood stock still when he saw his mam and dad looking so serious and stiff. 'Mam? What's going on?' he said.

'Both of you, sit down,' Mary began. Ruby and Michael did as they were told.

Arthur tightened his grip on Mary's shoulder.

'Mam?' Ruby said, worried now.

Mary looked at her bairns. 'I've not been feeling too well lately,' she began. 'I guessed a while back what it was, but I wanted to wait, just in case. And then I had to tell your dad first before I could tell anyone else.'

'Are you dying, Mam?' Michael asked, eyes wide.

Mary smiled and shook her head. 'No, love. I'm not dying.' She took a long breath. 'I'm going to have a baby.'

Chapter Four

Ruby stared open-mouthed. 'A baby?' Suddenly everything about her mam's odd behaviour over the last few weeks began to make sense.

Arthur looked at her. 'You're to help your mam about the house more.'

'She's a good lass, Arthur, she doesn't need to be told,' Mary said.

'A baby?' Ruby repeated, still in shock.

'It's come as a surprise to us both. I wasn't expecting to be in the family way again, not at my age. But it's happened and we have to deal with it. It's not going to be easy. We've got little enough money as it is, never mind having another mouth to feed. And there'll be blankets and clothes to buy. I gave all the baby clothes away after Michael was born. I thought I'd never need them again.'

Ruby knelt at her mam's side. 'I'll do everything I can to help, Mam,' she said. 'And I got the job at the Queen's Head, so I'll have money coming in.'

'You got the job, pet? Well done,' Mary said.

'Michael, do you have anything to say about your mam's news?' Arthur asked.

'I hope it's a boy. I want a brother. Sisters are sissies.' Michael smirked at Ruby.

'Is that all?' Mary said.

Michael shrugged. 'I suppose it might be all right.'

Arthur looked at both of them. 'Now listen, you two. Things are going to get worse for us Dinsdales when the new baby comes. We're going to have to pull together and do the best we can with the little we've got. You understand?'

'Yes, Dad,' Ruby and Michael chimed.

Mary stood and busied herself at the fireplace with the kettle and a small pan of vegetables boiling on the fire. 'It's chicken pie tonight with carrots and potatoes,' she said.

Arthur raised his eyebrows. 'Chicken, eh? Now there's a luxury. Here's me worrying about how we're going to feed ourselves in the next few months, and you're serving up chicken. Maybe I don't need to worry after all.'

'I got it cheap, Arthur, they were selling them off at the store,' Mary said quickly. Then she turned her head from her husband so that he wouldn't see the lie in her eyes. She hadn't bought the chicken; she could never have afforded such a thing. It had come from Bert Collins. He had called to see her while Arthur was at work, waiting in the back lane until the coast was clear before knocking on the door and offering her the freshly killed bird for free.

'You haven't stolen it from the store, Bert?' she had gasped.

'Course not, what do you take me for?' he replied.

'Then why are you giving it to me if you don't want money for it?'

Bert tapped the side of his nose. 'Ask no questions and

I'll tell you no lies,' he said mysteriously. 'But if you can put in a good word for me with Elsie Hutton in exchange, I'd be grateful, Mary. You and her are best friends, aren't you?' And with that he was gone.

Mary stood and stared at the chicken. She was about to close the door when Bert reappeared.

'Whatever you do, don't tell Arthur.'

'Why?' Mary asked.

But he'd gone again. Mary had held the chicken by its broken, scraggy neck and appraised the weight of it, trying to guess how much meat there might be under its feathers.

'Right, you,' she'd said to it as if it was a naughty child. 'You're going into a pie tonight, soup tomorrow, and sandwiches for Arthur and Michael's bait boxes for the rest of the week.'

Now Arthur rubbed his hands together with glee as Mary cut the chicken pie into slices. She piled three slices on to his plate, ladled gravy over and spooned potatoes and carrots on the side. He and the bairns tucked in, but Mary felt sick inside. So many worries whirled in her mind, as they had done for weeks. Would her skinny, weak body be strong enough to carry a baby in the coming months? Was she too old to give life to a healthy child at her age? There was no money for her to visit Dr Anderson to ask his advice. Besides, it wasn't the done thing to question being pregnant. Women had babies just as night followed day; it was the natural thing to do. She shouldn't worry, just let nature take its course, but still her anxiety gnawed.

'Eat up,' Arthur urged. 'You're eating for two now, you know.'

Eating was the last thing Mary wanted to do. She'd felt nauseous all day, couldn't remember the last time she'd felt normal. She picked up her fork and stabbed a piece of carrot, then slowly brought it to her mouth and chewed.

The following evening, Ruby prepared to set off to work her first night at the Queen's Head.

'What are they like, the people who run it?' Mary asked.

Ruby thought of the Hutchinsons: hard-faced, plump Polly and her husband Jim with his pipe hanging out of his mouth.

'I'm sure they'll be fine once I get to know them,' she replied. She kissed her mam goodbye.

'I hope it goes well, love,' Mary said.

Ruby headed out for the short walk to the pub. As she hurried along the back lane, she saw what she first thought was a pile of rags by the wall. But as she drew near, it was clear that it wasn't rags at all; it was the dog she'd seen the previous day. It was curled in a ball, shivering. Ruby crouched down. She looked up and down the lane in case its owner might be about, but no one was there.

'What's wrong, dog?' she said.

The dog tried to lift its head from its front paws, but it only had enough strength to raise its eyes.

'Are you tired?' Ruby asked. She stroked the dog along the back of its head, then stood up. She couldn't be late, not on her first night. If she'd had the time, she would have run back down the lane to ask Michael to take it into their yard. At least it'd be safe there, away from any passing horses and carts. But even if she could take the dog home, she knew her mam had enough on her plate without the added burden of a stray. Reluctantly she left the dog where she'd found it. As she walked away, she heard it softly whine.

When Ruby reached the Queen's Head, she was greeted by a tall young man she recognised immediately as Stan. His face had filled out since their school days, although he had the same freckles across his nose that he'd had when he was younger. But in all other ways he'd changed a great deal. He was no longer the gangly lad she remembered. He had grown into his limbs and fattened out – though, she was pleased to see, not as much as his mam. He was a strapping man, muscled, and a lot more handsome than Ruby remembered when he'd been just a shy boy at school.

'Stan, you're looking well,' she said when she entered the pub.

'It's nice to see you too,' Stan replied. 'I couldn't believe it when Mam said she'd taken on a new barmaid by the name of Ruby Dinsdale. I thought to myself, there can't be that many Ruby Dinsdales in Ryhope, and I was hoping it was you.'

A strange feeling fluttered in Ruby's stomach. Was he flirting with her?

'You're a hard worker, or at least you always used to be at school. I remember that much about you.'

Ruby chided herself. Of course he wasn't. Why on earth would she think anyone would?

'That's me, strong and willing Ruby Dinsdale,' she smiled. 'I can turn my hand to anything.' She thought about the last time her mam had tried to teach her how to bake bread and what a disaster it had turned out. 'Well, almost anything.'

'Come on in, let me show you around,' Stan said. He held the door open and Ruby stepped into the passageway.

'Snug's this way,' he said, directing Ruby into the small, cosy room at the front of the pub with its two bay windows. 'We don't have a select room in here like some of Ryhope's pubs. The Queen's Head is a bit rough and ready, did Mam tell you?'

'She warned me, yes,' Ruby said.

'And this is the bar,' Stan said, leading her to the room where she and Polly had talked. The place looked as dilapidated as she remembered, with its chipped paint, stained floor, flaking walls and rotten floorboards. Still, the tabletops were clean and the bar area tidy.

'Come through here.' Stan beckoned her behind the bar. 'This leads out to the yard and the netty,' he added as Ruby followed him to the back of the pub. He stopped at the bottom of a staircase. 'No customers are allowed up there; that's where we live. If you see anyone hanging around here, shoo them back into the pub. Mam keeps the door locked up there, but you can't be too careful.'

'Noted,' Ruby said.

'And this is the kitchen and pantry,' Stan said, as he pushed a door open. 'We use this as our family kitchen as well as for the pub. Mind you, Mam doesn't often cook food for the bar.'

Ruby was relieved to hear it. She was dreading Polly finding out just how bad her cooking was.

'But she'll be putting on a spread for Peace Parade day,' Stan continued.

Her heart sank.

'Nothing special, just pies and sausage rolls, that kind of thing. We usually buy in pies from the Forester's Arms; they've got a girl there, Sadie, who does their cooking now.'

Ruby had heard of Sadie Linthorpe. She had arrived in Ryhope out of thin air it seemed, told folks she was from Hartlepool and ended up with two jobs, working in the Forester's Arms pub and as a maid at Ryhope Hall. She was also the first lass in Ryhope to ride a bike or wear trousers, and she had set up her own pie-making business. Ruby felt in awe of such a capable girl, who wasn't much older than herself.

'Will your mam be buying pies from Sadie for Peace Parade day?' Ruby said. She crossed her fingers, hoping that Stan's answer would be the one she needed to hear. But instead he looked at her as if she was mad.

'What on earth for?' he said, surprised. 'She's got you now to do the cooking. It's one of the reasons she took you on, because you can cook so well.'

'But I . . .' Ruby began. She remembered that Polly had assumed she could cook, and she hadn't had the courage to put her straight for fear she wouldn't be given the job.

Stan dismissed her concern with a wave of his hand. 'Oh, don't be so modest, you'll be fine,' he laughed. 'Be warned, though, the coal oven's temperamental, but I'm sure you'll get used to it. You'll be cooking up a storm in no time.'

Ruby managed a very weak smile.

29

Chapter Five

Ruby's first night at work went smoothly. It was midweek, and although the pub was busy, the customers were, in the main, well behaved.

'It gets rowdy on a weekend,' Stan warned as they worked side by side at the bar.

Ruby was alert to any raising of voices, any signs of pushing and shoving in case a fight started. However, the atmosphere remained peaceful, if not entirely calm. Singing broke out once or twice, and one man even climbed on to a table to belt out a song that had his friends clapping and singing along, until Polly strode over and broke up their raucous behaviour.

'I won't have customers standing on my tables,' she said sternly. 'Now get down.'

Ruby watched, impressed at the respect Polly commanded. Whenever there was a sign of trouble brewing, no matter how trivial, it was the landlady who waded in. Jim stood at the bar, watching in case she needed him, his pipe hanging from his mouth as his beady eyes took in the scene. But he knew Polly could manage fine well on her own, as he told Ruby that first evening. One word from her and their customers usually behaved. If they didn't, he and Stan took the offending customer by the arms and threw him out on the street. Polly would follow, and as the hapless customer tried to pull himself together, she would give a satisfied sneer and say the dreaded words no drinking man wanted to hear.

'You're barred!'

Working in the pub alongside Polly, Jim and Stan, Ruby learned a great deal. Not just about the Queen's Head but about the Hutchinson family and how they worked as a team. Stan was the youngest of Polly and Jim's five sons. The others worked at the mine and were settled with families. None of the Hutchinson boys had gone off to war, choosing the protected profession of mining instead.

'Someone had to keep the country running, and the country will always need coal,' Jim was often heard to say. He was as proud of his mining sons as any father was of his soldier son returning home from the front.

Ruby liked Jim. He was straightforward and kind. He could reel off full sentences – hold a long conversation – without once taking his beloved pipe from his mouth. When he wasn't smoking it, she saw him stuffing it with tobacco, or cleaning it with a tiny soft cloth he kept in his waistcoat pocket. Sometimes she even caught him holding it to the light that streamed in through the pub's windows, admiring the smooth curve of the wood.

As for Polly, Ruby saw a different side to the pub landlady when the two women worked together. The Polly Hutchinson she'd met on the day she applied for the job was a harsh-faced harridan who'd put a chill in her heart. But in the bar on an evening, Polly's features were softened by the glow from the oil lamps. In daylight, her clothes strained against her ample bosom, her waist disappeared under rolls of fat. But by night? Ah, by night, Polly blossomed behind the bar. Her skin became luscious and warm, her features made prominent with a touch of lipstick, powder and rouge, her curves smooth and round. And her large bosom was no longer covered; instead, it oozed from a low-cut blouse that Ruby couldn't take her eyes off. She'd never seen a woman display herself that way before.

She often spotted Jim with his arm around his wife's shoulders, the two of them laughing at something private or sharing a joke with a customer. It was easy for Ruby to see that Polly was in her element working in the pub, and with the support of her husband and the hard work of her son, she ran a profitable inn. The sound of the till ringing in shillings and pennies was one Ruby soon got used to hearing.

As the nights went on and Ruby and Stan worked often together, she found herself warming to him. He was no longer the shy boy from school she'd barely passed the time of day with. He was generous with advice, and nothing was too much trouble for him as he taught her the peculiarities of working at the Queen's Head. He was funny too, and made her laugh with his impressions of their customers.

'See him over there?' he whispered to her as they shared a quiet moment. He nodded towards a corner of the pub where an old man sat with a pint of Vaux stout in front of him and a copy of the *Sunderland Echo* in his hands. 'That's Micky Talbot, used to work at the pit – retired now, poor old soul. Can't walk far but he manages to get in here most nights. Anything to escape from the missus. He sits there with his pint and his paper and he doesn't say a word to anyone.' He pointed out a group of three young men, all wearing flat caps and shapeless brown jackets, then glanced at the clock above the fireplace. 'They like a game of darts, those three. In fact, I'll bet you anything they come over here to ask for the arrows in three, two . . .'

Right on cue, one of the men strolled towards the bar.

'Got the arrows, Stan? Me and the lads fancy a game of darts.'

Stan winked at Ruby and her face broke into a smile. 'Told you,' he whispered as he handed over the three heavy darts with their red feathered tips.

'You know your customers well,' Ruby said.

'You get to know a thing or two about folk when you see them day in, day out,' he replied.

'How long have you been working with your mam and dad?'

'Feels like forever,' Stan said. 'We've always lived here. I grew up here, and as soon as I was big enough, Dad had me helping with the barrels and cleaning the yard. I started working behind the bar when I was at school.'

The mention of their school days made Ruby feel uncomfortable. She'd seen Stan back then, of course, but hadn't paid him any attention. She hadn't been friendly to him or reached out with a kind word. She'd simply ignored him; he'd been just a quiet boy she didn't know. And anyway, she'd been much more interested in forging bonds with her girlfriends Abigail and Jean, and the three of them remained close. She decided to clear the air.

'I'm sorry we were never friends at school,' she said.

'What's to apologise for?' Stan replied. 'I was a different lad back then, a bit too timid for my own good. I spent most of my time with my head stuck in a book, preferring that to talking to people, even girls.' He laughed out loud. 'Especially girls.'

'Do you have a girlfriend now?' Ruby dared ask.

If he was surprised by the question, he hid his feelings well. 'Not any more. I had a girl once, Veeda she was called, but she wanted to get serious too quickly and I don't mind admitting I'm not ready for that yet. Think I still prefer books, to be honest.'

Just then a customer approached the bar. Stan flicked a glass cloth from the shelf across his shoulder and greeted the man. 'All right, pal? What can I get you?'

When the customer had been served, Stan returned to Ruby's side.

'What about you? Got a boyfriend?'

The thought of having a boyfriend had never crossed Ruby's mind. Not an actual living, breathing boyfriend who'd kiss her and hold her like the men in the stories in *The Red Letter* magazine hidden under her bed. When would she ever have time for that, and all the preening that seemed to go with it? Anyway, if she believed what she read in the magazine's stories, boyfriends seemed more trouble than they were worth. Women were forever having their hearts broken and shedding tears over some unsuitable man before they found their Mr Right. No, she didn't think she wanted any of that. Her heart was perfectly fine as it was without it being smashed in two.

Besides, where would she even find a boyfriend in Ryhope? She didn't know any fellas. Michael's friends who came to the house were far too young, annoying too.

One of them once brought a frog into the house that he dropped down her back as a joke. He and Michael thought it a hoot and ran into the back lane crying with laughter while Ruby went white with shock. The only man she knew and liked apart from her dad and Michael was her dad's friend Bert Collins. Even if Bert wasn't busy trying to court Elsie, he was far too old for her.

She thought of the delivery men who sold their wares in the back lanes. The fish man, the egg man, the man who brought the meat from the store. She'd not given any of them a second thought. She knew their names, said hello and goodbye and was polite when she handed over whatever money her mam could afford to buy food, but that was as far as it went. One of the delivery boys, Ted, was courting her friend Jean, but the minute he'd turned up in her life, he was all Jean could talk about. It bored Ruby stiff. She and Jean hadn't seen each other in weeks, not since Ted came on to the scene. And according to her other friend, Abigail, all fellas were wrong 'uns and best avoided. Everyone in Ryhope knew that Abigail's mam had a string of fellas traipsing in and out of her house, and Abigail didn't have a good word to say about any of them. Ruby wondered how much her cynicism came from her troubled home life with her wayward mam.

Ruby sighed. She didn't know how or where she would ever meet a nice man, and in light of the baby news at home, she knew she'd soon be spending more time helping her family.

'A boyfriend? Me?' she said, startled.

'Why not? You're a bonny lass. Smart too,' Stan said.

Ruby felt the heat rise in her neck. She remembered Polly had called her a bonny lass too; it was one of the

35

reasons she'd been given the job, to pull in the punters. She'd never thought of herself as bonny. She was just Ruby Dinsdale.

'Bonny?' she laughed, shaking her head. 'Strong and useful, that's me.'

She turned away and busied herself cleaning glasses. She hoped her face hadn't turned as red as it felt.

Chapter Six

Ruby settled well into her new job. However, at home things were about to take a turn for the worse. Mary's pregnant stomach heaved each morning, leaving her exhausted every day.

'I'll be all right, love,' she said each time Ruby expressed concern. But it was clear from her ashen face and her loss of appetite that she was anything but. Ruby heard her crying in the night through the thin walls of their house. During the day, she helped her as much as she could with cleaning the house, keeping the fire burning and bringing in water for her dad's bath.

'I'm feeling fair done in,' Mary would say. It was the only complaint she made.

Something sinister weighed on Mary's mind, yet she'd kept the severity of her situation to herself. She hadn't breathed a word to anyone, not even Arthur. Now, however, she knew she had to take advice from someone she could trust. One morning when she and Ruby were sitting by the fire, Ruby offered to boil the kettle to make tea.

Glenda Young

'I can do that much at least, Mam, without getting it wrong,' she smiled.

But Mary declined her offer. 'Not for me, lass. I need to head out to see Elsie.'

'I'll come with you.'

Mary shook her head. 'I need a private word.'

Ruby looked at her mam, saw the discomfort she was in, noticed for the first time that morning how pale and wan she was. She saw her lips trembling. 'I'll go and get her, Mam. You stay there. You're in no fit state to visit Elsie or anyone else.'

Mary laid her hand on Ruby's arm. 'Tell her to come quickly,' she said.

As soon as her daughter left the house, Mary bent double in her chair and tears began to fall.

Within minutes, Elsie Hutton swept into the Dinsdales' kitchen. She wore a long black dress and a crumpled black hat. She whipped the hat off and threw it on the table, then set her large black handbag on a kitchen chair. As soon as she saw the state Mary was in, she spun around to Ruby.

'You stay outside, lass. I'll call you if I need you.'

'But Mam's not well,' Ruby protested.

'It's best if you leave us,' Elsie said. 'This is women's talk.'

'I'm a woman! I'm seventeen!' Ruby cried.

'Out, Ruby, please,' Elsie said. 'There are things a young girl like you shouldn't hear.'

Ruby didn't move. She wanted to be with her mam, to hold her hand, to fetch a cold cloth for her forehead if she needed one.

'Ruby, go,' Mary breathed.

Only then did Ruby turn and leave. She left the door open, hoping to catch some of the conversation between her mam and Elsie, to find out the truth about what was going on. But when she heard the door close behind her, she headed into the lane. Beside the gate was the large, flat stone she had used as a seat. She moved it back into position and plonked herself down, thinking how unfair it was that she couldn't stay with her mam. From the corner of her eye, she saw a movement at the end of the lane. She knew immediately that it was the black dog she'd seen before.

'Come on, dog,' she called. The animal obeyed her command and walked slowly, hesitantly towards her. As it neared her, she realised it was limping, favouring a front paw. When it reached her, it collapsed at her feet and whined. Ruby tenderly lifted its paw and saw that it was crusted with blood. She walked to the tap and the dog followed, limping. Turning on the tap, she cupped her hands under the flow. Then she lowered them and the dog greedily lapped the water.

'You'll be hungry, too, I bet,' she said. 'But there's nothing I can do about that.'

Meanwhile, inside the kitchen, Mary was in tears. 'I'm going to lose the baby, Elsie, I can tell. Something's not right inside.'

'Shush, love, don't talk like that.'

Elsie took her large handbag from the chair and rummaged inside. 'I've got something that'll help,' she said.

'Medicine?' Mary said. 'Something to get rid of it?'

'No, love,' Elsie said, shaking her head.

Mary couldn't believe her eyes when Elsie brought a tin of golden syrup from her bag and laid it on the fireside to warm. Then she pulled out a paper bag and produced two perfectly round home-made crumpets. Without asking, she lifted the fire poker, speared the two crumpets and toasted them over the flames.

'Bit of sugar, bit of something to eat, it'll help build you up,' she said.

'I can't keep anything down,' Mary told her.

Without missing a beat, Elsie slid the poker from the fire and with quick fingers pushed the warm crumpets free. 'Where are your knives?' she said.

Mary nodded at the rickety sideboard. 'Top drawer.'

Elsie quickly and deftly spread thick, sweet syrup on the crumpets and handed one to her friend.

Mary took it. 'I'm not sure I can eat it,' she said.

'Try,' Elsie urged.

Mary lifted it to her lips.

'We used to love these when we were girls, remember?' Elsie said.

'Those days seem a world away now.' Mary bit into the crumpet and the syrup dripped on to her fingers. 'Oh, it's good.' She smiled at her friend. 'Brings back lots of memories.'

Elsie sat back in her chair with her arms folded across her black dress. 'See, I told you that was all you needed.'

Mary took another small bite, then turned her face towards the fire. 'I haven't told you everything,' she said.

'Come on then, out with it,' Elsie urged.

Mary raised her gaze to meet Elsie's concerned face. 'I've been bleeding. I haven't told Arthur; it'll destroy him. Once he got over the shock of having another bairn, he's been soft about it since. But we can't afford it, and if it's trying to leave my body, surely that's the best thing?'

'Now listen, we'll have none of that talk, you hear?' Elsie said.

'But something's not right, Elsie.'

Elsie stayed silent, thinking. 'And you can't afford the doctor?' she said at last.

Mary shook her head.

'Then there's only one thing for it. We'll have to get you up to your bed. You're to rest.'

'I can't rest, there's work to do,' Mary cried. 'What about Arthur's tea? And his baths?'

'Your Ruby's a strong lass, she can help. And you've got Michael. Once you explain what's wrong, they'll understand, and I'll call in every day to see how you are.'

'I appreciate it, Elsie. But I can't lie up there in bed and let the bairns look after Arthur. You know our Ruby can't cook.'

'Then I'll come to help. Because if you don't rest, you risk losing more than just the baby. Look at you, you're skin and bone. Don't you ever eat?'

'Food goes to Arthur and the bairns first, you know that, and I take what's left. We can't afford much when there's a pile of bills need paying.'

'Why didn't you come to me before?' Elsie asked.

Mary sighed, resigned. 'Pride,' she said at last.

'Well, I'm here now, and I'm going to help. What are friends for?'

'You're a good woman, Elsie Hutton. It's no wonder Bert Collins is setting his cap at you.'

Elsie's hand flew to her heart. 'Me?' she said.

'Oh, don't act so coy,' Mary said. 'You know fine well

41

Glenda Young

he's been after you for ages. He calls in once a week with a fresh chicken for us, for free. It's the only meat we've been eating; I can't afford to buy any.'

'A chicken? What on earth for?' Elsie asked.

'On the promise of me putting in a good word with you about him.'

'Bert did that?' Elsie said, surprised. Then she pulled herself together. 'Now come on, finish your crumpets, then I'll help you upstairs and put you to bed. If Arthur's got anything to say about it—'

'He won't, I know my Arthur,' Mary said firmly.

'Well, if he does complain, send him along to see me and I'll have a word with him about you needing to rest.'

Mary lifted the crumpet to her lips and took another delicate bite. 'I can't eat both,' she said.

Elsie eyed the second one. 'You sure?' she said. 'Seems a shame for it to go to waste.'

Mary nodded. Elsie took the crumpet from the hearth and slathered it with more syrup before taking a huge bite.

'Ruby, get yourself in here, lass,' Elsie called into the yard. Ruby ran in, desperate to find out what was going on, leaving the dog in the back lane licking its paw. But when she entered the kitchen, there was no sign of her mam. And what was a tin of golden syrup doing on their hearth? They never had syrup in the house; it was a luxury they couldn't afford.

'Your mam's going to be in bed for a few days,' Elsie explained. 'You and Michael are going to have to do everything for her, you hear? You'll have to cook your dad's tea, starting tonight. I'll call in every day to see how she's doing.'

'Cook?' Ruby said, startled. Then she shook her head. 'What's wrong with her?'

Elsie laid her hands on Ruby's shoulders and looked into her brown eyes, choosing her words carefully. 'She's not as strong as she used to be, I think you know that. And when she had you and Michael, she was a much younger woman and a lot better in herself, in all ways.'

'Is she dying?' Ruby asked.

Elsie shook her head. 'No, love, but she needs looking after. She's got a look about her that I don't like. She reminds me of her mother, your Grandma Winter, and the way she was before . . .' She stopped herself saying more. 'Never mind. Listen. You and Michael have got to do all you can for her.'

Ruby swallowed hard. 'Can I go up and see her?'

'I think she'd like that,' Elsie said. 'But don't press her if she doesn't want to talk; just hold her hand and tell her you love her. Offer her a cup of tea – you know how much she likes her tea. But don't ask too many questions. She needs to talk to your dad first.'

'Elsie?'

'Yes, love?'

'What will I cook for Dad's tea?'

Elsie looked around the tiny kitchen. 'Let's see what your mam's got, shall we?'

She opened all the cupboards and every drawer, and scoured the pantry for food. All she found was a block of margarine, two onions, a packet of gravy browning, tea, a jug of milk covered with a tea towel, a pile of fresh pea pods and the remains of a cooked chicken, still on the bone. She rolled up her sleeves. 'Ever made a chicken stew?'

Ruby shook her head.

'Well, you're going to learn how to make one now.'

With Mary resting in bed, the Dinsdale house fell quiet. She was its soul and its spark, the person around whom all the action and emotion centred. Michael stepped up and took his chores more seriously when he came home from work. He helped Ruby clean and wash his dad's pit clothes, and fetched the water for his bath. As for the family meals, Elsie visited daily and repeated instructions to Ruby she'd heard many times from her mam. She showed her over and over again how to peel and boil carrots, how to make pastry, crumpets and bread, how to put a meal together from whatever she could find or afford. This time Ruby *had* to get it right; there could be no room for error. If she didn't cook, the Dinsdales didn't eat. Her efforts weren't great, and some were downright terrible, but when they began to be edible, she knew she was making progress under Elsie's tuition.

'Do it for your mam, Ruby!' Elsie advised.

Each afternoon before Arthur returned home, Ruby would sit at her mam's bedside while Mary guided her through the household expenses. She told her where the cheapest goods could be bought, which shops would give a discount and which of the delivery boys might be willing to give credit, or an extra rasher of bacon.

'Go shopping late in the day,' she advised. 'Take whatever's left and ask for it cheap. If you don't ask, they won't offer.'

Ruby learned her new role quickly, ashamed of herself

for not taking a deeper interest before her mam became ill. She shopped as Mary advised, late in the afternoon before the shops turned their signs to *Closed*. Bert arrived regularly with a chicken, and his visits were no longer a secret. Arthur despaired at his friend's antics and worried that the birds had been stolen from one of the village farms. Whether stolen or not, they meant that tasty meals could be served up to supplement thin broth or pease pudding sandwiches. Elsie helped out when she could, bringing a bit of cooked ham for Mary to help build her friend up and get her back on her feet.

The black dog in the lane disappeared and Ruby gave it no more thought, until one morning, some days later, she opened the back gate to find the animal standing to attention, waiting. A dead rabbit hung from its mouth, and two more lay at its feet.

Chapter Seven

Rabbits weren't the only dead animals the dog brought to the Dinsdales' door. One morning there was a duck, its neck bloodied and twisted. The dog nudged its offering towards Ruby with its nose. Another day it brought a large rat in its mouth. That day Ruby shooed it away. The Dinsdales were hungry, desperate for fresh meat, but even they had their limits.

When the dog first brought the rabbits, Ruby ran to Elsie's house, the animal bounding after her. Elsie showed her how to skin and bone them, while Ruby's stomach churned.

'You're too squeamish by far,' Elsie chastised her. 'Just think of the rabbit stew you can present to your dad when he comes in from work. And when you take a bowl of it upstairs for your mam, it'll do her the world of good.'

Ruby mellowed towards the dog. She began to allow it to stay in the yard overnight. She laid a bowl on the ground and filled it with water, and fed the animal titbits of cooked rabbit, the gristly bits she knew her mam and dad wouldn't like. The dog wolfed down every morsel.

'You ought to give that dog a name now you've taken it in,' Elsie said one morning, when she'd arrived to help Ruby bake bread. No matter how much advice Elsie gave her, Ruby's bread was still heavy and flat.

'I haven't taken it in,' Ruby said. 'It just moved in.'

While the bread dough was rising by the fire, Elsie and Ruby walked into the yard. The dog was sleeping, curled up in a corner, but as soon as it heard footsteps, it stood to attention, its tail wagging furiously.

'It's got the look of a lurcher about it, with something else mixed in,' Elsie said. 'What about calling it Lucky?'

The dog looked at her eagerly, as if awaiting a command.

Ruby shook her head. 'It needs a girl's name; it's a bitch after all.'

The dog turned its attention to her.

'Lady! I'm going to call her Lady!' Ruby cried.

The dog walked towards her and nuzzled its head against her hand.

'She knows we're talking about her,' Ruby laughed. She stroked the dog behind the ears, and Lady groaned with delight.

In the days that followed, Mary still didn't move from her bed. Ruby was disappointed to see food she'd cooked for her mother go untouched.

'Wasn't it nice, Mam?' she asked.

'It was fine, love,' Mary replied. 'You're definitely getting better. But I'm just not hungry. I can't seem to keep anything down.'

'It's Peace Parade day tomorrow,' Ruby reminded her. 'Polly wants me at the pub all day and I'll be there till late at night. I've cooked a chicken pie for Michael and Dad and baked some bread too.'

'How is your bread, pet?'

'It's coming on,' Ruby said as enthusiastically as she could. 'Elsie says I'm getting better. It's not as flat as before.'

Mary ran a finger gently down her daughter's cheek. 'You're a good lass, Ruby. You're a trier, if nowt else. Enjoy every minute of the parade. And see if you can nab yourself a good-looking soldier. There'll be some lovely lads back in Ryhope now they're all home from the war.'

'What do I need a lad for?' Ruby laughed. 'I've got you and Dad and Michael to look after.'

'Well, don't let Polly Hutchinson work you too hard,' Mary continued. 'Make sure you get out on to the street to see as much of the parade as you can. I want all the gossip and news when you get home.'

'Will I bring some food up for you before I go to work in the morning?'

'Just a cup of tea,' Mary said. 'I think I can manage some tea.'

The next morning, after Arthur and Michael had left for the pit, Ruby remembered her mam's request and took a mug of hot tea up to her. She knocked three times at the bedroom door.

'Mam?'

'Come in, love,' Mary rasped.

Ruby entered the darkened room, set the mug on the floor at her mam's bedside and opened the threadbare curtains to let in the light. Then she kissed Mary goodbye and headed out to work.

As soon as Mary heard the familiar sound of the gate

banging shut, she forced herself up out of bed. But when her bare feet hit the floorboards, pain shot through her body and her stomach cramped with what she'd feared for so long. She half walked, half staggered to the bedroom door, then pressed her hand to the wall to steady herself as she inched her way downstairs, one painful step after another.

Ruby's day went by in a blur. She'd already been shown around the kitchen by Stan and he'd explained how everything worked and how to get the best from the pub's big coal oven. But still she was scared about her mammoth cooking task. She had pastry to make, pies to fill, bread dough to knead and sausages to cook on the fire. With Elsie's instructions and her mam's words ringing in her ears, she took a deep breath, pushed her hair behind her ears and rolled up her sleeves.

'Come on, Ruby Dinsdale, you can do this,' she said out loud.

And with that, she began to cook.

The beer started flowing earlier at the Queen's Head on the day of the Peace Parade than it ever had before. And fortunately for Ruby, the more the customers drank, the less they cared how tough her pastry was or how doughy her bread. They never noticed the blackened sausages as they swigged back pint after pint in a celebration like no other. The surrounding shops and pubs were decorated with bunting. Union flags hung from the upstairs windows of the Queen's Head. Ryhope had never looked so joyful and jubilant.

Once her cooking was done and the kitchen made

Glenda Young

spotless, Ruby took her place behind the bar with Polly, Jim and Stan. The four of them worked flat out, taking money with one hand, pulling pints with the other. Polly had bought extra barrels from the brewery, and as soon as one emptied, Stan quickly replaced it with another from the yard. Soon the pounding of a big bass drum could be heard from the street, and a shout went up.

'Parade's started, lads!'

The customers streamed from the pub to watch the soldiers and brass bands go by.

Stan grabbed Ruby's arm. 'Come on, we're not missing this!'

Ruby didn't need to ask Polly or Jim for permission to leave, for they were heading out too, leaving an empty pub behind. Ruby stood close to Stan, watching in awe as the soldiers marched by, swinging their arms in perfect time to the beat. Banners were held high, showing the regiments the soldiers had served in. Ruby saw the banner of the Durham Light Infantry, carried by young men not much older than Michael.

'What a sight. Makes you proud and does your heart good,' Jim said, and his pipe jiggled in his mouth.

Dignitaries from the Ryhope churches marched by, schoolchildren in fancy dress, a horse-drawn cart decorated with ribbons of red, white and blue. And above the noise of people cheering and laughing came the sound of the Ryhope colliery brass band with its drums and trumpets, cornets and horns. People were dancing, swaying from side to side, clapping along to the music. Onlookers lined the street, pushing forward to get the best view. At one point, the crowd surged, and Ruby almost lost her footing.

'Don't worry, I've got you,' she heard Stan say. She felt an arm slip around her waist.

'Thanks,' she said. She felt a flutter in her stomach and knew the excitement wasn't caused purely by the parade.

On the marchers came, until the end of the procession was in sight. It was a sombre scene, a coffin carried on a horse-drawn cart. The coffin was draped with a Union flag, to represent the Ryhope men and boys who hadn't returned from the war. Men removed their flat caps and held them at their hearts. Women bowed their heads in respect and brushed away a tear when they thought of lost loved ones and friends. The parade made its way down the colliery bank, past St Paul's church to the village green. The road outside the Queen's Head was clear again.

'Best get back to work now,' Ruby said.

Stan let his hand drop to his side and nothing more was said between them.

The pub was busy for the rest of the day, and well into the evening. Polly had said it would stay open until the last drop of beer had gone. Before Ruby left to walk home, Stan invited her to join the Hutchinsons for a drink in the bar. When she took her seat, she noticed chunks of pastry on the floor. Some of the men hadn't been hungry – or drunk – enough to eat her pies. She knew her cooking still needed to improve.

Polly raised her glass of stout. 'Cheers, everyone,' she said.

Jim, Stan and Ruby raised their glasses too, and Ruby sipped the stout Polly had pulled for her. It wasn't to her liking, but she wasn't going to refuse a free drink, and she was tired and thirsty after such a long day.

'It's been a good day,' Stan said.

'With not a fight in sight,' Jim noted. He turned towards Ruby. 'Seems you're having a calming influence in here. Since the day we took you on, we've not had half as many fights. I reckon the lads get distracted by a good-looking barmaid. Best thing we ever did, giving you a job in our pub.'

'My pub,' Polly said sternly.

Jim took a swig from his pint. Ruby and Stan exchanged a shy smile, and it didn't go unnoticed. Polly had seen the way Stan behaved when he was with Ruby. He was clearly keen on the girl and she didn't like it one bit. Ruby Dinsdale was nowhere near good enough for her youngest son, and she was determined to put a stop to them becoming more friendly.

When Ruby returned home, she was humming a tune the brass band had played in the parade. She let herself in through the back gate and Lady came to greet her. She filled the dog's water bowl and let herself into the house. She'd expected everyone to be asleep. Her dad and Michael had to be up early for work. But there was someone sitting by the embers of the fire.

'Dad?' she said, confused. 'What are you doing up?' She stood in front of him, trying to make out the expression on his face.

'It's your mam, love, she's not well.'

'But when I took her tea in for her this morning she seemed all right,' Ruby said.

Arthur slowly shook his head. 'Ruby, love, she's lost the bairn.'

Chapter Eight

In the coming weeks, life changed in the Dinsdales' house. Mary became a shadow of her former self, barely speaking, staring out of the window, acting in a way that Arthur, Ruby and Michael had never seen before. None of them knew what to do. Not even regular visits from Elsie could cheer her up. When Mary sat by the fire on an evening, Michael sat close to his mam and held her hand.

Arthur, meanwhile, was more stoical. 'Come on, lass, you'll be all right,' he kept saying. 'It's just a matter of time. You'll pull round.'

Ruby wondered if her dad believed his own words or whether he was trying to convince himself. She saw the faraway look in her mam's eyes and she worried for her state of mind. She'd heard stories from Mary of her own mother, Ruby's Grandma Winter, who had suffered from melancholy. She prayed that her mam wouldn't go the same way.

One Monday morning in late September, Ruby was up early, ready to make a start on washing day. Before she began, she ate a breakfast of oats she'd bought from High Farm. They were the cheapest she could find, the ones the farmer fed his pigs with, but they were tasty enough for those who could afford nothing else. Mary refused her offer of breakfast.

'Cup of tea, Mam?' Ruby asked as Mary sat by the fire in her nightgown.

Mary stared ahead of her. 'Put a cinder in it,' she said softly.

Ruby was confused. 'A cinder, Mam?'

'A tot of something. Surely we've got something in the back of the pantry? A drop of Christmas sherry, anything will do.'

Ruby was shocked by the request. She'd never known her mam drink alcohol. The Christmas sherry was kept for the fruit cake they made once a year. She didn't know why Mary was asking for sherry now. Perhaps it was medicinal and could help? She walked to the pantry and opened it wide. Inside, the shelves were almost bare. On the floor were old boxes, nibbled by mice.

'Shove your hand all the way back to the wall; there should be something there,' Mary said.

Ruby moved boxes to one side. Sure enough, right at the back was a small green bottle.

'Found it, Mam.'

'Pour it in my tea,' Mary said.

Ruby took the stopper from the bottle and tipped a tiny amount into her mam's mug. She handed it over and Mary took it gratefully.

On the fireside, water was boiling in pans ready for Ruby to start the wash. Mondays were the toughest days of all. Usually, the back-breaking work was shared between Mary and Ruby. Yet even with two of them beating the coal from Arthur's pit clothes before they were washed, it was heavy, tiring work. Since Mary's baby had died, she'd lost the energy and motivation she once had. Ruby did the work on her own, with occasional advice from her mam.

'Remember to run the clothes through the mangle when you're done,' she'd say. As if Ruby would ever forget.

'If it's too worn and thin, brush it, don't wash it,' she advised. Ruby knew her mam's mantra off by heart, for many of their clothes were too shabby or threadbare to survive being scrubbed in hot water.

On that September morning, however, there was one thing that put cheer in Ruby's heart: the sun was shining, and the day was warm. Fair weather on washing day made the world of difference, for it meant that clothes could be hung across the back lane. On wet days and cold days when nothing would dry no matter how long it blew, everything had to be hung indoors, drying slowly over the course of a week. Tempers were short as everyone tried to dodge the clothes steaming up the house.

In the yard, Ruby rolled her sleeves up and set to work. Lady watched as she beat her dad's pit clothes against the wall before scrubbing them with as much hot water as she could boil. Each time she went into the kitchen to put another pan of water on the fire, her mam was still in her chair, still with her mug in her hands, long after her tea had turned cold. What Ruby didn't know was that when she left the kitchen again to head to the yard, Mary poured another nip of sherry in her tea. And another, and another, until the whole bottle had gone.

* * *

Ruby worked hard and fast, concentrating fully on her chores. She scrubbed blouses and nightshirts, skirts and socks, trousers and pants. And when they were as clean as she could get them, when they'd been put through the mangle to squeeze the water out, she took the washing line into the lane. Some women already had their washing pegged out, and clothes were flying high. Up and down the back lane, shirts billowed against the blue sky, men's long johns and flannels stirred in the breeze. Ruby's neighbour from a few doors away, Lil Mahone, was pegging out her bloomers. Lil was a short, thin, bird-like woman with brown hair that she often wore tucked under a green woollen hat.

'Morning, Lil,' Ruby called. 'Perfect washing day weather.'

'Couldn't have chosen it better myself!' Lil replied. 'Your mam not helping you today? I haven't seen her for a while, come to think of it. Everything all right in there, is it? She's not run away with the fish man, has she?'

Typical Lil, Ruby thought, as nosy as always.

'She's indoors,' she replied. That was all Lil was going to get. Lil Mahone was the worst gossip in Ryhope, and if Ruby told her about her mam losing her baby and her melancholy since, the Dinsdales' private business would be spread around the village by dinner time.

Ruby dropped one end of the washing line over a metal hook fixed to the wall by their back gate. Taking the other end, she walked across the back lane, tying it to the metal ring opposite. Then slowly, carefully, she pegged her family's clothes to the line. All done, she took a moment to admire her work. The clothes billowed and rippled in the gentle wind. All down the back lane, line after line of clothes was hung out to dry. It was easy to tell the washing belonging to the two Miss Huttons. No men's clothes hung there, just skirts, blouses and drawers, all of them black. Some women used long wooden poles to prop up their lines, sending the clothes higher, as if by reaching the sun first they'd dry quicker.

Ruby was about to head back into the yard when an almighty yell went up.

'Flaming heck!' a woman shrieked. 'They're at it again!'

Lady dashed out of the yard to see what the fuss was about and stood by Ruby's side. The precise and ordered lines of washing up and down the lane were under siege. At the far end of the lane, Ruby saw a horse and cart, and her heart sank.

'Why they have to come on a Monday, I'll never know,' Lil Mahone cried.

The cart moved into the lane, running straight down without a care for any of the hard work the miners' wives and daughters had done. Props were knocked over, washing lines snapped and clothes dragged through the mud. There was uproar. Women were yelling and swearing at the cart driver, a young lad who didn't know any better. Lady barked and chased the horse. Three angry women ran after the lad, threatening to chop off his manhood if they caught him next time. Worse was to come when the horse trampled on clean washing as it made its escape. For some of the women, all their washing would need to be done again. Ruby was luckier. Apart from having to peg fallen clothes back, her washing was otherwise fine. She'd be able to brush off any muck when the clothes were dry.

* * *

Although Ruby was exhausted after washing day, she still found herself looking forward to work at the Queen's Head that night. She didn't breathe a word to anyone, but she was glad to escape from the claustrophobic air the Dinsdales' house had taken on while Mary was going through what Arthur called 'pulling herself together'. Ruby hoped her dad was right and that Grandma Winter's disease of the mind hadn't made its way down the generations.

She'd made a leek pudding for tea. Mary had eaten a little, and Ruby was glad to see her efforts paying off. Even her dad paid her a compliment of sorts.

'Your cooking's not as bad as it used to be,' he'd said while chewing a lump of undercooked turnip.

There was no doubt that under Elsie's direction, Ruby's cooking had improved. But her skills at managing the family finances and buying food from the Ryhope shops left a lot to be desired. No matter how much she scrimped, or what scraps of food she brought in, the pantry shelves stayed empty. She bought food in the morning, cooked it in the evening and had to start over again the next day, worrying constantly about what she would put on the table. There didn't seem to be any let-up from the anxiety. If she wasn't fretting about buying food, her mind whirled with worry about cooking it.

Her mam needed feeding up, but ate little. Instead, she begged Arthur to buy her a bottle of stout from the Forester's Arms. 'It'll do me good,' she said.

Arthur, as keen as any of them to see Mary back to her old self, bought the ale with money they could ill afford.

It was an endless cycle. Ruby was running the household single-handedly. Oh, she didn't blame her mam. How could she? Mary was grieving the loss of her child, and the healing process would take time. But as the autumn days turned shorter and the memory of the Peace Parade disappeared, she was still in a bad way.

One night when Ruby walked into the Queen's Head, she was surprised to see pies and bread laid out on the bar.

'Had some free time, so I thought I'd do some baking,' Polly explained.

Ruby eyed the spread and her mouth watered. She hadn't seen so much glorious food in a long time. Polly caught her eye.

'You can stop that right now,' she said sternly. 'This is for the customers, to get them drinking more ale. If I so much as catch you looking at it again, I'll have your guts for garters.'

Ruby quickly turned away, forcing herself not to look at the food in case she was tempted to take something and stuff it into her mouth, or put it in her pocket to take home to her mam and dad. All night, as she worked, she tried to keep her eyes off it. But it was hard when it was right there in front of her. In fact, it was so hard it proved impossible. At the end of the night, when there were two slices of pie left on a plate, she did what she'd been thinking about all night. She'd thought she was alone in the bar. She thought she hadn't been seen.

'What the hell do you think you're doing?' Polly roared.

Ruby spun around. 'Nothing . . . I . . .'

'Put them back,' Polly ordered.

Ruby knew there was no point in lying. Slowly, reluctantly, she emptied her pockets and placed the slices back on the bar.

'It was for my mam and dad – Mam's not well,' she said, hoping she could find a chink in Polly's heart to make her understand.

'I've been watching you, Ruby Dinsdale,' Polly said slowly. 'And I know what you're up to here.'

Ruby had no idea what Polly meant. 'I've not been up to anything.'

'I've seen you with my Stan,' Polly said.

Ah, so that was it, Ruby thought. Well, whatever Polly imagined, she'd got the wrong end of the stick. 'We're just friends,' she said.

'Friends?' Polly roared. 'Don't give me that. You see my strong, strapping lad as a way out of your poverty-stricken little house on the pit row, don't you?'

'No!' Ruby cried.

'Don't lie to me, lass,' Polly said. 'I've known it from the minute you walked in here. You've turned his head.'

This was news to Ruby. She wondered if Stan had said something to his mam, or whether Polly was making it up as she saw it.

'You're trying to get your claws into him, aren't you? Well, this is my pub, and if you think I'd pass it on to a pit rat of a lass like you, you're sadly mistaken.'

Ruby took a step forward, hardly believing what was happening. 'Polly, no!'

'I've been wanting to get rid of you for a long time,' Polly said.

A chill went through Ruby.

'Time after time Jim told me to give you another chance. But he doesn't know you like I do. A lass like you from the pit lanes, you'll never amount to anything. You're pure evil, lass. And now you're stealing from us. I doubt Jim will be so keen to keep you on once he knows about this. Oh, and I'll make sure Stan knows too. He'll want nowt to do with you, I can tell you that now.'

Polly's words hit Ruby hard and she felt tears prick at her eyes. 'I'm not evil,' she found herself saying.

Polly nodded towards the pub door. 'Get out, and don't come back.'

Chapter Nine

Ruby walked from the pub into the night. She felt numb and confused. Where had Polly's temper flared from? What exactly did she mean about Stan? Ruby knew she hadn't encouraged him, flirted with him or acted inappropriately. They were friends, that was all. Oh, it was too confusing, too hurtful. And as for taking the pie, of course she knew she shouldn't have, but her stomach had been gnawing with hunger all day, her dad and Michael needed food to keep them going at work, and her mam needed sustenance if she was to recover. Had Polly been looking for an excuse to sack her? If she had, Ruby had stupidly handed it to her.

She balled her hands, determined. She was angry, and Polly's words about her never amounting to anything made her blood boil. She didn't know how, not yet, but she vowed to herself that one day she would prove the woman wrong.

She looked across the road to the pit lanes. Behind was the coal mine, and although it was late, the pit was still working, still bringing up coal from underground, its railway running, the winding gear turning. Production never stopped. But for Ruby, time stood still. How could she go home and tell her mam she'd lost her job; worse than that, that she'd been sacked for stealing? She'd lost the tiny bit of money she was bringing into the house when her family already couldn't make ends meet. She couldn't head home in such a state; she had to calm herself down. Her dad might still be up, smoking his pipe by the fire. She didn't want him to see her with a tear-stained face.

She walked slowly, wiping her eyes, going over each word Polly had flung at her. None of what she'd said about Stan made sense. Ruby didn't love him or want him in the way Polly assumed. She wondered if she should try to speak to Jim the next day; maybe he'd have a word with his wife, persuade her to take her back? But Ruby's heart sank the more she thought her plan through. It was Polly's name above the door of the pub. It was Polly who called the shots.

She shivered. Although the day had been warm, a fine day for washing, it was a cold night that carried the threat of worse weather to come. She crossed Ryhope Street towards the pit lanes, going over in her mind what she'd tell them back at the house. She couldn't lie, she wouldn't, not to her mam and dad. But she felt the weight of their disappointment as she worked out exactly how to phrase what she needed to say.

'You shouldn't be out this late, miss.'

Ruby turned to see a man, a miner on his way to work, his face and hands pale in the moonlight. She noticed a thick black moustache falling over his lips, almost covering his entire mouth. His eyebrows were black and bushy too, and his eyes heavy and dark. Her first reaction was that it was the face of a man without a woman in his life. For if he had a wife or a mam, even a sister, they would have nagged him into having a shave. He wore a flat cap, as most miners did – it was their only protection under-ground – and carried his lamp, bait bag and a bottle to fill with water at the pit head.

'I've just finished work. I'm heading home,' she explained.

'Got far to walk?'

She pointed to the pit lanes. 'Just to Tunstall Street.'

'Come on, I'll walk with you. Tunstall Street's on my way to the pit. I'll walk up the back lane and see you safely home. You never know what strange fellas might be lurking at this time of night.'

He began marching in the direction Ruby had pointed and she ran to catch up with him. She was about to explain that she felt safe enough, that she'd walked home late from her job many times. But there was something reassuring about the man's words, and her instinct told her he seemed harmless enough. Besides, there were others about in the streets, groups of miners heading to the pit to work the night shift. She walked in step with him, their feet hitting the pavement at the same time, and when he turned to smile at her, she took heart.

'My dad works at the pit, and my brother,' she said.

'Oh aye, what's their names?'

'Arthur Dinsdale, he's my dad. And our Michael's just a lad; he works at the pit top but he's going underground when he turns fourteen in November.'

'And what's your name?' he asked.

'Ruby Dinsdale.'

'Gordon Fisher,' he said, beaming at her. 'Pleased to meet you.'

When he smiled widely, his face changed. His moustache lifted, his eyes creased at the sides and he suddenly looked vulnerable. Ruby realised he was a lot younger than she'd first thought.

'How long have you worked at the pit?' she asked. It was a sure-fire way of finding out how old he was without coming out and asking him, which might have seemed rude.

By the time Ruby reached her back gate, she knew a lot about Gordon Fisher. He was nineteen years old and lived in a room at Mrs Sowerby's lodging house on Burdon Road. She had guessed right about him being a bachelor. His family lived in Seaham, he said, but then he clammed up and changed the subject. He didn't explain what had brought him to Ryhope, and Ruby didn't press him – well, they'd only just met, and she didn't want him to think her too forward.

'This is my house,' she said when they reached the back gate. 'Thank you for walking me home.'

Gordon raised his cap. 'It was my pleasure,' he said. 'Nice to meet you, Ruby Dinsdale.'

Ruby put her hand on the gate, and it swung open. Lady came to greet her from her corner of the yard.

Gordon gave a polite cough. 'If I was to call sometime, like? I mean, next time I have a day off, if I came to ask you out for a walk, might you come?'

Ruby felt herself blushing and was grateful for the darkness so that he wouldn't see how much his question had flustered her. She'd never been asked out before. 'I might,' she said.

'Could I call this weekend?'

'That'd be nice,' she said with a smile.

'Evening, Ruby, sleep tight,' Gordon said. As he walked away down the back lane, Lady bared her teeth and growled.

Ruby now had the difficult task of telling her parents what had happened in the pub. She thought she'd keep quiet about Gordon for now. One thing at a time. She took a moment before she pushed the kitchen door open and stepped inside, ready to face whatever was coming her way when she gave her mam and dad the bad news.

Chapter Ten

Money became tighter than ever for the Dinsdales once Ruby lost her job. The news had not gone down well with Arthur and Mary, just as she had feared. She suffered her dad brooding over it for more than a week. She'd let her parents down in the worst possible way, and all for the sake of two pieces of pie. There was little hope of her getting another job while she had the household to run single-handedly.

The autumn days turned cold and dark. Bitter winds whipped off the North Sea and rain and sleet roared in. At the end of October, Ruby turned eighteen. But there was no celebration in the Dinsdale house, and the day went unmarked apart from a peck on the cheek from Arthur. Mary rarely left her bed, and when she did venture downstairs, she sat in her chair by the fire, demanding a jug of beer or stout be brought from the Forester's Arms. At first, Arthur had given in, believing it might settle her mind, the better to help her cope with the loss of the bairn. But as her requests became more frequent, he pleaded with her to lay off the ale. Ruby heard her Grandma Winter's name invoked, something he rarely did.

'Do you want to end up like your mother?' he yelled at Mary one night. 'You know what the drink did to her, and still you persist in asking me to buy it.'

'But Arthur . . .' she pleaded.

'But Arthur nothing! I won't have it, Mary. I'm not going to lose you to the ale the way your dad lost your mam.'

He refused to buy more beer for her, told her he'd rather throw his money in the gutter. He told her she was ruining herself, but Mary didn't listen. All she wanted was the ale. Arthur begged and pleaded with her, while she would cajole him, tease him, promise him the earth, say that she just needed one more drink, just a little one, and then she'd stop and have no more. Arthur's love for his wife meant he hated to see her in pain, but he knew he couldn't give in to her demands. He told Ruby and Michael never to buy ale for their mam, no matter how much she begged. Mary raged against the injustice and took to her bed, sleeping during the day and only coming downstairs when Arthur returned home from work.

One evening when Mary was in bed, Arthur and Ruby were sitting by a fire burning low in the hearth. Arthur was smoking his pipe and Ruby was darning socks. The tension had finally thawed between dad and daughter after Ruby's sacking.

'Dad, do you know a fella at the pit called Fisher?' she asked. 'Gordon Fisher?'

Arthur took his pipe from his lips. 'Fisher?' he said, thinking. 'Doesn't ring a bell.'

'He's got a big black moustache,' Ruby said.

'So have half the men in Ryhope,' Arthur laughed. 'Why do you ask?'

Ruby had been out with Gordon twice now, just for a walk around the village. Plenty of people had seen them out together and she felt certain that gossip would reach her dad in due course. Nothing stayed secret in their small village for long. She kept her gaze firmly on her work. 'I've been getting quite friendly with him.'

'Friendly?' Arthur said. 'You mean you're courting?'

She lifted her gaze to him. 'I suppose we are, yes.'

'My little lass, eh? And here you are, eighteen years old. How time flies. How long's it been going on between you and this Fisher lad?'

'A few weeks,' Ruby said. 'It's not serious or anything, we just walk around the village and talk.'

'How old is he? Who's his family? Is he a Ryhope lad?'

Ruby told her dad everything she knew about Gordon. It was a relief to get her friendship with him out in the open. She'd kept quiet about him so far as she didn't know where it might lead, or if it might lead anywhere at all. But she'd warmed to him and found herself looking forward to seeing him again. They'd even talked about him coming to the Dinsdale house and meeting Arthur and Michael. And if Mary felt up to it, Ruby would introduce him to her mam too. When Ruby had explained to Gordon how the Dinsdales were fixed, that money was tight and there was nothing spare to feed an extra mouth at their table, he had offered to bring slices of ham if he was invited to tea. This was news Ruby passed to her dad.

'Ham, eh?' Arthur said, licking his lips.

'What do you think, Dad? Can I invite him for tea?'

'I don't see why not, lass. It might just be the tonic your mam needs.'

* * *

In the following weeks, Gordon became a regular visitor to the Dinsdale house, where he was respectful to Arthur and Michael, courteous to Mary when she made it downstairs, and charming, even loving towards Ruby. He spoke to Michael about life at the pit, and told him not to be scared when Michael expressed his worries about working underground as soon as he turned fourteen. He quickly became a part of the family, chipping in with parcels of fresh beef or ham from the store. He brought an ounce of tobacco once a week for Arthur, who accepted the gift with good grace.

'What do you think of him, Dad?' Ruby asked one night.

Arthur lifted his pipe from his mouth. 'Brings good baccy,' he said without a trace of emotion.

'Is that it?' Ruby said.

He shrugged. 'Seems a decent sort. Mind you, he could do with a bloody good shave.'

Ruby thought the same thing herself. She and Gordon had kissed now, more than once, and although it was every bit as thrilling as the stories in *The Red Letter* magazine promised, she didn't like having to fight her way through his bristly moustache. Oh, but once her lips found their way there, his kisses were welcome and sweet. As their relationship deepened, she took the magazine from under her bed. She hoped to find the advice she needed about having a boyfriend and what might happen next. Would she have her heart broken, or would she live happily ever after, like some of the lucky ones did?

* * *

News spread around the village about Ruby and Gordon, and one morning when Ruby was sewing by the fire, there was a knock at the kitchen door. She opened it to see two faces she hadn't seen in a very long time.

'Jean! Abigail!' she cried.

The girls flung their arms around each other.

'Come on inside, out of the cold,' Ruby said.

Jean and Abigail headed straight to the fire to warm their backsides. Lady trotted behind them and slunk away under the table, which was fast becoming her favourite place to lie.

'Let me look at you both. I haven't seen you in ages,' Ruby said.

Jean looked as beautiful as ever. She'd always appeared older than her years due to the powder and paint she wore on her face. Her dark hair was curled prettily, her lips sharp with red lipstick and her cheeks pinched pink by the cold air outside. Abigail, as always, looked more robust. She was a no-nonsense lass, with thick arms and calves, and long fair hair tied in a ponytail that fell down her back, though Ruby noticed that her normally ruddy complexion was pale and wan. 'Still playing football, Abigail?' she asked.

'Of course,' Abigail replied. 'I'm captain of Ryhope ladies' team now. We had a cracking win against Silksworth this summer.'

'Will you have some tea while you're here?' Ruby asked.

'Please,' Jean said. 'We need something to warm us up before we head back outdoors. It's perishing out there. How's your mam?' she asked. 'We heard she wasn't well.'

'She has good days and bad days,' Ruby said. 'Losing

71

the bairn knocked the stuffing out of her. She's been bad with her nerves ever since.'

'Wasn't your Grandma Winter bad with her nerves?' Jean asked with concern.

'I think Dad's worried Mam might turn the same way,' Ruby said sadly. 'Anyway, I'm sure you didn't come to hear about my problems. How's *your* mam, Abigail?'

'Oh, same as always. You know her. Fellas come and go in our house. Mam can't seem to keep any of them longer than a couple of weeks. Nothing changes.'

Ruby looked at her friend. 'How are things between you and her these days? Do you get on any better?'

'Not really,' Abigail said quickly. 'She leaves me to my own devices just like she's always done since I was a child.'

Jean tutted. 'It's shameful the way you were brought up.'

'Why do you think I started playing football?' Abigail said. 'I had to get out of the house, away from Mam.'

Suddenly she began coughing. She covered her mouth with her hand and turned her face away. A look of concern passed between Ruby and Jean as the cough shook her body.

'You all right?' Ruby asked once Abigail was silent.

'Can't seem to shake this cough,' she said at last. 'Any chance of a drink of water?'

Ruby lifted the jug with fresh water in it and poured some into a mug.

'What's your Michael up to these days?' Jean asked.

'He's going underground at the pit next month, as soon as he turns fourteen,' Ruby replied.

'Poor lad,' Abigail said softly. 'I'll always be thankful for being a lass and not having to work underground. It must be hell for them. Can't think it'd do my chest any good being underground; feels like I'm coughing all the time as it is.'

'It brings the money in, though,' Jean said. 'My brothers hate every minute working at the pit, but there's not much choice for Ryhope lads. Ted's lucky he got himself a job as a delivery boy at the store.'

Ruby thought of Stan, working behind the bar in his parents' pub. He was one of the lucky ones too.

'How is Ted?' Ruby asked.

Jean began twirling a lock of hair around her fingers. 'Oh, he's fine,' she said coyly.

'And what about you, Abigail, have you got a fella yet?'

Abigail gave a mischievous smile. 'There's no one special, just a couple of fellas I go to when I want a night out at the pictures or dancing in town. I'm not going to get tied down too soon. I like to keep my options open.'

'You need to be careful. You'll get a bad name carrying on like that,' Jean warned.

Abigail ignored the remark and turned to Ruby. 'Are you still working at the Queen's Head?'

Ruby shook her head. 'I'm looking after the house until Mam gets better.'

'Is that why you left the pub?'

'It's a long story,' Ruby sighed, then she brightened slightly. 'You'll never guess who works there. Stan Hutchinson! Remember him from school?'

'Stan? The tall, quiet lad with freckles?' Jean said.

'That's him,' Ruby replied. 'Except he's not so quiet now. He's a big strapping lad, handsome too.'

She smiled when she thought of her friend, and cursed his mam for keeping them apart. She'd managed to speak to Jim since Polly had sacked her; she'd bumped into him on the colliery bank one day while out shopping for her mam. He had been kind and honest but told Ruby there was little chance of changing Polly's mind once it had been made up.

'Do you fancy him?' Abigail asked, cutting into Ruby's thoughts.

'Who? Stan?'

'He sounds just like the type of fella I'd go for,' Abigail continued. 'Who wouldn't want a tall, handsome, strapping lad who runs his own pub? Seems like just the ticket to me. I wouldn't mind getting my hands on someone like him.'

'Abigail, behave yourself,' Jean warned.

'His mam and dad run the pub; Stan just works there,' Ruby explained as she busied herself making a pot of tea.

Jean leaned closer. 'Talking of fellas you fancy, who's this one you're courting?'

'Come on, Ruby, you can tell us, we're your friends,' Abigail urged.

Ruby looked into their eager faces and laughed.

'I don't see either of you for weeks, and as soon as there's a whiff of gossip in the air, you're straight in here sticking your noses in where they don't belong.'

'Well, if you're going to be like that,' Jean sniffed.

'Don't be angry, Ruby,' Abigail wheedled. 'Me and Jean are working full-time at the store; we rarely get a minute to ourselves, never mind having spare time to visit.

But it's our day off today and we wanted to come and see you.'

'You mean you wanted to hear all about my fella,' Ruby said.

Abigail put her arm around Ruby's shoulders. 'Every single word.'

Chapter Eleven

In early November, with still no improvement in Mary's condition, Arthur made a firm decision. One cold, frosty morning he headed to the miners' hall.

The miners' hall was a large room where union meetings took place. It was also where miners went to enjoy a spot of rest and relaxation when they weren't at work and the pubs weren't open. Pipe and cigarette smoke hung heavy in the air. As he entered, Arthur removed his cap. At one end of the hall, he saw Gladys Smith, a stout woman in a green dress, bustling about with a large brown teapot. She was filling cups and setting them out on a table beside a plate of ginger biscuits. At smaller tables scattered around the hall, groups of men were playing cards or dominoes. A dartboard hung on the wall.

'Morning, Arthur!' a man called as Arthur walked further into the hall. He acknowledged his friend Taffy with a smile and a wave, but inside, his heart sank. He'd been hoping to avoid anyone he knew. He should have known better.

'What you up to in here, then?' Taffy asked.

'Come to see Stuart Brown,' Arthur said. 'Just want a quiet word with him, like.'

'Union business?'

'Aye,' Arthur said. He hated lying, especially to the men he worked with, the men his life depended on in the hell of the underground mine.

'He's over there, near Gladys,' Taffy said, pointing in the direction of the woman with the teapot.

Arthur saw Stuart sitting at a table concentrating on a pile of paperwork. He walked towards him and stood quietly until Stuart realised he was there and raised his head.

'Dinsdale,' he said with a smile.

Arthur gripped his flat cap with both hands. He was nervous. He felt as if everyone was staring at him, wondering what his business was. He glanced around the room. No one was looking at him. Card games continued and he heard the click-clack of dominoes hit the tables.

'Well, what is it?' Stuart asked.

Arthur put his hand on the back of a chair. 'Can I sit down, Stuart?'

Without waiting for an answer, he pulled out the chair and positioned it so that he had his back to the men in the room. What he wanted to speak to Stuart about was not for their ears. He laid his cap on the table. Stuart moved his pile of paperwork to one side, called Gladys over and requested two cups of tea and a couple of ginger biscuits. He waited for the woman to shuffle away out of earshot before he leaned across the table to Arthur.

'Now then, what can I do for you?'

Many times Arthur had gone over the words he wanted to say. They were there, on the tip of his tongue, but he couldn't seem to set them free. Stuart sensed his discomfort and sought to put him at ease. He hadn't been elected chief union official without learning a thing or two about the behaviour of the men he represented. These were hard-working men, more used to the dark horror of toiling underground than sipping tea and eating biscuits with something on their mind.

'Whatever you tell me remains confidential,' he said.

'Aye,' Arthur replied. He took a sip of his tea and grimaced. Pulling the sugar bowl towards him, he dropped three large teaspoons of sugar in, gave it a stir and tried again. Then he set the cup on the table and locked eyes with Stuart. 'You've always said that we can come to you for advice.'

'Any time, Arthur. That's what I'm here for, always willing to help where I can. What is it? Want to move to a different seam? Is it the waterlogged seam you're working on? The amount of complaints I get about that. You know Ryhope Coal Company are bound by law to move—'

'No.' Arthur shook his head. 'It's not work. It's something else, something personal.'

Stuart leaned back in his chair. 'Go on,' he said.

Arthur pulled at the cuff on his jacket. 'I've got a mate, like,' he began.

From Stuart's experience dealing with Ryhope miners and hearing many tales begin this way, he doubted very much there was a mate. He let Arthur carry on.

'And his missus, she . . .' Arthur faltered. It felt like he was betraying Mary, the love of his life. But he had nowhere else to go, no one else to ask. 'She lost a bairn some months ago and she's not been right since. He wants

78

his wife back, you know?' There, it was out in the open. He'd said it. He felt his hands tremble.

'Bad with her nerves?' Stuart asked. It was the cover-all term for women's ailments that men could never hope to understand.

'Her own mam went the same way, bad with her nerves too.'

'It happens more than you'd think, Arthur,' Stuart said sagely. He chose his next words carefully. 'It sounds like your friend loves his wife very much.'

Arthur held his gaze. 'He does.'

'Does she have friends who can help? Someone to call in to see how she is?'

Arthur thought about Elsie. 'I'll have a word with my pal and suggest it,' he said.

'I could have a word with Reverend Daye,' Stuart offered. 'He could call to give words of comfort.'

'My friend's not a churchgoer,' Arthur said quickly.

Stuart thought for a moment. 'Then I'll make enquiries.' He leaned across the table. 'There might be other wives who can offer support. If I find someone to help, which address will I send them to?'

Arthur picked up his cap. It was a delicate balance between getting help for Mary and betraying her, giving details of their private lives to folk outside of their family. He decided to say nothing more. 'I'll pass on what you've said to my pal,' he said. 'And if he wants to take it further, I'll send him to see you.'

'Arthur, wait!' Stuart called. But Arthur was already striding out of the hall.

Outside, the cold wind whipped his face. He pulled up the collar of his thin jacket and nestled his chin into it, burying as much of his face as he could. He had to get to work and turned left to head up to the pit. He walked with his head down, barely looking where he was going, knowing his route off by heart. The wind blew harshly around him and rain began to spit. He walked faster, blood pounding in his ears. He heard the cry of seagulls overhead and then a noise that caught him by surprise. A woman's laughter, a throaty laugh, out of place on such a wet and cold day.

He looked ahead to see a young couple walking on the other side of the road. The woman's auburn hair blew across her face and she brushed it away. Arthur recognised her painted face. He knew who she was, or at least he knew of her. She was called Annie Grafton, and was one of the women who worked the pit lanes offering their womanly charms in exchange for cold, hard cash. Her black stockings were laddered, her boots down at heel, her jacket unsuitable for the weather. But it wasn't the sight of the woman that turned his stomach. It was the man at her side, the man who was holding her around the shoulders and planting kisses on her face as they walked. A man with a thick, heavy moustache.

The shock hit Arthur hard. He stood still as the couple walked by. They were oblivious to him, lost in their own world. His instinct was to give chase, to thump Gordon on the nose and demand he stay away from his daughter, tell him he was no longer welcome in their home. But he didn't move; he couldn't. He felt as if he'd had the stuffing knocked out of him. He continued walking up the bank to the pit, wondering how on earth he'd tell Ruby what he'd seen.

* * *

For a few days, Arthur battled with his conscience. When he finally resolved to tell Ruby that he'd seen Gordon with Annie, he chose his moment carefully. He and Ruby liked to sit by the fire on an evening while Arthur smoked his pipe and Ruby busied herself with sewing. With just the crackle of the flames, the house was calm and still. Ruby had already prepared a hot bath for Michael, who was due home from his first day underground. The tin bath was waiting in front of the fire. Lady lay at Ruby's feet and Mary was in bed. Arthur decided to ease into a conversation with his daughter as tactfully as he could before Michael returned.

'Fancy our Michael working underground already, eh?' he said. 'I can't believe my two bairns are growing up so fast. Won't be easy for you now, looking after two miners in the house as well as your mam the way she is. There'll be two baths to prepare and we'll be working different shifts, so it'll be a case of getting one bath over and done with and another one ready. The water needs to be on the boil all day.'

'I know, Dad,' Ruby said quietly. She'd already given it much thought.

'Two sets of pit clothes to wash,' Arthur continued.

'I'm strong, Dad, I can do it.'

'Michael's wages won't go up much, you know,' he warned. 'It'll be as hard as ever for us all. There's still no hope of affording the doctor to see your mam.'

'I'm getting better at managing the money, Dad.'

'Make sure any debts are paid off,' Arthur said.

Ruby laid her sewing on her knee and looked at him. 'I'm doing my best.'

'You're a good lass, and a daughter to be proud of.' He

paused. 'And that's why I need to say something that's been on my mind.'

Ruby shot him a look. He looked serious, anxious even. A shock went through her. Was he about to say that *he* was ill? Was it something about her mam that she needed to know?

'What is it?' she said.

'This fella of yours . . .' Arthur began. But before he could say any more, there was an almighty clatter in the yard. Ruby leapt from her seat. Lady followed, with Arthur behind.

'Who's there?' Ruby called.

'Just me.'

She was relieved to hear Michael's voice.

'What are you making all that racket for? You'll wake Mam,' she said.

She stepped into the yard and faced her brother. His face was pit black, his hands too. His clothes were greasy and dirty, every inch of him blackened with coal. She was used to seeing her dad like this after a day down the pit, but it seemed wrong on someone as young and innocent as Michael. He was just a lad, her little brother. Her heart went out to him.

'Hey, onion face,' she said. 'Your bath's ready, then there's rabbit stew.'

Michael glanced at Lady. 'Rabbit? Again?'

'It's better than going hungry,' Ruby said.

He walked into the kitchen.

'Your first day underground,' Arthur said. 'How was it?'

Michael stood rigid, as black as the ace of spades. Then, silently, he began to cry.

Chapter Twelve

In bed that night, Ruby was kept awake by the sound of Michael's sobs. She hadn't known him cry since they were little.

'Michael?' she whispered.

The crying stopped. There was silence. She tried again. 'Michael, are you asleep?'

'Yes,' he replied.

She smiled to herself. Typical Michael, trying to make a joke of things to cover up his true feelings. 'Is everything all right?' she whispered. She didn't want her words to make their way to their parents' room. The walls were thin and she would hate to wake them; they both had enough on their plate.

Silence.

'Michael?'

'What?'

'You can tell me what's wrong. I won't tell anyone.'

'Promise?'

'I promise.'

She turned on her side to face her brother's bed and listened to his tale about his first day underground. She heard how scared he had been, the youngest one there, the smallest of them all. She heard about the open cage that he'd been crammed into with much older, bigger men, to be lowered into the mine. He told her it was like a different country down there, a place with its own rules, even its own language – known as pitmatic – the miners using words he didn't understand. It was dark, of course, he'd expected that. The hours were long, but he was used to that too. It was the crushing lack of space he'd felt keenly and hadn't been prepared for, working on his hands and knees for twelve hours in a cramped space.

'I don't want to go back,' he gasped through his tears.

Ruby wished she could say something that might help. But both of them knew he had to go back the next day and all the days for the rest of his working life. He simply had no choice.

Each night when Michael returned from work, after he'd eaten whatever meal Ruby had been able to cook and had his bath by the fire, he went straight to bed. Ruby often heard him crying. He became withdrawn, no longer the happy, cheeky lad he'd once been. Working underground meant that he was now spared the drudgery of domestic chores. He was a man now, a miner, and his priority was the pit. Ruby had always known that was how it would be. And as her dad had warned her, she had two baths to fill and empty, two sets of pit clothes to bash against the wall to beat the coal dust from them, two sets to wash each Monday in the yard and peg out in the lane to dry. But with the cold, wet November days, the washing was increasingly taken indoors to dry in front of the fire, where it steamed up the windows in the small house.

Whenever Mary came downstairs these days, she wore her nightgown under her clothes. She'd sit by the fire, arms crossed, demanding that Ruby spike her tea with a cinder. But Ruby would never give in to her demands, no matter how much her mam begged. There was no alcohol in the house now; Arthur had made sure of that in an effort to get Mary sober. It seemed to have worked, but Mary's will to help Ruby with the chores, or take an interest in herself and her family, had waned. She didn't know Michael was struggling with the demons that came with his new job. She didn't know Ruby and Gordon were growing close. It was all she could do to drag herself downstairs each day from her bed to the fireplace, drink tea and nibble at whatever Ruby could encourage her to eat.

Ruby did her best for her mam – she helped wash her and brush her hair – but there was little she could do to ease the troubles in her mind. And now with Michael crying each night, she was at a low ebb. She felt useless, unable to help either her mam or her brother. Cooking and cleaning for her family had always been hard, not that she'd ever complain. Her cooking skills still weren't great, but she kept everyone fed and the house clean. However, what she couldn't do was mend the pain and sorrow behind her mam's eyes, and the fear in Michael's heart.

Christmas approached, and displays of fruit cakes and marzipan filled the shop windows. Sweet mince pies went on sale, bottles of sherry and brandy were sold. But in the Dinsdale house, no celebrations were planned. The money just wasn't there. After much deliberation, Arthur had decided to hold his tongue as far as Gordon was concerned. He didn't want to hurt Ruby, not when she was working hard to keep their home together. But he did make enquiries about Gordon at the pit, determined to find out more about the man courting his daughter.

'Anyone know a fella called Fisher, works the Betsy seam?' he asked at work one day.

'Fisher?' a strong lad called Joe called out. 'Gordon Fisher, the fella with the moustache?'

'That's him,' Arthur said.

'I know him. What about him?'

Arthur crawled along the shaft to sit beside Joe so he didn't have to shout his business for all and sundry to hear. 'Where's he from?'

Joe shrugged. 'Seaham, I think, by the harbour.'

'Who's his dad?' No matter how many times Arthur had asked Gordon about his background, he'd always been evasive.

'He never talks about his family. From what I understand, there was a bit of a falling-out and he moved to Ryhope. Lives in a lodging house, by all accounts. What do you want to know for?'

'Because our Ruby's keen on him,' Arthur said. He thanked Joe.

But Joe wasn't finished. 'There's something else, Arthur. I've got a mate on the Betsy seam. He often works with Gordon.' He leaned close, so close he was almost touching Arthur's ear with his lips. 'I've heard things about him.'

'Oh aye?' Arthur said.

'He's a token slinger.'

Joe's words were delivered with the seriousness they deserved. Token slinging was a sackable offence, something that only the lowest of miners would do. Once coal had been hewn and shovelled into tubs, a token was hung on each tub. Each token bore a number to identify the miner who had filled it. The more tubs the miner filled, the more money he earned. Token slingers were those men who changed the tokens to claim the tubs for themselves.

'No!' Arthur cried.

Joe tapped the side of his nose. 'That's what I've heard.'

'Why doesn't your mate report him?' Arthur asked.

'He's handy with his fists, Arthur. Nobody wants to go up against that.'

Arthur's heart sank. Gordon was a liar, a thief, a womaniser. But there was even worse to come.

'He's already been in trouble with the gaffers,' Joe said.

'What for?'

'Kicking the pit ponies. He almost booted one of the poor things to death.'

In the days before Christmas, Ruby asked Arthur if Gordon could join the Dinsdales for Christmas Day dinner.

'Isn't he going home to his own family to celebrate Christmas with them?' Arthur asked.

'He said his mam's got a houseful already and he's planning to go the day after,' Ruby replied.

Arthur had so far kept quiet about what he knew about Gordon; it was gossip after all, second-hand news. But still, he felt uneasy and was against having the man in his house. That was, until Ruby revealed that Gordon had offered to bring a turkey.

On Christmas Day, Gordon duly arrived and Arthur glared at him as both men sat by the fire. Michael was at work after another sleepless night. Ruby had hoped that her brother would become used to conditions underground and settle down. But Michael's mood had continued to darken.

She boiled a pan of potatoes, the only vegetables in the house, and made gravy in the turkey tin. The scent of the roast meat filled the air and lured Mary downstairs. She was wrapped in an old cardigan over her nightgown, her feet bare, her hair matted. When she saw Gordon by the fire, she put her hand to her head. 'Sorry, Gordon. The state of me, eh? I didn't know we had company.'

Gordon was his usual charming self with both Ruby and Mary. Arthur watched him keenly. Every move Gordon made, every word that he said came under scrutiny now. And yet no matter how hard he tried, Arthur couldn't find fault. He saw the polite and respectful way Gordon spoke to Mary, flattering her even, putting a rare smile on Mary's face. He saw how Ruby lit up each time he offered to help with the dinner. Was this really the same man he'd heard about? The same man he'd seen with his own eyes out with a common tart? He was having a hard time reconciling the two versions of Gordon he knew. Gordon even offered to take Lady for a walk, to get her out from under Ruby's feet until dinner was ready. But when he made a move towards the dog, she bared her teeth and growled.

'Lady, don't do that,' Ruby chided. She turned to Gordon with an apologetic smile. 'She's not like that with anyone else.'

'Maybe it's my moustache she's not keen on,' Gordon joked.

'She might have a point,' Arthur said sternly.

The smile dropped from Gordon's face. 'What are you saying, Arthur?'

Ruby and Mary looked at Arthur too, waiting for him to explain.

'What I mean is . . .' Arthur began. 'Your face is a mess, lad. You need a bloody good shave.'

Ruby's hand flew to her mouth to stifle a giggle, but Mary had no such qualms about upsetting Gordon and she burst out laughing.

'Dad!' Ruby chastised.

'Well, it's true,' Arthur said. 'It's as if he's hiding behind that thing on his face. Get rid of it and show us the real Gordon Fisher. I dare you.'

Ruby held her breath.

'All right,' Gordon said, squaring up to Arthur. 'If that's what you want. Fetch your razor. I'll do it right here, right now.'

'But I'm just about to serve dinner,' Ruby cried.

'Dinner can wait another ten minutes,' Arthur said. 'Mary, go and fetch the razor and a bar of soap. Gordon, you can shave in the yard.'

'Dad!' Ruby exclaimed again. She couldn't believe this was happening. What had got into the men?

Fifteen minutes later, Gordon took his seat at the table and Ruby couldn't take her eyes off him. His face was pink and shorn; he looked different, younger, more vulnerable. In Ruby's opinion, he was even more handsome.

Gordon glared at Arthur opposite him. 'Happy now?' he sneered.

'A little better,' Arthur replied, pleased to have won a battle against the man he was going to watch like a hawk from now on.

After dinner had been eaten and a plate of food left in

the oven for Michael's return, Ruby washed the pots and pans. Arthur was due up early for work the next day, so he soon went to bed, and Mary followed him up. Left alone downstairs, Ruby and Gordon sat by the fire with Lady lying at Ruby's side. Ruby ran her hand across Gordon's face, delighting in the touch of his smooth, soft bare skin. She leaned forward for a kiss, a different kiss to any she'd experienced before. Gordon's lips were welcoming and ready. They kissed until Lady began to growl, and Gordon gently pulled away.

'Even without my moustache, she's still baring her teeth,' he joked.

Ruby stroked Lady's head and the dog snuggled against her hand.

'Can I smoke, Ruby?' Gordon asked.

Ruby nodded. Her dad regularly smoked his pipe and she didn't mind at all that Gordon wanted to have a cigarette. She enjoyed the fact that he had asked her permission. It felt as if he was letting her take control, giving her a choice.

They sat and talked by the fire until it was time for Ruby to bring water in to prepare Michael's bath. Gordon wouldn't hear of her fetching the water herself and insisted on doing it for her. When it was set to boil and Gordon had brought in the tin bath, doing all he could to help, he flicked his cigarette butt towards the fire and reached for her to kiss her goodbye. They kissed for a very long time, Ruby delighting in the touch of Gordon's clean-shaven face. When they finally released each other, she walked into the back lane with him to see him off into the night.

Both of them were unaware that his cigarette had missed its target and was now smouldering on the rug.

Chapter Thirteen

Ruby shivered in the night air as she watched Gordon walk away down the back lane. She heard a dog bark behind her but ignored it at first. The barking became louder, more incessant, and before she knew it, Lady was running rings around her, barking for all she was worth.

'What is it, girl?' Ruby asked. 'You'll wake up half the street.'

She had never seen the dog so agitated. Each time she tried to take a step forward, Lady was in front of her, barking, nudging her shins with her nose. 'What, girl?' she said. 'What's wrong?'

Lady darted away as if running back to the Dinsdales', then stopped, barked again and returned to Ruby. Ruby was worried the dog was injured or had eaten something it shouldn't. She followed Lady to the yard, but as soon as she neared the kitchen door, the dog backed away, fearful. Ruby looked into the kitchen and her heart fell to the floor. Flames were licking up from the hearthrug. Without thinking, she ran inside, lifted the bucket of water that was standing by the fireside ready to be heated for Michael's bath and threw it on to the flames. The fire on the rug and in the hearth died instantly, sizzling away, and black smoke filled the air.

Ruby sank to her knees. She was numb with shock; she couldn't move, could hardly breathe. Her heart pounded and blood rushed in her head. She felt something brush her arm and saw Lady sitting beside her, both of them staring at the water pooling on the floor. Ruby forced herself to take a good look at the rug. It was all but gone, just a blackened strip left. She thought of her mam and dad upstairs. If the dog's barking had woken them, they'd have come down to find out what was going on. She listened for the creaking of floorboards. Was someone on their way down the stairs?

It was Mary who came into the room, and her face fell when she saw the devastation caused by the fire. Ruby turned, ready to explain and apologise, but Mary had no time for words. She sprang into action, cleaning and tidying, sweeping away the burned and charred rug, mopping up water. The two women worked quickly together, and only once they'd finished clearing up did Mary demand an explanation. Ruby knew there was only one way the fire could have started. She remembered Gordon smoking, flicking his cigarette to the fire, but she couldn't recall seeing it land in the flames; they'd been too busy kissing.

'He's not to smoke in our house again, do you hear?' Mary said sternly once Ruby told her what had happened. 'And we'd best keep the truth from your dad. If he finds out Gordon caused the fire, he'll not let him back into the house. Just leave him to me. I'll speak to him first thing in the morning.'

'You'd do that for me? For Gordon?' Ruby asked.

'I can see how much you like this Gordon fella,' Mary

said. 'He's put a sparkle in your eye. I'm sure the fire was just an accident, but your dad might not be so generous. I'll soften him up and tell him a lump of coal fell from the hearth.'

Ruby put her hand on Mary's arm. 'Thanks, Mam,' she said.

'Oh, don't thank me, love. It's me who should be thanking you.'

Ruby shot her a puzzled look. 'What do you mean?'

Mary sank into her chair by the hearth. 'I came downstairs because I could smell smoke and I thought . . . I thought it was because of something I'd done. I thought I'd left the fire burning after I'd been drinking.'

'But dad doesn't allow any beer in the house now, he's been trying to help you get sober, Mam. Have you been getting beer from somewhere else?'

Mary closed her eyes and tears made their way down her tired face. 'Just every now and then, when things get too hard to cope.'

'Who's been buying it for you?' Ruby demanded. 'I know you don't have enough money to waste on buying ale.'

Mary gulped. 'Ann Hutton bought it for me. I begged her, Ruby, it wasn't her fault, don't think badly of her. I was desperate for something to take the pain away. But now . . .' Mary waved her hand towards the hearth. 'This has scared the life out of me. I know how far I've gone with the ale in the last few months, how lost I've been since the baby died. And I know I wouldn't be able to forgive myself if my drinking caused something to happen to my family. If I thought for one moment that I'd caused the fire because I'd been drunk . . .' She shook her head and cast her gaze at the sodden floor. 'I couldn't bear it, Ruby. This has given me one hell of a shock.'

'But it's not your fault, you mustn't think like that,' Ruby said.

Mary raised her eyebrows. 'Mustn't I? It's about time I pulled myself together. I've been trying, lass, really I have, and it's not been easy. But this . . .' She looked at the hearth and the burned rug. 'This is a warning of what could have happened, what might still happen if I keep on drinking. I'd get careless, sloppy. I could put my family in danger. It's got to stop now before it gets out of hand.'

There was a noise behind them, footsteps, then Michael was at Ruby's side.

He surveyed the scene in front of him. 'What happened?' he said.

'The rug caught fire,' Ruby gasped.

'How?' Michael said. 'Did coal fall out on to the floor?'

Ruby and Mary shared a look. Ruby sighed. If only it was as simple as that.

Michael kept his filthy pit clothes on while he ate his meal of Christmas turkey at the table. Meanwhile, Ruby set the fire in the hearth again with paper and wood and a shovel of coal. It took a long time to catch, having been doused with water, and she had to be patient. And all the while she thought of Gordon's cigarette and of what might have happened if Lady hadn't raised the alarm.

The new year arrived quietly at the Dinsdale house – there was no money for a celebration – but during the early weeks of 1920, Gordon and Ruby became even closer and he visited the house more often. He apologised over and over again when Ruby told him what had happened with the fire. Despite his remorse, whenever he asked her if he could smoke, she shook her head and banished him to the yard with his cigarette, though she was sure he wouldn't be so careless again.

One Monday morning in spring, a weak sunshine greeted Ruby when she woke. Her heart leapt to see light struggling its way through the clouds. It was washing day, the first one of the year when there was the possibility of drying clothes in the lane instead of cluttering up the kitchen and steaming up the house. After the chaos caused by the kitchen fire, Mary had been true to her word about her drinking, shocked into giving it up. No more did she beg Ruby to put a drop of something in her tea. No more did she plead with Arthur for a jug of beer. Without the ale to slow her thoughts and clog her mind, she was beginning to get better, and, although not fully back to her old self, she got dressed each day and helped Ruby with the chores. But still there was a sense of sadness about her, and Ruby often caught her staring out of the window into the pit lane, in her own world. It was as if she was searching for something out there, keeping vigil for her lost child.

On that warm spring morning, Ruby did the bulk of the washing, scrubbing and cleaning coal dust from her dad and Michael's clothes. Mary helped where she could, but she didn't have the strength she'd once had. Lady lay down in the lane, having learned the hard way to keep out of Ruby's way on washing day, otherwise she'd be splashed with water. Once the clothes were washed and mangled, Ruby and Mary carried them out to peg them on the line. All up and down the back lane, lines were strung from yards to the opposite wall. Washing blew in the breeze, shirts flying like kites, bloomers billowing like barrage balloons. Women chatted with neighbours and bairns ran barefoot under flapping clothes. Ruby caught sight of the two Miss Huttons and waved a cheery hello. Elsie headed towards them, threw her arms around Mary and hugged her.

'How are you, love?'

'I'm on the mend, Elsie. And thanks for your visits while I was holed up in my bed. It felt good to be reminded that life went on outside of my own four walls, outside of my own mind.'

Elsie shrugged. 'What are friends for?'

'Will you come in for a cuppa?' Ruby offered.

'I'm in the middle of stringing our washing out,' Elsie said. 'I can't leave Ann on her own.'

'Come in when you're done,' Mary said. 'Bring Ann if you like. I want to hear all your news.'

'News?' Elsie gave a throaty laugh. 'There's not much to tell.'

'Not even about you and Bert Collins?' Mary smiled.

Ruby loved to see her mam smile. It warmed her heart that she was taking pleasure from life again.

Elsie was just about to head back to finish pegging out her washing when an almighty yell went up from Lil Mahone a few doors down.

'He's flaming well back again!' she shrieked.

The women in the back lane stopped what they were doing. Bairns stood still in the street. Everyone glared at the distant horse and cart as it turned the corner at the top of the lane and came trundling into view.

'The cheek of the lad!' Elsie cried.

'Lasses?' Lil Mahone called. 'Are we going to just

stand here and let this lad trample our washing to the ground again?'

'No!' Ruby shouted.

'Over my dead body,' Elsie said. 'Come on, Ruby, let's sort him out.'

'Me? What can I do?'

'Follow me,' Elsie commanded.

Ruby matched Elsie step for step as the older woman stormed up the lane towards the lad on the cart. Women came out from each yard and followed them. Some were carrying bairns. Some were holding hands with toddlers, pulling them along. Others walked with their hands on their hips, fury written all over their faces. One woman even picked up a stone and held it tight, ready to throw.

'Now there's no need for that,' Elsie said with a warning look, and the woman dropped the stone.

A small army marched up the back lane behind Elsie and Ruby. Mary hung back with Lady at her side. She didn't have the strength to go marching with the women, but she wasn't going to miss watching the action unfold. The cart driver brought his horse to a halt as soon as he saw the women trooping towards him.

'What's up, lasses?' he called.

The women stood in a line across the lane, blocking the horse and cart. They crossed their arms and glared at the young lad. And he *was* young, inexperienced too, sent by the older men from the store who knew only too well the risks of trying to deliver goods in the pit rows on washing day.

'Now listen here, you,' Elsie said sternly. 'You're to turn around and come back any day but Monday, when there's no washing out.'

'I can't do that,' the lad laughed. 'I'll get sacked if I don't make my deliveries.'

Without turning, Elsie called to the women behind her. 'Any of you lasses want a delivery today?'

'No, Elsie,' one of them cried.

'Not me.'

'Not today.'

'Never on a Monday.'

'You heard them,' Elsie told the lad. 'Now scram. And don't you ever come down here on a Monday again.'

'But I've got deliveries that'll go off if I leave them for another day,' the boy spluttered. 'I can't go back to work without dropping them off.'

'Then leave your horse at the corner and walk down the lane,' Elsie said. 'You can't go undoing all the hard work we do on a Monday by bringing your cart through the washing.' She took a step forwards and pointed at the women around her. 'And if I or any of these lasses see you with that horse and cart again on a Monday, we'll have you next time, lad. You hear?'

The delivery boy gulped. The pit lanes were narrow, and it was difficult to turn the cart around, but he knew he had no choice.

'Take as long as you need to get that horse away, but you're not coming down here,' Elsie said.

The women walked away, linking arms, laughing, enjoying their victory. Their washing would be safe from now on. Elsie put her arm around Ruby's shoulders.

'Now then, Ruby. Give me a few minutes to help Ann hang the washing out, and then weren't you about to put the kettle on?'

Chapter Fourteen

'I hear you've got a fella, Ruby,' Elsie said as she sipped her hot tea.

Ruby smiled, as she did each time she thought about Gordon.

'Hope he's treating you well.'

'He is,' she said.

'Never mind our Ruby, what's happening with you and Bert?' Mary asked.

Ruby made herself as comfortable as she could in the spindly wooden chair. Oh, how she'd missed these cosy chats with her mam and Elsie during the long months her mam had taken to her bed. Mary was sitting by the fire; Elsie and Ruby had each pulled a chair from the table and the three of them sat facing each other. Lady lay between them on the floor. Ruby closed her eyes for a second to savour the moment, then took a mouthful of tea as she listened closely to what Elsie had to say.

'Bert? He's a nice enough fella. And I appreciate you putting in a good word on his behalf, Mary.'

'I had no choice,' Mary laughed. 'I wasn't going to pass up the chance of getting free chickens.'

Elsie's brow furrowed. 'I'm still not certain they weren't stolen, you know.' Then her face clouded over. 'But I'm far too old to be courting Bert, or anyone.'

'Nonsense!' Mary said.

Ruby thought it nonsense too. Elsie was nowhere near as old as her mam.

Elsie shook her head.

'I am, Mary. I'm too stuck in my ways. What do I need a fella for anyway? I'm not one of those women who . . .' She stopped short and sent a sly look towards Ruby. 'Well, let's just say I'm nothing like your friend Abigail's mam.'

Mary tutted and shook her head. 'She's got a terrible reputation, that woman.'

'And her daughter's going the same way,' Elsie said, casting another glance at Ruby.

Ruby knew only too well what Elsie and her mam meant. For as long as she had known Abigail, gossip had been rife about her mother, Kate, being a bit too free and easy, welcoming men into her home. The talk had started as far back as when Ruby and Abigail were just girls at the village school. Kate had left Abigail at home on her own to fend for herself while she stayed out overnight. Ruby remembered it being something of a scandal at the time. She wondered how true Elsie's words were about Abigail turning out the same way. She'd long assumed that Abigail's energy and passion were directed into playing on the ladies' football team, rather than toying with fellas. But there'd been something a little indelicate, smutty even, in Abigail's comments about fellas when she and Jean had visited. Ruby turned back to the conversation as Elsie continued.

'No, I can manage quite all right without a fella, thank you very much. Me and Ann live an easy life, with no problems. We trust each other implicitly, always know what the other one's doing or thinking. What good would it do to bring a fella into our lives to change that?' Elsie shook her head and Ruby noticed a sadness creep into her voice. 'I've got to do what's right by Ann. She's looked after me all my life. I can't let her down.'

'Ann would understand, though, wouldn't she?' Mary asked. 'What about love and marriage, Elsie? Don't you want any of that? A bit of romance, perhaps?'

'Romance?' Elsie laughed. 'I'm past all that nonsense, love.'

Mary winked. 'Bert doesn't seem to think so.'

Elsie nodded towards Ruby, keen to change the subject. 'Anyway, what about you and your miner? Any sign of a wedding coming up?'

Ruby felt herself blush. She and Gordon hadn't talked about their future.

'Now that your mam's on the mend, you should be thinking about spreading your wings, girl,' Elsie said. 'Making a life of your own, getting wed and having bairns.'

'Elsie,' Mary chided. 'Leave the lass alone. She's been good to me the last few months, the best daughter anyone could ask for. She's looked after house and home, fed Arthur and Michael, done all the chores, managed the money, paid the bills. She's a little star, our Ruby.'

'How *is* your cooking these days?' Elsie asked.

'Well, I haven't burned a pan of potatoes in a long time,' Ruby laughed.

'I can understand you won't want to lose her,' Elsie told Mary. 'But you know what they say. You lose a son when they get married, but you never lose a daughter; you just gain a son-in-law.'

'Would you stop talking about me as if I'm not here, the pair of you?' Ruby said. 'I can speak for myself, you know.'

'Course you can, love,' Mary said.

'Where does he live, this fella of yours?' Elsie asked, blunt as ever.

'A lodging house on Burdon Road,' Ruby replied.

'Is it clean, decent?'

Ruby shrugged. She'd never been to the house where Gordon lived, never seen it, had no idea what it was like.

'I don't know,' she said.

Elsie set her mug on the hearth. 'What do you mean, you don't know?' she said sternly.

Ruby glanced at her mam for support. 'I've not been invited.'

Ruby saw the look that passed between Elsie and her mam, and felt unnerved by it as Elsie continued.

'How long have you been courting him? Weeks, now? Months? And you've still not seen where he lives?'

Ruby wondered what Elsie was getting at.

'How much do you really know about this lad you're going out with?'

'Elsie,' Mary chided. 'Gordon's a good fella, the two of them were made for each other. He makes our Ruby happy and that's good enough for me.'

Ruby looked at her. 'No, it's all right, Mam. Elsie's right. There *is* a lot I don't know.'

She remembered the way Gordon always swerved her dad's questions when he asked about his background or his family. He'd often done the same thing to her when she'd pressed him about his family, telling her it wasn't important. How could family not be important? Ruby couldn't understand Gordon sometimes. His evasiveness had niggled at her, she had to admit, but she'd been so enamoured by him and wrapped up in the rush of feelings she'd developed for him that she'd pushed it to the back of her mind.

'Then you need to start asking him,' Elsie said. 'Meet him at the lodging house and ask to see inside. It'll tell you a lot about the man when you see what state he lives in.'

'Elsie, no,' Mary said. 'Respectable lasses like our Ruby don't meet fellas in their rooms.'

'And respectable fellas don't keep secrets from their girls,' Elsie said sternly. 'If he lived at home with his parents, they'd be itching to meet their son's girlfriend. Ruby would have been invited to tea before now.'

'That's true,' Mary said, looking at her daughter. 'Elsie might just have a point.'

'I'll speak to him,' Ruby said. 'I will.'

The following day, Ruby baked fresh bread and made vegetable soup under the supervision of her mam, who called out instructions and advice from her chair by the fire.

'Don't put too much onion in it; your dad's not keen on onion,' she said. 'And make some dumplings if there's suet in the pantry.'

'There's none left, Mam, and there's been no money to buy any more.'

Mary was silent a few moments, and then spoke the words she'd been thinking for a few days. 'It might be time for you to go back out and start earning,' she said.

Ruby wiped her hands on her pinny and sat down next to her mam. 'Are you sure?' she said.

'We need the money. It's as simple as that.'

She thought for a moment. 'But are you sure you're well enough to cope here at home on your own?'

Mary took hold of her hands. 'I'll manage,' she said.

'Dad's worried about you,' Ruby said softly. She looked into her mam's eyes. 'He thinks . . . We worry, Mam, in case what happened to Grandma Winter happens to you.'

Mary rubbed her fingers along her daughter's smooth hands. 'It won't,' she said. 'I promise.'

The two of them sat in silence in the warmth of the kitchen. Outside, the sun began to peek through the clouds.

'Then I'll go and see if there's any jobs to be had in the village. I'll take Lady for a walk this afternoon.'

At the mention of her name, the dog raised her head from the floor.

'I'll call at all the pubs and shops, see what I can find.'

'What about the store?' Mary said. 'Why don't you have a word with Jean or Abigail – they both work there, don't they? They'll be able to tell you if there's a job going spare. And if there's nothing in the village, buy a copy of the *Sunderland Echo* to see what jobs are advertised there.'

'We can't afford to buy the paper any more, Mam,' Ruby said.

'Then I'll ask your dad to read it in the miners' hall; they always keep the day's paper in there. He'll write down the jobs and bring a list home for you.'

'Are you sure you're up to managing things in the house if I go back to work?'

Mary squeezed Ruby's hands. 'I'm sure, love. And I'll tell you this for nothing. I'm going to get some cloth scraps from Pemberton's Goods and make a new mat for the hearth. I miss that old one we had. Your Grandma Dinsdale made it.'

Ruby stayed quiet and bit her lip.

Later that day, Ruby walked up the pit lane with Lady. Her plan was to make her way from the colliery bank down to the pretty village green. It was a warm spring day and leaves were budding on the trees. Around the green were pubs and shops, and she intended to call at each one to ask for work. She could turn her hand to anything now; she even felt confident enough to offer her skills as a cook – well, as long as the cooking that was needed was basic.

She headed to the Albion Inn first, the pub she'd once worked in. It was locked, and she knocked hard at the door. She crossed her fingers and hoped it would be Hetty and not Jack who answered. However, she was to be disappointed. An upstairs window was pushed up, and Jack's miserable face loomed out.

'What do *you* want?' he barked.

Ruby took a step backwards and shielded her eyes with her hand against the spring sunshine as she squinted up at him. 'I've come looking for work, Mr Burdon,' she said.

'*You?*' he laughed. The window slammed shut.

She stood there for a moment, willing Hetty to come to the window or unlock the pub door. If only she could explain. But the door and the window stayed closed.

Next she tried the Railway Inn, and spoke to the landlady, Molly Teasdale.

'I wish I could help you, love,' Molly said. 'But I've got enough staff as it is.'

It was the same message at the Ship Inn; the Salutation Inn too. At Watson's Grocers, Ruby was given short shrift by bad-tempered Renee Watson, who seemed in a particularly foul mood. There was no work at the Grand Electric Cinema either. As she headed to the Guide Post Inn, she hesitated. The pub was on the corner of Ryhope Street and Burdon Road. Burdon Road was where Gordon lived; it was the address of his lodging house. Dare she go and take a look? Should she? What harm would it do to see the place from outside if she walked past with her dog? It wasn't as if she was spying on him. It was a free country, after all, and she could walk where she liked, couldn't she?

She turned left along Burdon Road with Lady at her heel, glancing at each house as she passed it. Which one could it be? She had no clue as to the number of the lodging house where Gordon lived. Ahead of her, she saw a young woman walking down the garden path of a house at the end of the street, a woman with fair hair tied in a ponytail that ran down her back. Ruby recognised her immediately.

'Abigail! Wait!' she called. She was confused. Why wasn't Abigail at work at the store? Abigail turned and began walking along the pavement away from Ruby. She didn't look round, and Ruby's words were lost on the air.

Chapter Fifteen

Ruby continued along Burdon Road, and when she reached the house Abigail had emerged from, she slowed down and took a good look. It was a terraced house, respectable in every way. There was a small, neat garden with clusters of daffodils standing to attention around a patch of grass. The curtains at the windows looked decent and the windows themselves were clean. The brick-built house appeared more solid than the cottages on the pit rows. An elderly woman with a shopping basket over her arm walked towards her and Ruby smiled.

'I'm looking for the house that takes lodgers in. Do you know which one it is?'

The woman pointed to the house where Abigail had walked from. 'But if you're after a room, Mrs Sowerby's full. She's got a miner living in now.'

As the woman walked on, Ruby's thoughts ran wild and her heart pounded. What on earth had Abigail been doing at the house where Gordon lived? Elsie's words came to her. Had she been trying to warn her? Surely not! Gordon wouldn't cheat on her . . . would he? It didn't make sense. Abigail had given no indication that she knew

Gordon when Ruby had told her about him. What on earth was going on? There was only one way to find out.

Ruby lifted the sneck on the gate and walked towards the green front door. She knocked hard, three times, and when the door was flung open, she was greeted by a short woman with greying hair and steely blue eyes.

'Mrs Sowerby?'

'I don't take animals,' Mrs Sowerby replied, looking at Lady. 'And my room is rented right now.'

'I haven't come about the room.'

'Then is it about the tap?'

'Sorry?'

'I've been waiting all day for the fella to come and fix my tap. I've got no water in my yard. Has he sent you, is that it? I expect you're wanting payment in advance.'

'No, I'm nothing to do with that either.'

Mrs Sowerby leant against the door frame and crossed her arms. 'Then what?'

Ruby swallowed. She hadn't planned what to say; she'd acted on impulse. And now that she was standing at the house where her boyfriend lived, she felt more than a little foolish. Still, she was here, and she might as well make the most of it. 'Is your lodger a man called Gordon Fisher?' she asked hesitantly.

Mrs Sowerby nodded. Ruby felt her heart jump. She tried to focus her thoughts, to give a plausible explanation as to why she was asking. But it was Mrs Sowerby who spoke first.

'He's at work.'

'Oh,' Ruby said. Relief flooded through her, and a bubble of happiness rose in her chest. How stupid she'd been, thinking that Abigail and Gordon were up to something. Abigail was her friend; she'd never betray her like that. And Gordon, sweet Gordon, was loving and kind and her own. It felt as if the pieces of the jigsaw of her life were snapping back into place.

'He's in demand today, though,' Mrs Sowerby went on. 'You're the second young lass who's asked to see him this morning.'

She could only mean Abigail, Ruby thought. And suddenly the jigsaw fell apart.

'She brought him a ticket for a football match,' Mrs Sowerby said. 'Ryhope Ladies are climbing the league.'

Ruby relaxed again. That was all it had been, an invitation to one of Abigail's football games. How could she have been so daft as to think it was anything more? Gordon had never given her any reason to feel insecure. Her emotions were running away with her and she needed to get them in check. It had been Elsie's words that had unsettled her. She gave her head a shake and took a deep breath.

'Will I give Mr Fisher a message from you?' Mrs Sowerby asked.

'Could you tell him that Ruby called, please?'

As Ruby walked back to the road, Mrs Sowerby watched her go before glancing from right to left to make sure that no neighbours were watching. It wouldn't do for anyone to see two young girls calling on her lodger. She ran a respectable lodging house and didn't enjoy being gossiped about.

Ruby returned home with bad news. Although she'd asked in every pub and shop, even at the cattle market and High Farm, she hadn't found any work. There were either no jobs to be had or a strong lad was wanted, not a girl. Mary made a cup of tea for them both and they sat down to talk. Ruby mentioned, as casually as she could, that she'd taken Elsie's advice and walked past Gordon's lodging house to see where he lived. But she kept quiet about Abigail, for she felt a fool thinking there could have been an ulterior motive for her friend's visit.

'Mam? Can I ask you a question?' she said.

'Course you can, love.'

'What do you think about Gordon? I mean, *really* think about him?'

'Well,' Mary began. 'He puts a smile on your face, treats you well.'

He did, Ruby thought, there was no denying that. And he treated her family well, too, bringing ham for tea and helping feed her dad and Michael when the Dinsdales' money wouldn't stretch that far.

'He's polite and decent and looks a heck of a lot better since he got rid of that moustache,' Mary continued. Then she looked directly at Ruby. 'And he doesn't appear to take liberties with you.'

Ruby felt yet another stab of guilt over the burned rug, for it had happened when she'd been oblivious, lost in Gordon's kisses. Still, her mam was right. Gordon had never laid a hand out of place or pushed her for more when they'd kissed. He'd been a gentleman through and through.

'And he's a hard-working bloke.'

Ruby couldn't disagree with that either. The niggle of doubt that had settled in since her visit to Burdon Road finally began to dissolve. She'd speak to Gordon, she decided, and tell him about meeting Mrs Sowerby in her curiosity to see where he lived. She wanted to be honest with him, for what use was being otherwise if they were going to continue their relationship, even develop it into something more?

It was later that week when Ruby saw Gordon again. He called at the house one evening and asked if she'd like to walk to the beach. The spring air was warm and Ruby jumped at the chance.

'I'll need to be back within the hour to get Michael's bath ready,' she said.

'I can do that,' Mary said. It was the first time she had offered to bring in buckets of water for months.

'Are you sure you're feeling up to it, Mam?' Ruby asked.

Mary assured her she would be fine, but Ruby wasn't convinced. Gordon insisted on bringing in the first bucket himself.

'Get yourselves away and have fun,' Mary said. 'I want to do this; I need to get my strength back.'

As they walked past the church and the village school, Ruby told Gordon about her visit to the lodging house. Gordon wasn't in the least surprised, as Mrs Sowerby had passed on her message.

'My landlady told me you'd called,' he said. Then he cast a sidelong glance at Ruby. 'In fact, you weren't the only visitor I had that morning.'

Ruby looked at him. 'Oh?'

'You told me you had a friend called Anna,' he began.

'Abigail,' Ruby corrected him.

'Of course, that's right,' he said. 'Well, she called at Mrs Sowerby's house to offer me free tickets for the football. We should go and see her play one afternoon when I'm off work.'

Ruby breathed a sigh of relief. But still, she wondered how Abigail knew where Gordon lived.

She took Gordon's hand. They rounded the village green, and before they reached the Railway Inn, they headed to the road that led through the cliffs to the beach. Ahead of them the sea rolled and broke on the shore. They found a place to sit on the sands.

'Why did you come to my lodging house, Ruby?' Gordon asked.

'To see where you lived, of course. You've never invited me there.'

'And if I was to invite you in, Mrs Sowerby wouldn't let you past the front parlour, you know that?'

Ruby was shocked by his forthright tone. 'The front parlour's as far as I'd be willing to go,' she said. 'What do you take me for, Gordon Fisher?'

Gordon hung his head. 'I'm sorry,' he said.

They gazed out at the waves.

'She's a funny old stick, Mrs Sowerby,' he said. 'She's having trouble with her tap in the yard. Causes me no end of bother when I come in from work. Sometimes there's not enough water for a full bath.'

'Do you have to bring the water in for your own bath and boil it yourself?' Ruby asked.

'No, she does it for me. It's included in my rent. But there's not as much water as there should be with the broken tap. I'm having little more than a cat's lick right now.'

An idea came to Ruby. 'Then come to ours for your bath until the tap's fixed.'

'Your house?' Gordon began laughing. 'Me sitting in your kitchen in the nuddy? Your mam'd have a fit, and anyway, you might want to peek.'

Ruby hit him playfully on the arm. 'Me and Mam will be out in the yard or upstairs until you're done. I won't look,' she laughed. 'As long as your shift ends at a different time to Dad and Michael's, I reckon I could manage.'

'It'd be welcome. I haven't had a decent wash in days,' Gordon said.

He leaned close to Ruby and laid his arm across her shoulders, and she snuggled into his side. Any remaining doubts and suspicions about Abigail melted away.

'I love you, Ruby Dinsdale.'

It was the first time he'd said it, the first time Ruby had ever heard those words from anyone other than her mam. The power of them made her heart flutter as if a tiny butterfly was inside her chest.

'I love you too,' she breathed.

Then Gordon gently tilted her face and kissed her on the lips.

Chapter Sixteen

As the mild weeks of spring turned to warm summer days, Ruby felt like she was walking on air. She loved Gordon with all her heart and thought of him constantly. He was the first thing on her mind each morning when she woke and the last thing on her mind at night. He came to tea at the Dinsdales' house twice a week now, and Mary was always pleased to see him, not least because he brought something good to eat each time he visited.

'Nice bit of ham for you to cook, Mary,' he'd say, offering her a parcel of meat that she'd take from his hands as if it was a priceless gem.

Arthur still kept a watchful eye on Gordon, but never saw him put a foot wrong. Oh, he still had reservations about the lad after what he'd been told at the pit, but as he'd heard nothing further, he dismissed what he'd learned as pit gossip.

As for Ruby, she admired the way Gordon advised Michael about how to overcome his fear of working underground at the pit. She never knew what he said, as the two of them whispered by the fire. By now, Michael had learned the unwritten rules of the coal mine and understood pitmatic, the language the miners spoke underground, with its short, sharp words. But still he suffered. He had a haunted look about him most days, but when he spoke to Gordon, she saw a little of the old Michael come back.

It wasn't just Michael who Gordon got on well with. Gordon was helpful around the house and Mary appreciated this more than anyone when he'd bring in buckets of coal and water. However, Ruby noticed that Arthur was less enamoured. She'd watch her dad and Gordon having long conversations about their work at the pit, about the unions and the coal company. But that was as far as it went. Gordon never offered to take Arthur to the pub, the way she expected, even wanted, so that the two men could talk as friends. She caught her dad sometimes looking at him slyly, as if he was trying to weigh him up, and she wondered what was going through his mind. Did he feel threatened by the arrival of a younger, stronger man settling in under his roof? She was too happy, too much in love with Gordon to give it further thought, but still something niggled.

Fortunately, she didn't have to worry too much. The men's shifts at the pit meant that Arthur, Michael and Gordon were often working at different times and were rarely all together at the Dinsdale house. The fire burned constantly, the tin bath in regular use. Ruby wondered if she'd made a rod for her own back offering Gordon the chance to take his bath at their house until Mrs Sowerby's tap was fixed. It was hard enough work lugging in buckets of water to heat for Michael and Arthur's baths. Then there was Mary's bath once a week, with Ruby stepping into it afterwards. Now, with Gordon bathing there,

Ruby's arms ached from the extra work. When she wasn't preparing baths, looking after the house or cooking for her family, she worked with her mam. Both of them took in sewing now, after Ruby's efforts to find a job had failed.

She'd had a word with Jean and Abigail at the store to see if there were any jobs going there. Surely there must be something she could do? When she'd gone to enquire, she'd told Lady to stay by the door, but the dog tried to follow her and Ruby had to reprimand her. When she finally got her to stay, she heard Lady whine as she walked away. Inside the store, the smell of freshly baked bread floated on the air and Ruby's stomach ached with hunger. Polished walnut counters gleamed under sunlight flooding through the large windows. There was a counter where fresh meat was sold. Next to it, a store assistant in a white blouse and blue skirt was cutting butter on a marble slab. Sugar was being scooped from large sacks to be weighed carefully into strong paper bags. Ruby watched the assistants shaking the sugar down into bags and folding the edges over.

Onward she walked, past the ladies' and gents' clothing for sale – boots and shoes, blouses and skirts – past the household supplies and furniture, none of which her family could afford. In one corner of the store a sign for funerals caught her eye, a service the store was well known for. Everyone knew that if you wanted a decent send-off, you'd get one here. There was even a banking and finance counter. She looked around, desperately seeking the counter where Jean and Abigail worked. And there it was, ahead of her, selling soaps and pomanders, bags of scent, face powders and lipsticks in pink and red. She spotted Abigail serving a customer and saw Jean in conversation with an older man with oiled hair. He wore a well-pressed suit, a white shirt and a sombre blue tie. As Ruby walked towards them, she caught snippets of their conversation.

'A horse?' Jean was saying. 'How can a horse go missing?'

'That's what I'm trying to work out,' the man said sternly. 'But when we did the stock check this morning, we're one horse down. I'll be having words with the delivery lads this afternoon.'

Ruby hung back, not wanting to interrupt Jean while she was talking to another member of staff. Once she was free, Ruby stepped forward and a smile spread wide on Jean's face. Abigail caught sight of her from the corner of her eye and nodded briefly before returning her attention to her customer.

'Hello, you.' With a dramatic flourish, Jean waved her arm across the soaps and perfumes on the counter. 'And what can I help madam to purchase today?'

'You know I can't afford any of those,' Ruby said. She leaned across the counter. 'I was hoping you might know if there are any jobs coming up?'

'For you?' Jean said.

'Of course for me. Who did you think I meant?'

'I thought you were looking after your mam?'

'She's getting better,' Ruby said, relieved.

'I'm pleased to hear it,' Jean said. 'But the only jobs I've heard of are in the stables, or delivery work – nothing you'd be suitable for.'

'I can ride a horse,' Ruby said with as much confidence as she could muster. The truth was, she'd never ridden a horse in her life, but surely it couldn't be that hard to learn?

'You know fine well those jobs aren't for girls,' Jean chided. 'But if I hear of anything going, I'll let you know.'

'Thanks, Jean,' Ruby said.

Once Abigail's customer had left, Ruby waited, expecting Abigail to join her and Jean as they talked, if just for a moment or two. But Abigail stayed where she was with her gaze fixed ahead.

'Have I said something to upset her?' Ruby whispered.

Jean glanced at Abigail and shook her head. 'Don't you worry about her,' she said with an anger that surprised Ruby. 'She's got something on her mind. Some fella she's got herself involved with.'

There was something not right, Ruby thought. And she felt it acutely when Abigail turned her back on her and Jean.

That evening, when Ruby went upstairs, she took *The Red Letter* from the box beneath her bed. She knew it word for word, she'd read it that many times. But this time she studied it more closely than before, scouring the stories for advice on what to do about fellas, friendship and love. At last she sighed, closed the magazine and slid it under her bed, then let her head fall back on the pillow.

Chapter Seventeen

'Isn't it about time you returned to taking baths in your lodging house, lad? Surely the tap's fixed by now?'

Gordon twisted around at the sound of Arthur's voice. He was more than a little surprised to see anyone there. Normally bath time was a wholly private affair. But he knew only too well he was under Arthur's roof and had to play by Arthur's rules. Arthur had caught him naked and exposed; perhaps that had been his plan in order to press home his point while Gordon was vulnerable. Water splashed from the bath to the kitchen floor.

'Watch what you're doing,' Arthur warned.

Gordon grabbed tight to the block of carbolic soap and rubbed it between his hands, trying to work up a froth in the hard water. Then he soaped his arms and muscled chest. He knew Arthur was watching him, waiting for a reply. He didn't want to take advantage of the Dinsdales' hospitality, but the baths Ruby made him were far and away better than any he'd had at Mrs Sowerby's. The bath was bigger for a start; he could almost stretch his legs out. And it was deeper too, able to hold more water. The truth of it was that the tap at Mrs

Sowerby's house had been fixed weeks ago, but Gordon had kept the news quiet.

'I've got used to coming here, Arthur,' he said. 'I've come to think of this house as my home.' He rubbed soap furiously up his leg, ignoring the older man as best he could, which wasn't easy as Arthur loomed at his side. He glanced up and noticed Arthur was searching for something on the table.

'Got it,' he said at last. 'I just came in for my pipe. But think on, Gordon. You wouldn't want to outstay your welcome, would you?'

And with that, he walked from the kitchen, leaving Gordon deep in thought.

He'd been making himself very comfortable at the Dinsdales' house and wasn't ready to give up his hot baths. If Ruby and her mam were happy to prepare them for him, he certainly wasn't daft enough to refuse their hospitality. But neither did he want to get on the wrong side of Arthur. He had to keep things on the level there, especially if he wanted to keep courting Ruby. As he thought of innocent, sweet Ruby, he ran his tongue around his lips. There were many joys to courting Ruby Dinsdale, Gordon thought. He'd been taken by her looks, her bonny face and bobbed brown hair, and the friendly way she had about her. She'd proved to be a strong lass, not one to shy from hard work. He liked that about her too. She didn't ask too many questions either, and for that he was grateful, for the less she asked, the less he had to lie. He'd managed so far to deftly turn any awkward conversations about his mam and dad in other directions. Or he'd simply stop her questions with a kiss. And each time he kissed her, Ruby accepted his lips. Yes, there was a lot to like about Ruby, Gordon thought, including her friend with the long blonde hair.

Ablutions done, he stood and picked up the coarse cloth that Ruby had left for him over a chair. He smiled when he thought about Ruby's kindness. But then he thought again about her friend Abigail, and a wicked grin spread wide.

The following week, Ruby and Mary were in the kitchen enjoying a welcome cup of tea as they took a break from their chores. Their reverie was broken by a loud rattling deep inside the hearth.

'Oh blimey,' Mary said, startled.

Ruby recognised the noise immediately and her heart skipped a beat. It was a noise they hadn't heard for some time, a warning that came from their next-door neighbour rattling her fire poker on the back of her hearth. In this way word went from one home to another along the pit row. There was only one thing it could mean. A stranger was in the back lane, someone to be dealt with at the earliest opportunity. Strangers were uncommon in the pit lanes, where everyone knew everyone else. They were seen as a threat.

'Go and tell her on the other side,' Mary urged.

Ruby ran into the yard and called over the wall to next door, so that they in turn could rattle their pokers and warn more neighbours. Before she ran back to her mam, she peered out into the lane to see who was there. Many of the miners' wives were out there wondering the same thing. She saw a man with dark hair and a rugged, weather-beaten face. He wore a blue shirt tucked into brown trousers, and around his neck he wore a red scarf.

As Ruby watched, her mam joined her, Lady by her side.

The two Miss Huttons were the ones who approached the man. Ruby and Mary walked closer to hear what they said. Women all up and down the lane inched forward. Ruby heard snatches of conversation as Elsie demanded to know who the man was and what he was up to. He'd been caught sneaking into their back yard, where he hadn't been invited.

'Is he a thief?' Ruby whispered.

'Not sure, love. But he's a whippet man. You can always tell a whippet man because of the red handkerchief around his neck.'

'A whippet man? Then where's his dog?'

'These men don't keep the dogs; they're gambling men. They arrange bets on dog races.'

'What's he doing here?'

'Shh,' Mary said, putting a finger to her lips, trying to catch what was being said. 'Elsie will give us chapter and verse once she's given him short shrift and sent him away.'

However, what happened next surprised everyone watching, for the man wasn't sent away. He was invited indoors by Elsie and Ann.

'What's going on?' Ruby asked.

Mary shook her head. 'No idea, love. But you can be sure I'll find out.'

Later that day, Mary and Ruby walked to the house where the two Miss Huttons lived, Lady trotting obediently behind. It was a fine summer day with an eggshell-blue sky. When they reached Elsie and Ann's back yard, they found Ann sitting on a chair in the yard with a wooden frame on her knees. A square of hessian was stretched inside the frame, and she was deftly pushing scraps of coloured cloth through the holes with a small wood and metal stick known as a progger. Ruby watched entranced as a rag rug formed under Ann's fluttering fingers.

'Hello, Ann. Is Elsie in?' Mary said.

Ann nodded towards the door that led to their kitchen. The bottom half of the door was closed and the top open to let air inside. She glanced at Lady. 'Leave the dog in the lane. I'm not having it in the house. I've had enough of dogs today to last me a lifetime.'

'The whippet man?' Mary said.

Ann raised her gaze from her work and looked at her. 'Oh, you saw him, did you?'

'Everyone saw him,' Mary said. 'The pokers were rattling all the way along the lane when he turned up. Everything all right?'

Just then Elsie leaned over the half-door and greeted Mary and Ruby. Lady lay down at Ann's feet, but was rewarded with a gentle nudge from her boot. She stood, walked away and found a safer space.

'You'll be wanting to know who he was,' Elsie said straight away. She looked at her sister. 'Will you tell them or shall I?'

Ann laid her progger down. 'Nothing to tell,' she said.

'Nothing to tell?' Elsie laughed. 'My sister, mistress of the understatement, as always.'

'Elsie, it's no one's business but mine.' Ann spoke sternly.

'Mary won't breathe a word,' Elsie said.

'I promise,' Mary said.

'Me too,' Ruby added.

And so Ann began her tale. It turned out the man they'd seen in the back lane, the man with dark hair and a red neckerchief, was an old flame of hers.

'A very old flame,' she said. 'I was just Ruby's age when we were courting, and I haven't seen him since. He left me for another girl.'

Mary raised her eyes and exchanged a look with Elsie.

'He broke my heart,' Ann carried on. 'I've kept myself to myself ever since. Fellas. You can't trust them, not one of them.'

She stared hard at Ruby when she said this, and her gaze was unsettling. Ruby shook her head as if to once more dismiss her doubts over Abigail and Gordon, doubts that had an unfortunate way of refusing to settle. The shiver from Ann's words lasted a split second longer than she would have liked.

'What's he doing here after all this time?' Mary asked.

Ann picked up the progger and started poking scraps into the hessian with more vigour than before. It was Elsie who picked up the story.

'His wife died not long since,' she said, 'and it turns out he's always had our Ann on his mind. Always.'

'Never did a bloody thing about it, though, did he?' Ann muttered.

'And he's telling you this now? The cheek of the fella!' said Mary.

'Well, he laid his heart on the line in front of us, so we know what his feelings and intentions are. He said he'd like him and Ann to be friends.'

'Friends? At our age?' Ann huffed. 'There's too much water gone under that bridge.'

Mary laid a hand on her heart. 'My goodness, what a shock,' she said. 'Will he come back, do you think?'

Ann shook her head sharply and turned back to her work.

'Who knows?' Elsie said.

Mary and Ruby bade their friends farewell and headed home with Lady. As they did so, Elsie returned to her work in the kitchen. Meanwhile, alone in the yard with her mat on her knees, a tear ran down Ann's face.

It was time for Ruby to get Gordon's bath ready for his return from the pit. He'd still not moved back to having his baths at his lodging house, despite Arthur's less than gentle hints.

'Leave the lad alone,' Mary had told him in the quiet of their room one night when Arthur complained Gordon was taking liberties. 'He brings ham for tea more often than ever. The least we can do is let him have a good wash. And he and our Ruby are getting serious too; he's as good as family, Arthur.'

Ruby picked up the metal bucket and walked towards the tap in the lane. She saw Jean heading towards her and waved.

'Just on my way home,' Jean said. 'Thought I'd walk down the back lane. I was hoping I'd see you.'

'Oh?' Ruby brightened. 'Is there a job going at the store?'

Jean shook her head. 'I'm sorry, Ruby. Nothing. Just more lads' jobs, I'm afraid.'

Ruby's heart sank. 'Will you let me know as soon as there's anything?'

'Course I will,' she said.

Ruby and Jean watched the water gushing from the tap.

'It's for Gordon's bath,' Ruby explained.

Jean bit her lip. 'Is everything all right between you two?' she asked.

Ruby beamed, as she did every time she thought about Gordon. 'Never better,' she said. 'Why do you ask?'

'Oh . . . no reason.'

But Ruby knew her friend well and picked up on Jean's unease. 'Is everything going well between you and Ted?'

At the mention of Ted's name, Jean smiled. 'He's a keeper. I'm trying to get him to set a date for our wedding. Dad takes him fishing at the beach on a weekend. Mam thinks the world of him, and he gets on with my brothers too.'

'Even your Jimmy?' Ruby asked, thinking of Jean's youngest brother, the most wayward of them all.

'Especially our Jimmy,' Jean said.

Ruby felt the familiar disappointment that her dad hadn't fully accepted Gordon into their family the way she would have liked.

'I got talking to Stan Hutchinson the other day,' Jean said. 'He came into the store doing some shopping for his mam. He was asking after you.'

Ruby missed Stan's friendship. But there was no way she'd be welcomed back inside the Queen's Head. She didn't know how or when she'd see him again. Anyway, she had Gordon now and he might get jealous if she was friendly with another lad. She quickly changed the subject. 'How's Abigail?'

'I've told you, don't worry about her.'

'Should I go and talk to her? See if I can make things up with her? I hate to think she's upset at something I might have said or done.'

Jean kicked at the muck on the lane with the toe of her boot. When she glanced up, she laid her hand on Ruby's arm. 'I'm here for you, Ruby. If you ever need me, you know where I am.'

And with that she walked away, leaving Ruby more than a little confused.

Chapter Eighteen

The following day, Ruby's routine followed its familiar pattern. It began in the dark early hours when she cooked a hearty breakfast of oats and milk for Michael and her dad. While they ate, she laid slices of cold cooked ham between thick slabs of bread and packed them in their bait boxes. Then she polished their boots in front of the fire. When all was done, she waved them off to work.

'Keep your eyes peeled, onion face,' she tried with Michael. He didn't respond, didn't even acknowledge that he'd heard.

After they'd left, Ruby made sure her mam ate breakfast too. She felt it vital to keep Mary's strength up to stop her dipping into melancholy again. She was only too aware of her mam's quiet moments and she kept a watchful eye.

With the men out at work, it was time for Mary and Ruby to work through their chores before making a start on the sewing that provided an income, no matter how small. Monday was washing day; Tuesday was for baking bread. The upstairs bedrooms were swept on Wednesday, and on Thursday the kitchen was cleaned. Friday was

Ruby's least favourite day, the day when they had to tackle the netties. There were three ash closets in the lane, and the neighbours took it in turns to scrub them. When it was her turn, Ruby held her nose and did the best job she could on the most horrid of chores. Saturday, money permitting, was another baking day, when Ruby and Mary would roll up their sleeves to make pies for the family. If Gordon had been generous with his parcels of fish or meat, some of this might go into the pies too. The oil lamps were filled weekly by Ruby, who trimmed the wicks and washed the glass. Mats were lifted and dusted each day. Sunday was a quiet day, not that the Dinsdales were religious; a day of much-needed rest.

That evening, Arthur and Ruby were joined in the kitchen by Mary, who often came and sat with them now that she was feeling better in herself. Michael was out with his friends, fishing at the beach. It was a warm summer night and the fire had burned out – there was no need to keep it going as there were no more baths to prepare or water to boil. Arthur tapped his pipe against the hearth and cleared his throat, looking towards Ruby. 'Your mam tells me Gordon's still having his bath here,' he said.

Ruby and Mary exchanged a look.

'I told him last week he wasn't to come here any more for that,' he continued. 'It's got to stop, Ruby.'

'Arthur, the lad's only—'

'But Dad—'

Arthur held up his hand to silence them. This was something he rarely did, and Ruby knew how serious his words would be.

'This is my house and you'll listen to me,' he said. 'It's

not right. I don't want Ruby getting a bad reputation as a cheap and easy lass, not like her friend Abigail and her slattern of a mam. You know how people talk.'

'Arthur, give over,' Mary joked. 'Gordon gets his privacy. All Ruby does is bring the bath in for him; she's always with me when he's in here getting washed. She gives the lad the same privacy as she gives you and Michael. What's the problem?'

'I don't like it,' Arthur said. 'It's not decent. What'll folk think?'

'Dad, please,' Ruby said.

Arthur shook his head. 'No, Ruby, it stops now. He's got his own lodgings and he should have his bath there. The tap must be fixed by now.'

'But he'll be expecting his bath when he finishes his shift in the morning,' Ruby said.

'The lass is right,' Mary said, trying to soothe Arthur. 'He can have one last bath here, surely?'

Arthur looked from his wife to his daughter. He knew when he was beaten. A smile reached his lips and the lines around his eyes creased in the familiar way Ruby loved.

'All right then,' he said. 'One last bath and that's it. He can't keep coming here for such a personal reason when he's not part of the family. It's not right. Now if he'd proposed to you, Ruby, that'd be different, but he hasn't even had the decency to do that, has he? So you be sure to tell him when he turns up in the morning that he's to return to his lodging house and that'll be that.'

Ruby accepted her dad's words with a sigh. She'd enjoyed looking after Gordon, preparing his bath for him. She'd even entertained a fancy notion that she was practising for when they got wed, for if she married him, she'd have to make his bath every day. Not that Gordon had ever mentioned anything about marriage. Arthur's words about him not having proposed yet stung her more than she let on. Surely, if what she read in the stories in *The Red Letter* was true, it could only be a matter of time before he asked her dad for her hand?

The following morning, after Arthur and Michael had left for work at the pit, Ruby started lugging in heavy buckets of water to heat. She took the tin bath from the wall and set it in front of the flames. She found the block of carbolic soap and laid it on the hearth, ready for Gordon. She'd have to let him know what her dad had said about him taking his baths at his lodging house, and she wasn't looking forward to it. But there was no choice other than to give him the news. She had to abide by her dad's word. Arthur didn't put his foot down very often in the house, but when he did, they all knew he meant business.

She took a breather and sat in the back lane on the flat, smooth stone with Lady by her side. Mary was spending the morning with the two Miss Huttons, helping them with their baking. They were putting on a spread for Bert Collins and the whippet man, who'd both been invited to tea. Ruby couldn't wait to hear all the gossip when her mam returned after preparing the food.

She waited in the sunshine for Gordon. He was due any time and she kept glancing along to the end of the lane, watching for him rounding the corner and walking towards her. A group of miners appeared, and she scanned them as they approached, but none of them were Gordon: too short, too fat, too tall. But suddenly there he was; she recognised him immediately, his familiar gentle amble, even though his hands and face were covered in coal dust. Her heart leapt, and she ran into the kitchen and began filling the bath with hot water.

Gordon greeted her with a wave as he came in. How Ruby wanted to hug him and kiss him, throw her arms around him and squeeze him tight. But she couldn't, not when he was black with coal.

'Thanks, Ruby,' he said when he saw the steaming hot bath. A cheeky grin came to his face. 'Don't suppose you want to stay and wash my back?'

Ruby felt herself blushing. She glanced behind her, just in case her mam had come home unexpectedly and heard his teasing words. 'You know I can't,' she said quickly.

'Can't blame a man for asking,' he joked.

Ruby left him alone and headed to the yard, where Lady was waiting. There was nothing else to do now except wait for Gordon to wash before the arduous task of emptying the bath would begin. She decided to walk to Elsie and Ann's house and offer to help her mam.

As Ruby walked away with Lady at her side, a woman entered the lane. She stood by the wall, watching Ruby disappear into Elsie and Ann's back yard, then she made her move. She knew where Ruby lived; she'd been inside the house many times. And she knew Gordon was in there right now. She'd waited at the pit gates for him, out of sight, and followed him here. Slowly she made her way along the lane until she was standing outside the Dinsdales' yard. She cast a final glance over her shoulder to ensure Ruby wasn't on her way back, then took a deep breath to calm her racing heart. What if Ruby's mam was indoors, or her dad or brother? But she had to speak to Gordon. He'd been ignoring her, sending his landlady to answer the door, to say he wasn't in when she knew he was. Well, he couldn't ignore her now. Bumping into any of Ruby's family was a risk she'd have to take.

She walked into the yard, her footsteps barely making a sound. The kitchen door was open to the sunny day outdoors. She stepped inside, doing her utmost to be quiet. Gordon was sitting in the bath, his back turned towards her. He had no idea she was there. She moved slowly. The sound of her boots on the kitchen floor were lost in the noise of the splash of water as he soaped his legs. She approached him and saw the rippling muscles in his shoulders glistening in the firelight. The sight of his naked body sent a shiver of delight running through her.

Suddenly the block of soap shot out of Gordon's hands.

'Blasted thing!' he yelled.

He reached out to pick it up from the floor, but she got to it first. Behind him, she laid a hand against the back of his head, turning his face forwards.

'Who the devil . . . ?' Gordon cried.

'Shh.'

He froze. 'Ruby?'

There was silence. The woman kneeled behind him. She dipped the soap into the water and turned it in her hands. Then she laid her soft hands on Gordon's body and began to caress his back. Gordon dipped his head forward, letting her touch and the soap work their way into the muscles of his neck.

'Are you sure your mam won't come in?'

Still silence. The woman's hands worked the soap over

Gordon's broad shoulders and down to the dark hair on his chest. She stood so she could reach further down to soap his stomach, and he groaned with pleasure.

'Ruby,' he whispered.

Further down her hands went, until they were under the water. Gordon's breath turned fast and shallow.

'Ruby!' he gasped.

He turned and looked up, and his face twisted with horror.

'You!' he cried. 'What the hell's going on?'

He leapt from the bath, sending water splashing on to the floor. He grabbed the coarse towel Ruby always left for him and held it to his groin.

'What are you hiding it for, Gordon? I've seen it before,' the woman teased.

'Get out,' he growled.

She didn't move. 'Why won't you speak to me, Gordon?' she demanded. 'I've been to your lodging house, but you turn me away.'

'Are you mad? Get out of here. Now!' he yelled.

'But I thought you wanted to see me again,' she said. 'You wanted to see me that night you sneaked me into Mrs Sowerby's.'

'Well, you thought wrong,' he said quickly. 'Get out before anyone comes in. Get out. I'm warning you.'

She took another step forward and ran her fingers across his damp chest. He lashed out with his free hand and she stumbled back against the table. She was too stunned to say anything. Pain seared in her back where the table had broken her fall. She bit back her tears and walked from the room. But Gordon wasn't finished with her yet.

'Abigail,' he growled.

She turned, crossed her arms and tilted her chin in defiance. 'What?'

'Breathe a word of this to Ruby and I'll . . .'

Abigail crossed her arms. 'You'll what?'

The pain in her back gave her the answer. She knew exactly what Gordon might do. She walked out without a word.

Chapter Nineteen

'Ruby! Don't forget the milk!' Mary called down the stairs.

Ruby rushed to the hearth, where she'd put a pan of milk and oats to cook on the fire.

'Oh blimey!' she cried when she saw the state of the pan. The milk was frothing right to the top. She whipped it off the heat and immediately the milk simmered down. She heard her mam's footsteps on the stairs as Mary made her way to the kitchen.

'I thought I was getting better at cooking,' Ruby sighed. 'But I still can't even cook oats without almost burning the milk.'

'Don't give yourself such a hard time. You're doing all right in the main,' Mary said kindly. 'It's just that sometimes you take your eye off things and you don't see what's under your nose.'

Just then Michael bounded in.

'What are you up to today, then?' Mary asked him.

'Going fishing on the beach this morning and playing football with Bobby and the lads this afternoon. Got to make the most of my day off work.'

Ruby noticed that he was beaming. The only time she saw him smile these days was when he wasn't at work; otherwise he was sullen and quiet. His body was changing too, her little brother turning from a boy into a man. Standing in the Dinsdales' small kitchen, he seemed to use up more space now. The muscles he was developing as a pitman showed lumpily under his shirt. His trousers hung a few inches away from his shoes.

'Just look at the state of your trousers,' Mary said. 'Give them here and I'll unpick the hems. You're growing faster than ever these days.'

'I haven't got time, Mam,' Michael said. 'The lads are waiting for me.' He kissed her on the cheek. 'Can I take Lady with me?' he asked Ruby.

'Course you can,' she said. 'She'll enjoy a run on the sands.'

'Keep your eyes peeled, onion face!' he called to her with a cheeky smile.

'If I see you first, you're the worst,' Ruby replied, relieved to see her brother happy.

Michael left with the dog by his side, leaving Ruby and her mam in the house. The kitchen door was open, as it always was when the weather was fine, to let the coal smoke escape to the yard. It was a dry autumn day, with clouds scudding across the sky.

Mary gazed out of the window. 'Hope it stays fine for washing day,' she said.

Ruby was busy serving the oat pudding breakfast into bowls for herself and her mam. She handed a bowl and spoon to Mary and both of them sat by the fire.

Mary winced when she took her first spoonful. 'Needs a bit of sugar,' she said.

Ruby shook her head.

'There's no sugar?' Mary cried. 'Your dad'll have a fit. You know how much he likes his sweet tea.'

'I could buy some from the store this morning, if there's any money for it,' Ruby offered.

'There might be a little cash spare, but there are cheaper places than the store,' Mary said.

They carried on eating.

'When are you seeing Gordon next?' Mary asked.

'Not sure, but he's talking about taking me on a tram ride into town, maybe seeing the sights.'

Mary glanced at her daughter's face. 'You've been courting a while now, the pair of you.'

Ruby looked at her mam. There was something in her tone she couldn't detect. What was she getting at?

'Oh, don't look at me like that, Ruby. You know fine well any decent fella would have offered to take things further by now. You've known him for months and he's not so much as had a quiet word with Arthur about asking for your hand.'

Ruby lifted her spoon to her lips and chewed, letting her mam's words sink in.

'If he wants a future with you, he needs to do more than offer you a tram ride,' Mary continued. 'You need to speak to him, find out what his plans are. You need to know what's going on.'

'And what about *my* plans? What about what I want? Or don't I get a say?'

Mary laid her bowl on the hearth and sat back in her chair. 'Come on then, what *do* you want?'

Ruby swallowed another spoonful. Her mam was right. She wanted nothing more than for Gordon to propose. There were times when she'd thought he might, moments when they'd been kissing and she'd felt his hot breath on her neck, moments when he'd told her he loved her.

'I want to be happy,' she said.

'And do you think you can be happy with Gordon?'

Ruby nodded. 'I'm certain.'

'Ruby, you're young,' Mary began carefully.

'I'm almost nineteen.'

'But you've not had much experience with lads,' she went on. 'I want you to be sure in your mind that Gordon's the right one for you. Don't let him string you along.'

'He's not stringing me along. I like being with him. It hurts when we're apart.'

Mary picked up her bowl and started eating again. 'Your dad's right, it's not decent for a girl to be courting a fella for so long without him offering commitment.' She lowered her voice. 'You don't want to end up like your friend Abigail.'

Ruby shot her mam a look. 'What about her?'

Mary's face darkened. 'You don't know? Jean hasn't told you?'

Ruby shook her head.

'Abigail's pregnant.'

Ruby's hand paused mid-air. She gripped the spoon tightly and stared at her mam. No, this couldn't be true! Not Abigail, surely? She wasn't even courting, as far as Ruby knew. She let her mam's words sink in. Abigail? Pregnant? A million questions rushed through her mind, but only one word left her lips. 'What?'

'You heard well enough,' Mary said.

'Pregnant?' Ruby breathed. 'How? I mean . . .'

'How?' Mary laughed. 'I think you're old enough to know about the birds and the bees. Heaven knows I did my best telling you about those things over the years.'

'No, Mam. I mean how do you know?'

'Your dad told me last night when he came home from work. He said Abigail's mam is always a topic of gossip underground when the lads get to sharing stories about women. You know what Kate's like. And when her name was mentioned yesterday, one of the lads said that he'd heard from her that Abigail was in the family way.'

'Then it might just be gossip,' Ruby said, trying to make sense of it.

'Did they say who the father was, or who Abigail's courting?'

'No, all I know is what I've told you,' Mary said.

'There was no mention of a fella, or a wedding?' Ruby asked, desperate to know more.

Mary pursed her lips. 'Nothing. But I'll tell you this, she won't be playing football for a while. Look, why don't you go and see her, find out for yourself? She could probably do with a friend to talk to.'

Ruby felt sick. Why hadn't Abigail told her? Why hadn't Jean said anything? Perhaps Jean didn't know either, she thought. She wasn't sure what kind of reception she'd get if she called at Abigail's house, but there was only one way to find out the truth.

'I'll call on her today after she's finished work at the store.'

Abigail and her mother Kate lived at the end of Railway Street, in a tiny cottage that shook when trains rattled by.

Ruby straightened her shoulders, knocked at the door and waited. It was Abigail's mam who opened it, and Ruby was shocked by what she saw. She remembered Kate as a handsome woman, with her long fair hair tied in a plait just like her daughter's. Men would stare at her in the street. Women would admire her beauty, then gossip about what kind of mischief such looks got her into. The woman who stood in front of Ruby now had a doughy face with a thick layer of powder and rouge carelessly applied. Her eyes were smudged black, whether from lack of sleep or dark make-up, Ruby couldn't tell. Her hair, previously so well cared for, hung oily and lank. The whole effect jarred with Ruby's memory. She balled her hands into fists and forced herself to speak.

'Is Abigail in?'

Kate looked her up and down and took her time before she replied. 'No.'

'Could I wait until she gets home?'

'It'd be best if you didn't.'

Ruby struggled to understand why her request had been denied. Did Kate have a man in the house, someone she was *entertaining*, as the Ryhope gossips would say? She heard a noise inside the house. Someone was coughing; a woman. Was it possible Abigail was inside and had told her mam not to let Ruby in? Ruby's stomach turned over. Why was her friend ignoring her?

'Will you tell her I called?'

Kate nodded sharply, then slammed the door in Ruby's face.

Ruby stood on the pavement, staring at the door. It had shut so abruptly she felt like she'd been slapped. She was upset at not being able to talk to Abigail and find out what was going on. And she was angry too; angry at Kate for not allowing her to wait, angry at Jean for not telling her what was going on.

Jean. If she couldn't speak to Abigail, then she'd have to speak to Jean the following day. She started to walk away, keeping her gaze fixed ahead. But if she had turned, she would have seen the twitch of a curtain in an upstairs bedroom. And she would have seen Abigail watching.

Chapter Twenty

'Jean,' Ruby whispered across the counter at the store. 'Jean!'

Jean spun around. Not only was she surprised to see Ruby, she was shocked at the distraught look on her friend's face.

'What's wrong?'

'Have you heard about Abigail?'

Jean glanced around to make sure that no customers were within earshot and no supervisor was watching as she gossiped with her friend. She leaned forward and said in a too-loud voice, 'Perhaps madam would like to see it in a different shade?'

Ruby stared at her as if she'd gone mad.

'Pretend I'm serving you,' Jean said quickly. 'If I'm caught chatting, I'll be for the chop.'

Ruby made a show of looking over a tray of face powders that Jean laid on the counter. Heads together, the two girls whispered urgently.

'Yes, I've heard,' Jean said.

'Why didn't you tell me?'

'She didn't want anyone to know.'

'But I'm not just anyone! The three of us have always been close.'

'I've already told you, don't worry about Abigail, she's big enough to look after herself.'

'But . . . a baby?' Ruby said. 'I didn't know she was courting. Whose is it? Who's the father?'

Jean swallowed hard. She lifted the tray of powder from the counter and moved another into its place. 'Would madam prefer to see it in pink?' she said loudly.

'Is she going to keep it?'

'Look, I don't know. All I know is what she's told me. She was at work, then she went off sick. She's sent word to our supervisor that she's feeling too ill to leave home and doesn't know when she'll be back.'

'Do you need help in the meantime?' Ruby said. 'I could apply, couldn't I? There must be someone I can speak to about stepping in until Abigail returns.'

'No, Ruby, please,' Jean said.

'Why not?'

'Just leave it. It's best if you don't.'

Ruby stared hard at her friend, a familiar feeling of dread making its presence felt in her stomach. First Abigail's mam had turned her away, and now this. Something wasn't right and she needed to know what it was.

'What's going on, Jean? What is it you're not telling me?'

'I can't speak now, not here.'

'Then when?'

'Tonight, as soon as I finish work. I'll come to your house. I'll tell you everything.' She laid her hand on Ruby's arm and looked her in the eye. 'But it won't be what you want to hear, love,' she said. 'You need to prepare yourself for what I've got to say.'

Ruby pulled her arm away. She and Jean stood a few moments in silence. Eventually Jean spoke.

'You'd better go, Ruby. I've got a customer waiting and I don't want to get into trouble.'

Ruby walked from the store. Her heart hammered and the blood pounded in her ears. What on earth could Jean have to tell her that was so important?

She was so lost in her thoughts of Abigail, she didn't notice the two Miss Huttons entering the store, drifting straight past her as she walked out to the street.

'Looks like she's got a lot on her mind,' Elsie noted.

'She seemed miles away,' Ann replied. 'She's a lovely girl, is Ruby, but she often reminds me of Mary's mam when she was a girl. Let's hope she doesn't turn out like her.'

Elsie pursed her lips. 'I wouldn't wish that on anyone.'

Ruby had intended to head home. She'd promised her mam she'd learn how to make a panackelty stew with ham. But that didn't seem important now. She needed someone to talk to in confidence about Abigail. Why was her friend freezing her out? What had she done to upset her? And what was Jean about to tell her that she wouldn't want to hear? It was all too confusing and hurtful. She couldn't make any sense of it. And so, instead of heading home, Ruby turned right when she came out of the store, and walked down the colliery bank.

She walked past the rhubarb field, past the Prince of Wales and the Duke of Wellington pubs and the tiny Italian ice-cream shop that was always dark and cold inside no matter how warm the day. When she reached the Guide Post Inn, she turned right on to Burdon Road. She had to speak to Gordon. She knew which shifts he worked at the pit by now and reckoned there was a good chance of finding him home. She prayed he wouldn't be sleeping, for she knew how much her dad and Michael hated being woken after working nights.

Taking a deep breath, she headed up the path to Mrs Sowerby's lodging house. She knocked three times at the green-painted door. When it swung open, she plastered a smile on her face.

'Hello,' she said as brightly as she could. 'I was hoping Gordon might be in.'

Mrs Sowerby looked her up and down. 'You again?'

'I'm Gordon's girlfriend,' Ruby said proudly.

She didn't notice the way the landlady gripped the door handle.

'*You're* his girlfriend?' Mrs Sowerby said. 'But I thought . . .'

'Thought what?' Ruby asked, confused.

Mrs Sowerby shook her head, dismissing the memory of the long blonde hairs she'd found on her lodger's pillow when she'd stripped his bed to wash the sheets. 'Sorry, love,' she said quickly. 'Yes, he's in. Let me just see if he's up and dressed. He's been working the night shift and sleeping all day.'

'I know what shifts he works,' Ruby said with authority.

Mrs Sowerby bustled inside. Ruby waited on the doorstep and peered around the door, trying to catch a glimpse within. From her spot on the step, all she could make out was a neat and tidy room with two well-stuffed armchairs in front of an open coal fire. Presently she heard heavy footsteps, and Gordon appeared. His face looked freshly shaved, scrubbed pink and clean.

'Well, this is a surprise. Come on in,' he said.

Ruby stepped over the threshold. It was the first time she'd been inside the house where he lived, and she was curious. She followed him into the living room she'd seen from the doorstep. Gordon sank into one of the chairs by the fire and indicated for Ruby to sit in the other.

As she made herself comfortable, Mrs Sowerby appeared and hovered by the door. 'Will your lady friend be requiring tea, sir?' she asked in an affected, over-polite voice that made Ruby smile.

'Yes, please, Mrs S,' Gordon replied.

'It's Mrs Sowerby, Mr Fisher. How many times do I need to tell you?'

'Tea for two and a couple of biscuits sounds perfect, Mrs Sowerby,' Gordon said, chastised.

'Well, I think I can do better than biscuits,' Mrs Sowerby said. 'I'll bring you both a slice of my cocoa cake, fresh out of the oven just now.'

'She gives you cake?' Ruby whispered once the landlady had bustled away.

'She'll give me anything as long as I pay for it. That cake'll be on my bill at the end of the week. But it's not such a bad place to live. What are you doing here, anyway? It's not that I'm not happy to see you, of course.'

'I'm sorry, Gordon, I . . .'

He reached for her hands. 'Hey, no need to apologise. It's a nice surprise, a good surprise,' he said.

'Really?'

'Really,' he assured her.

Ruby fidgeted in her seat. 'I needed to speak to someone, to you.'

'What on earth for? Is everything all right?'

Ruby laid her head against the back of the chair. Now that she was here, with Gordon in front of her, it seemed silly to tell him she was worried about her friend. What would he think of her? That she was just a foolish girl?

'Come on, Ruby,' he said gently. 'Whatever it is, you know you can tell me.'

She was about to explain about Abigail when Mrs Sowerby returned carrying a tray. On it was a teapot covered with a knitted red cosy, two brown cups and saucers, a matching bowl of sugar lumps and a tiny white jug filled with milk.

'Mr Fisher, would you do the honours?' the landlady asked.

Gordon knew what was expected after living in the lodging house for so long. He stood and walked out of the room, and returned carrying a small wooden table, which he placed in front of Ruby.

Mrs Sowerby laid the tray on the table. 'I'll be back in a moment with the cake,' she said before disappearing again.

Ruby lifted the teapot and smiled at Gordon. 'Shall I be mother?' she said.

The words hung between them. Too late Ruby realised how her innocent remark might have sounded.

'Sorry, all I meant was shall I pour?' she said quickly, trying to cover her mistake. But when she looked at Gordon, she was relieved to see him smiling.

'Yes, you be mother. In fact, I think you'd make a good mam,' he said.

She felt her heart flutter at his words. Had he been thinking of their future together after all? She carefully poured the tea and added milk and sugar to both cups. Mrs Sowerby returned with generous slices of dark cake on rose-patterned plates.

'Now, you know my rule on visitors – no later than six p.m.,' she said before she left the room.

Gordon got up from his chair and closed the door firmly so that whatever he and Ruby spoke of couldn't be heard by his landlady.

Ruby glanced at the clock on the mantelpiece. It was five thirty. She didn't have long to tell Gordon her news. She bit into the warm, gooey cake, washing it down with a mouthful of tea. How wonderful it felt to eat such rich, sweet food and to drink tea made for her, from a cup with its own saucer too. What a treat it was.

'What's wrong, Ruby?' Gordon asked.

'Now I'm here, it feels like nothing, honestly. I was upset before and wanted to speak to someone who would understand. But I'm fine, really.'

'Come on, you can tell me,' he said.

Ruby took a deep breath. 'It's Abigail,' she said.

He picked up his slice of cake, took a huge bite and chewed furiously. 'Who?'

'Abigail, my friend. The one who plays football.' She leaned forward and whispered, 'She's pregnant.'

Gordon spat his cake on to his plate and began coughing as if he was choking. Ruby was alarmed; she stood over him and patted him hard on his back. After a few minutes, his coughing subsided, his breathing returning to normal.

'I think it went down the wrong way,' he said weakly.

'Hard to digest, isn't it?' Ruby said.

'You can say that again.'

'Here, drink some tea, it'll help.' She handed him a cup, and he sipped from it, taking his time before meeting her eyes.

'You've gone very red in the face,' she said.

'Did she say . . . I mean, has she mentioned whose baby it is?'

Ruby shook her head. 'She won't see me. And that's the thing, Gordon. She's my friend, and she's snubbed me. I don't know what I've done wrong.'

Gordon set his cup and the remains of his cake on the table, then leaned towards her.

'Never mind Abigail or any of your friends. Don't concern yourself with them.'

'But—'

'No, Ruby, listen to me. Your life is with me now.'

Ruby was confused. Why was he saying these things? Why now? 'My life?'

'If you'd like it to be,' he said sweetly.

Oh, I would, Ruby thought, I would. She wanted nothing more. She kept quiet, though, waiting to hear what he'd say next.

'Well, *would* you like it?' he asked.

She nodded.

'Then that's all fixed,' he said.

Ruby looked at him. His face was still red from his choking episode, his hands were shaking and his left knee bobbed up and down.

'What's all fixed?' she said.

'You and me, we'll get married.'

'Married?' Ruby cried.

150

She heard a noise, a scuffle at the door. Gordon heard it too, and both of them turned. Was Mrs Sowerby listening outside?

'Married?' she said again.

'Don't you want to get wed?' Gordon asked.

'Yes,' Ruby said cautiously. 'Of course I do.'

'Well, you could sound happier about it. Here's me laying my heart on the line, offering you my life, till death us do part, and all you can do is sit there. Come here and give me a kiss.'

'No,' Ruby said firmly.

Gordon's face dropped. 'No?'

'Not until you ask me properly.'

She glared at Gordon, daring him to do the right thing, the thing that she wanted – needed – him to. He nodded slowly, as if thinking it through. Taking his time, he wiped cake crumbs from his fingers, then stood, looming over Ruby, before kneeling on the floor in front of her chair.

Ruby sat up straight in her seat. She was ready; more than ready. Her stomach fluttered, her heart pounded and a wide smile made its way to her lips. She'd read about this moment; over and over she'd read about it in the pages of *The Red Letter* magazine. And now, finally, it was happening to her. She could hardly believe it.

Gordon took her soft hand in his roughened fingers and looked deep into her eyes.

'Will you marry me, Ruby Dinsdale? Will you do me the honour of becoming my wife?'

'Oh yes. A thousand times, yes.'

* * *

Gordon's head spun. He closed his eyes. He couldn't look at Ruby; he needed to pull himself together. Flaming Abigail! If the baby was his – and there was every reason to think it might be – then he needed to lie through his teeth to protect his future. His roving eye and appetite for pleasure had nearly cost him everything. One stupid night with Abigail wasn't going to ruin his life with a decent lass like Ruby; she was respectable, and this was something he craved to make him appear more worthy in public.

He knew there was only one way out of this now.

Chapter Twenty-One

'Mam! Dad! I've got some wonderful news!'

Ruby ran into the kitchen, pulling Gordon by the hand. She'd expected to see her parents there, knowing her dad's shift at the pit had already finished. But although the kitchen door had been left unlocked, there was no one indoors. There was only Lady snoring under the table.

'Where is everyone?' Gordon asked.

Ruby bounded up the stairs, taking them two at a time. 'Mam! Dad!'

But the two rooms upstairs were empty. She walked slowly back down. 'I don't understand it,' she said. 'They should be here.'

The coal fire was burning, but there were no pans boiling potatoes or peas, nothing in the oven either. From under the table Lady gave a long sigh. Ruby watched as the dog stood and shook itself before stretching its front legs along the floor.

'There's only one place they could be,' Ruby decided. 'Gordon, stay here. I'll run down to Elsie and Ann's to see if they're there.'

* * *

Ruby left the kitchen, leaving Gordon alone with the dog. Lady bared her teeth and a low growl made its way from her throat. Gordon glanced at the kitchen door to ensure there was no chance of Ruby reappearing, then quick as a flash he lifted his leg and landed his boot on Lady's back end. She yelped with pain, shook herself, then growled deeply and began to bark. Gordon started to back away, realising he'd gone too far.

'Come on now, nice doggy,' he cooed, trying to calm the animal. But if anything, the sound of his voice seemed to incense it more. He retreated towards the door, but by now Lady had worked herself up into a fury. He readied himself to run as soon as his boots hit the yard. But the minute he stepped outside, the dog fell silent and still. She simply sat down and blocked the doorway to the kitchen, keeping an eye on him.

Gordon took a moment to breathe deeply; he'd had a lucky escape. He heard the chatter of voices and looked into the lane. Ruby was walking towards him, linking arms with her mam and dad. The three of them were smiling and happy.

'Why are you standing out here in the cold?' Arthur said when he saw Gordon.

'Just wanted a breath of fresh air,' Gordon replied, glaring at Lady.

Ruby and her mam and dad walked into the kitchen; Lady trotted after them as they went straight to the fire to warm through. Gordon followed, keeping his eyes on the dog, who had now slunk back under the table.

'Come on then, what's your news? What's got you so excited?' Mary said, glancing from Ruby to Gordon.

Ruby grabbed hold of Gordon's hand. 'Will you tell them, or shall I?'

Gordon shifted from one foot to the other. 'There's something I need to say first, to your dad, before we announce the news,' he said. He turned to Ruby's father. 'Arthur,' he said gravely. 'I know I should have come to you first to ask permission, and I want to apologise for not doing so. But—'

It was too much for Ruby, who was bursting with excitement to tell her mam and dad. 'We're getting married!' she yelled.

Mary and Arthur were stunned into silence. Then Mary rushed forward to Ruby and hugged her daughter tight. 'Oh love, that's wonderful news,' she said. 'It really is the best news ever.'

Gordon offered his hand to Arthur. Arthur looked at it for a few seconds, leaving Gordon waiting, before he took it and shook it briefly.

'Congratulations, lad. Welcome to the family,' he said flatly.

Ruby and Mary were lost in their embrace. Tears of joy streamed down Ruby's face. Arthur took a step towards Gordon and whispered in his ear.

'Harm one hair of her head and you'll have me to deal with. You hear me?'

Gordon locked eyes with the older man. Oh, he'd heard him all right. But before he could react, he found himself being spun around by Mary.

'Come here, lad,' Mary said as she planted a kiss on his cheek. 'I know you're going to make our Ruby very happy.'

Gordon hugged her close. As he did so, he looked over

her shoulder and locked eyes with Arthur. 'I'll do the best I can.'

'This calls for a celebration,' Mary said. 'Ruby, what about going across to the Queen's Head to see if you can sweet-talk Stan Hutchinson into giving you a jug of ale before the pub opens?'

Ruby felt dizzy with excitement. The Queen's Head and Stan Hutchinson seemed a world away from the Ruby Dinsdale she now felt herself to be. She was so caught up in her joy that she'd missed the significance of her mam asking for ale. It was something she hadn't requested in months. But Arthur had heard Mary's words and Ruby saw the look that clouded his face.

'We don't need ale to celebrate,' he said. 'A cup of tea will do just fine.'

Mary put her hand on Arthur's arm. 'It will indeed,' she said. 'The longer I stay away from the ale, the better I feel.'

Arthur patted Mary's hand affectionately. Ruby sank into a chair next to Gordon while Mary put the kettle on to boil. She kept tight hold of Gordon's hand, happier than she'd ever been. With all the excitement of everything that had happened that day, the only thing she'd eaten in hours had been Mrs Sowerby's cake. Now her stomach growled with hunger.

'What's for tea, Mam?' she asked.

'Your dad and me have eaten already. That's what we were doing at Elsie and Ann's. They laid a tea on for us, we had home-made crumpets with syrup and lots of chat and laughter.'

'Aye, it's been grand,' Arthur agreed as he lit his pipe.

'And now coming home to hear your news, Ruby, it's the perfect end to a wonderful day,' Mary said. 'I can warm some stew for you as long as you leave some for Michael. Gordon, have you eaten? I hope you have, lad, because I wasn't expecting you and there's not enough to go round.'

'I had beef and potatoes at the lodging house,' Gordon said.

'And a slice of warm cake,' Ruby piped up.

Arthur began to suck on his pipe. When he took it from his mouth, he looked long and hard at Gordon.

'When do you plan to tell your parents?' he asked.

Gordon glanced quickly at Ruby. 'Soon,' he said.

'I'm looking forward to meeting them.' Ruby smiled at him.

'You don't mention them much,' Arthur said, his gaze unwavering from Gordon's face.

'I see them now and then. They live at Seaham; it takes a bit of organising, getting train tickets and so on.'

'Seaham?' Arthur raised his eyebrows. 'It's only one station on from Ryhope East. What's to organise?'

'Oh, you should invite them here,' Mary urged, cutting into the conversation.

'Don't be daft, lass,' said Arthur. 'There's not enough room to swing a cat in here, never mind invite people in.'

'But they'll be family once these two are wed,' Mary said. 'It'd be good to meet them at least once before the wedding.'

'Got a date in mind?' Arthur asked, glaring at Gordon. 'Because I'll tell you this now, you know fine well there's no money in this house, so whatever wedding you hope for, you'll have to fork out for it yourself.'

'I'll take care of everything, Arthur, don't you worry about that.'

Arthur snorted. 'On a pitman's wage? Good luck with that, lad.'

Ruby looked at her dad's worn and lined face. There was a sadness about him, a resigned air. His shoulders drooped as he sucked on his pipe. While Mary was jubilant and full to the brim with excitement, Arthur seemed distant. Was this how things would be between her dad and Gordon, even when he was her husband? Oh, she knew Arthur was a proud man who'd worked at the pit since he was Michael's age and yet still had nothing to show for it. Just a dilapidated roof over his head and sticks of furniture in their pit cottage. Was he hurting because he couldn't afford to give his daughter the wedding he'd hoped he could? The wedding he felt, as the bride's father, he should provide?

'I'll help pay. I'll find work soon,' Ruby said brightly, trying to convince herself. 'There's got to be work going somewhere. I'll look beyond Ryhope if I have to, at Grange Paper Works, or even in town.'

A knock at the kitchen door stopped any further conversation. Ruby leapt up. 'I'll get it.' She swung the door open.

'Jean!' she cried. She'd forgotten all about Jean's promise of a visit. The afternoon had gone by in such excitement, what with Gordon's proposal, she'd given no further thought to Jean or Abigail, fully wrapped as she was in her own joy. 'Come in,' she said, holding the door wide.

Jean looked into the kitchen, but as soon as she saw Gordon sitting there, she took a step back into the yard.

'No, I'd best not,' she said.

'Don't be daft, lass, get yourself in, it's chilly out there,' Mary called.

'I won't come in, Mrs Dinsdale. I've got to get home, my mam's expecting me.'

'But our Ruby's got good news to share! You'll never guess, she's getting wed!'

Jean rocked back on her heels. Her mouth hung open.

'Gordon's proposed and I've said yes!' Ruby beamed.

Jean snapped her mouth shut and tried to force a smile.

'Isn't it wonderful?' Ruby carried on. 'Oh, I've never been so happy, Jean. I'm engaged! Can you believe it? I mean, I haven't got a ring yet, but I know Gordon will buy me one just as soon as he can.'

'Ruby . . .'

'Oh, listen to me prattling on. Of course you already know how special love is. You've got Ted and now I understand what it's all about too. Will you share my news with Ted and your parents and your brothers?'

'Ruby, don't—'

'You'll all be invited to the wedding just as soon as we can afford it. It'll probably not be for months yet, maybe even longer.'

'Ruby, please—'

'And would you be my bridesmaid, Jean? I'd ask Abigail, but you know how things are between us right now. But maybe when I tell her my news, she'll start speaking to me again. Jean?' Ruby looked at her friend. 'Jean? What is it?'

Jean glanced into the kitchen again and locked eyes with Gordon.

'You said you had something to tell me about Abigail. Is she ill? Is it the baby? What is it?'

Jean shook her head. 'It's nothing. Really it's not. It's not important any more. I've got to go. Mam doesn't like it when I'm home late.'

With that, she turned and walked quickly away.

Chapter Twenty-Two

'Hello, Arthur. Haven't seen you in here for a while. How's that family of yours?' Stuart Brown asked when Arthur walked into the miners' hall.

'They're all well,' Arthur replied. 'Our Michael's not long turned fifteen, and Ruby's nineteen now.'

'I hear your Ruby's getting married, is that right?'

Arthur took his cap off and raindrops fell from it to the floor. 'Don't get me started on that wedding of hers. It's all she ever talks about.'

'Is she still with the same fella, the Fisher lad from Seaham?'

'Aye, that's him,' Arthur said. He wondered why Stuart was asking and hoped that Gordon hadn't been caught changing tokens on the tubs. Arthur had lived with the knowledge of Gordon's deceit ever since the lad had started courting Ruby, and it made him uneasy knowing what his future son-in-law was capable of. He'd kept quiet for Ruby's sake; he'd never seen his daughter so happy as when she was with Gordon.

He worked his fingers around the thick buttons on his

coat and laid it over the back of a chair. It was soaked through from the rain outside. 'Heaven only knows when the wedding will happen,' he sighed. 'They haven't got two ha'pennies to rub together, the pair of them, and me and Mary can't afford it. I told Ruby right from the start she was on a hiding to nothing if she thought I'd be able to chip in and pay.'

'Expensive things, weddings,' Stuart said. 'With four daughters I should know. Be grateful you've got just the one.'

'Ah, she's a good lass, our Ruby.'

'Is she working yet?'

'Her and Mary take in sewing. It helps us get by.' Arthur sank into the chair opposite Stuart.

'What can I do for you, Arthur?'

Arthur straightened. 'I've come on behalf of the lads I work with. We want to know what's going on. Rumours are flying around about strike action coming. I've been sent to ask if you have any news.'

Stuart waved his hand dismissively. 'There's always talk about strikes. It's the rumour mill working overtime. Don't pay it any heed, Arthur.'

'So you haven't heard anything?' Arthur asked.

Stuart shook his head. 'Nothing official, not yet.'

'And will there be a meeting called if the rumours turn out to be true?'

'As soon as we've got information, you know we'll let the lads know.'

'I can't afford to strike, Stuart. None of us can. If we don't work, our families don't eat.'

Stuart glared at him. 'Arthur Dinsdale, I hope you're not telling me that if push comes to shove and the union calls a strike, you'd have second thoughts about where your loyalties lie?'

'Course not,' Arthur huffed. 'What do you take me for? I'm no blackleg.'

'I'm glad to hear it,' Stuart said, relieved.

Arthur stood, slid his arms back into his wet jacket and put his cap back on his head. 'I'll be seeing you, Stuart,' he said.

'Arthur? Before you go?'

He stopped in his tracks.

'How are things these days . . .' Stuart paused, 'with your friend?'

'Friend?' Arthur said, puzzled.

'Some time back, you came in and we had words about a pal of yours who was having a spot of trouble with his wife after she'd lost her bairn.'

'Oh, *that* friend,' he said, remembering. He shifted uncomfortably. 'It's all sorted, thanks.'

'I'm pleased to hear it. But know that I'm here for any advice your friend needs.'

Arthur quickly walked to the door. When he pushed it open, the rain and sleet blew at him. He turned his collar up, pulled his cap down and began the walk up to the pit. He wished he'd had more courage, wished he'd been able to take Stuart up on his offer of help for Mary when she needed it most. His job as her husband was to protect her as best he could, but he never could have risked having her gossiped about. What if someone had overheard him in the miners' hall? What if Stuart had told his wife at home, and she'd told a friend, and the next thing anyone knew local gossip Lil Mahone had got hold of the news and started telling all and sundry? No, he would never have risked putting Mary through that. Thankfully she seemed brighter these days, stronger in herself, the girl he fell in love with coming back day by day. Arthur lowered his head as he walked to stop the icy rain stinging his eyes.

Later that morning in the house on Tunstall Street, Michael and Ruby were sitting by the fire with Mary.

'I don't feel well, Mam,' Michael moaned.

Mary laid her hand to her son's forehead. 'You feel perfectly fine to me.'

'I'm too hot.'

'Then move away from the fire. But if you think you're going to stay off work, you're mistaken.'

'I'm allowed to stop off if I'm not well.'

'There's nothing wrong with you,' Mary said sternly.

Ruby watched the exchange. She knew her mam would never let Michael stay home from work. He'd have to be half dead before she'd even consider it. No work meant no pay. Besides, Ruby wasn't entirely convinced by her brother's performance.

Mary walked out into the yard.

'What's wrong, onion face?' Ruby asked Michael once their mam was out of earshot.

'I'm ill,' Michael said dully.

'No, you're not,' Ruby said. 'You're putting it on so you don't have to go to work.'

Michael laid a hand to the side of his head. 'I get all dizzy in here.' He laid his other hand on his stomach. 'And sick in here.'

'Do you feel that way now?' Ruby asked.

He shook his head. 'Just when I'm at the pit.'

'You've worked there for over a year,' Ruby said

gently. 'Has anything changed that's making you feel worse now?'

Michael turned his gaze from her and stared into the flames. 'I can't do it. I can't go back.'

Ruby put her hand on her brother's arm. 'You have to,' she said softly. 'If you don't work, we don't have any money. Mam needs you to work; we all do.'

'But you don't know what it's like. You don't understand.'

'Then tell me,' she said.

Michael's eyes flickered towards her. He swallowed hard. 'We have what's called cavel day,' he began.

Ruby nodded. She'd heard of cavel day from Gordon.

'The coal company draw lots to see where we'll work at the pit for the next few weeks. It was cavel day last week and I got put on the seam where no one wants to work.'

'The seam full of water?' Ruby asked.

Michael locked eyes with her.

'Gordon's told me about it,' she said.

'We dread it,' Michael said dully. 'Brings our arms and legs out in boils.'

'And you're starting work on that seam today?'

He nodded.

'What if you worked with Dad? Would that help? Can't you ask to be moved to work with him?'

Michael shook his head. 'They never let men from the same family work together. Just in case.'

'You mean in case there's an accident?'

He nodded again. 'Besides, I couldn't ask to be moved. They'd laugh at me, tell me to man up and pull myself together.'

Just then, Mary returned, putting an end to further talk.

165

'What are you two plotting?' she laughed. 'Thick as thieves you are; always were.'

'Think of what you'll do on your next day off work,' Ruby whispered to Michael. 'Think of fishing with your friends, playing football on the beach.'

The mention of football made her think of Abigail. It'd been weeks since she last saw Jean, and she'd not heard a word from Abigail. However, her mam brought gossip from Elsie and Ann. Abigail was growing heavy with the baby and looked done in, by all accounts. As for the fella who'd put her in the family way, Kate had spread word that he was a traveller from Stockton who'd stayed overnight at the Albion Inn. Apparently he'd upped and left the next morning and had never been seen again.

Ruby felt a stab of anxiety each time she thought about Abigail and Jean. She'd tried to see Abigail again, but Kate had turned her away as she'd done before. And whenever she called at the store, Jean told her she was too busy to talk, even when there were no customers at her counter.

'Ruby? Are you listening to me?' Mary's voice cut into her thoughts. 'I said you need to go and deliver the finished sewing to . . .'

A sound pierced the air, and her voice trailed off into nothing. Ruby and Michael stared at each other. It was the pit buzzer, sounding three times. It was the worst kind of noise, one Ryhope folk lived in dread of, for it signalled a death at the pit.

The emergency signal ended, and in the silence that followed, no one dared speak. To speak would be to admit what they all feared in their hearts, for both Arthur and Gordon were at the pit.

Chapter Twenty-Three

They all remained frozen for a few moments, then Michael leapt from his chair and Ruby dashed towards their mother.

'Come on, Mam, we've got to get up there. We've got to find out what's happened,' Michael cried.

Mary stood rooted to the spot.

'Mam!' Ruby cried.

Mary slowly reached out to her two bairns and brought them close to her.

'No,' she said softly. 'Your dad and I have spoken about what to do when the pit buzzer goes. It's not the first time I've heard it and I daresay it won't be the last.'

'But we've got to get up there, now!' Ruby cried.

'Your dad wants me here in the house. It's what we decided long ago. He wants me kept safe, out of harm's way. There'll be crowds up there soon, pushing and shoving, women crying and desperate to know what's gone on. I'm staying here, for your dad. Ready for him coming home.'

Ruby and Michael exchanged a look.

'But Dad's underground, Gordon too. They might be hurt,' Ruby urged.

Mary was firm. 'We're staying here, all of us. If there's bad news to come, we'll hear it in time.'

But no sooner had the words left her lips than Michael ran out of the kitchen with Lady at his heels.

'Michael!' Mary cried, but it was too late, he'd gone.

'He's desperate to know,' Ruby said. 'You can understand, surely?'

'Oh, I understand pit life only too well. But I'll never get used to its dangers. Men go into that hell to work; they give their sweat and their blood. And when the buzzer sounds, it means that someone has given their life.'

Outside on the lane, women were pouring from their yards, everyone running to the pit, hoping, praying it wasn't their husband, brother or son. Inside the Dinsdales' kitchen, Ruby pulled her mam to her and they stood with their arms wrapped around each other as the minutes ticked slowly by. A lot went unsaid, for to speak it would be to admit how frightened they were. Mary didn't know what she'd do, how she'd cope if she ever lost Arthur.

'What if it's Gordon, Mam?' Ruby whispered.

Mary stroked her hair. 'Shush now. I won't have that sort of talk. It does no one any good.'

'But what if it *is* him, or Dad?'

'It could be any one of the thousands of men working there. Now come on, we've got to be strong.'

Ruby sank into a chair as her legs turned weak. She felt as if she might faint.

'Whatever happens, we'll get through it. We're Dinsdale women, we're strong.'

But right then, Ruby felt anything but.

There was a knock at the back door, and without waiting for an answer, Elsie and Ann stepped inside. Elsie immediately went to the fireplace and set the kettle on to boil.

'Tea. That's what we need while we wait for the news,' she said.

'I could do with something stronger,' Mary muttered. Ruby glared at her.

'Oh, don't give me that look, Ruby. At a time like this, how can you refuse your mam a drink?'

'Mary, I don't think it's wise,' Elsie said, remembering Arthur's words in confidence to her after Mary had taken to her bed.

'We've got nothing in, anyway,' Ruby pointed out.

Mary crossed her arms in front of her stomach and turned her head away.

'Is Michael at the pit too?' Elsie asked.

'He's gone to find out what's happened,' Mary explained. 'He's not working today. Just Arthur.'

'And Gordon,' Ruby added quickly.

Ann reached out and held Ruby's hand. 'We'll wait with you until news arrives, one way or the other.'

Elsie made the tea, then she and Ann pulled chairs from the table to join Mary and Ruby in front of the fire. Every so often, Ruby went out to the lane and looked up and down, but no one was about.

'Any news yet?' Mary called.

'Nothing, Mam, no.'

The morning passed slowly. But still Mary was resolute: she would do as Arthur had bid. He had been adamant. Whether he returned home safely on his own two legs or, heaven forbid, on a cart pulled by the coal

169

company's horse, Mary was to stay home and wait. She had promised, and she'd keep her word. She sipped her tea. There was nothing else she could do.

It was almost noon when Ruby heard a noise at the door.

'Gordon? Dad?' she yelled.

She ran to the door and flung it open. Mary, Elsie and Ann crowded behind her, desperate for news. Three pitmen were there, their faces and hands streaked black. They were standing in the yard, a respectful distance from the door. Ruby scanned their faces; she didn't recognise any of them. But men from the pit at their door today of all days could only mean bad news.

Mary pushed her way forward and the men slowly removed their flat caps.

'I'm the woman of the house. If you've got news, I'm ready to hear it,' she said.

Ruby was surprised by the strength of her mam's voice. She gripped tight to Mary's hand. The man in the middle stepped forward. She saw his thick fingers clutching his flat cap to his heart as he worked up the courage to speak.

'Missus, I'm awful sorry to have to tell you that it's your man who's been killed at the pit.'

The blunt words hit them as if they'd been shot through the heart. Mary slumped against the door frame. Elsie and Ann grabbed her before she fell to the floor.

'My Arthur . . .' she breathed.

The pitman gave a start. He looked from Mary to Elsie, to Ann and Ruby.

'No, lass, not Arthur. The dead man's name is Gordon Fisher.'

Ruby couldn't move. She couldn't speak. She didn't see Michael bound into the yard, red in the face, breathless after running from the pit. She didn't see her dad walk in after him, taking Mary in his arms and burying his face in her neck. She didn't see Elsie and Ann quietly leave. She felt empty and numb. She didn't feel her mam's hands on her, helping her to walk, guiding her to the chair by the fire. She didn't see her dad bring a glass of brandy from Elsie's house for her. She didn't feel the glass at her lips as her mam encouraged her to drink. The shock paralysed her. Only when the brandy had made its way down her throat did her world begin to come back into focus, bit by rotten bit.

'No,' she cried, shaking her head wildly. 'No, it can't be Gordon. Are they sure? Did they check it was him? Make them check, Dad. Go back to the pit and insist. It can't be him.'

Arthur bit his lip. 'The doctor's been down there; they're sure it's him,' he said.

'But why? Why him of all the men who worked there? Why my Gordon? What did he ever do wrong?'

'He knew the dangers,' Arthur said softly. 'We all do. Every time we go down there, we know we might never come back.'

Ruby took another sip of the brandy, and it burned in her throat.

'What about his mam and dad?' she said quietly. 'I need to tell them.'

'The coal company will write to them,' Arthur said. 'That's the way these things are done.'

She shook her head. 'No, I'll do it. I need to. His parents would have become my family.'

Mary stroked her arm. 'Ruby, love, how will you get there? They live at Seaham. We can't afford the train fare.'

'I'll walk,' Ruby said. 'I don't care how long it takes.'

Arthur and Mary exchanged a look.

'We'll get the money for the train from somewhere,' Arthur said. 'I'll ask in the miners' hall tomorrow. There are funds available for such things in the event of a . . .' He stopped. The word *death* was left hanging between them. 'There might be enough money to cover the cost of two tickets. No one can expect you to go on your own.'

'I'll come with you,' Mary said. 'We'll go as soon as you feel able.'

'I want to go tomorrow, as soon as Dad gets the money,' Ruby said firmly. 'Gordon's parents need to know from me, not from the cold, harsh words of a telegram.'

With the last of the brandy gone, she set the glass on the hearth. The shock was working its way through her and her numbness had given way to a raw, unbelievable pain. She reached out to her mam and dad, and the three of them hugged as Ruby's tears began to fall.

The following day, Arthur received a promise at the miners' hall that money would be found to cover the train fares.

'It's the least we can do, under the circumstances,' Stuart Brown said.

Secure in the knowledge that the money was forth-coming, Arthur handed Ruby coins from his own pocket to cover the tickets. It was icy cold outside, and Ruby and Mary wrapped up as warmly as they could. As they walked down the colliery bank, men raised their caps in respect, to acknowledge Ruby's loss. She was adrift in her grief and could barely put one foot in front of the other without hanging on to her mam.

Before heading to the railway station, they called first at Mrs Sowerby's house to give her the news about her lodger, in case gossip hadn't reached her yet. Mrs Sowerby was also their only hope of finding out where Gordon's parents lived.

'I'm awful sorry to hear it,' Mrs Sowerby said when Mary told her what had happened. Ruby couldn't bring herself to say the words, for speaking them aloud would make it real. Mrs Sowerby invited the two of them indoors while she wrote down the address of Gordon's parents in Seaham. He'd given her the details when he'd first moved in.

'I never take in a lodger without knowing who their next of kin are. You can't be too careful. You need to know who to go to if someone does a runner without paying the rent. What will I do with his belongings?'

Ruby gasped. She hadn't given it any thought. Gordon's death had been too sudden; she still felt too raw.

'We'll come back to sort through them,' Mary said.

'Well, make it quick,' Mrs Sowerby replied. 'I'll need to get the room cleaned and prepared so that I can take in another lodger.'

Mary shook her head in despair at the woman's insensitive words.

With Gordon's parents' address written on a slip of paper, Ruby and Mary headed to Ryhope East railway station. Once on the train, Ruby took a window seat and looked out at the grey North Sea.

'I always wanted to meet his mam and dad,' she said. 'But never in my darkest dreams did I think I'd meet them under such circumstances.'

'Did he speak of them often?' Mary asked.

Ruby shook her head. She remembered how she'd tried to ask Gordon about his home life in Seaham, and how quickly and easily he'd closed her questions down.

'Never.'

'His poor mam,' Mary sighed. 'I can't imagine the pain she'll go through.' She laid her hand to her daughter's knee. 'You'll get through this, love,' she said. 'I know it doesn't feel like it at the moment, but each day will bring its own challenges, and joys, in time.'

Ruby didn't hear her mam's words. She stared out of the window, lost in her grief.

When the train stopped at Seaham, Ruby and Mary alighted. The cold air pinching their faces, they huddled close together and Ruby read the address again. Following directions from the stationmaster, they headed towards the harbour, to a street with grand houses three storeys high. It wasn't what Ruby had expected. She'd thought Gordon's family was just like hers, living in a terraced house, struggling to make ends meet. In the absence of information from Gordon, had she assumed too much and managed to get it all wrong?

She and Mary walked up the garden path arm in arm. There were lawns to each side. Heavy curtains hung at the windows on all three floors. A leaded square of red and green glass decorated the imposing front door.

Ruby raised her eyes to her mam. 'I can't do this,' she said.

Mary knocked hard at the door. 'You can.'

The door was opened by a stern-faced housekeeper. She wore a grey dress with a white pinny, black stockings and polished shoes. Her grey hair was scraped back in a bun.

'I'm here to see Mr and Mrs Fisher,' Ruby said.

The housekeeper stared at her long and hard. 'Who are you?' she demanded.

'Ruby Dinsdale. And this is my mam, Mary. We've come from Ryhope, on the train.'

'Ryhope?' the housekeeper said.

Ruby nodded. 'I'm afraid I bring the Fishers bad news.'

'I'm sorry we didn't make an appointment to see them,' Mary added quickly. 'It all happened so quickly, you see.'

The housekeeper's face grew grim. She stepped to one side and held the door open.

'I'm Mrs Fisher. I think you'd better come in.'

Chapter Twenty-Four

Mrs Fisher walked along a wide hallway.

'We can talk in the scullery,' she said.

Ruby and Mary followed her into a cold, functional room lined with shelves holding glass jars and dishes alongside plates and crockery of all shapes and sizes. A scent of lavender floated in the air. In the centre of the room was a small wooden table with four chairs.

'Sit yourselves down,' she said. She didn't offer tea.

They did as instructed, and Mrs Fisher pulled out a chair for herself.

'Now, what's all this about?' she said.

Ruby and Mary looked at one another.

'Mrs Fisher, I . . .' Ruby began. On the train this morning she'd practised what she was going to say, going over the words in her mind. But now that she was here, with Gordon's mam in front of her, they just wouldn't come. She glanced at the housekeeper and saw Gordon's dark eyes staring back.

'Shall I tell her?' Mary offered.

'Tell me what?' Mrs Fisher demanded. 'What's going on? Just who the devil are you and what do you want?'

Ruby shook her head. 'I need to tell her myself, Mam.' She straightened in her chair. 'Mrs Fisher, I'm sorry to tell you this, honest I am. I wish we could have met under different circumstances.'

'Spit it out, girl.'

'I'm afraid I'm here to tell you that Gordon . . .' She faltered. Mary reached for her hand.

Mrs Fisher's shoulders slumped. 'Gordon? What the hell's he up to now?'

Ruby's lips trembled. Having to say it out loud was difficult enough, but to deliver the news to Gordon's mother threatened to send her into another torrent of weeping.

'Gordon is dead.'

She wiped her eyes with the back of her hand and looked at Mrs Fisher, waiting for her reaction. What happened next took her by surprise. She'd expected tears, at least. This was his mother after all, the woman who'd brought him into the world, had raised him, looked after him. The woman who loved him, surely? But Mrs Fisher simply nodded and brought her hands together under her chin as if she was about to pray.

She was silent for a few moments, thinking. 'Was it a fight he was in?' she asked at last. 'I always knew those fists of his would be the death of him.'

'A fight?' Ruby was confused. 'No. He died at the pit. There was an accident, a rock fall.'

Now it was Mrs Fisher's turn to be surprised. 'The pit? He was a miner?'

'You mean you didn't know?' Mary asked. She wondered what sort of a mother Mrs Fisher was if she didn't even know what her own son was up to.

'I haven't seen Gordon in over five years,' Mrs Fisher said, eyeing Ruby closely. 'Anyway, who are you to come here to bring me this news? The pit won't have sent a young lass.'

'Gordon didn't mention me at all?' Ruby asked.

'Not only have I not seen him, but I've not heard a whisper from him in all that time either. And that's the way I preferred it.'

'But he's your son!' Mary cried. 'I'm sorry, he *was* your son.'

Mrs Fisher shook her head. 'He was a bad lot, was Gordon. I threw him out not long after his father died.'

Ruby gasped. Whenever she had asked Gordon about his parents, not once had he told her that his mother was a widow. And what did Mrs Fisher mean about him fighting, and his fists? What else didn't she know about the man she'd loved?

A sadness clouded Mrs Fisher's stern face.

'Gordon went off the rails as a boy. He was always up to no good. Always in trouble with the coppers. Me and his father, we did our best, but there was no stopping him. Running with a bad crowd, he was, out fighting and stealing and . . .' She stopped herself. 'Were you a friend of his?' she asked.

Ruby bit her lip to stop herself from crying, but it didn't help, and her tears came fast.

'She was his girlfriend,' Mary explained. 'They were engaged. Gordon proposed and they were planning to wed.'

Mrs Fisher gave a long sigh. 'Then I'm sorry for your loss,' she said. 'Because I daresay you'll feel his passing deeper than I ever will.'

Mary handed Ruby a cotton handkerchief to dry her eyes and blow her nose. Slowly Ruby managed to pull herself together. Just then, a brass bell sounded. All eyes turned to the wall: a service bell had been rung from one of the rooms above.

'If you'll excuse me,' Mrs Fisher said. 'I'm wanted back at work.'

'Of course, we'll go,' Mary said. 'Would you like me to write to you with details of the funeral when it's all arranged?'

Mrs Fisher shook her head. 'I've already said my goodbyes to Gordon,' she said coldly. 'He's been dead to me for years.'

Ruby and Mary walked from the house and heard the heavy door close behind them. They huddled close against the wintry day as they made their way back to the station. As they walked, Ruby struggled to make sense of everything she'd been told, everything she'd learned about the man she'd thought she knew. The man she'd thought she loved.

'His own mam disowned him,' she said. 'And he lied about his dad; he never told me he was dead. As for fighting and stealing . . . What kind of man was he?'

Mary comforted her daughter. 'He was loving and warm and generous, that's the kind of man he was with you. And that's how you should remember him.'

Ruby snuggled into her mam's side as they walked. She remained silent all the way home.

Mary, meanwhile, remembered what Arthur had told her about Gordon, the things he whispered to her in the dead of night when they were both abed. It was gossip he'd heard about him attacking a pit pony, about him taking credit for work that others had done. What was it Arthur had called it? Token slinging, she recalled. Mary had kept quiet about it all; well, it was just gossip after all and nothing had been proved about Gordon. And although she'd never mention it to Ruby now – not while she was grieving, and perhaps not ever – Mary couldn't help wondering now if Gordon's death had provided her daughter with a lucky escape from a future with a violent man.

Gordon's funeral took place at St Paul's church on a dark, cold December day. It was a pauper's funeral, held early in the morning and paid for by funds raised at the miners' hall. Ruby was sitting at the front of the church, with Arthur and Mary on either side. Michael was at work at the pit. Local gossip Lil Mahone was there, for she never missed a funeral and liked to tell anyone who'd listen who'd been in attendance, what they'd worn and what hymns had been sung. Lil had chosen the pew by the door, to keep an eye on everyone coming and going. Elsie, Bert Collins and Ann sat in the same pew as Mrs Sowerby. Jean and Ted were there too, holding hands. Jean had insisted on attending to support Ruby, no matter what she knew about Gordon.

Once everyone else had been seated and was facing the vicar, a lone figure crept into the church. She wore a long coat to disguise the slight swelling of her belly, and took a seat at the back, at the end of a pew.

Reverend Daye opened his Bible. He began with a few words about Gordon that Ruby had helped him prepare. But as his voice echoed around the church, Ruby wondered again how much of what she knew about Gordon was true.

The vicar looked out into the sparse congregation. He saw a woman sitting alone at the back, a woman with long fair hair tied in a plait. Once the final hymn was sung, she crept out of the church. She thought she'd been unseen by anyone at the front, but Lil Mahone's well-trained radar never missed a thing. When the service was over and everyone filed out, Lil and Mrs Sowerby fell into conversation by the door. Lil kept glancing towards Ruby, raising her eyebrows as Mrs Sowerby told her about the miner lodging with her until his untimely death.

Ruby and her mam and dad headed down the church path.

'Ruby, wait!' a voice called. It was Jean. 'I want to say how sorry I am for your loss.'

'Thanks for coming, Jean. And you, Ted,' Ruby said. 'Look, we're going to the Miss Huttons' house for a bite to eat, if you'd like to come.'

'Ted?' Jean offered.

He shook his head. 'I've got to get to work.'

'I'll come,' Jean said. 'I've got the whole day off from the store.'

Arthur and Mary were chatting with the vicar, saying their goodbyes. At the same time, Lil Mahone and Mrs Sowerby rounded off their gossipy chat.

'Have you seen Abigail?' Ruby asked Jean. 'How is she?'

Jean shook her head. 'I don't have anything to do with her these days,' she said. 'But I hear the baby's due in the spring.'

'A baby?' Lil Mahone said from behind Ruby.

Both girls spun around.

'It's someone we know, that's all,' Jean said. 'Not that it's any of your business.'

'Oh, I agree,' Lil sniffed. 'It's none of my business at all. But it should be *her* business.' She nodded towards Ruby.

'Mine?' Ruby said.

'Mrs Mahone, please!' Jean snapped. She couldn't believe that Lil Mahone would be cruel enough to reveal the news that Jean had managed to keep quiet from Ruby so far.

'No, if she's got something to say, let her say it,' Ruby said.

'Mrs Mahone, this is neither the time nor the place!' Jean hissed.

Ruby looked from Lil to Jean. 'What's going on? I demand to know.'

Lil Mahone looked her in the eye. 'I think you should have a word with your friend Abigail.'

Chapter Twenty-Five

'Jean? What does she mean?' Ruby cried.

Jean took hold of Ruby's arm and pulled her away, shooting Lil Mahone a look that could have curdled milk. But it was like water off a duck's back to Lil, who simply shrugged and walked away. She thrived on receiving and delivering gossip, and what she'd just heard from Gordon Fisher's landlady had been worth its weight in gold. Fancy him courting the Dinsdale lass while sneaking her friend Abigail into his room at night. Well, as Mrs Sowerby had said, there wasn't much anyone could hide from a landlady. And now Abigail was pregnant and it certainly seemed there was a good chance of the baby being Gordon's. Mrs Sowerby had kept quiet about all of this so far, she'd told Lil, but now that Gordon was dead and buried, what harm could there be in sharing what she knew?

Lil had thanked her for letting her know. She was buzzing with her news and couldn't contain herself, couldn't resist bustling over to Ruby and Jean when she'd heard a baby mentioned. Oh, she loved to dip her nose into other people's business. It made her feel alive. Heaven knows, she had precious little else in her life. She had no bairns of her own, which some said was a blessing, for who would want someone as gossipy as Lil as their mam? Other, kinder folk, said that Lil's childless marriage and her unloving husband were the reason she gossiped, and she should be pitied for it. Being the font of all knowledge, whether right or wrong, about the goings-on in Ryhope was the only reason she had friends. Everyone knew that if they wanted to find out what was going on, they only had to ask Lil Mahone.

She'd always had gossip to spread about Abigail's mother, Kate, for she was a woman who had more men in and out of her front door than most people had hot meals. And now it seemed the apple hadn't fallen far from the tree. Kate's daughter Abigail was in the family way. Lil had suspected it for a while. She recognised the signs of a pregnant woman many weeks before a swollen belly gave the game away, spotting the subtle changes that most people missed. If there was a Ryhope lass looking a little flushed around the face or laying a hand to her stomach every once in a while, Lil watched her more keenly the next time she saw her. If a woman's blouse looked a little tight across the breast, or her ankles were swollen, that was a giveaway too. And the mere mention of sickness, especially early in the morning, as good as confirmed it. But this? What she'd just been told about the dead miner, his fiancée and her friend was currency that would buy time with people who flocked to her pretending to be her friends just so they could find out the latest news. As Lil walked from the church, she wondered who she'd tell it to first.

* * *

'Jean, tell me what's going on,' Ruby demanded.

'We need to get you home,' Jean said.

Ruby pulled her arm free. 'I'm not going anywhere until I know what Lil meant. What is it about Abigail that I need to know?'

'Nothing, really.'

'Look, Jean, I'm not stupid. Abigail won't speak to me and you've been acting strange for ages. I need to know.'

'Ruby, please—'

'Jean!' Ruby snapped.

Jean froze as Arthur, Mary, Elsie and Ann walked towards them.

'Girls?' Mary said. 'Are you coming for a bite to eat at Ann and Elsie's?'

'Later, Mam,' Ruby said, glaring at Jean. 'Jean and I need to talk.'

'Well, don't be too long,' Mary said.

Elsie reached her hand towards Ruby. 'Are you sure you're all right?'

Ruby nodded. 'Thanks, Elsie.'

Mary and Arthur headed down the church path, followed by the Hutton sisters. As they walked away, Elsie turned a couple of times, glancing curiously at the two girls.

Once they were alone, Ruby beckoned Jean behind the church.

'We'll talk here, out of sight,' she said.

The day was cold and the sun was low in the sky. The building provided welcome shelter from the wind. Ruby stood with her back against the wall. Ahead of her were fields, and beyond them the sea, grey against the blue winter sky.

'Beautiful, isn't it?' she said, staring at the view.

Jean shot her a look of concern. Ruby had been agitated just a moment ago, and now she seemed overly calm. Jean moved to stand next to her with her back against the wall too, and the two of them stared ahead. They were silent for a few moments until Ruby began to speak.

'Remember when we were little and our Michael got his head stuck in the railings up by the store?'

Jean stayed quiet but her heart was hammering so hard she was afraid Ruby might hear it. She knew she had no choice but to tell Ruby the truth about Abigail's baby. If Lil Mahone knew – and it seemed from her earlier remark that she did – then half of Ryhope would have heard by nightfall. She had to be the one who told Ruby; she couldn't let her learn about it from anyone else. It was going to be hard enough for Ruby to hear it from her friend, never mind a washerwoman pegging clothes in the lane, or a drunken fool staggering from one of Ryhope's pubs.

'And do you remember the day the fair came to the village green? And the ribbon seller who rode in on a donkey?' Ruby went on. 'I've still got one of those scarlet ribbons.' She turned towards her friend. 'We've known each other all our lives, Jean. I know when you're keeping things from me.'

'Ruby, I—'

'No more excuses. Please,' she begged. 'Just tell me the truth.'

'Ruby, you've just come out of Gordon's funeral. Are you sure you want to know now? Can't it wait until you get home and your mam and dad are with you?'

Ruby leaned against the wall again and stared out

ahead at the sea. She shook her head. 'You tried to tell me before, didn't you? When you came to our house. But Gordon was there and you couldn't do it. Well, he's not here any more. What is it, Jean?'

She took a gulp of cold air. Both girls looked out at the fields. Jean reached for Ruby's hand and their fingers entwined.

'Abigail's baby . . .' she began.

Ruby screwed her eyes tight. She pressed her back hard against the wall.

'It's Gordon's, isn't it?' she said quietly.

Jean gasped. 'You knew?'

Ruby crumpled as if she'd had the life punched out of her. Her legs gave way and she slid down the wall to the rough patch of ground. Jean got down on her knees in front of her friend and laid her hands on her shoulders.

'You knew?' she repeated.

Ruby didn't reply. She just stared ahead. 'It's like he's died all over again,' she whispered.

'What do you mean?' Jean asked, worried.

'The pain, the rawness inside,' Ruby said. 'I can't take any more.'

'You'll get through, Ruby. You're young and you're strong. You've got your whole life ahead of you. You're a bonny lass, you'll find someone else.' Jean could have bitten her tongue off the minute the insensitive words left her lips. 'Oh my God, I'm sorry, Ruby, that came out all wrong.'

Ruby struggled to stand. Jean tried to help her, but Ruby shrugged her arm away. She hadn't known for sure. How could she? She'd thought Gordon had been faithful to her, just as she'd been to him. She'd trusted him with her heart and soul, with her life, her future. And he had betrayed her in the worst possible way. Doubts had started to creep in after her visit to Gordon's mam. She'd begun to wonder about the man she'd thought she'd loved. What else might he be capable of that she didn't know about, if he'd hidden his past from her and lied about his dad? But that was all they had been, just doubts. Now her darkest fear had been confirmed.

'It's too much. I can't bear it,' she said, her voice rising.

'Ruby, calm down,' Jean said. But Ruby paid her no heed. She stormed away from Jean and the church, towards the fields.

'Ruby!' Jean called.

Ruby didn't turn. Jean hurried after her, calling her name, begging her to stop, but Ruby walked more quickly, and then she began to run. The black hat she had worn for Gordon's funeral, her Grandma Winter's old hat, flew from her head. Jean picked it up and ran with it in her hand.

'Ruby, stop! Wait!'

Her words were lost in the cold air. Not once did Ruby turn; she just kept running through the field, stumbling over clods of earth. Faster and faster she went. Jean couldn't match her pace, but she managed to keep her in her sights.

At the end of the field the earth gave way to a stony track that led through the cliffs to the beach. Once Ruby reached the track, she ran faster, pulling away from Jean. Jean stopped calling her name and put all her energy into running as fast as she could, but still she couldn't catch Ruby. It was as if her friend was possessed, racing to get to the beach. Jean struggled on, panting furiously, until the sea came into view. The tide was out and a broad stretch of coal-blackened sands lay ahead. She paused to catch her breath, bending low and trying to breathe deeply. But when she straightened and looked ahead, Ruby was no longer in sight. Jean forced herself on, her legs burning, her lungs about to burst. She caught sight of Ruby ahead of her on the sand. She was running more slowly now, but still moving forwards. Jean stood a moment, watching in disbelief as she ran towards the waves.

'No,' she breathed. 'No!'

She threw the hat to the ground and let her arms fly out, propelling herself forwards, her feet hitting the damp sand. She had to get to Ruby before she entered the sea. She had to.

'Ruby!' she yelled as she ran, but it was no good, her cry was lost in the roar of the waves. Blood pounded in her ears and the bitter wind nipped at her face as her boots sank into the wet sand. She was gaining on Ruby, who had slowed when she reached the shoreline. Jean breathed a sigh of relief. Ruby was almost within reach now; she'd stopped dead. Did she want Jean to catch her? Did she even know she was being followed?

Jean called out again, but Ruby didn't turn. Instead, she calmly and slowly walked into the sea. Jean watched in shock, then ran forward, calling out, but Ruby didn't heed her words. Jean reached the water and waded in after her, the icy waves soaking her skirt and pulling at her legs. Now the water was up to her waist, dragging her forward, pushing her back; then it was up to her breasts, her neck.

Jean had never learned to swim; no one had taught her. All she could do was walk forward on tiptoe, keeping her head up, away from the waves as they crashed on to her. She ploughed on towards Ruby, pushing her way through the breakers, spitting salt water from her mouth. Her friend was there, right in front of her; all she needed to do was lift her arm and grab her. She reached out; she was almost there, she almost had hold of Ruby's jacket, but she was being pushed by the waves into a different direction to the one she needed to go. She was dragged away, and as she fought her way back, Ruby disappeared under a wave.

Chapter Twenty-Six

Jean's limbs were screaming with pain, but she forced herself forward. She saw Ruby being tossed by the waves; not fighting against them, just letting them take her away. Wave after wave crashed in, each one pushing and pulling, too strong for Jean to fight. And then it happened: a breaker came rolling in that threw Ruby's body in front of her. She wasted no time. She fastened her arms around Ruby's waist and began stumbling backwards, dragging her out of the churning sea.

After what seemed like an age, they reached the shallows, the water at their knees. Jean sank exhausted to the sand, and Ruby fell at her side.

'Breathe, Ruby, breathe,' Jean urged.

Ruby spat out salt water and took great gulps of air. The two girls sat together, soaked and frozen to the bone.

'Ruby! Jean!' a voice called.

Jean spun around, surprised and relieved to see Elsie running down the beach. Elsie picked up her skirt, exposing her black stockings to the knee, and strode into the water. When she reached Ruby, she hooked her hand under her right arm. Jean took the other arm.

'Get her on to dry sand,' Elsie ordered.

'How did you know we were here?' Jean gasped.

'No time for that now. Come on, help me lift her.'

The two women stumbled out of the water, dragging Ruby. They laid her down on dry sand, but Ruby forced herself up into a sitting position and began coughing up seawater. Elsie threw an arm around her shoulders and cuddled her. Both girls were shivering violently.

'Whatever got into you, Ruby?' she whispered.

'Elsie, leave her be,' Jean said. 'We can talk later. The main thing is that we get her home.'

'I was halfway home myself, but something kept niggling at me,' Elsie explained. 'I knew Lil Mahone had said something to upset Ruby. I walked back to the church to speak to her, but there was no sign. I asked Reverend Daye if he'd seen her, and he said he'd seen you both running towards the beach.'

'Thank heavens you came,' Jean said, then she looked at Ruby. 'Can you stand, Ruby? Do you think you can walk?'

Ruby nodded. Elsie and Jean stood and took her by the arms. Together the three women walked slowly from the beach, water dripping from their sodden clothes. They reached the track that led back through the cliffs.

'We need to get her to the doctor,' Elsie said.

'No!' Ruby cried. She couldn't lay the cost of a doctor's bill on her mam and dad when there wasn't any money to spare.

'Then we'll keep walking,' Elsie urged. 'Jean? Are you going to be all right?'

'I think so,' Jean said through chattering teeth.

Elsie and Jean held tight to Ruby as they walked, and

with each step Ruby's strength began to return. They skirted along the edge of the village green, past the school and the church, the police station and the Grand Electric Cinema. And what a sight they looked, Ruby and Jean soaked through, their hair bedraggled. Elsie stared down anyone who looked their way.

'Mind your own flaming business!' she growled.

The freezing wind bit into Jean and Ruby through their wet clothes, and by the time they reached the colliery bank, it was all they could do to find the strength to put one foot in front of the other. Slowly they went, step by painful step.

'Come on,' Elsie urged. 'We're nearly there.'

The store came into view, and beyond it the Queen's Head. A man came running towards them. Elsie was just about to give him short shrift, tell him to mind his own business, when she realised it was Stan Hutchinson. Fortunately, he asked no questions, although what must have been going through his mind at the sight of the two girls, Elsie could only guess.

'Stan, take her arm,' she said quickly. 'Jean, you get yourself home, get warmed through. Stan and me will take Ruby home.'

Jean didn't need to be told twice. She had never felt so cold in her life. All she wanted to do was run home and have a hot bath in front of the fire. She kissed Ruby goodbye, nodded towards Stan, then turned to Elsie.

'We'll speak later, yes?'

'Yes,' Elsie said.

Jean headed for home. She knew she'd have some explaining to do to her mam and dad when she returned in such a state.

* * *

With Stan's help and his strong arms, Elsie managed to get Ruby the rest of the way home to the Dinsdales' house.

'Front door or back?' Stan asked.

'Back,' Elsie said. The only time anyone in the pit lanes used their front doors was when they were heading to the church, either in their finery for a wedding or in a box to the cemetery.

They rounded the corner of the back lane and walked the remainder of the way in silence. When they reached the Dinsdales' back yard, Lady walked towards them with her tail wagging.

'Not now, Lady. Down!' Elsie commanded. The dog slunk away to its corner.

'Do you want me to come in?' Stan asked Elsie.

'Please, lad,' she said.

'I'm fine,' Ruby said weakly, but Stan still wasn't prepared to let her walk on her own. He held tight around her waist, while Ruby's arm was looped over his shoulder for support.

The three of them manoeuvred their way into the yard. Elsie thumped the back door as a warning that they were coming in, then pushed at it with her free hand. Stan loosened his grip, Elsie stepped back, and when the door swung open, Ruby fell into her mam's arms.

'What on earth?' Mary cried when she saw the state of her daughter.

'It's a long story,' Elsie said. 'But the main thing is that she's safe. She's in shock. She might need something to drink.'

'I'll bring brandy from the pub,' Stan said.

'Good lad,' Elsie said.

As Stan left and headed to the Queen's Head, Mary led Ruby to the chair by the fire, then kneeled in front of her and held her hands.

'Oh lass, just look at you,' she cried. 'What happened? Where did you go when we all left the church?'

Ruby's eyes flickered from her mam to Elsie. 'Elsie?' she whispered. 'I need to talk to Mam alone.'

'Course you do,' Elsie said. 'And if there's anything you need, anything at all, either of you, just say the word, you hear?'

'Thank you,' Ruby murmured.

'Bless you, Elsie,' Mary said.

Once Elsie had gone, Mary began to peel Ruby's wet clothes from her body. She dried her and wrapped her in a knitted blue blanket, then set to bringing in buckets of water to boil up for a bath. At the tap in the lane, she saw Stan walking towards her carrying the brandy he'd promised. With every ounce of self-control she could muster, she forced herself to resist looking at the bottle, to do the right thing, to take it from Stan and give it to Ruby. But as it came closer, her determination dissolved. She began thinking of the taste of the brandy on her lips, imagining the burn in her throat as it slipped down, the warmth of it in her belly, the ease it would bring to her mind. She swallowed hard. Stan walked closer.

'Shall I take it in for her, Mrs Dinsdale?' he said.

Mary's breath caught in her chest. She wanted to rip the bottle from his hands. Her mouth went dry. She was trying, really trying, not to look at it, but it was there, in his hand, right in front of her face. Why did he have to bring it so close? She saw the liquid sloshing at the bottom of the bottle. If she took just a sip, Ruby wouldn't know. There was enough in there for both of them to have a drink.

'Mrs Dinsdale, the water,' Stan said.

He leapt towards the tap to turn it off, and Mary realised that her bucket was overflowing. She'd been too lost in her thoughts about the brandy to care. She grabbed for the bottle.

'I'll take it,' she said.

Stan went to pick up the bucket. 'Then let me carry this for you.'

Mary got her hand to it first. 'No,' she said harshly. 'I'll do it. You go.' She held the brandy bottle high. 'Tell your mam and dad thank you for this. And I'm grateful for all you've done to help Ruby.'

'Maybe I could call to see her when she's better, like?' Stan asked.

'Maybe you could,' Mary said, barely paying attention to his words. Now that she had the bottle in her hand, there was only one thing she wanted to do. She had to get away from the back lane as quickly as she could. Desperate as she was for the taste of the spirit in her mouth, she wouldn't give her neighbours the satisfaction of seeing her drinking.

She walked into the yard with the heavy bucket in one hand and the brandy in the other. The minute she was safely away from prying eyes, she set the bucket down on the ground. Lady came towards her and started to lap the water. Mary pulled the stopper from the bottle and lifted it to her lips. The smell of it hit her, and made her mouth water. She wanted the taste of it on her tongue. But she knew that she mustn't. It was for Ruby. Her daughter needed it. Her own flesh and blood. Battling with her thoughts, she lowered the bottle. Then, with every ounce of strength she possessed, she pushed the stopper back in, picked up the bucket and walked into the house.

'Stan brought this for you,' she said, showing Ruby the bottle, thrusting it as far away from her as she could reach, as if by holding it close there was a chance she might change her mind and drink it herself. 'There's enough in here to warm you through.'

Ruby slowly sipped the brandy as Mary went back and forth to the tap with the bucket. The water was heated on the fire and she finally sank into the bath. She let her mam wash her hair, soap her shoulders and caress the skin on her back.

'You said you wanted to talk, love,' Mary said softly. 'Did it all get too much at the funeral?'

'It all got too much.' Ruby repeated her words.

'You know, love . . .' Mary began cautiously, 'when I lost the bairn, it all seemed too much for me too. But you'll get through it. You have to. We women don't have any choice.'

Ruby stared into the flames. 'How *do* you carry on, Mam, after your life's been torn apart?'

'You take it one day at a time,' Mary said. 'And if that seems too hard, take it one hour at a time. Take it slowly, gently. And before you know it, a whole day has gone by, and then another. Your heart will still be broken, but you're alive and you'll keep going, because you have to. You're a Dinsdale lass, Ruby. Nothing and no one keeps us lot down.'

'Grandma Winter didn't keep going,' Ruby said.

Mary's eyes flickered to the brandy bottle before

197

returning to her task of washing seawater from Ruby's hair. 'Your grandma had her problems; we've never made any secret of that.'

'Have I inherited her mind?' Ruby asked. 'What happened today, Mam, it scared me. It felt like I had no control over what I did.'

'You're not Grandma Winter. What happened to her was different.'

'How?' Ruby asked.

'She only had Grandad in the end, and he couldn't cope. We've got each other. Us Dinsdales will look after each other. Grandma never spoke about what was bothering her. She kept everything inside, never once let on when she was feeling out of sorts. She took to drinking instead, and that was when her problems began. Whenever *we* have problems, we'll talk to each other, more than ever before, Ruby. We need to help each other through difficult times. Maybe a little bit of madness runs in us all. The trick is not to let it overwhelm us. I let it get to me too much when I lost the bairn.' Mary faltered.

'I'm sorry, Mam, I didn't mean to drag things up from the past,' Ruby said.

Mary soaped her daughter's hair. 'At least you'll always know Gordon loved you,' she said.

Ruby was silent for a moment, then she turned her head to her mam. Tears glistened in her eyes. 'No, Mam,' she said sadly. 'The more I learn about him, the more I doubt he did.'

Chapter Twenty-Seven

Ruby sat up into the early hours talking to her parents by the fire. She told them about Gordon and Abigail and how betrayed she felt by them both. The next morning, after Michael had gone to work, Mary was busy toasting bread to serve with a scraping of beef paste for breakfast.

'How are you feeling today, lass?' Arthur asked.

'I didn't sleep well, if that's what you mean,' Ruby replied. 'I just keep thinking about Abigail. How could she do such a thing to me? I'm her friend, as good as her sister. When she was little, she spent more time here with us than she did at home with her mam. You fed her, Mam. You looked after her. I let her share my bed. And she goes and does this to me.'

'You've had a terrible shock,' Arthur said. 'You've barely got over your lad's death, and now the news about Abigail will be all over the village. After what happened yesterday, we won't expect too much of you, not until you pull yourself round.'

Mary shot Arthur a warning look to be careful about what he said next.

'Me and your mam, we're worried about you,' he

continued gently. 'It's not like you to let the darkness in the way you did yesterday, walking off into the sea. What were you thinking?'

Mary handed slices of hot toast to Arthur and Ruby and set mugs of tea on the hearth.

Ruby picked her mug up and warmed her hands on it. She raised her eyes to meet her dad's. 'I don't know what I was thinking,' she said. 'I wasn't thinking anything, yet it seemed everything was in my head. I had to escape it somehow, get away from the truth about Gordon. The only thing I could do was run. And once I started, I couldn't stop. The thoughts were in my head and I couldn't leave them behind, no matter how fast I went.'

'I called on Jean first thing this morning,' Mary said.

'You did? Is she all right?'

'She'll survive, just like you. You lasses are tougher than you look.'

'She saved my life,' Ruby said.

'She said . . .' Mary paused, looked at Arthur, who nodded his head, her cue to carry on. 'She said you slowed down when you reached the sea. She said it was as if you were trying to decide what to do, and that you made the decision to walk in.' She locked eyes with Ruby. 'Is that true?'

Ruby hung her head. 'I wish I could answer. But the truth is, I don't know. I was angry and hurt and my head was full of it, the anger and grief all mixed up. I couldn't think straight. I still can't.'

'I daresay you'll be up and down for some time,' Arthur said sagely. 'Gordon's got a lot to answer for.'

'I just ran and ran.' Ruby carried on as if she hadn't heard her dad. 'And when I reached the sea, it seemed the right thing to do, to carry on, as if the waves would wash the thoughts away, wash the truth away and all that had happened.'

She began crying again, and Mary laid her hand on her arm. 'Now, lass, come on. You're safe now, you're home. We'll take care of you.'

Ruby sipped at her tea and stared into the flames. 'I'm going to Mrs Sowerby's today,' she announced.

'Are you sure you're up to it?' Mary said.

Ruby nodded. 'I need to empty Gordon's room of his belongings. There's no one else to do it. I don't suppose his mam cares what happens to his things, not now we know the truth.'

'I think you're right about that,' Mary said. 'She said that he's been dead to her for years.'

'His clothes, that kind of thing?' Arthur asked.

'I don't know what else there will be,' Ruby replied.

'Well, he was a big fella, and I know our Michael needs new trousers – he's a growing lad,' Arthur said.

Mary shot her husband a very dark look. 'Arthur Dinsdale! I hope you're not suggesting what I think you are. Surely you can't expect any of . . .' she steeled herself, '*that man's* clothes to make their way into our home? After what he did to our Ruby? Shame on you.'

'Our Michael needs trousers that aren't halfway up his legs, and there'll be Gordon's pit clothes going spare. That's all I'm saying, love.'

'No, Arthur,' Mary said firmly, glancing at Ruby. 'No.'

Ruby began to eat her toast and took another sip of tea.

'Do you need me to come with you to the lodging house?' Mary asked.

Ruby had thought of little else all morning before reaching her decision. 'I want to go on my own.'

'Are you sure?'

'I'm sure,' she said.

'Just make sure you get a good price for anything the landlady wants to keep.'

'What if there's rent to be paid on his room?' Arthur said.

Ruby straightened in her chair, took a huge bite from her toast and thought carefully. Then she looked from her mam to her dad. 'If there's any money due, if Gordon's left debts, Mrs Sowerby can whistle for them. I'm not covering his mistakes for him.'

Arthur winked at her. 'That's my girl.'

After breakfast, Ruby set off on her walk to the house where Gordon had lived. She kept her gaze low to avoid speaking to anyone who might recognise her. She couldn't take their pity; she had enough going on in her head. Whether folk knew about Abigail's baby or not, they would know about Gordon being killed at the pit, and she couldn't face anyone talking to her about him.

When she arrived at Mrs Sowerby's house, the landlady opened the door.

'I've been expecting you,' she said. There was no exchange of pleasantries, no cup of tea offered, no chance for Ruby to warm by the fire after her walk in the winter air. Mrs Sowerby was all business, her priority getting her lodger's room cleared and rented out again. 'His room is up the stairs, first door on the right.' She indicated the staircase behind her.

Ruby stepped inside. On her way to the lodging house

that morning, she'd been determined to stay strong. She'd sworn to herself that she wouldn't waste more time crying over the man who'd deceived her, betrayed her in the worst possible way. But once she stepped over the threshold into the hallway, her tears came again. The last time she'd been there was when Gordon had proposed, and the memory of it threatened to overwhelm her. She nodded politely at Mrs Sowerby and then took the stairs slowly.

'If you need me, I'll be in the kitchen,' Mrs Sowerby said.

Ruby gripped the handrail as she walked up the stairs. Gordon's proposal. His words echoed in her mind. How stupid she had been, how foolish not to have made the connection. He'd proposed just minutes after she'd told him about Abigail being pregnant. They'd been eating Mrs Sowerby's cocoa cake, she recalled. She remembered the gorgeously gooey and sweet cake, and how Gordon had almost choked on it when she'd told him the news. His proposal hadn't come from the heart at all. She felt such an idiot. Rage burned in her with each step she took towards his room.

When she reached the landing at the top of the stairs, she saw that there were two doors on her right. She walked to the first one, turned the handle and opened the door.

The room was smaller than she had imagined. She looked around, taking it all in. A single bed was pushed against the wall under the window. There was a wooden chest with three drawers, and a small table by the bed. Ruby saw a shaving kit and a block of carbolic soap on top of the drawers. The room smelled metallic and cold.

Thin brown curtains hung at the window, and the floor was bare, just a blue mat by the bed.

She felt numb and daunted by the task ahead. Her mam was right: she wouldn't be taking Gordon's clothes home for any of her family to wear. She'd never do that; they'd forever be a reminder of what he'd done to her. But neither would she deny her family the money that the garments might bring once they were sold. She knew she could offer them to Meg Sutcliffe, the girl who ran the rag-and-bone round. However, she didn't know when she'd see Meg next, for the girl seemed to keep the most peculiar hours and was rumoured to be out on her horse and cart before the sun rose each morning. Plus, the anger she felt over Gordon's betrayal wouldn't allow her to see further than getting rid of his belongings as quickly as possible. She wanted no reminder of him in her life.

She pulled the drawers open, throwing shirts and socks, underpants and vests on to the bed. She'd offer all of it, every last handkerchief, to Mrs Sowerby, and she'd have to trust that the woman would share the profits with her. She'd have to bargain, for she knew that the landlady wouldn't give her the money up front; she was too canny for that. She'd try to come to some arrangement where half the money was paid now and half when the items were sold.

When she pulled the bottom drawer open, there were papers tucked under the clothes. She sat on the bed and sorted through them. There was a letter from the Ryhope Coal Company confirming Gordon's appointment with them when he'd first arrived in the village. There was a letter giving details of his wages, along with empty pay packets. She decided she'd ask her dad what to do with those, and whether the coal company might need them returned.

Just as she was about to bundle the whole lot together and take it all downstairs, she spotted a sheet of pale blue paper. She pulled it out. It was a letter addressed to Gordon and covered with rows of delicate slanted handwriting. As she read it, her hands began to shake and she sank back down on the bed, her stomach turning over. It was from someone named Clara.

Whatever Ruby had known about Gordon before she entered his room, however much of a swine she'd thought him, nothing could have prepared her for this. The words settled like a rock in her heart. She could hardly believe what she was reading, and yet deep down she knew that after what had happened to her, nothing she learned about him could shock her. On she read, taking in Clara's words as she wrote of her love for Gordon, begging him to return home to Seaham, to her.

When she had finished reading, Ruby folded the letter and stared at it for a long time, unsure what to do with it. At last she made her mind up, and with trembling hands she tore it into shreds.

Chapter Twenty-Eight

The harsh weeks of winter felt like they'd never end. Sleet blew in on an icy wind. Snow banked against the walls in the pit lanes, mixing with coal dust to form a dirty grey sludge. Fires in the miners' homes were banked high; flames roared day and night to keep the frosty chill from kitchens, if from nowhere else in the small houses. In the bedrooms at the Dinsdales' house, ice formed on the inside of the windows.

As Christmas drew close, Ruby twice visited Mrs Sowerby's house to ask for the remainder of the money from the sale of Gordon's clothes. But each time she called, there was no reply from within. She wondered if she'd made a mistake in not selling the clothes to Meg Sutcliffe herself, for if she'd done that, she'd have had the money by now, however little it might have been.

Christmas Day in the Dinsdale house was celebrated with pigeon pie, using a plump dead bird Lady brought to their door. As the year turned to 1921, Ruby carried on as she'd always done, taking sewing in for her and her mam, delivering their finished goods around Ryhope and collecting payment for their work. Michael and Arthur slogged at the pit. Every penny they earned was pooled and counted once a week at the kitchen table by Arthur. Mary was given money to pay the bills and clear the debts, and then some was set aside as housekeeping to buy food, soap and necessities.

Ruby had said her goodbyes to Gordon during many long, sleepless nights when she'd shed tears over the pain of his betrayal as well as the shock of his death.

'It's time to look to the future,' Mary often said. Ruby wondered what kind of future there might be for a girl like her.

She scoured the *Sunderland Echo* each time her dad brought home the paper he'd picked up in the miners' hall. The only jobs on offer in Ryhope were for boys and men, heavy lifting work at one of the village farms, and there were always jobs at the pit.

The rain, sleet and snow forced Ruby and Mary indoors in the early weeks of the year. Washing day was unbearable; wet clothes were hung in front of the fire, cluttering the small house and steaming up the windows. Tempers were frayed and the family were tetchy with each other. Lady kept out of the way and hid under the table. Even Ruby, normally calm and even-tempered, found herself getting irritable as the cold, dark days seemed like they would never end. Worse was to come, though, when early in the year, Arthur brought bad news.

There'd been rumours going around Ryhope for months about a strike at the pit, and now the rumours were gaining ground. Arthur read in the *Sunderland Echo* that coal prices had tumbled across the country. In

Ryhope, as elsewhere, this meant local coal companies were forced to cut costs.

'It's going to be bad, Mary,' he warned one night as they lay in bed. It was so cold in their bedroom that they'd piled two moth-eaten overcoats on top of the eiderdown, blankets and sheets to try and keep themselves warm. 'The only economy the coal company understands is lower wages. They've already posted notices at the pithead announcing drastic wage cuts.'

'How will we manage?' Mary asked.

'Heaven only knows. But Stuart Brown's told me he's heard of wages being cut by half at mines in places like South Wales.'

'No!' Mary gasped.

'I don't know what'll happen, lass. But if wages are cut like that here, Stuart says we won't have any choice but to come out on strike.'

Mary nestled against Arthur's shoulder. He put his arm around her and cuddled her close, but neither of them slept well that night.

As the harsh winter dissolved into spring, Ruby let Gordon disappear from her heart. She let Abigail go too. Her friend had betrayed her just as much as Gordon had, and it had hurt Ruby very much. As for Jean, Ruby was beyond grateful to her for saving her life. For she feared that without her, she would have kept on walking into the sea.

'I'm living with the curse of Grandma Winter hanging over my head,' she told Jean when she visited one day.

Jean laid her hand on Ruby's arm. 'No, Ruby. You're not your grandma or your mam. You're you. What goes on in your mind is down to you. You would have turned back, I'm sure.'

'Would I?' Ruby said. She wished she felt as certain as Jean. Inevitably, their talk turned to their mutual friend.

'How will you feel if you see Abigail out walking with the baby one day?' Jean asked. 'You need to prepare yourself for it. In a village as small as Ryhope, your paths are bound to cross.'

Ruby heeded Jean's words. It was hard to imagine how she might feel – it hurt too much to think about it – and she tried to push the subject to the back of her mind.

She headed to Mrs Sowerby's house again to ask if the landlady had been able to sell Gordon's clothes. She knew there wouldn't be much money coming her way, but it was money the Dinsdales were desperate for. However, as had happened the last time she had knocked on Mrs Sowerby's green door, there was no reply from within.

In the coming weeks, leaves began budding on trees around the village green. The sky turned from grey to white, with clouds scudding on the spring breeze. Washing days were brighter, with wet clothes pegged on the lines in the back lane instead of indoors. There was an optimism in the air that had been missing for a very long time. Ruby made the decision to head to Mrs Sowerby once a week until she received the money she was owed from the sale of Gordon's clothes. Each time, she banged hard at the door and called through the letter box, but Mrs Sowerby proved impossible to find at home. Ruby took Jean with her on one visit, and Arthur came with her on another. But no matter how long they waited there, or how hard they knocked at the door, Mrs Sowerby was nowhere to be seen.

* * *

Meanwhile, there was trouble brewing. At the end of March, Stuart Brown presided over a throng of men, some on their way to work, some on their way home, with coal-blackened skin. Standing on a table at the front of the miners' hall, he brought the meeting to order.

'Men of Ryhope,' he called. 'As you know, for some time now there's been a vexed question of national wage agreements that has brought the country to a crisis over coal.'

On he went, repeating words that most in the room knew by heart, as they'd been following the news closely in the *Sunderland Echo*. But what they heard next put fear in everyone's hearts.

'The coal companies have rejected our demands not to cut wages,' he told them. A murmur of dissent went around the room. He held his hands up to quieten them. 'Therefore, miners' unions all around the country are rejecting new terms offered by regional coal companies. And this means that as of Wednesday the second of April, strike action will begin.'

Men muttered darkly between themselves as the news sank in. Arthur rocked back on his heels and put his hand on the wall, bracing himself against the shock.

'It's been a long time coming,' Taffy said.

'Aye, I know,' Arthur sighed. 'We need to feed our families!' he yelled from the back of the hall.

Men turned to see who had spoken out, then looked back towards Stuart, everyone needing to know what he was going to say. For if they went on strike, there would be no money and no coal. There would be no fires to keep their homes warm, no way to cook what little food they could afford. Coal was the life blood of Ryhope. Without it, there was nothing.

'We'll feed your families,' Stuart said. 'We're going to set up a soup kitchen right here in this hall. We'll call on the farmers to offer what they can. And if you're growing vegetables in your garden – leeks, onions, carrots, whatever you have – bring them here. We're a community that cares; we'll do what Ryhope has always done when times have hit hard. We'll come together!'

'Yes!' The cry went up.

'We'll help each other,' Stuart continued. 'For if we don't, then what does it say about us as miners? As men? As human beings with hearts and minds and the goodness in us to do what we can?'

'I agree!' yelled a voice.

'All those able and willing to help, say *aye*,' Stuart said.

The response was overwhelming, deafening, as the men in the room roared as one.

'Aye!'

Stuart called out over the din. 'If you have wives and daughters at home who can help, let them know that we need their productive hands. And tell everyone that Reverend Daye at St Paul's church has offered refuge for those who need shelter, day or night.'

Taffy nudged Arthur in the ribs with his elbow. 'Thank the Lord for that,' he joked.

'Shush,' Arthur said, concentrating on Stuart's words.

'I know that with the full support of every Ryhope miner, we will get through this,' Stuart continued. 'We'll stick to our guns, never give up on our demands for the wages we need.'

Another roar went up. Stuart climbed down from the table, and men began to file out of the hall.

Arthur was caught up in the crowd, and he and Taffy walked out together.

'Guess I'll go home and tell the missus the bad news,' Taffy said. 'Although what she'll have to say about me being at home under her feet until this strike's over, I don't know.'

The two men parted at the door. Arthur turned left to head home. As he walked, he tried to form in his mind the right way to break the news to Mary. But the minute he walked into the kitchen, it was clear that word of the strike had reached her already. She had more of a resigned air about her than usual, and was slumped in her chair. Ruby was standing at her mam's side.

'Jean's little brother Jimmy called in to tell us,' she explained. 'He was first out of the hall and news has already spread.'

Arthur sank into the chair opposite Mary and took her hands in his. 'We'll get through this,' he said firmly.

Mary raised her eyes. 'How?' she asked dully.

Ruby watched her mam and dad. She saw the tender way her dad stroked her mam's hands, heard the words he used to try to reassure her. But she also saw her mam's tired, lined face and knew what worries would be going through her mind. Up and down the pit rows, the scene would be the same. Husbands, brothers, fathers returning home to give the news that no wages would be coming into homes where poverty already scarred too many lives.

'There's to be a soup kitchen at the miners' hall,' Arthur explained. 'They're looking for lasses to help. It'll be you women who'll help us win the strike. You women who'll keep the homes running and the bairns fed.'

Mary nodded thoughtfully. Then, with a determined look in her eye she straightened in her seat.

'I want to help too,' Ruby said.

Arthur and Mary both looked at their daughter. Ruby's words had put a smile on Mary's face.

'Eeh, lass. I remember when you couldn't cook to save your life,' she said lightly. 'All those times I tried to teach you, and now finally you get a chance to put your skills to good use again.'

Ruby smiled. 'I promise I'll do my best.'

Chapter Twenty-Nine

Knowing how hard life would be without the men's wages coming in, the people of Ryhope came together as they'd done during the Great War. Except this time the enemy was right there at home: the coal company itself. Rumours flew that the company had threatened to cut off the water in the back lanes to force the miners back to work. But it was a threat they didn't carry out, much to everyone's relief.

At the pit, all was quiet and calm, all work called to a halt. Without the constant grinding of the gears and the steady clouds of smoke polluting the air, Ryhope became a different place. Without industry, its heart stopped beating. Pit ponies were brought up to the surface to graze on common land. Many of them were blind after years underground and were a pitiful sight, unsure of what to do and wary of their new surroundings.

'Where do you want us, Gladys?' Mary called the first morning she and Ruby walked into the miners' hall.

Gladys Smith had worked at the hall since before anyone could remember. She was as much a part of the place as the bricks and mortar, woven into its history like the miners' banner that hung on the wall. She was a stout woman with grey hair swept up in a bun. She had thick calves and strong arms. And after serving up tea for miners and keeping the hall in order for most of her working life, she took no nonsense from anyone.

Now she looked around the hall and started issuing commands, counting each item off on her fingers. 'I need chairs, tables – put them in rows over there. I need as many pots and pans as you can find in the village. Get the women to bring them in. I need meat bones begged from the butcher. I need someone to sort through sacks of vegetables. And I need ladles and at least five tin baths bringing in.'

'Tin baths?' Ruby said, confused.

'We're going to be making a lot of soup,' Gladys explained. 'The baths are the biggest things we have. They'll all need scrubbing out first. Think you're up to the job?'

Ruby pushed her shoulders back. 'I know I am,' she said.

With every day that passed, Gordon slipped further from Ruby's mind and the knot of anxiety in her stomach over his betrayal finally began to loosen. What had happened at the beach on the day of his funeral was never forgotten, however. Ruby became more aware of her moods and feelings, alert to any changes in her emotional state. She spoke again to her mam about Grandma Winter. Was she about to follow the path her grandma had walked and lead a life with a fragile mind?

'You'll be fine, Ruby. You'll see,' Mary reassured her. 'We'll keep talking, remember? We'll keep each other right.'

Ruby read her copy of *The Red Letter* magazine again, this time looking for words of comfort, anything to confirm she wasn't going mad. But all the stories she read seemed to confirm that her own life held more danger and drama than any of the fiction within.

Her work at the miners' hall meant that she now had something else to concentrate on, which came as a blessed relief. She returned to Mrs Sowerby's house every single week, banging at the door, desperate to know if there was any money from the sale of Gordon's effects. But as ever, there was no reply.

At the miners' hall, Gladys took charge, issuing commands to everyone who came to help. Within days, a small army of women and girls, men and boys had been organised into various tasks. Some were peeling potatoes, others scrubbing baths clean. The local farmers were true to their word and donated fresh produce from their fields; the village bakery donated bread. Miners who had served in the Great War and had experience of field cooking were called into action. Six boilers were brought in and manned by those men as their expertise in feeding large numbers was put to use. Other men rose early in the morning to light the fires in the hall ready for breakfast to be prepared and served.

Everyone chipped in where they could. As the strike wore on and food became scarce, some miners went out hunting to feed their starving bairns, catching and killing chickens, pheasants and rabbits; even stealing pigs. Others gathered in gangs to pilfer coal at the pit. This was dangerous work, and if caught, the men would face jail. Arthur never went coal picking; he wouldn't risk it for fear of the consequences. Miners' wives threw themselves into the fight to support their striking men. Some walked all the way to Sunderland to sell their jewellery, even offering their beloved wedding rings in exchange for cash to buy food. There was no shame in begging when they had hungry mouths to feed.

'Our priority will be the bairns,' Gladys announced to everyone in the miners' hall. 'Them's the rules that's come down from above. And we'll have set times for meals. I'll chalk them up on a board at the door so folk know when we're open and what meal they can have. We'll offer them breakfast – a cup of cocoa with a slice of bread and marge. Dinner will be soup, a broth of meat and potatoes, or even dumplings if we have the makings. That's the basics we'll do. Anything else we get given will be a godsend. And we'll have tea on the boil constantly for them who needs it, but remember, we feed the bairns first.'

The two Miss Huttons came to the miners' hall each day to help where they could, working alongside Ruby and Mary. Many of the women sang as they worked, to keep spirits high. Bairns ran around the hall playing catch or hide-and-seek. Older children and boys from the pit helped their mothers and sisters by stirring soup in the tin baths or laying plates and cutlery on the tables. Michael helped too, scrubbing pots and pans, happy in his work. Ruby was pleased to see the old Michael return, the cheeky lad she'd grown up with, the one with a ready smile. How different, how happy he was when he wasn't working underground. He hadn't cried at night since the strike began. Meanwhile, Arthur spent his days with his mining friends. They'd congregate on street corners, smoking their pipes, catching up on the latest strike news.

One day while Ruby was working at the hall, she picked up a gnarled turnip.

'What do I do with this, Mam?' she asked.

Mary was too far away to hear her daughter's request, busy making stock for the soup. It was Elsie who came to Ruby's aid.

'Start by cutting any diseased bits off, as carefully as you can,' she said. 'Then chop it into small chunks. It'll be tough, so watch your fingers with that sharp knife.'

Ruby began chopping the turnip, and she and Elsie worked companionably together until Elsie asked if she'd yet caught Mrs Sowerby at home. Ruby paused with her knife in her hand.

'The woman's deliberately avoiding me, I'm sure,' she said.

'Anything I can do to help?' Elsie asked.

'I'm not sure what to do for the best,' Ruby replied. 'I've taken Dad with me as back-up, and Jean came with me one day, but Mrs Sowerby never answers the door. I'm not going to give up, though. No matter how long it takes me, I'll get the money out of her.'

'Good for you, girl,' Elsie said.

Ruby returned to her work and was concentrating so hard she didn't notice that someone was walking towards her. She felt a gentle nudge at her side from Elsie.

'Hey, lass, you've got a visitor.'

She looked up into the friendly, smiling face of Stan Hutchinson. She hadn't seen Stan in months, not since the day of Gordon's funeral, when he'd helped Elsie carry her home after she'd walked into the waves. He was carrying a cardboard box in his arms, and as he walked, she heard the unmistakable chink of bottles.

'Stan, what a nice surprise,' she said. She laid down her knife and held out her hand to greet him. Stan took it.

Elsie watched the exchange, and noticed how the two of them held on to each other's hands just a fraction longer than necessary.

Stan set the box on the table and the bottles rattled again. 'How are you?' he asked.

Ruby pushed her hair behind her ears. 'Better,' she said. 'And thank you again for all your help with . . . you know, that day . . .' She trailed off. She felt embarrassed to be speaking to him in this way, afraid he might judge her for what she'd been through.

'You're looking well,' he said.

She looked into his eyes, relieved to see no awkwardness there and no questions for her about her episode at the beach. She appreciated how straightforward he was.

At Ruby's side, Elsie carried on with her work, pretending she wasn't listening.

'I'm really busy, Stan,' Ruby said, looking around. 'I can't talk long. There's soup to be made.'

'I won't stop. I've brought you these, from the Queen's Head. Thought they might be a treat for anyone who'd like one with their dinner.'

He lifted the cardboard top from the box and Ruby saw eight bottles of Vaux stout inside.

'I'll hand them to the girls looking after supplies,' she said.

She turned her gaze back to the turnip. Stan shifted from one foot to the other.

'Well, I guess I'll be going then,' he said.

Ruby glanced up. 'See you, Stan.'

He nodded at Elsie. 'Bye, Miss Hutton.'

Elsie smiled. It was painful to watch. Stan was being so kind and courteous to Ruby, and yet Ruby didn't seem to be picking up on the fact that he was obviously keen on her.

'Ruby? Would you like to take a break, maybe walk Stan out to the door?' she suggested hopefully.

'I'm sure he knows where the door is,' Ruby said, confused as to why Elsie would suggest such a thing when she was so busy.

However, Stan took up the offer enthusiastically. 'That'd be nice,' he said, nodding eagerly.

Ruby looked at him again, really looked this time. His brown eyes, his freckles, the familiarity of his features calmed her. They'd been good friends when she'd worked at the pub; there was no reason why they couldn't be friends again. She wiped her hands on her pinny. 'All right,' she said. 'I think I can take a break for five minutes.'

Elsie winked at Stan. 'Take ten,' she said with a mischievous glint in her eye.

Ruby followed Stan as he made his way through the busy hall. At the door that led to the street, they stood to one side to allow in a woman leading a small child by the hand. Ruby noticed that the child's feet were bare and its legs were dirty.

'Is there cocoa left?' the woman asked. 'Am I too late to get breakfast?'

'Ask for Gladys,' Ruby replied. 'There might be some left. And ask her about clothes for your bairn. We've been given donations and there might be something that fits.'

Once outside, Ruby and Stan shuffled around each other, unsure of what to say.

'How are things at the Queen's Head?' she asked at last.

'We've been shut since the strike began,' Stan replied. 'There's no point in keeping it open; no one's got money to spend. We've been cleaning the place from top to bottom so it's in a decent state for when it reopens. Have you heard how long the strike might last?'

'Nothing official,' she said. 'They reckon it could go on for a full year.'

Stan blew air out of his mouth and slumped against the brick wall. 'A year? That would put us out of business.'

'How are your mam and dad coping?' Ruby asked.

He stood up straight, less self-conscious now their conversation was flowing. 'Dad's wanting to open the pub on weekends to give the fellas somewhere different to come and sit. Even if they don't buy any beer, they'll be grateful to get out from under their wives' feet at home. Not many fellas in Ryhope are used to being cooped up in the pit houses. But Mam's against opening without beer being sold. Me and Dad are trying to win her round.' He glanced shyly at Ruby. 'I'm sorry about the way Mam treated you,' he said, his face earnest and kind. 'She should never have said those things. Dad told me all about it. I didn't know why you left, you know. Mam wouldn't talk about it.'

Ruby felt herself going red with embarrassment. Would Stan believe she wasn't a thief? 'I didn't steal anything, not really,' she said quickly. 'It was just slices of pie left on the bar at the end of the night. We were that hungry at home, I wouldn't have done it otherwise. I hoped your mam might understand, but she sacked me on the spot.'

'She rules that pub with a rod of iron,' Stan said. 'But still, what she did, what she said, it was wrong.'

Ruby turned towards him. 'And you, Stan? How are you?'

He shrugged. 'Oh, you know.'

She looked at his face, his open expression, his friendly smile. In that moment, she realised how much she missed talking to him, and how much she missed working at the pub, hearing the chatter of the customers and keeping up with everyone's news.

'I was sorry to hear about Gordon,' he said.

Ruby lifted her hand and Stan said no more. 'Please don't mention his name again,' she said firmly. 'He wasn't the man I thought he was and I won't have him talked about.'

A silence hung between them for a few moments until Stan finally plucked up the courage to say something that had long been on his mind. 'Ruby, I . . .' He paused. 'I know now might not be the right time and I'd understand if you said no, and of course I'm not pushing, but if you think there's a chance, just a small chance, of you coming out on a date with me perhaps, and . . .'

'Yes,' Ruby said.

'. . . if you did want to, and you need me to ask permission from your dad, then I'll ask him, although I know you're of an age now when you can do things on your own, women these days have got a mind of their own, but still, some miners are old-fashioned that way and . . .'

'Yes,' Ruby repeated.

Nervous Stan carried on. '. . . it wouldn't be a date anyway, not really, we already know each other, it'd just be as friends, we could take a walk to the beach. No, not the beach. Why did I say the beach? I'm sorry, Ruby, I'm that nervous I can hardly speak straight, I'm getting my mixed words all up.'

Ruby burst out laughing. She put her hand on Stan's arm. 'I said yes, Stan.'

'You did?'

'More than once,' she smiled.

Just then the door of the miners' hall swung open. Mary stood there with her hands on her hips, her face red and flustered. 'Ruby, we need you inside,' she called.

'I'll be right there, Mam,' Ruby replied.

The door swung closed. Ruby and Stan locked eyes.

'Ruby?' Stan said. 'Can I kiss you?'

Ruby felt her heart flutter in a way it hadn't done since . . . well, since the early days when she fell for Gordon. She laid a finger on her cheek. 'Here,' she said, offering her face to Stan. He inched towards her. She felt his warm breath on her skin, and a delicious tingle ran through her. And that was when she quickly and deliberately turned her face so that he missed her cheek and his lips ended up on hers. He pulled back in surprise, but when he saw the cheeky grin on her face, he smiled.

'Got you!' she laughed, as she felt her neck and face burning up. She pointed to the door of the miners' hall. 'I'd better go.'

'Me too,' Stan said.

As he turned to leave, he waved at her. 'I'll be seeing you, Ruby Dinsdale.'

Ruby walked back into the miners' hall with a huge grin on her face.

Chapter Thirty

In May of that year, it was five months since Gordon's funeral, and despite visiting Mrs Sowerby's house regularly since he'd died, Ruby had never managed to find the lodging house owner at home. Once she thought she saw a movement behind a curtain at the front of the house when she walked up the garden path. But no one had answered her call at the door. However, she remained determined not to give up.

On Ruby and Stan's first date, at the end of May, they walked with Lady to the village green and sat on a bench under a sycamore tree. They sat slightly apart and Lady lay contentedly at Stan's feet. At first Ruby was afraid to let her guard down with him, fearful that if she allowed herself to fall for him in the way she wanted to, he might hurt her as Gordon had done.

But as they talked that first night, and got to know each other better, her concerns began to dissolve. They talked in a way that had been impossible when they'd worked at the Queen's Head. They were more open and honest with each other now. Ruby felt comfortable with

Stan. Better still, she trusted him. They'd as good as grown up together, gone through school at the same time. They talked freely; they laughed a lot too, especially when Stan did impressions of customers at the Queen's Head and made Ruby guess who they were. There was a sweetness to him that there'd never been with Gordon, and best of all, he was a Ryhope lad, not like Gordon with his secret past in Seaham.

At the edge of the village green was the track through the cliffs to the beach. Several couples walked past Ruby and Stan, arm in arm, heading to the beach for a stroll.

'It's a perfect night for a walk on the sands,' Stan mused as he watched them.

Ruby shook her head. 'I don't think I could face the beach, Stan,' she said. 'I haven't been since . . .'

He reached across the bench and took her small hand in his own. 'I understand,' he said gently.

Just then the bells of St Paul's began to chime.

'Come on,' Ruby said, standing. 'It's about time I got myself home. I told Mam I wouldn't be out long.'

They walked from the green past the school and the church and began the slow climb up the colliery bank. As they walked, Ruby felt Stan's arm brush against hers. She turned to look at him and smiled. He offered her his hand and they walked hand in hand all the way up to Tunstall Street. At the corner of the pit lane, he turned to her.

'I suppose this is goodnight, and goodbye for now.'

'For now,' Ruby smiled. 'But I'd like to do it again. Would you?'

'Not half,' Stan laughed.

She tilted her face up towards him. 'You can kiss me again if you'd like.'

'Oh, I'd like very much.'

A mischievous smile played over Ruby's lips. 'Just here,' she said, tapping her cheek. 'Kiss me here.'

Stan leaned in for a kiss, and just as before, Ruby moved in the nick of time so that his lips met hers. At the same time, both of them began laughing. Stan slipped his arms around her, and they hugged one another, lost in their own happy world. But when they finally moved apart, a worried look crossed Ruby's face.

'What'll you tell your mam if she asks where you've been?'

'Don't you worry about Mam.'

'She won't be happy when she discovers you're courting me.'

'I'll tell her when the time is right. I just need to pick my moment, that's all.'

And with that, Stan headed across the road to the Queen's Head, while Ruby turned into the lane. When she reached her back gate, Ruby sat down for a few moments, making herself comfortable on the stone outside the gate. With the pit silent, she heard birdsong in the evening air. Lady sat next to her and laid her head on her lap. Ruby scratched behind Lady's ears, her favourite spot, and the dog gave a contented sigh.

Ruby laughed. 'You sound as happy as I feel.'

Ruby and Stan arranged to meet twice a week, but with no money coming into the pub, Stan couldn't afford tickets to the picture house or a fish and chip supper. And Ruby could hardly invite him in for tea at the Dinsdales' house when they had no food for themselves, never mind anyone else.

One morning, while Arthur and Michael were still asleep, Ruby and Mary were getting ready to head to the hall to prepare breakfast for the families of striking miners.

'Are you seeing Stan tonight?' Mary asked.

Ruby glanced out of the window. 'If it stays fine, we'll be out for a walk.'

Mary slipped her arms into an old knitted jacket. 'Can't you and he spend time together in his family's room above the pub?' she asked.

'Not until his mam knows he's stepping out with me,' Ruby said. 'I'm not risking meeting Polly again until she's forgiven me.'

Mary tutted. 'Fancy falling out over a few pieces of pie. I should have gone over there when it happened and given Polly Hutchinson what for.'

'Let's talk no more about it,' Ruby said. 'No use raking over old ground.'

She stuck her feet into her boots and was about to begin tying up the laces when there was a knock at the door. It was a gentle knock. A woman's knock. Ruby knew it wouldn't be either of the two Miss Huttons. Elsie and Ann were as good as family; they would have knocked and walked in without waiting She and Mary shared a look.

'Not expecting anyone, are we?' Mary said.

Ruby pulled her laces tight, then stood and walked to the door. She pulled it open, and froze when she saw who was there. She stared at the figure in front of her, unable to make sense of what was going on. The woman's hair, usually long and fair and tied in a plait, was dirty, dishevelled and fell in clumps. Her face was bloodied with scratches and scars, her bare arms were bruised black and blue. And underneath a thin cotton dress, her pregnant belly strained.

Ruby gasped with shock. 'Abigail!'

Chapter Thirty-One

'Who is it?' Mary called.

Ruby could hardly breathe, never mind tell her mam who was at the door. She blinked hard, unable to comprehend what was going on. Was it a dream she would wake from? But no, the woman in front of her was still there.

'Ruby?' Mary called. This time Ruby stood to one side and held the door open. Without a word, Abigail walked into the kitchen. Ruby saw her mam's face drop. She knew it wasn't just the shock of Abigail turning up out of the blue; it was the state she was in.

'Water,' Abigail whispered. 'Can I have some water?'

Ruby and Mary looked at each other for a second, then Ruby lifted a brown porcelain jug from the table. She removed the cloth from the top and poured water into a mug, which she handed to Abigail. Abigail snatched it greedily, held it with both hands and gulped it down without stopping for breath. She was standing close to Ruby, so close that Ruby could smell the stench coming from her. This wasn't the Abigail she knew. What on earth had happened?

She glanced at Abigail's swollen belly, and a flicker

of something passed through her. Immediately she knew what it was. It wasn't jealousy, not that; she wasn't envious of Abigail carrying Gordon's child. It wasn't even hurt over Gordon's betrayal; that had long since disappeared with her grief. It was, she realised, the betrayal by her friend. Ruby, Abigail and Jean had been inseparable when they were young. They were more like sisters than friends. Many times Ruby had struggled to comprehend how Abigail could have deceived her. Many times she told herself she was done with her friend after she'd found she'd been carrying on with Gordon. But here Abigail was, looking much the worse for wear, stinking to high heaven of something Ruby didn't dare name. She wondered if she had been sleeping rough. Had her mother thrown her out? Her dishevelled appearance certainly suggested she might have spent a night outdoors. So many thoughts whirled in Ruby's mind and she couldn't make sense of a single one.

'More?' Abigail said, thrusting the mug towards her.

'Of course,' Ruby said. She poured more water and watched Abigail gulp it down.

When Abigail had finished, Mary stepped forward and took the mug from her hand. Gently she led her to the chair by the empty fireplace. 'Sit down, love, you look done in,' she said.

Abigail sank heavily into the chair, supporting her stomach with both hands. Ruby's feet felt like they were stuck to the floor. Mary, dressed and ready to head to the miners' hall, began to unbutton her coat.

'Ruby, run down and tell Elsie and Ann we won't be at the hall to make breakfast.' She nodded towards Abigail. 'Tell them something's come up, something important.'

Ruby forced herself out of the kitchen and into the back lane. Lady stood lazily from the corner of the yard, gave herself a shake and followed her to the two Miss Huttons' house.

'Abigail?' Elsie gasped when Ruby gave her the news. 'What's she doing at your house?'

'We don't know. She just arrived a few moments ago. But you should see her, Elsie. She's a mess. Bruised, scratched, and the stomach on her, she's enormous.'

'Tell your mam we won't breathe a word.'

Ruby ran all the way home. When she stepped inside the kitchen, the first thing she saw was her mam kneeling on the ground. At first she thought Mary had dropped something and was searching for it. But then she saw water on the floor below Abigail's splayed legs. Her cotton dress was ruched around her thighs, and her breathing was coming quick and deep, accompanied by soft moans.

'Ruby! Go and get Elsie. Now!'

'But I've just been—'

'Now!' Mary screamed. 'Tell her to bring towels and water, hot water if she's got any coal. She'll know what to do. The baby's on its way.'

Ruby did as she was told and ran outside. Her mam was right. If anyone could help, it was Elsie; she'd worked at Ryhope Hospital before the war. But had she delivered a baby? Her mam had faith in Elsie and that was enough. Ruby wondered if Abigail had known she was about to go into labour when she turned up at their door. Was that why she'd come, knowing Ruby and Mary would help her just as they'd done many times in the past?

Ruby quickly gave instructions to Elsie and ran home

again, followed by Elsie with Ann in tow. The sisters began work the minute they set foot in the house. Ruby felt useless. She had no experience of bairns or pregnant women and didn't know what she could do.

'Mam?' she said. Her head was foggy; she was still trying to make sense of it, still hoping it was a dream that she'd wake from at any moment.

'Get the bloody dog out,' Mary ordered.

Ruby shooed Lady away and closed the kitchen door, watching the scene unfold in front of her.

'Abigail, look at me,' Elsie ordered.

Abigail raised her eyes and swallowed hard.

'We're going to lie you down on the floor, all right?'

She nodded. Elsie and Ann took her arms to help her stand, and then, with Mary's help, they carefully laid her on the bare floor.

'Ruby, go and get hot water. There's a pan boiling on our fire,' Elsie said.

Ruby gave her head a shake to spur herself into action and did as Elsie commanded.

In the hour that followed, as Abigail went into labour on the kitchen floor, Elsie took control. Mary and Ann mopped Abigail's brow with a piece of cotton soaked in cold water. Ruby fetched and carried, doing whatever she was told.

'Knife, Ruby,' Elsie demanded, getting everything ready that she'd need.

Ruby went to the basket of sewing that she and her mam were working on. There was a small, sharp knife they used for cutting cloth. She laid it on the floor between Elsie and Abigail. Abigail's breathing became louder, quicker, as the pain rocked her body.

'Good girl, keep going,' Elsie said.

Ruby saw the anxious looks that passed between her mam and Ann. Then she watched as Elsie, determined, rolled her sleeves up and spoke to Abigail firmly.

'Abigail? Push down, love. Do you understand? Push down.'

Abigail began grunting, making noises that Ruby had never heard before. Ann held her hand. Ruby stepped forward and knelt at Abigail's side. She looked at her friend's face, tortured with pain, then reached for Abigail's other hand and held it, letting her squeeze her fingers as the pain gripped her.

Just then, the door that led upstairs swung open and Arthur and Michael wandered in, bleary-eyed, having woken from their dead sleep.

'What's causing all the noise?' Arthur demanded. He stood stock still when he saw the scene in front of him. Abigail heaving with pain, knees raised, lifting her head and yelling, screaming. Mary and Elsie at her feet, urging her to push. Ruby and Ann holding her hands. He did a quick turn, bumping into Michael as he pushed his son out of the kitchen.

'Oh bloody hell,' he said.

'What's going on, Dad?' Michael asked, trying to peer over Arthur's shoulder.

Arthur shook his head. 'It's women's business, son. That's all you need to know.'

As the two men headed back upstairs, Abigail pushed and pushed and Elsie encouraged her. On it went until Abigail was exhausted.

'I can't push any more,' she gasped.

'You can, Abigail. You have to,' Elsie said firmly.

Abigail grunted, and tried again, and then her body slumped back as the baby made its way into Elsie's capable waiting hands.

'It's a girl,' Elsie breathed.

Ann made the sign of the cross. Ruby peered at the bloodied baby in Elsie's hands. She'd witnessed a miracle; a new life was in the room, six of them now instead of the five of just a moment ago.

'Knife,' Elsie called.

Mary passed the sewing knife, and in a flash Elsie cut the cord thick with blood. Ruby watched in awe as Elsie made sure the baby was breathing and counted its fingers and toes. Then she sighed with relief and her shoulders relaxed.

'She's well,' she said. 'Blanket, Mary?'

Mary handed over a cotton sheet and Elsie swaddled the baby tight, then wrapped her in a blue knitted blanket. It was the same blanket Mary had wrapped Ruby in the night she'd returned from walking into the sea.

All eyes were on the baby as Elsie laid the precious bundle on Abigail's chest. Abigail's hands automatically went to her daughter; she put her arms around her and tears streamed down her face.

'Thank you,' she whispered.

Elsie nodded and took a long, deep breath. Ann laid her hand on her sister's shoulder.

'Well done, our Elsie,' she said.

Then Abigail turned her tear-stained face towards Ruby and said the words Ruby had thought she'd never hear.

'I'm sorry.'

Chapter Thirty-Two

Elsie began issuing more commands to help Abigail off the floor and make her decent.

'Leave her a while,' Mary said. 'She's in no fit state to be moved. She's exhausted, poor love. Let her rest.'

Ruby headed upstairs and walked into the bedroom she shared with Michael. She found her brother sitting on his bed reading a comic.

'When will it be safe for me and Dad to come down?' he asked.

Ruby pulled the eiderdown off her bed. 'Shift,' she told him.

Michael stood and Ruby pulled the eiderdown from his bed too.

'We'll cover her, make her comfortable, then you can come down. But it's best if you don't stay in the house; she needs some time with her baby with no fellas around. You and Dad head to the hall for your breakfast. Tell them that me, Mam, Elsie and Ann have been caught up in something at home, but don't tell them what. And don't mention Abigail. It's no one's business what's gone on downstairs.'

Michael laid his comic on the stripped bed and gazed shyly at Ruby, who was bundling the eiderdowns together. 'Is it true, then? Is the baby Gordon's?'

Ruby stopped in her tracks. 'Who told you that?'

Michael shrugged. 'Fellas were talking at the pit, before the strike.'

'It's true,' she said softly.

'Do you wish it was yours?' he asked.

Ruby started at the blunt question. It wasn't like him to be so direct. But he was growing up now; he was more of a man than a boy. She studied him for a moment. His face was set hard, serious, no trace of the cheeky smirk of the boy she'd grown up with. She decided to answer his question with an honest reply, speaking words that she had only ever thought before, words she hadn't even told her mam or Jean.

'I wouldn't want to be in Abigail's shoes, bringing a bairn up on my own.' She paused, swallowed hard, surprised at the bubble of emotion still inside her. 'I've been given a lucky escape from that evil man.'

'There's been more talk at the pit, you know,' Michael began slowly. 'About Gordon.'

Ruby shook her head. 'I don't want to hear it.'

'I think you should.'

'Did he have another woman on the go? A third one? A fourth? Is that what you heard?' she said angrily. 'I don't think I need to be reminded of how much of a fool that man made of me, Michael.'

The bedroom door inched open and Arthur walked in, looking from his son to his daughter.

'Hear the lad out, Ruby,' he said. 'There are things you should know. Things that will make you realise how much of a bad 'un he was.'

Ruby dropped the eiderdowns on the bed and put her hands over her ears. 'No!' she said. 'I won't listen. If it's about another baby, another woman . . .'

'No, lass, it's none of that,' Arthur said. 'It's something to do with the pit; I heard it from lads who worked with him. You and him were happy together, see, and I didn't want to spoil things for you. So I didn't say a word, but I did keep my ear to the ground.'

He didn't tell Ruby about the other reason he'd not said anything: his weakness for the ham that Gordon brought with him each time he was invited to tea.

Ruby's heart began to hammer. What kind of monster had Gordon really been if her own dad had kept things from her? She sank on to her mattress. Arthur sat next to her and laid an arm around her shoulders as he told her about the token slinging, about Gordon taking credit and payment for other men's work, money that should have gone to feed their families and bairns. He told her about his cruelty to the pit pony, and she felt sick when she learned what he'd done. How had she not noticed his cruel streak herself? How had she missed it? Had she been so blinded by her love for him that she'd chosen not to see it? Even his own mam had disowned him. And yet Ruby had been unable to see behind his fake smile. The realisation settled like a stone in her stomach.

'That lass downstairs deserves your pity,' Arthur said. 'For if her bairn's got an ounce of Gordon's evil in it, then heaven help the poor little mite.'

Ruby kissed her dad on the cheek, then carried the eiderdowns downstairs. She found her mam kneeling on the floor beside Abigail, who had her eyes closed and her arms tight around the tiny baby. Elsie and Ann had gone. Ruby rolled up one of the eiderdowns and slid it under Abigail's head, then unfolded the other to cover her bloodied dress and legs. Then she called up the stairs for Arthur and Michael, who tiptoed down and out through the kitchen, making their way to the miners' hall.

'Ann's gone to help at the hall and Elsie's gone home to fetch more hot water,' Mary told her.

Ruby looked at Abigail's face. She appeared to be sleeping, her head lolling to one side against the folded eiderdown. Mary gently lifted the baby from her chest and Abigail didn't move.

'She's done in,' Mary said.

'Did she say anything, while I was upstairs?' Ruby asked.

'Enough,' Mary said.

'Did she say why she came to us?'

Mary stood carefully, holding the baby tight, and made her way to a chair at the kitchen table. Ruby stood too and pulled out a chair to sit next to her mam.

'Kate threw her out,' she said. 'Or to be more accurate, Kate's new fella threw her out.'

'But he can't do that; it's not his house, it's Kate's,' Ruby said.

Mary nodded towards Abigail. 'From the little she said, it sounds like he's taken over the place. He's a bully.'

'Does that explain her bruises, the scars?' Ruby asked.

Mary nodded. 'She hasn't been home for three days. She's been wandering the streets, sleeping on the village green, in a cave at the beach, anywhere she could find shelter. She said she'd tried to come here to talk to you before but couldn't pluck up the courage. She wasn't sure if you'd want to see her again.'

Ruby's heart softened and she stared long and hard at Abigail's sleeping face. Then she turned her gaze to the baby in her mam's arms.

'Can I hold her?' she asked.

'Are you sure you want to?' Mary sounded surprised.

'I need to, Mam. It's important,' Ruby said. 'Abigail and me have got a lot of making up to do, but the little 'un is innocent in this. She knows nothing of what's gone on.'

Mary handed the baby over, instructing Ruby how to hold her, how to support her with her hand against her head. Ruby leaned back in her chair with the baby facing her chest. Her tiny face was bloodstained and raw. Her eyes were tight shut, her nose and lips perfect and pink. Ruby glanced at Abigail to make sure she was still asleep.

'If she's been chucked out at home, we can hardly take her in here, can we? We've got no money, or food, no coal to heat water, no fire.'

'I don't know what else we can do,' Mary said. 'There's the asylum, of course; that's where women like her usually end up.'

'No, Mam, not the asylum, please,' Ruby said.

'Oh, don't worry, pet,' Mary said quickly. 'I wasn't suggesting it, not for a minute. After what happened with your grandma, I wouldn't wish the asylum on anyone. But we have to face up to the facts. It might be her only choice and one I'm sure she's given thought to already.'

Ruby felt the baby squirm against her chest. Michael's question to her earlier ran through her mind. Did she wish the baby was hers? Well, did she? 'No,' she whispered.

'What was that, love?' Mary said.

Ruby shook her head as if to dismiss Gordon from her heart and her mind. 'Nothing, Mam, just something I was thinking.'

She looked again at the baby and the same word came to mind. No. Over and over again it came to her. No, she did not wish she had carried Gordon's child and brought it into the world. And no, she did not wish to be in Abigail's position, not for all the coal in the world. She wanted her *own* bairns, her *own* family. She wanted to spend her life with a man she could trust. Someone who was good and decent and kind. A man who didn't kick pit ponies. A man who didn't cheat his colleagues out of money that was theirs by right. A man whose own mam hadn't disowned him.

She handed the baby back to Mary, who cradled the child to her chest as it began to cry. The sound woke Abigail, who opened her eyes and looked wildly around the room.

'It's all right, love,' Mary said gently. 'Baby's here, she's fine.'

The back door swept open and Elsie walked in carrying a large bowl with a cloth draped over the top. Out in the yard, Lady sat obediently by the kitchen door. Ruby walked to the door and shut the dog out.

'Abigail?' Elsie said, getting down to business immediately. 'I'm going to start cleaning you up, do you hear me?'

Abigail nodded.

'Ruby, you get a cloth and help your mam wash the baby,' Elsie ordered.

Ruby did as she was told and began gently cleaning

blood from the baby's face, arms and legs. How tiny she was, how precious, she thought. Her mind whirled with emotions she'd never felt before, and despite it all – despite Gordon and his evil, despite Abigail's betrayal – her heart surged with love for the child in her hands.

The women worked quickly and quietly together. Then Elsie disappeared again, back to her own house. When she returned, she carried a tray with four steaming mugs of tea. There was more too: a plate of crumpets soaked with golden syrup.

'Abigail can have mine,' Ruby said. It was the least she could do. If her friend had been living on the streets and sleeping rough at night, she doubted she'd have eaten much, if anything.

Abigail took the food gratefully and began tearing off chunks of crumpet. She gulped her tea, using both hands to lift the mug. Then she began coughing, great hacking coughs that caused her to struggle for breath. Elsie tended to her until the cough subsided. Mary gently laid the baby on to a folded eiderdown at Abigail's side.

'Abigail, you can stay with us for a while, until things get settled at home,' she said.

Abigail kept quiet, knowing her fate was in their hands.

'Our Michael could sleep downstairs and Abigail and the baby could take his bed,' Ruby suggested.

Abigail gave Ruby a wry smile. Her offer would mean the two of them sharing a room, no mean feat when there was a lot of making up to do.

'Nonsense,' Elsie said firmly. 'You can't have the lass here. You've got no coal, the place is too small as it is for the four of you, and it wouldn't be fair on Arthur and Michael, no matter how much they'd say they didn't mind.'

Mary nodded. Elsie had a point. Abigail stared wildly at Elsie and found her voice at last.

'Don't send me to the asylum. Please.'

Elsie laid her hand on Abigail's arm. 'Never the asylum, lass. No, what I had in mind was somewhere a lot closer to where you are now.'

Mary and Ruby shared a puzzled look.

'How would you like to move in with me and Ann until you get yourself sorted?' Elsie asked.

'Oh Elsie, yes. Yes. Thank you,' Abigail said fervently.

Ruby gave a sigh of relief. It was too soon for her and Abigail to be at such close quarters. They needed time to talk.

'Will you come to visit?' Abigail asked, staring hard at Ruby. 'There's a lot we need to say.'

Ruby glanced at the baby at Abigail's side. It was Gordon's child, there could be no getting away from that fact. But it was a baby nonetheless, an innocent, sweet child, and Abigail was her friend, who'd fallen for Gordon's manipulative charm. Oh, she wasn't blameless, Ruby knew that. But how could Ruby deny her comfort given the sorry state she was in? The home she'd been brought up in had never been a safe haven, due to Kate's neglect when Abigail had been a child. Now that she was a grown woman, it still wasn't a safe place to live. She was friendless too and would be gossiped about in the worst possible way, being unmarried with a child.

Ruby lifted her gaze towards Abigail and they exchanged a smile.

'Of course I'll visit,' she said.

Chapter Thirty-Three

On the day of Ruby's first visit to Abigail and the baby, the two Miss Huttons tactfully disappeared from their small cottage. With no end in sight to the strike, the women were continuing to help at the miners' hall, preparing food and cooking.

'Are you ready yet, Ann?' Elsie yelled up the stairs as she slid her arms into her black jacket.

Ann walked into the kitchen and the sisters headed out arm in arm, leaving Abigail and Ruby alone. A clock ticked on the mantelpiece, the only other sound the crackling of the coal as it burned in a very low fire. Ruby held her hands out towards the flames, for although it was May, it was a cold day outside.

'I'd almost forgotten what it felt like to be warm,' she said as she gazed at the glowing coals.

'The strike's biting everyone hard,' Abigail said.

Abigail shifted in her seat. Ruby watched as she laid her daughter into a cot fashioned from an apple box from Watson's grocers, made soft with blankets inside. They sat in silence for a few moments. Ruby felt a knot of anxiety in her stomach. There was so much she wanted to say, so many questions she wanted to ask.

It was Abigail who spoke first. 'Ruby, I . . . I don't know where to start.'

Ruby gazed at the sleeping baby. 'Me neither,' she said gently. 'But Mam taught me something when I was little. She said that when she had a day ahead of her filled with chores, she did the worst one first, the one she hated the most. It was usually cleaning the netty in the back lane. She said she had to get it done and out of the way otherwise it'd sour her whole day if it was left on her mind. Maybe . . . well, perhaps we should do that too.'

'You mean say his name and get it over and done with?' Abigail said.

'That's exactly what I mean.'

Abigail dropped her gaze, unable to look Ruby in the eye.

'Abigail, please,' Ruby said. 'He's dead and buried now.'

Abigail bit her lip, then cautiously began to speak. 'I saw you and him, how happy you were,' she began. 'And I was jealous, Ruby. I wanted to be as happy as you. I wanted a fella.'

'But you had fellas!' Ruby cried. 'You could have had any man in Ryhope you wanted. Why did you go after mine?'

'I didn't want just any fella. I wanted one to make me as happy as you were. So happy that you glowed the day me and Jean came to visit.'

'You wanted Gordon,' Ruby spat. His name hung like a drop of poison between them.

'I've never had a decent man of my own,' Abigail said. 'And so I asked around, found out where he lived, and I went there with a ticket for the football. I thought—'

'You thought about yourself, Abigail,' Ruby said sternly. 'Did you ever think about me?'

The ticking of the clock became louder, more insistent in the silence as Ruby waited for Abigail's reply.

'You and Jean,' Abigail began, 'you're both from good families; your mothers love you. You know how I've suffered my mam's neglect. Ever since I was little, it's always been the same. You and your mam took me in each time mine left me on my own. Kate's not fit to call herself my mam. She cares more about her fellas than she's ever cared for me.' She winced as the painful memories came flooding back. 'That's why I started playing football; it was a way to get out of the house, away from Mam and her men. All I wanted was someone to love me, someone I could love back.'

'And *did* you love him?' Ruby asked.

Abigail shook her head. 'It was just the once, Ruby. I wanted to know what it was like. I never thought I'd end up with a baby. He told me girls couldn't get pregnant their first time.'

Ruby winced.

'I know, I'm an idiot,' Abigail said.

'You hurt me,' Ruby said, with a catch in her voice. 'You were my friend, Abigail. And you betrayed me.'

Abigail reached her hand to Ruby's arm. Ruby's instinct was to pull away. So many times over the last months she'd gone through in her mind what she'd say to Abigail if she ever met her again. In her imagination, she'd flung words at her, sworn at her, told her she never wanted to see her again. But here she was sitting right in front of her, and she was surprised by how calm she felt.

But then she glanced at the baby lying asleep. What would be the point in raised voices and shouting now? What had been done could not be undone. Abigail, her friend, the girl she'd grown up with. Abigail, Ruby and Jean, the three of them always together, always close. Or at least they had been once. She forced herself to keep her arm where it was.

'Can you ever forgive me?' Abigail said. 'Because I'd understand if you walked out now and I . . . *we* never saw you again.'

Ruby looked at Abigail's tiny baby in the box. Deep emotions she'd never felt before pulled at her heart as confusion whirled in her mind.

'Does she remind you of him?' Abigail asked. 'If it's too painful to see her, I can take her upstairs while we talk.' She covered her mouth with her hand and turned her face away as she began to cough. Then she lifted a mug of water from the hearth and sipped it slowly.

'Leave her where she is,' Ruby said quickly. 'And no, she doesn't remind me of him. She reminds me of all that is good in the world. A new start. A new life.'

Abigail looked at her baby too. 'I wonder what sort of life she'll have when she grows up. Will she live in the pit lanes? Will she suffer through a miners' strike?' She turned to Ruby. 'Sorry, Ruby. I'm nervous. I talk too much when I'm nervous.'

'You always did,' Ruby smiled.

'I don't deserve you being here,' Abigail continued. 'I don't deserve your friendship. Jean's given up on me, but I can't undo the past, it's done. This little one will always be Gordon's child; there's nothing I can do to change that.'

'No,' Ruby said firmly. 'That's where you're wrong.'

Abigail sat up straight in her chair, waiting to hear what Ruby meant.

'She'll never be Gordon's child. He's dead, Abigail. Gone. But even now I'm discovering secrets about him that make me realise I should never have got involved with him in the first place. He didn't just betray me with you; he was a bad man through and through, the worst kind of man. I've heard stories about him from Dad and Michael. He fooled us both.' Ruby thought of Clara, the girl in Seaham who'd written the love letter she'd found in Gordon's room. Clara had been fooled too. 'So please, when you look at your gorgeous baby, remember one thing. She's not Gordon's child. She's yours.'

Abigail reached her hands towards Ruby's, and slowly Ruby let herself be held. They sat in silence, holding hands, until Ruby began to form more questions.

'How long are you going to stay here?'

Abigail shrugged. 'Elsie's said I can stay a whole week. I don't want to take advantage, but I've nowhere else to go.'

'You can't go home at all?' Ruby asked.

Abigail bit her lip. 'Mam's got a new fella; he's moved in. I couldn't stay there, not with the way he was treating us.'

Ruby ran her finger along Abigail's arm, where her pale skin was spotted with bruises. 'Did he do this?'

Abigail nodded. 'And worse,' she said. 'He's angry all the time, shouting and screaming and lashing out with his fists. Mam says it's just his way of showing her he loves her. But when he started hitting me, I had to get out. I wouldn't let him harm the baby.'

'And so you came to our house?' Ruby looked at Abigail and saw her eyes brim with tears.

'I'm sorry, Ruby. I didn't know what else to do.'

'Will you . . .' She paused, glancing at the baby. 'Will you keep her?'

Abigail wiped the back of her hand across her eyes. 'I want to, very much, if I can. Do you think I'm mad?'

'Not mad, no. But it's not going to be easy.'

'I know. But you can't let them put me in the asylum, I couldn't bear it. They'll take her away from me in there and I'll never see her again.'

'You'll never get out again, either,' Ruby said, and a shiver went down her back thinking of the stories she'd heard about her grandma. Everyone in Ryhope had heard tales of what happened to women taken there, whether young girls with babies, or older women as they struggled with the change in mid-life.

'But where will you live?' she said. 'If not at home or the asylum?'

Abigail struggled to hold back her tears. 'I've got nowhere to go.'

Ruby thought for a moment and an idea came to her. 'I could ask Mam if she'll make enquiries at the miners' hall. Someone might know a kind soul who'll take you in.'

'I'll be gossiped about!' Abigail cried.

Ruby laughed. 'It's a bit late to worry about that. Leave it with me. Mam'll be discreet.'

'You'd really do that for me?'

Ruby glanced at the baby. 'I'm doing it for you both. Thought of a name for her yet?'

'Emily,' Abigail said proudly. 'It was my grandma's

name. But she won't be christened. I can't see the vicar letting an unmarried lass like me into the church with my bairn.'

'You'd be surprised,' Ruby said. 'Reverend Daye is a vicar with an eye to the future.'

'Well, we'll see, but I won't hold out much hope.'

Just then, the baby began to cry. Abigail picked her up and cradled her in her arms. 'I've got to feed her now,' she said.

Ruby stood. 'I'll go then.'

'You'll come back, though?'

'Perhaps.'

'Are we friends again?'

The girls exchanged a look.

'Sorry. I'm sorry,' Abigail said quickly. 'I'm expecting too much, too soon.'

Ruby didn't know how she felt. It was hurtful and confusing to think she could forgive Abigail so quickly. But what lay ahead in her life if she didn't? Dark days and nights with the past burning inside her, letting Gordon ruin her life from beyond the grave? She needed time to think, to talk to her mam, to try to make sense of it. Hadn't her mam said they must talk to each other more than ever now?

'I'll be back tomorrow,' she said evenly. 'Let's leave it at that for now.'

Chapter Thirty-Four

Later that week, Ruby and Mary were in the kitchen at Tunstall Street, where Mary had given Ruby some news.

'Gladys?' Ruby said, surprised. 'Abigail's moving in with *Gladys*?'

'That's what Elsie's just told me,' Mary said.

Ruby was pleased to hear that her friend had been found somewhere to live, but was surprised it was Gladys who'd offered. She'd thought of Gladys as organised, yes, but also cold and aloof when she'd worked with her at the miners' hall.

'She'll be looked after but not mollycoddled,' Mary said.

'Has Gladys got the room to take Abigail in?'

'She's a widow woman, love. She's got an empty house and an empty heart; both of them need filling. I think Abigail and the baby—'

'Emily,' Ruby chipped in.

'Is that what she's calling her?'

Ruby nodded.

'Well, I think Abigail and little Emily are lucky to have Gladys on their side. Abigail's going to be working at the miners' hall, and Elsie said her bairn's coming too. Some of the other women take their babies there; they take turns to look in on them. She'll be safe enough.'

'I'll see Abigail every day, then?' Ruby asked.

'If you're working the same meal shifts you will. Will that be a problem? I thought you two had made up.'

'We have, I suppose,' Ruby said. 'It's just . . . I don't know, Mam. How can things ever be the same between us after everything that's happened? I need to speak to Jean as well. Abigail said Jean had given up on her. It's about time the three of us forged a bond again.'

Mary gave her a peck on the cheek. 'I'm proud of you, love. I know none of this has been easy.'

'Have I done the right thing, Mam? Moving on, trying to forgive Abigail?'

Mary sighed deeply and put her arm around Ruby's shoulders. 'Well, the way I see it is that you had two choices. You could have gone through the rest of your life filled with hate and a darkness that would have eaten away at you every single day. Or you could have done what you did. So yes, you've done the right thing. Abigail has to live with what she's done too. She knows how lucky she is that you've given her a second chance.'

'Do you think so?'

'I know so.'

Ruby gave her mam a puzzled look.

'We've had words, me and Abigail,' Mary explained. 'I called in to see her at Elsie's yesterday. You and her will be fine, in time.'

Ruby hugged her tight. 'I'll go and speak to Jean after I've finished at the miners' hall,' she said. 'It's about time she knew what's happened.'

'Gossip's rife about Abigail. I daresay she might already know.'

'But she won't have heard the truth. You know what rumours are like.'

Mary put her hands on her daughter's shoulders. 'You're a good lass, Ruby. Abigail and Jean should both be proud to call you their friend.'

'After I've seen Jean, I'm going to walk down to Mrs Sowerby's house again.'

'She's a bad 'un, that one,' Mary hissed. 'Keeping money from you all this time. It's been months now. If I see her on the colliery, I'll give her a piece of my mind.'

'All I can do is keep trying, and make sure she never forgets that she owes me something, no matter how little it might be.'

'Do you want your dad to go with you again? Or how about taking Stan?' Mary asked.

'No, Mam, I need to do this on my own.'

'Well, if she doesn't pay up this time, tell her you'll be back with your father, and she can bloody well answer to him.'

Ruby didn't get her money on that visit to Mrs Sowerby's house either, as once again, no one answered the door. She banged on the green door, she called through the letter box, but still no one came. She left with a heavy heart and more than a sneaking suspicion that Mrs Sowerby was deliberately avoiding her, again. But why? The landlady had agreed that she would pay Ruby her share of the money from the sale of Gordon's possessions. Had he owed rent and she had taken what was hers? But why hadn't she told Ruby this? She'd had plenty of time to do so in the months since Gordon died.

Ruby headed home feeling dejected, trying to tell herself that it didn't matter. There couldn't have been much money from the sale of Gordon's effects. What little there might have been wouldn't have gone far in the Dinsdales' house anyway, once outstanding bills and debts had been paid. Just like every mining family in Ryhope during the strike, they were being fed three times a day at the miners' hall. It was nourishing food, soup or broth freshly made each day and ladled from tin baths into bowls and mugs. The quality was high, although portion size was low, and Ruby craved variety after eating the same thing every day. But no one complained.

She continued to work hard at the hall, often with Abigail, showing her how to chop and peel vegetables, for Abigail hadn't a clue. And when they took a break together, they'd sit outside the hall on a patch of rough grass overlooking the silent pit. Abigail would hold Emily in her lap and the baby would smile at them both. When Abigail's cough got the better of her, she'd hand Emily to Ruby, who let the baby grip her finger, surprised at the strength in her tiny hand. As she and Abigail talked, they slowly rekindled their friendship and built up trust again. Emily's little face lit up each time she saw Ruby, and she always seemed to be laughing and gurgling whenever she was in Ruby's arms.

As the warm weeks of early summer passed, rumours of an end to the strike spread. Urgent talks were held at the hall. At the beginning of July, Stuart Brown called a packed miners' hall to order and confirmed the news that the strike was over. But it was no victory for the miners, alas.

'One million miners!' he called from his position at the

front of the room. 'One million of us around the country have been out on strike for three long and desperate months. It has been more difficult than any of us could have known. We have stood alone. The railway workers and transport workers refused to join us in our war against wage cuts.'

'Shame on them!' men called.

'Without their support, it has been a long and lonely battle. A hungry battle.'

'Aye!' a shout went up.

'And it's a nation's shame that we are being forced back to work,' Stuart went on. Then he took a deep breath before delivering the words he had been dreading speaking. 'The road ahead will become darker, my friends. It will become even more desperate than it was before the strike began.'

Squashed in the throng of men were Arthur and Michael, standing shoulder to shoulder. Michael's heart felt heavy with the confirmation that he would have to return underground. Worse than that, he felt sick, dizzy; there didn't seem to be enough air in the room. If he wasn't squashed in so tight between his dad on one side and Taffy on the other, he feared he'd faint dead away. His legs felt weak and his heart pounded.

'Dad?' he said.

'Shush, lad,' Arthur said, concentrating on Stuart.

'Dad, I need to get out.'

Arthur stood to one side, barely glancing at his son, concentrating fully on the grave news that Stuart was announcing. Michael pushed his way through the crowd, tripping and falling, stepping on men's boots, gripping their arms as he half walked, half stumbled out of the hall.

As he did so, he heard fragments of Stuart's speech and the savage words *wage cuts*. When he finally reached the door, he pushed it open with both hands and staggered out on to the street, taking great gulps of air. He was shaking, terrified at the thought of going back underground. The last three months had been an escape from his personal hell. He couldn't go back! He wouldn't! His chest heaved as he tried to stop himself crying. He slid to the ground, sat on the pavement and buried his face in his hands.

The next day, miners' wives up and down the pit rows were shaking out their husbands' work clothes and polishing their boots. Food from the miners' hall was ladled into bait tins for those who wanted it on their first day back. It was with heavy hearts that the miners returned. They'd been promised safer conditions, better wages, but none had been forthcoming. Their strike had been a lost cause.

As the first miners headed to the pit, women lined the streets, clapping their men back to work, showing their support. The Ryhope colliery brass band led the way with the colliery banner flying high. Once the band reached the pit head, they stopped, laid their instruments down and gave the miners a rousing round of applause. Then each man picked up his instrument again, and the conductor at the front gave a sharp nod and raised his right hand. A haunting, mournful hymn floated out on the air as each miner filed past.

The band played until the last man descended to the coal face. Arthur was one of those men. Meanwhile, back at the Dinsdales' house, Michael was nowhere to be seen.

Chapter Thirty-Five

That evening, before Arthur returned from work, Ruby and Mary walked to the pit to collect coal for the fire. Now that the strike was over, folk turned up with wheelbarrows, even babies' prams, to carry coal home. All Ruby and Mary had were tin buckets, and filled with coal, they were so heavy they could only carry one each.

'It'll be enough for tonight,' Mary said. 'Got to get the water heated up for your dad's bath.'

'What'll we do for food, Mam, until Dad gets his first pay packet?'

'The miners' hall is staying open for a few more weeks for those who need it,' Mary replied with a sigh. 'And I daresay we will need it until your dad and Michael start bringing money in.'

'Where is he, our Michael? I haven't seen him since he left the house this morning.'

'He'll be with his friend Bobby, I expect,' Mary said, but a worried look crossed her face. 'Mind you, he should have been home by now. He's got to get ready for his first shift back tonight.'

Ruby knew how much Michael hated working at the

pit, and working nights had always been particularly hard on him. Her heart went out to him. How she dreaded hearing him crying in the night again once he went back to work. For although he was growing from a boy to a man, he was still her little brother. She knew how scared he was when he worked underground, and how much he suffered. She'd spoken to her mam about his fears at the pit, but as Mary pointed out, where else could he go? There was little else for a boy to do but follow in his father's footsteps. Jobs at the village farms paid a lot less than pit work, and without a decent education behind him, Michael's future at the pit was sealed.

When Ruby and Mary returned from collecting the coal, Michael was still not home.

'Ruby, you know where Michael's friends live,' Mary said. 'Go and find him, round him up. He needs to be back here to get dressed for work or he's going to be late, and we can't afford to lose wages, not when they're being cut as it is.'

Ruby went out into the yard. She called for Lady, who trotted obediently behind her as she headed into the back lane. Michael had three close friends that Ruby knew of, and she called at the home of each one. But no one had seen him all day. Worried, she walked to the village green, hoping that he might be there, for it had been a warm, sunny day and the green offered shade under the trees. But he wasn't there either.

Suddenly Ruby heard her name being called. She looked across to the Albion Inn and saw landlady Hetty Burdon at the door. Hetty's auburn hair was piled messily on top of her head, wisps escaping around her kind, soft face. She beckoned Ruby over.

'You all right, girl?' she asked. 'You look a bit flustered.'

'I'm looking for our Michael. I thought he might be resting on the green.'

'Michael? I saw him a while back. It looked like he was heading to the beach. I've been cleaning windows all day. Now the strike's over, we're opening up. I can't tell you how relieved me and Jack are to be earning again.'

'What time did you see Michael pass by?' Ruby asked.

'About an hour since.'

'Was he on his own?'

Hetty nodded. 'I shouted hello, but he had his head down, ignored me. He seemed lost in his own little world.'

'Thanks, Hetty.' Ruby pushed her bare feet forward in her old boots. 'Hetty?'

'What, love?'

'I don't suppose there's any chance of me having my old job back, is there?'

Hetty glanced behind her into the doorway of the pub. 'I'd love to have you back, but . . .'

'Jack wouldn't?' Ruby guessed correctly.

Hetty nodded. 'Sorry, love. He's not the forgiving type, and you know he runs a tight ship and checks the money religiously. That blasted barmaid's dilemma, it's got a lot to answer for.'

Ruby waved Hetty goodbye. Then she picked up the hem of her skirt and set off for the beach road, with Lady at her side. As she ran, Ruby's heart began to pound. Why had Michael been heading to the beach? Memories of her own broken day there came to her. Surely he wasn't in the same sorry state she'd been in? No, please not Michael, she thought. He was braver than her, he wouldn't do anything daft, surely? On she ran, along the path that meandered through high, grassy cliffs at each side. She heard the roar of the sea ahead of her; the tide was in, crashing against the cliffs. She saw a couple of men walking towards her. They carried a box with handles between them, and as she passed and slowed down, she saw a movement: silvery grey cod slithering inside. She recognised the men; it was Mick Carter, who worked on the railway at the paper mill, and his dad. She called out to them.

'Is there a boy down there on the beach?'

'No, lass. No one. Tide's all the way in now,' Mick replied.

Still Ruby carried on; she had to see for herself. Ahead of her the path ended, swallowed up by foaming sea as the waves rolled and crashed. If Michael wasn't on the beach, then where was he? Lady began to bark. Ruby turned and saw the dog scrambling up the slope of a hill. She looked in the direction Lady was headed and gasped. Michael was standing on the hilltop, staring out over the sea.

'Michael!' she yelled, but her words were drowned by the roar of the waves. There was only one thing for it. She began following the dog as best she could.

It wasn't easy; the slope was steep and rocky, and she wasn't used to climbing. She went slowly, using her hands to pull her up as she went. She slipped many times, lost her footing, scraped her hands, but at last she reached the top and fell exhausted on to the grassy knoll where Lady was waiting. Michael was just in front of her. She stood and slowly made her way towards him. He was inches from the edge, looking straight ahead, lost in his thoughts.

She couldn't startle him, for he might turn and fall. What was he thinking? What was he doing? Was he planning to jump? Or had he climbed the hill without knowing what he was going to do, just as she had blindly walked into the sea to escape the turmoil of her mind on the day of Gordon's funeral?

She heard the toot of a whistle behind her as a train made its way along the Hartlepool to Sunderland line. To her right, the clifftops ran all the way to Seaham, and to her left the coast led to Sunderland docks. She felt dizzy being so high, and forced her boots hard into the earth to steady herself.

'Michael, it's Ruby,' she said calmly. He didn't move. Had he heard her? She said his name louder, but still he didn't turn. Then before she could stop her, Lady trotted forward.

'Lady,' Ruby called quietly. The last thing she wanted was for the dog to scare him. But she needn't have worried. Lady didn't bark or whine; she simply walked towards Michael and sat at his side. Ruby stayed where she was. She saw Michael's head turn; he'd seen the dog. Would he know she was there too?

'Michael?' She tried again.

This time he slowly turned to face her. He was crying. His cheeks were red and blotchy and he didn't attempt to hide his tears. Ruby gingerly stepped forward and took him in her arms. Gently and carefully she pulled him from the edge, away from danger, and they sank to the grass. Michael wiped the back of his hand across his eyes. Lady sprawled on the grass and laid her head on his leg. Neither Ruby nor Michael spoke.

Finally Ruby put her hand on his arm. 'Mam'll be

worried about us. We've got to get home.' She didn't mention the fact that he was due at the pit. She knew what horrors would already be in his mind when he thought about work.

He took a deep breath and looked out to sea. Ruby glanced at his tear-stained face. 'Were you going to jump?'

He kept his gaze fixed on the water. 'I don't know what I was going to do,' he said sadly, shaking his head. 'All I know, all I'm certain about, is that I can't go back to the pit. I won't.'

He had said this many times before, and yet they both knew he had no choice. But there was something in the way he spoke this time, a determination, an anger Ruby hadn't heard before. She slid her arm around his shoulder. Michael smiled at the gesture. Their dad did the same whenever either of them had something on their mind and he wanted to offer advice.

'Then don't go back,' she said. 'Life's more precious than coal.'

'Easier said than done,' Michael said flatly.

'Difficult maybe, I agree. But it's not impossible.'

'Mam'd have my guts for garters, and Dad . . . well, I know Dad wouldn't understand. I've tried talking to him about it before.'

'Don't worry about Mam and Dad,' Ruby said. 'I'll help you as much as I can. We'll talk to them together this time. But you need to think about what you *are* going to do if you're not going back to the pit.'

'You mean give them good news instead of bad?'

'Exactly,' Ruby said.

She thought of what Hetty had told her about the Albion Inn reopening now the strike was over. Jack

Burdon might not want Ruby back, but there might be a chance of a job there for Michael.

'The pubs are reopening in the village,' she said. 'They might have some work. We could call in at each one on the way home. Start with the Railway Inn. You're a strong lad, Michael, there's always call for help in the cellars or stables. Then there's the cattle market, we'll ask there, and I know the money's not great working on the farms, but they're always taking lads on. We'll ask everywhere we pass.'

'No we won't,' he said flatly, and Ruby's heart dropped. But then he turned to her with a playful smile on his lips.

'I'll go on my own. You've just said Mam'll be worried. Tell her that I'll go to the pit office tonight to let them know I'm not going back. And tell her . . . tell her I'll come home the minute I've found another job. She's not to worry about me. She knows I can look after myself, but I won't be a burden at home, not while I'm not earning. I'll go and stay with Bobby; his mam can never resist my cheeky smile.'

Ruby gave her brother a playful punch on his arm.

'Seriously, Ruby, tell Mam what's happened, but whatever you do, don't tell her I was up here on the hill.'

'She'd have kittens if I did,' Ruby said. 'Especially after my episode down there in the waves. She hates to let me out of her sight; thinks I'm about to run into the sea every time I get upset.'

Michael's smile dropped. 'And are you?' he asked.

'No,' Ruby said firmly. 'I'll never do anything like that again.'

Michael returned his gaze to the churning sea. 'What is it with us Dinsdales?'

'Do you ever think of Grandma Winter?' Ruby asked.

He nodded. 'A little. I mean, she died when we were young, I can't really remember her. But I think about what happened to her.'

'And do you ever worry we might end up like her, living out our days in the asylum, being weak in the mind?'

'I don't know,' Michael said as a troubled look crossed his face. 'I think my mind is sound enough. But if that's the case, would I be up here on the hill? Would I suffer so much underground when most men in Ryhope have no such concerns?'

They sat in silence for a few moments.

'Do you think about her too?' Michael asked.

'More often than I used to,' Ruby admitted. 'Since the day I walked into the sea, she's been on my mind a lot. Promise me, Michael, that if you ever feel you need to come here again, or you're feeling anxious, you'll talk to me first.'

'Only if you promise you'll do the same.'

Ruby held her little finger out, and Michael wrapped his own little finger around it.

'I promise,' he said.

'I promise,' Ruby repeated.

They dropped their hands and stared ahead under the darkening sky.

'The beach is a healing place,' Ruby said gently. 'Don't you feel calm here, content when you're near the sea? Perhaps that's why you came here, to ease your troubled mind.'

Michael nodded. 'I suppose I hoped the sea might wash my pain away,' he said.

'And has it?'

'For now,' he replied.

He stood and offered her his arm. Slowly and carefully, with Lady ahead of them, they picked their way down the hill. Then they began walking along the path that would lead Ruby home and Michael to a new beginning.

When they parted, he called out, 'Keep your eyes peeled, onion face!'

'If I see you first, you're the worst,' she replied.

Chapter Thirty-Six

'He's gone *where*?' Mary was livid.

'Let the lass speak,' Arthur said, trying to calm his wife.

Ruby looked from her mam to her dad. She saw Mary grip the back of the chair, so tightly that her knuckles turned white.

'That's all I know, Mam,' she said. 'He said he's going to the pit tonight to tell them he's not going back.'

Arthur hung his head and gazed at the kitchen floor, remembering the times Michael had told him how scared he was underground. And yet there'd been nothing Arthur could have done, no advice he could give. Mining was in his blood; it was all he knew, and he couldn't understand why Michael had been so afraid.

'And he's not coming home until he can bring news that he's got another job.'

Mary's hand flew to her heart. 'How long does he think that'll take? Jobs aren't exactly ten a penny around here.'

'He's going to stay overnight with Bobby,' Ruby said, remembering what Michael had told her about switching on the charm with Bobby's mam. 'He's too embarrassed to come home without being able to bring money in.'

Mary snapped her attention to her husband. 'Go and find the lad, Arthur. Bring him home and give him a good talking-to. He can't give up his job at the pit. It's a job for life, for heaven's sake! He's going to throw good money away and I won't have it.'

Arthur sighed heavily. 'Don't you see, it was the thought of having his job at the pit for life that means he's not here now,' he said gently. 'He struggles with life underground. He's tried to talk to me plenty of times about it and I just never knew how to respond. I blame myself for letting things get this far. If only I'd talked to him, if only I'd listened and tried to understand. How can he be afraid of the dark?'

'It was much more than a fear of the dark, Dad,' Ruby said.

'But Arthur,' Mary pleaded, 'he's just a boy, out there on his own tonight, and who knows how many more nights, until he gets a job elsewhere.'

Arthur held his hand up to silence her. 'He's a man, love. Almost sixteen. We've got to let him do what he thinks is right.'

Ruby watched the exchange between her mam and dad. She knew how worried Mary was. She'd kept quiet, as she'd promised Michael she would, about finding him on the hilltop above the crashing sea.

'He'll be all right, Mam,' she said. 'I'm certain of it.'

Mary turned her gaze towards her husband. 'Arthur?'

'Ruby's right. Michael will be fine. It's not as if he'll be sleeping on the streets, now is it?'

Ruby just hoped that her brother's cheeky smile would

work its magic on Bobby's mam and secure him somewhere to stay.

Two days later, Mary and Ruby were sewing outdoors
under a blue sky. They were sitting on chairs they'd
carried from their kitchen. Lady lay in the shade cast by
their shadows. The two Miss Huttons were close by, Ann
darning stockings and Elsie totting up their household
accounts in a small blue book. As they worked, the four
women talked freely. Topics of conversation ranged from
the price of eggs at the store to how Abigail was getting
on with Gladys Smith. Finally the conversation turned to
men. Elsie wanted to know all about Ruby's Stan and
whether they were getting serious. Ruby didn't mention
that she hadn't been back to the Queen's Head since she'd
started courting Stan for fear of meeting Polly again. She
knew she'd have to face her one day, when the time was
right. Then Mary asked after Bert Collins, and Elsie broke
into a smile.

'Oh, Bert's doing all right,' she laughed. 'But I wouldn't
say we're courting. At our age? The best we can hope for
is a little friendship, that's all.'

'And what about you, Ann?' Ruby asked. 'Whatever
happened to your whippet man who turned up out of the
blue?'

Ann laid her darning in her lap. 'Like Elsie says, it's
friendship and nothing more. Let the gossips make of that
what they will.' Then she took up her darning again and
carried on, a little more forcefully than before.

Ruby knew only too well what the gossips in Ryhope
said about the two Miss Huttons. Spinster sisters, who'd
lived together for as long as anyone could recall, now

being visited by men, one for Elsie, one for Ann? The gossips were having a field day. Rumour was rife that Ann's whippet man liked gambling a little too much, and risked more than he earned. There was even talk of him arranging fights between men and taking bets on the winner. These were dangerous bare-knuckle fights held on a patch of rough ground everyone called the Blood Pit. It lay behind the Toll Bar hotel on the road from Ryhope to Grangetown, and was a seedy place of violence and, it was rumoured, even death. Ruby wondered if Ann thought she was better off without a man who made his living that way. And as for Elsie's friend, Bert Collins, he wasn't innocent in helping fuel gossip. Ruby had often seen him out on his horse and cart, delivering goods from the store. When women called to him and waved, he'd wave back and tell them to let Elsie know he was thinking of her, saying that he only had eyes for Elsie, she was the only girl for him.

'Bert's got a lot to answer for,' Mary whispered so that only Ruby could hear her. The two of them shared a secret smile and then Mary returned to her sewing.

'When are you going to pay Mrs Sowerby another visit?' Mary asked.

'She's proving impossible to catch at home,' Ruby replied. 'I've been twice in the last week, but there's never any answer when I knock at the door.' She'd even wondered about heading to Mrs Sowerby's house early one morning or late at night, to catch the landlady at home.

'Keep trying, love,' Mary said. 'Don't forget you're entitled to anything she's managed to get.'

Ruby glanced at her. Mary looked happy and content, although Ruby knew she was worried sick about Michael.

She wondered if she still suffered her cravings for ale. It was something Ruby didn't like to speak about; it felt as if she was prying into a part of her mother's life that she had no right to. All through the miners' strike, when they'd worked together at the hall, she'd sensed that her mam had been aware of the bottles Stan donated regularly from the Queen's Head. She knew for a fact, though, that Mary hadn't touched a drop, because all the bottles had been handed out to miners; she'd seen it with her own eyes. Had her demons finally left her alone? Ruby crossed her fingers, closed her eyes and hoped it might be true.

Suddenly Lady leapt to her feet and began barking. Ruby glanced up and saw a familiar figure walking towards them.

'Mam, look,' she said.

Mary gasped and threw her sewing to one side. Ruby caught it before it hit the ground, then watched as her mam ran along the lane towards Michael. Elsie and Ann turned to watch too. When she reached her son, she flung her arms around him and they hugged for a very long time.

When she finally let go of him, Mary threaded her arm through Michael's and walked with him towards their back yard, bringing him home like a trophy she'd won at the fair. Michael greeted the two Miss Huttons with a respectful hello. Then he looked at Ruby.

'Okay?' she said.

His smile in return told her everything she needed to know.

Mary bustled him indoors, determined to make him a cup of tea and offer him something to eat, whatever she could find. Ruby and Lady followed them in.

'Stop fussing, Mam,' Michael laughed. 'I'll take a mug

of tea, but I'm not hungry. Bobby's mam cooked me sausage and eggs for breakfast.'

Mary walked towards him and laid her hands on his face, stroking his cheeks, brushing his hair from his eyes. 'Where have you been, son?'

'Doesn't matter,' Michael said. 'The question you should be asking is have I got myself a job.'

'Well, have you?' Mary said.

'No,' he said flatly.

He winked at Ruby. She saw the beginnings of a smile playing around his lips, and a flash of mischief in his eyes. How she'd missed seeing him this relaxed, looking so free.

Mary, however, wasn't in on the joke. She grew red in the face and planted her hands on her hips. 'No? You disappear for two days and come home without explaining where you've been, then you have the bloody nerve to stand there and tell me you still haven't got a job?'

'No, I haven't got a job,' he said. 'I've got two.'

Ruby burst out laughing, and it took a moment or two for Mary to join in once she realised her son had been stringing her along.

She hugged him again. 'Oh, you little bugger! Sit down. Have some tea and tell me all about it.'

'Well done,' Ruby said. She pulled a chair from the table and made herself comfortable. This was going to be quite some tale. Two jobs? She was looking forward to hearing what Michael had to say.

'Come on then, where are these jobs and how the devil are you going to do two? You can't be in two places at once, son, not unless you want to split yourself in half,' Mary said.

'I would've split myself into ten pieces if it meant not going back to the pit.'

Mary busied herself at the fireplace with the kettle and teapot as Michael revealed his news.

'I'm going to work with Ralphie Heddon at High Farm three days a week,' he began. He shot Mary a look. 'Now I know what you're going to say, Mam. And you're right, it doesn't pay well, nowhere near as much as I was getting at the pit. But it's hard work and I'll learn. I'll be working outdoors, that's what matters.'

Mary bit her lip. How would she tell Arthur that Michael was going to be bringing in a pittance?

'And the other job?' Ruby asked.

Michael smiled widely and shook his head, as if to stop himself from breaking into laughter.

'You'll never guess,' he said.

'Michael, tell me,' Ruby urged.

'Got myself a bar job,' he said. 'Humping barrels around in the cellar, pulling a few pints, doing a bit of cleaning, helping in the stables at the back.'

'Where? The Railway Inn?' Ruby asked.

He shook his head. 'Somewhere a bit closer to home. See if you can guess.'

There was something about the way he was beaming at her. And then it dawned on her why he was teasing her.

'You're never going to be working at the Queen's Head, are you?' she said.

He sat up straight. 'I am indeed,' he said proudly. 'Stan's taken me on for a trial to see how I do. I'll be working at the pub on the days I'm not at the farm.'

'And when will you get time off?' Mary wanted to

know. 'You can't be expected to work all the hours of each day, surely?'

Michael stood, looming over his mam, then slid his arm around Mary's shoulders and gave her a peck on the cheek. 'Mam, can't you see how happy I am?'

Mary softened. 'Course I can, lad. I'm just worried about you, that's all.'

Ruby and Michael shared a smile, unseen by Mary. But although Ruby was happy for her brother, something was bothering her. 'You know the Queen's Head has a bad reputation, don't you?' she said. 'Did they tell you? Grown men fuelled with ale battle it out in there. I saw it with my own eyes when I worked there. It can be a dangerous place.'

Michael shrugged. 'Stan's told me all about it. He's going to show me what to do when a fight breaks out.' He was full of bluster now, Ruby noticed. 'It's nothing I can't handle.'

She looked at her brother and hoped he was right.

Chapter Thirty-Seven

Michael began his new life, and Ruby saw the change in him immediately. No longer did he cry himself to sleep. Instead he slept heartily, and she heard him snoring as soon as his head hit the pillow. She was pleased to see him settled and happy, back to his old ways. She often caught him singing around the house or humming a tune to himself. And she heard him laughing when he played with Lady in the yard, rolling stones for the dog to retrieve.

One warm, sunny day in August, Mary and Ruby were working in the kitchen. A cotton sheet covered the kitchen floor and on it lay a pile of sewing they were working their way through. The door to the yard was open and they could see Michael and the dog outside.

'It's a relief to see him cheerful again,' Mary said.

Lady began barking. It wasn't her normal playful bark, but something deeper, louder.

Mary raised an eyebrow. 'Sounds like someone's coming in.' She stood and walked towards the door. 'Ruby,' she called excitedly. 'Look who's here.'

Ruby laid her sewing down and walked outside. It was the pram she saw first, a big battered black thing with enormous wheels and a thick wooden handle for pushing. Abigail stepped forward and opened her arms. Ruby hesitated a moment before finally accepting her hug.

'Hello, little cheeky chops,' Mary cooed at baby Emily in the pram.

And then Ruby caught sight of Jean, who was waiting outside in the lane. Her heart leapt with joy at seeing her again after so long. 'You two are friends again?' she asked.

'I made her apologise, and I hope you did too,' Jean replied sternly.

Ruby pointed at the pram. 'Where on earth have you got this old jalopy from?'

'Some fella I know gave it to me,' Abigail said.

'A fella?' Ruby teased. 'You don't waste any time, do you?'

'I'm a free woman,' Abigail said firmly.

Mary looked up from the pram. 'Be careful, love, you'll get yourself talked about, carrying on with a fella now you've got yourself a bairn.'

'Can't do right for doing wrong, can I?' Abigail sighed. Suddenly she began coughing, and covered her mouth with her hand as her body convulsed with great spasms. Mary and Ruby exchanged a look of concern. Abigail pulled a handkerchief from her skirt pocket, and turned away until her coughing had eased. Then she stood a moment, gathering her wheezing breath.

'Oh dear, that doesn't sound good,' Mary said.

'I've had it for ages, but it came on bad a few days ago.'

'You used to suffer from a bad chest when you were little,' Mary continued. 'I remember being worried in case you passed it on to Ruby, as you two were always together. You were here so often when you were a bairn, it was like having another daughter.'

Abigail began coughing again, and it took a few moments for her breath to ease.

'Has Gladys got onions in her pantry?' Mary asked.

Abigail nodded.

'Ask her to cook one in boiling water for you, then drink the water; it'll do your chest good.'

Abigail took in a long, slow breath of air. 'I think I'm all right now. It comes and goes.'

'Were you and Jean just passing?' Ruby asked.

Abigail shook her head. 'Thought you might like to come for a walk with us. Jean's got the morning off work.'

'I'd love to,' Ruby said, but then her heart sank. 'I can't, though. I've got a whole load of sewing to do before dinner time, and then I've got to call at Mrs Sowerby's house.'

'Don't worry about the sewing,' Mary said. 'I'll finish it for you. We're almost done as it is. You go and get yourself out for a walk with your friends.'

'Are you sure, Mam?'

'I wouldn't have offered if I wasn't.'

Ruby kissed her mam on the cheek and headed into the lane towards Jean, who was looking as bonny as ever, with her hair curled prettily around her face. She slipped her arm through Jean's and the girls headed off, Abigail pushing the pram carefully, manoeuvring it over the bumpy cobbles, trying not to get the wheels stuck in dried ruts of mud. Just before they reached the end of the lane, Lady came bounding after them, with Michael running behind, calling her name. They stopped, turned and waited for him to catch up.

'Stupid dog,' he said, catching his breath. 'She wants to follow you, I think.'

'Then let her,' Abigail said.

'Why not come too?' Jean offered.

'What?' Michael teased 'And listen to you three gossiping like old women?'

Abigail affected shock. 'Gossip? Us?' she laughed.

'And who are you calling old?' Jean added playfully. 'Come on, Michael. You can walk behind us if you're too embarrassed to be seen out with three of the best-looking lasses in Ryhope.'

'When you see these three bonny lasses, will you let me know who they are?' Michael teased.

The girls walked on, Lady at Ruby's side. Michael decided to follow, but stayed a respectable distance behind. He didn't want any of his friends to see him and think he'd gone soft, out walking with lasses. He had his reputation to think about now he was working at the Queen's Head.

'How's life with Gladys?' Ruby asked.

'She's all right,' Abigail said sadly.

'Just all right?'

'She keeps me on a short lead. I have to sneak out to see my fella. She's kind, I suppose, and she's letting me live with her in exchange for doing housework and cooking.'

'I hear she's a stickler for discipline,' Jean chipped in.

'Well, that's one way to describe her,' Abigail said. 'She means well. But she's always giving me advice, telling me what to do; always thinks she knows better than me. I don't like it, but I don't have any choice. I just say "Yes, Mrs Smith, no, Mrs Smith." Oh, she vexes me something rotten. But I have to bite my tongue and stay quiet or else I'll be back on the streets.'

'You still can't go home?'

'Not while Mam's fella lives there.'

'Is it anyone we know?'

'Ronnie Clarke,' Abigail said, but the name meant nothing to Ruby.

Suddenly Abigail stopped walking and began coughing again. Ruby took the pram from her as she rummaged in her pocket for her handkerchief.

'She needs to see the doctor,' Jean whispered.

But both Ruby and Jean knew Abigail could never afford a visit to Dr Anderson.

'I'm all right,' Abigail said once she could breathe easily again. 'Come on, we'll walk on.'

Ruby kept tight hold of the pram as Abigail seemed in no hurry to take it back. She pushed it forward, feeling the weight of it in her hands and the responsibility of Emily in her care. She wondered what folk would make of her, Abigail and Jean when they saw them walking together. Would she receive pitying looks because the baby wasn't hers? She held her head high. Folk could think what they wanted. She knew the truth. One day she'd push a pram with a bairn of her own inside. She looked at Emily, and despite it all, the baby's smile melted Ruby's heart. Emily was untainted and innocent.

'What are you going to Mrs Sowerby's house for?' Abigail asked.

'Oh, just a bit of business,' Ruby replied. She gritted her teeth when she thought of banging on the green door again, waiting for Mrs Sowerby to answer. The last time she'd called, the next-door neighbour had come out and told her she'd just missed Mrs Sowerby heading out moments earlier. Ruby had wondered whether this was true, or whether Mrs Sowerby barricaded herself indoors every time she saw her walking towards her front door. It had been many months since Gordon had died, and in all of that time, Ruby had seen neither hide nor hair of the landlady. She shook her head to dismiss the lodging house for now.

'Has your mam seen the bairn?' she asked.

Abigail nodded. 'I meet her once a week. It's the only time she gets away from Ronnie. We have to meet in secret; he doesn't want her having friends or anything to do with me.'

'In secret?' Ruby cried. 'But that's awful. Where do you meet?'

'The asylum grounds. I'm heading there now, and with a bit of luck Mam'll be waiting, if she's managed to get away from his grip.'

'The asylum grounds?' Jean said. 'But the village green is closer.'

'The air there is good for Emily, Gladys says.'

Ruby smiled. 'And if Gladys says it, it must be true, right?'

Abigail laughed. 'I daren't disagree with her. She'd be in a huff for days.'

'I'll walk as far as the asylum with you,' Ruby offered.

'Me too,' said Jean.

'It's a nice walk through the trees, and there's a little stream too,' Abigail said.

'But the asylum's scary,' Jean said. 'The people there, some of them hang out of the windows, shouting at you when you walk by. It's horrible. I wouldn't want any of my family in there.' Her hand flew to her mouth. 'Oh, I'm sorry, Ruby. Your Grandma Winter . . . I wasn't thinking.'

'It's all right. I don't mind talking about her.'

'How did she end up in there?' Jean asked. 'You've never really told us the full story.'

Ruby felt Jean's arm slip through hers as they walked. 'Grandad dragged her there by the arm and left her at the gates,' she said.

Both Abigail and Jean turned to stare at her.

'No!' Abigail cried.

'That's what men did back then,' Ruby said. 'I've heard about others doing the same. When their wives became too much for them to handle, when they broke down in hysterics or turned sad after giving birth, they took them to the asylum gates and left them there.'

'It's horrible,' Abigail said, shaking her head. 'Can we change the subject? It's scaring me. I want to talk about something else.'

When the girls reached the village school, they headed up Stockton Road. Ahead of them, turrets poked through the trees. Anyone who didn't know better might think it was a country home or rural retreat. But the imposing building set in its own grounds was in fact the Sunderland Borough Lunatic Asylum. It lay on the outskirts of the village, surrounded by fields, well away from houses, people and everyday life. On close inspection, bars could be seen at the windows, making prisoners of the four hundred or so patients inside: alcoholics, like Ruby's grandma had been; those suffering from melancholy, paralysis and epilepsy, or insane from syphilis; unmarried pregnant girls, and ex-soldiers driven mad by shell shock.

But although the building was dark and forbidding, the grounds in which it sat were lush and green, a perfect place of serenity and peace. Open to all, they expanded into a valley that ran down to the sea. Sadly, Ruby knew from reading the *Sunderland Echo* that some patients escaped and were later 'found drowned'. It was a kinder way to report a suicide, for the phrase could imply that the patient had been involved in an accident, rather than intending to take their own life.

As the girls headed into the grounds, Michael followed, trailing a stick along the ground.

'You all right?' Ruby called.

'I'm fine, onion face,' Michael replied.

'What did he call you?' Jean laughed.

'Ignore him, you know what brothers are like.'

Ruby was only too aware that being here, so close to where their grandma's sad life had ended, might set Michael thinking of his day on the hilltop. Her own memories of her day at the beach came rushing at her and she struggled to push them away. She breathed in deeply, taking in the warm summer air and the sweet scent of cut grass.

'I've got some news for you both,' Abigail said with a wry smile. 'It's about my new fella. But don't tell Gladys, whatever you do. She'll chuck me out if she knows.'

'Come on then, who is he?' Jean asked.

'He works at Grange Paper Works. I met him when I was walking Emily one day.'

'He knows you've got a bairn and he's still interested?' Ruby asked, shocked.

'He got me this pram, didn't he? Said he found it abandoned on the beach; someone had left it there after they'd been collecting sea coal. Gladys showed me how to scrub it up and it's come out all right. Anyway, why shouldn't I have a bit of fun? Just because I've got a baby doesn't mean my world's got to come to an end. He's taking me out dancing next week.'

'Dancing?' Jean cried. 'But you can't just leave Emily at home with Gladys. If you start taking her for granted, she'll not be happy.'

'Oh, don't worry about Gladys. I'll get round the old bat somehow.'

Ruby and Jean shared a look. Then Abigail raised her hand and waved at a woman sitting on a wooden bench ahead.

'There's Mam!' she cried excitedly.

Abigail's mother looked as unkempt and unwashed as the last time Ruby had seen her, when she'd tried to speak to Abigail at Railway Street. As she nodded towards Ruby and Jean, Ruby noticed the bruises on her bare arms. Kate folded her arms defensively across her body, running her hands over them as if she was trying to rub the damage away.

'I'll leave you two to talk. It's about time I headed home,' Ruby said.

'And I've got to get to work,' Jean said, excusing herself too.

Ruby leaned into the pram and gently ran her finger down baby Emily's cheek.

'Bye, Emily,' she said. 'See you soon.'

Emily gurgled and kicked her legs.

As Ruby and Jean began to walk away, they heard Abigail coughing again.

Ahead of them, a group of nurses in starched white

uniforms and caps were taking a breather on one of the benches. Some of them were smoking, one was eating an apple and another was flicking through the pages of a romance magazine. As Ruby and Jean neared them, polite good mornings were exchanged and Ruby noticed that one of the nurses was younger than the rest of the group. She was a bonny girl with a round face and fair hair, and was smiling directly at Michael. Ruby looked at her brother. Was she mistaken, or was the pink in his cheeks a nervous blush of emotion?

'Go and talk to her,' she whispered.

'What'll I say?' Michael whispered back.

'You'll think of something. Take Lady.'

Ruby and Jean walked on, leaving Michael standing awkwardly next to the nurse with Lady at his side. Ruby saw the nurse shuffle along the bench, creating space for Michael to sit next to her, then she reached out to stroke the dog.

Chapter Thirty-Eight

'What's her name?' Ruby asked when Michael returned home.

'Who?' Michael replied with a smirk.

'You know who I mean. You two seemed to be getting on well when Jean and I left you sitting on the bench.'

Michael slapped his hand against his forehead. 'Oh *her*,' he said.

'Michael?'

He began pushing his feet into his boots and doing up the laces, getting ready for work at the Queen's Head. Behind him, Mary was piling dinner plates into the large bowl she used for washing up.

'She's called Grace,' he said.

'Who's called Grace?' Mary asked, half listening to their conversation.

'Michael's girlfriend, that's who,' Ruby teased.

'She is *not* my girlfriend,' Michael said, shooting her a look.

'But you'd like her to be, wouldn't you?' she said.

'Might do.'

'Are you seeing her again?' Ruby asked.

Michael shrugged. 'If she's lucky.'

'Well, just you treat her right,' Mary warned. 'I'm not having my one and only son gossiped about in Ryhope. It was bad enough our Ruby being talked about when Gordon . . .' She stopped dead and looked at Ruby. 'I'm sorry, love, that came out all wrong.'

Ruby began helping with the plates. 'It's all right, Mam, no need to apologise. But please never mention his name again.'

Mary pulled Ruby to her and gave her a hug. Then she wiped her hands on her pinny and handed Michael a clean handkerchief from a drawer in the sideboard. 'Here, stick this in your pocket.'

Michael finished doing up his boots. He stood and kissed his mam on the cheek. 'I'm off to the pub then. I'll see when I see you.'

'If I see you first, you're the worst,' Ruby smiled. Then she looked seriously at Michael. 'Be careful.'

'I will. Anyway, I've got Stan to protect me.'

As he left, Ruby watched him proudly. How tall he looked these days, how broad across the shoulders. He seemed to walk with a spring in his step, and as he headed into the yard, she heard him whistling a tune.

'I might go and have a word with Polly tonight,' she said. 'It's about time she and I cleared the air. I haven't seen her since me and Stan started courting.'

'Speaking to her while she's at work? Is that wise? Shouldn't you wait until she's a bit more rested?'

Ruby remembered the change she'd seen in Polly when Polly worked behind her bar. The stern-faced harridan had been softened by the subtle light in the pub, her mood lightened too. The bar was Polly's domain, the place she felt most happy.

'I know what I'm doing, Mam.'

'Well, be it on your own head.'

Ruby set off for the Queen's Head soon after Michael had left. When she arrived, the pub door was locked. She knocked on the window and peered inside. She saw Stan and Michael busy setting up the bar, cleaning tables and getting ready to open up. Stan's eyes widened when he saw her, and he rushed to open the door, welcoming her in with a smile and open arms. Ruby was only too willing to walk straight to him, feeling safe, protected and loved in his embrace.

'Hey, you!' he said. 'What have you been up to today?'

'Went for a walk with Jean, Abigail and the baby,' Ruby replied.

'How's Abigail's little 'un coming on? Emily, isn't it?'

'Oh, she's gorgeous, Stan, a real bonny bairn. She never cries, you know. She's always laughing and she seems to connect with me for some reason; she gurgles when she sees me and kicks her tiny feet. And when Abigail lets me hold her, she looks deep into my eyes and I swear she can see my soul.'

'Sounds like you're as fond of her as she is of you.'

'I enjoy seeing her, Stan. She's not to blame for what happened. She's pure and untouched by the truth of who her dad is.'

'Do you think Abigail will tell her, when she's older?'

Ruby shrugged. 'That's up to Abigail. But for now, I'm more than happy being Aunt Ruby to such a gorgeous child.'

Stan kissed her on the cheek. 'Anyway, to what do I

owe the pleasure of this unexpected visit?'

'I've come to see your mam,' Ruby said.

Stan dropped his arms and looked into her eyes. 'Are you sure you want to do this tonight? Mam's been in a foul mood today. She's having some trouble with one of the customers, a fella who's been causing a bit of bother.'

'If not now, then when?' Ruby said. 'If there's to be a future for us, Stan . . .'

'There's no *if* about it. I love you, Ruby,' he said.

It was the first time she had heard those words from his lips. Her heart skipped a beat.

'You do?'

In that moment, she felt more loved than she'd ever done in her life. Nothing that Gordon had ever whispered in her ear came anywhere close to how Stan's words made her feel. It made her more certain than ever that she and Polly had to make peace. For if she couldn't get along with Polly, then what future could she hope for with Stan?

'Stan, I . . . I love you too. But we can't plan a future if your mam and I are at odds. I've got to speak to her.'

He pulled two stools from one of the small round tables in front of the window that looked out to the street, then sat opposite Ruby and held her hands tight.

'I've told her about us, obviously,' he began. 'And to be honest, she hasn't taken it well.'

'We never expected her to,' Ruby said. 'But surely she must see—'

'She?' barked a voice behind Ruby. 'Who's she? The cat's mother?'

Ruby recognised the voice only too well. She stuck a smile on her face, stood up and turned around.

'Hello, Polly.' She tried to keep her voice even, despite

the fact that her heart was pounding. She noticed that Polly was dressed for work, wearing a low-cut dress that emphasised her ample curves. Her hair was curled and her face was powdered and rouged. 'You're looking well,' she added, and it was true; the whole effect was pleasing. When Polly made an effort with her looks and her clothes, the change in her appearance, if not her demeanour, was startling.

'Stan, leave us alone for five minutes,' Polly said.

Stan put his arm around Ruby and kissed her full on the lips. 'I'll be at the bar if you need me.'

'Sit down, lass.'

Ruby sank back on to her stool. Polly took the stool where Stan had been sitting. The two women faced each other, and Ruby felt herself being appraised by Polly's critical eye.

'He's told me what's going on,' Polly said, nodding towards Stan at the bar. 'And of all the lasses in Ryhope, Ruby Dinsdale, I think you already know you wouldn't have been top of my list for my Stan. After all those things I've been hearing about you and that miner who died.'

Ruby felt a hardness grow inside her as Polly carried on.

'He got another girl pregnant and she's got the nerve to walk around Ryhope showing the bairn off to all and sundry. What does that say about you? Do you think I want a lass like you for our Stan? Think again, little Miss Ruby.'

Ruby glared at her.

'Cat got your tongue?' Polly sneered. 'I thought you'd try to defend yourself at least, like you tried to do the night you stole from my bar.'

Behind Polly, Ruby saw Stan's father Jim walking towards them. His pipe was hanging from his bottom lip.

'That'll do, Poll,' he warned. 'You've said enough. Let the lass speak.'

He sat down next to his wife. Ruby cast a glance towards Stan, a silent cry for help, but he was busy setting up glasses in neat rows. She turned back to face Polly and Jim, took a deep breath and began to speak.

'Everything you've heard about Gordon Fisher is true. Yes, the baby is his. Yes, he was untrue to me, betrayed me in the worst possible way. And now he's dead and buried, and none of it matters any more.'

'Don't be so daft, lass. Course it matters. Your reputation's ruined by association with . . .' Polly paused and took a deep breath before spitting out her final words, 'that man and what he did.'

'Polly, let her continue,' Jim said sternly.

Polly tutted, turning her head away as Ruby carried on.

'None of it matters any more because it's all in the past. It's over and done with. My future is with Stan and I intend to do the best for us both and make him as happy as I can.'

'You're still a thief,' Polly huffed.

Ruby sat up straight, pushed her shoulders back and looked the older woman squarely in the eye, speaking with a passion that surprised both Polly and Jim.

'I was starving, Mrs Hutchinson. My family were starving. I was doing the only thing I could do to help my brother and my mam and dad. And so help me, if I'm lucky enough to share the rest of my life with your son, and he was ever in that situation, starving, desperate for food, I'd steal to feed him too.'

Just then, Stan walked towards them and sat next to Ruby.

'All right?' he said.

Ruby nodded.

'Mam, you've had your say and you've heard what Ruby's said too. Whatever you think of what she's done in the past, or about what's happened to her, there's something I want to tell you both.' He took hold of Ruby's hands. 'I love her, Mam,' he said, locking eyes with Polly.

Ruby felt a warmth spread up the back of her neck to her face. She squeezed Stan's hands tight. Polly's mouth hung open in shock as Stan continued.

'I'm telling you, Mam. It doesn't matter what you think of Ruby, it's what I think that matters.'

'Good lad,' Jim said, his pipe jiggling at the side of his mouth. 'Polly, close your mouth.'

Polly snapped her mouth shut, lost for words.

'Can we be friends, Polly?' Ruby asked.

'Course you can,' Jim said, then he gently nudged his wife with his elbow. 'Can't you?'

Polly breathed in deeply. 'For the sake of our Stan, yes,' she said, but the look on her face suggested that every word was torture.

Jim clapped his hands together. 'That's settled, then. Let's have a drink.' He called over to the bar. 'Mikey lad!'

Ruby smiled. She'd never heard anyone call her brother Mikey before. But Michael didn't argue or complain; in fact Ruby noticed that he seemed to enjoy his new identity just as he was enjoying his new life.

'Four beers over here, and bring one for yourself.'

Michael brought three pints of Vaux best for the men

and two half-pints for Ruby and Polly. He set the drinks on the table.

'Well, Mam?' Stan said.

Polly raised her glass. 'To our Stan,' she said through gritted teeth. 'And Ruby.'

Jim removed his pipe while he took a sip of beer. 'You pull a decent pint, Mikey,' he said. 'And you'll get more practice tonight. It looks set to be a busy one.'

'I just hope that tall, stringy fella doesn't come in again,' Polly moaned. 'He's causing all sorts of bother with his gambling and betting. Fellas don't like losing money like that, and once they start kicking off, all hell breaks loose.'

'What's he called?' Ruby asked.

'Gamblers tend not to give names,' Jim said sagely. 'They usually do a bit of business in the pub, then disappear for a very long time after they've taken money from drunken, foolish men.'

'He always wears a red neckerchief,' Polly said. 'He turned up out of nowhere a few months ago.'

Ruby thought for a moment about the man who had started paying visits to Ann Hutton. 'Has he got a rugged, weather-beaten look about him?'

'That's him,' Polly said. 'Why? Do you know him?'

'No. But I know someone who does. I can ask her to have a word with him so that he'll take his gambling business elsewhere.'

'You'd do that for us?' Polly said, surprised.

'Of course. I've told you. I'll do all I can to help family and those I love.'

Jim lifted his pint. 'Well, I'll drink to that.'

Chapter Thirty-Nine

Once Ruby had left to walk home, Polly took her place behind the bar. With Jim and Michael serving customers, Stan's job was to keep order, wading in to break up arguments when he heard raised voices. And that night, tucked away in the snug, there were many drunken voices.

Stan's presence when a fight looked in danger of breaking out meant that men soon settled down once he'd threatened to throw them out or stop serving them. But there was one man, a big fella called Ronnie Clarke, who thought he was above the law. Both Jim and Stan had trouble controlling him. Ronnie drank too much, too quickly, and was usually already three sheets to the wind by the time he arrived at the pub after drinking elsewhere. That night, he'd staggered in looking to see who was there, who was easy pickings if he wanted a fight. And Ronnie always wanted a fight. Now he was holding court with a bunch of villains in the snug, and Ann Hutton's friend the whippet man was with him. Their jovial banter had turned increasingly loud. The more ale they sank, the louder and more raucous they became.

When Stan walked into the snug, Ronnie raised his full

pint of ale to his lips and drained every last drop in one gulp.

'Here comes trouble,' he said, playing to the audience of his drinking pals. 'Has your mammy sent you in?' he called out in a sing-song voice, making fun of Stan.

Stan walked calmly towards him, and as he did so, Ronnie stood.

'Sit down, Ronnie, or get out,' Stan said.

Ronnie put his hands on either side of his face and in a high-pitched voice mimicked Stan word for word. Those sitting around him roared with laughter. All of them, that is, except for the whippet man. He was waiting to see what might happen next.

Stan stepped forward. 'Ronnie. Sit.'

'Say please.'

A nervous titter went up from the men at the table. Some of them looked at each other, sucking air through their teeth, shaking their heads.

'Sit down, Ronnie, and mind your manners. You know Mam doesn't like a rowdy pub.'

Ronnie looked at each of the men. 'Oh! Would you just listen to him! His mam doesn't like a rowdy pub!'

Stan stood firm. 'Ronnie, sit down and shut up. Or . . .'

Ronnie made a pretence of being scared, flapping his hands in front of him. His drinking pals were lapping up the performance, swigging back their pints, waiting for his next move. Only the whippet man stayed silent, watching, weighing up the opportunity that was presenting itself. Suddenly Ronnie snapped. He lunged forward and grabbed Stan by his shirt, yanking him towards him. 'Or what?' he growled. 'You'll set your mam on me? She might not want a rowdy pub, but she's got a right dump of a place here.'

In one swift movement, Stan threw his arm around Ronnie's shoulder and twisted the man away from him. Ronnie's hands dropped to his sides.

'Go on there, lad!' one of his mates shouted.

Another jumped to his feet. 'Ronnie! Come on! Give him what for!'

But Ronnie couldn't move.

'A dump of a place – is that what you think of this pub?' Stan hissed.

'It's a pigsty,' Ronnie spat.

Stan strengthened his grip on the older man, getting ready to march him to the door and throw him out. But Ronnie wasn't finished yet. The pair of them twisted this way and that, shoving and pushing, until Ronnie broke free.

'Good lad, Ronnie!' one of the men called. The whippet man took a penny from his pocket and held it tight in his hand.

Ronnie stood glaring at Stan, breathing hard, his face full of fury. 'You've gone too far, mammy's boy,' he hissed. 'No one takes Ronnie Clarke on and gets away with it.'

Stan lunged forward again, trying to get a grip on Ronnie so that he could push him towards the door. But Ronnie stood firm, like a rock, immovable against Stan's best efforts. The whippet man laid his penny on the table. None of the men saw him do it; he brought no attention to himself. As the two men tussled, the whippet man stood. Still no one turned towards him; they were too busy watching the beginnings of what they hoped would be a good fight.

'Get another round in,' one of Ronnie's mates said to another. 'This is going to be good.' The man disappeared to the bar.

Stan was having trouble controlling Ronnie, but he couldn't, wouldn't back down, especially not in front of Ronnie's mates, who were all egging their man on. Stan felt his heart pound, the blood rush in his ears as he struggled. Then suddenly, with no warning, Ronnie stepped aside, letting his hands fall as if defeated. Another man stepped forward and Stan found himself looking into the eyes of the man with the weather-beaten face and the red neckerchief.

'Fancy a game of heads or tails?'

Stan glared at him, catching his breath. The whippet man carried on without waiting for a reply. 'Heads says you two fight at the Blood Pit. Tails says you don't.'

A roar went up from the men at the table. Ronnie banged his fists against his chest and nodded at the whippet man. 'I'm in,' he said, glaring at Stan.

'Stan?' the whippet man said. 'Heads, fight. Tails, walk away. Are you in or are you out?'

Stan wanted to be anywhere other than where he was right then. But one look at the men's faces told him he couldn't back down. He'd be a laughing stock if he did. And yet . . . there was still time to do the right thing, the decent thing, and walk away. He was on the verge of walking; he was calming down now, seeing Ronnie for the drunken fool he was. He opened his mouth to tell them, the words right there on the end of his tongue. He was about to say he was out; he was about to say he wouldn't fight, when Ronnie sneered in his face.

'Scared, are you? Frightened to take me on?' He spun

around to his mates and they fell silent, watching Stan's reaction.

'I'm not frightened of you,' Stan said. 'I just want a quiet life.'

Ronnie exploded into laughter. 'A quiet life? Quiet's not what I've heard about you, lad. Quiet's not what the gossips in Ryhope say about you and the Dinsdale lass.'

Stan felt a red rage building in him. How dare Ronnie bring Ruby into this? How bloody dare he? He felt his heart begin to pound as Ronnie carried on.

'Couldn't you find a decent lass of your own? Is that why you had to take second pickings after that dead miner had already had a go at her?'

Stan's fist swung out and caught Ronnie square on the jaw. Ronnie rocked back on his heels. There was silence in the pub. The whippet man suppressed a wicked smile, then stepped forward, his sparkling blue eyes dancing with mischief.

'Heads or tails? In or out?' he asked Stan.

Stan glared at Ronnie and spat out the word. 'In.'

A drunken whoop of delight went up. The men banged their fists on the tabletop and stamped their feet on the floor. The whippet man threw his penny up in the air. He caught it, slapped it to the back of his left hand and covered it with his right. Stan felt his heart skip a beat. He felt sick. He was a big lad, and strong when he had to be in the pub, but he'd never fought before.

The whippet man looked from Ronnie to Stan, then dropped his gaze to his hands. He lifted his right hand to reveal the head of King George. Stan's heart sank to the floor.

'It's heads!' the whippet man yelled. 'Heads says they fight!'

'Fight! Fight! Fight!' The men cheered as they brought their fists down on the table.

'What's going on?'

Stan turned to see his mam in the doorway.

'Your little boy's going to take part in a fight,' Ronnie sneered. 'With me.'

'A fight? Over my dead body. Not in my pub!'

'No, not in your pub,' the whippet man said coldly. 'At the Blood Pit. Midnight on Saturday. And I'm taking all bets now.'

Chapter Forty

While the drama played out in the snug of the pub, Ruby was making her way home, unaware of the danger Stan had put himself in. When she walked into her back yard, she saw Lady in the corner, eyes raised sheepishly. Her mam only ever put the dog in the yard to keep her away from a visitor to the house. Ruby wondered who on earth it could be. She pushed the door open, hoping it might be one of the two Miss Huttons. She hadn't seen either of them for a while. Besides, she needed to speak to Ann about the whippet man and ask if she had any influence over him, as she'd promised Polly. But it wasn't Elsie or Ann sitting at the kitchen table with Mary. It was Abigail's landlady, Gladys Smith. And in Gladys's arms was baby Emily, fast asleep.

'What's going on?' Ruby asked, looking from Gladys's stern face to the tiny baby. She was confused. Gladys had never been to their house before. She wasn't a friend of the family, not even a neighbour; just a woman they'd worked with at the miners' hall. 'Where's Abigail?'

'Sit down, love,' Mary said.

Ruby pulled a chair from the table. 'Is Abigail all right?'

Her mam and Gladys exchanged a look.

'No, Abigail is *not* all right,' Gladys said archly. 'If she was all right, do you think I'd be sitting here now with her child?'

'Now, Gladys, don't you take that tone with our Ruby. None of this is her fault,' Mary scolded.

'What's happened?' Ruby asked.

Gladys drew herself up in her chair and carefully repositioned Emily. She stared directly at Ruby, reminding her of a coiled spring with words wound tight.

'Your friend Abigail has left me holding the baby,' she began, then paused before delivering her final blow. 'Again.'

None of it made sense. Ruby was feeling angry at Gladys and wished she would get to the point.

'Did you know she was going out tonight?' Gladys closed her eyes as if to protect herself from what she was about to say next. 'With a *man*?'

'Tonight?' Ruby struggled to understand. 'No, no, I didn't know.'

All she knew was that Abigail had mentioned a new fella, the one who'd got her the pram. Hadn't she said that he'd offered to take her dancing the following week? She'd mentioned nothing about going out that night.

'She just upped and left, without a word,' Gladys said.

'How do you know she went out with a man?' Ruby asked.

'She thinks I don't know what she's up to; she thinks she can fool Gladys Smith. Well, she needs to think again. Next time you see her, tell her I'm not as green as I'm cabbage-looking.'

Ruby wondered why Gladys was taking in riddles.

Was whatever she had to say so difficult that she couldn't come straight out with it? She looked at her mam, hoping that she'd be able to chip in with something to let her know what was going on. But when Mary looked content to let Gladys speak, Ruby piped up instead.

'Well, she said she had a new fella, but she said nothing about seeing him tonight. Perhaps her plans changed.' Ruby felt as if she was defending Abigail from an accusation she didn't understand.

'Which man?' Gladys demanded, her voice getting louder. 'There's a different one every night, Ruby!'

Ruby sank back in her chair. She looked at her mam for support, but Mary nodded gravely.

'What do you mean?' Ruby said. But she wasn't a child any more. She knew only too well what Gladys meant. She felt sick to her stomach. How could Abigail turn against Gladys, the woman who had taken her in when she'd nowhere else to go? She felt let down by her friend, but disappointed in herself too, for giving her the benefit of the doubt.

'She's out every single night with a different fella, that's what I mean,' Gladys said. 'How much plainer can I make it? Your friend Abigail goes out with all kinds of men in all kinds of weather. And I won't have it.'

'She's . . .' Ruby paused, trying to find an angle to offer Gladys so that she wouldn't be so harsh on Abigail. 'She's been through a lot in the past, what with her mam and the way she was brought up . . .' She saw Mary shake her head, a silent warning for her not to go on, but there was no stopping her. 'Her mam did the same, she always has. It's all she knows.'

Gladys glared at her. 'And did her mam ever leave her

as a baby, in a room on her own, hungry and crying, dirty, wet through, while she was out kissing and canoodling every bloke on the colliery bank?'

'No . . .' Ruby breathed. 'She wouldn't . . . She didn't . . . ?'

'She did, love,' Mary said softly. 'And it's not the first time she's done it either. Gladys told me all about it while you were at the pub.'

'I caught her with a fella in her room last weekend,' Gladys continued. 'She knows I don't allow that sort of thing under my roof. I had to throw him out, after . . .' Gladys paused, her eyelids fluttering closed as if she was shutting out the words she was about to utter next. 'After he'd put his trousers on.'

Ruby was shocked to the core. The more she learned about her friend, the more she wondered if she'd done the right thing forgiving her after what she'd done with Gordon. Shocked as she was, though, the way Gladys delivered her words made her want to laugh, and she had to put her hand over her mouth to stifle a smile. When she glanced at her mam across the table, she saw a smile playing around Mary's lips too.

'Oh, you both think it's funny, do you?' Gladys barked.

'No, Gladys. Of course it's not funny,' Mary said as her smile disappeared. 'It's shocking, that's what it is. But I don't know what we can do. Abigail's a grown lass and she has to make her own mistakes.'

'Oh, she's making plenty of those,' Gladys said. 'But it's the little 'un I fear for. She can't just up and leave the bairn on her own.' Gladys looked into Emily's sleeping face. 'I've had to change her, clean her, feed her, care for her. It's not what I signed up for when I said I'd take Abigail in. She was only supposed to stay until things were better at home and she could go back to her mam.'

Ruby thought of the bruises on Kate's arms, and the battered state Abigail had turned up in on the night she'd given birth. Going home wasn't an option for her, Ruby knew that; heaven only knew what Kate's fella might do to baby Emily if his temper was as vicious as she'd heard.

'And she's not well, you know,' Gladys continued.

'The baby?' Ruby asked, worried.

'Abigail,' Gladys said sharply. 'Coughing all night long. It's a wonder she gets any sleep.'

'She can't go home,' Ruby said. 'Her mam's fella, he's a bad 'un. He knocks Kate about, and he used to do the same thing to Abigail, even when she was pregnant. That's why she had to escape. It's why she was living rough in the days before she gave birth. You can't send her home, Gladys.'

'Then where do you suggest I send her?' Gladys said with rising anger. 'Here? You'll take her in here, will you? You'll put up with her ways, look after the baby?'

Ruby glanced at Emily. Now that she and Abigail were friends, how comforting it would be to care for the child, to look after her until Abigail sorted herself out. At that moment, Ruby realised she'd become fonder of Emily than she could have known. She gave a sharp shake of her head to dismiss the thought. How foolish she was for even thinking such a thing.

'I'll make another pot of tea,' Mary said. 'I think this conversation's going to run all night.'

* * *

The clock on the mantelpiece ticked the hours away as Gladys, Mary and Ruby turned over the difficult situation, looking at the ways they might be able to help Abigail. Or if not Abigail, then surely there must be a way to help Emily.

'There's the asylum, of course,' Gladys said.

Both Mary and Ruby shot the idea down as soon as Gladys raised it.

'I could speak to her, if you think it'd help?' Ruby offered. 'I had no idea things had taken a turn for the worse.'

She recalled the events of the day, the walk with Abigail and Jean to the asylum. How carefree their talk had been, catching up on gossip, sharing news. She'd felt happy in a way she hadn't done for some time, enjoying being with her friends. And all the while, Abigail had been keeping the dark truth from her and Jean. She'd been neglecting her child in the worst possible way. The thought of baby Emily sleeping in soiled clothes, crying from hunger, was too much to bear.

'Can I hold her?' she asked Gladys.

Gladys looked at her as if she'd gone mad.

'It's all right. I've made my peace with Abigail,' Ruby said gently. 'And whatever's happened between us, the child doesn't deserve the blame.'

'Well, that's a big statement to make, Ruby. I applaud you,' Gladys said as she transferred Emily over.

'She's getting heavy,' Ruby said as Emily settled into her arms. She gazed into the baby's face and saw her eyes blink open. Emily stared up at her, and Ruby felt as if her heart would melt.

'Hello, little one,' she said softly.

Emily's tiny rosebud mouth opened wide in a yawn.

'What's he called, this fella of Kate's?' Mary asked. 'Maybe I could send Arthur to have a word with him.'

'Dad?' Ruby said, shaking her head. 'Dad's no match for a bully of a man.'

'No, but he might be able to talk sense into him,' Mary suggested.

Ruby thought back to what Abigail had told her earlier that day. 'He's called Clarke, I think.'

Gladys's eyebrows shot up. 'Ronnie Clarke?'

'Yes, that's him.' Ruby nodded. 'Do you know him?'

'Oh, I know him all right, and he's rotten through and through. He's a fighting man. Used to be a boxer as a lad, if I remember correctly.'

'A boxer?' Ruby said. 'It sounds like he can't control his temper or his fists.'

'You should have seen the bruises on Abigail the night she gave birth,' Mary said to Gladys. 'We can't send her back home, not while Ronnie's there.'

'Then what will we do with her?' Gladys asked, desperate.

There was a noise in the yard and Lady barked softly. Mary glanced at the clock.

'That'll be our Michael coming home. Arthur's not due back until the early hours.'

Michael stumbled through the door, eyes wide. He had a nervous look about him, Ruby noticed.

'What is it?' she asked.

He put his hand to the wall to steady himself. 'There's going to be a fight at the Blood Pit,' he breathed. 'Saturday at midnight.'

'Stupid fools,' Gladys said dismissively. 'Men and their tempers. Will they never learn?'

'It's Stan,' Michael said, shooting Ruby a look. 'Stan will be fighting.'

Ruby gasped and pulled baby Emily to her chest, trying to make sense of Michael's words. Her gentle Stan was going to be involved in a fight? Was this some sort of terrible joke?

'Stan? In a fight?'

Michael nodded. 'Against Ronnie Clarke.'

Ruby's mouth dropped open in shock.

Chapter Forty-One

The next morning, Ruby sat by the fire with Lady. Arthur was in bed after returning from work in the early hours and Michael was at work at High Farm. She tore a chunk off the soft white stotty bread her mam had baked earlier. Mary's bread was always tastier, better risen than any Ruby baked. She pierced it with the fire poker, then held the poker above the flames, gently toasting the bread. She was lost in her thoughts about Stan and the news Michael had given her. She'd asked her brother if he knew of a reason for the fight, as she was struggling to understand why mild-mannered Stan would have become involved. But Michael said he didn't know; just that there'd been a bit of bother in the pub.

Ruby knew she had to stop Stan from fighting. As big and strong as he was, he was no match for someone like Ronnie Clarke, if what Gladys had told her was true. Hadn't Gladys said Ronnie had been a boxer as a lad? He'd make mincemeat out of Stan! Stan wasn't a fighter. He was used to throwing rowdy drunken fellas out of the Queen's Head, but that was as far as it went. He wasn't a violent man; he'd never pick a fight. He didn't have a quick temper or a bad bone in his body. Ruby shook her head. No, she couldn't allow him to get hurt. Somehow she had to make him call the fight off.

However, little did Ruby know that the first bets had already been placed. Money had begun to change hands and the odds were firmly stacked in Ronnie's favour. As daylight broke on that late August morning, news began to spread around Ryhope about the fight at the Blood Pit on Saturday. Nothing and no one could stop it now. Not unless one of the fighters pulled out, and there was little chance of that happening when there was pride – and money – at stake.

As Ruby toasted the bread, her thoughts ran to Abigail and Emily. She felt heartbroken for Emily and disappointed in Abigail after finding out the truth. How could her friend neglect her baby like that? How could anyone leave such a helpless creature alone in the dark, crying and in need of love? Was Abigail's problem simply that she didn't know how to care for her child? Was her own upbringing, being neglected by her mother, repeating itself now? Or was there something deeper going on? Ruby shook her head; she didn't know what she could do to help other than talk to her friend. But if Abigail had her mind set on going out with men, would anything Ruby said make any difference? How complicated it was. And at the heart of it all, baby Emily was the one who suffered. Ruby's heart went again to the child.

'Ruby! The bread!' Mary called.

Ruby snapped to attention and yanked the poker from the fire. The bread was charred black. Smoke curled into the kitchen.

'Get rid of it,' Mary advised. 'It's no good for eating now.'

Ruby pushed the burned bread from the poker and was about to throw it into the flames when Lady began to whine. She dropped the bread on the floor, where the dog devoured each blackened crumb.

'Sorry, Mam, I was miles away.'

'Again?' Mary muttered. 'How many times have I told you to concentrate when you're cooking?'

'I was thinking about last night, about Stan, and about Abigail and the baby.'

Mary sank into a chair opposite her. 'Me too,' she said. 'What Abigail's doing is wrong. She could have her bairn taken off her if she's not careful. I was so churned up about it that I didn't get much sleep. And what about Stan? Are you going to talk to him to see if he'll pull out of the fight? I daresay his parents won't want him to be involved. The three of you can work on him, surely, and make him see sense?'

'I'll try,' Ruby said. 'But there must be a reason he's agreed to do it. I just can't think what it might be. Stan, fighting? It's not in his nature, Mam. And as for Abigail, I don't know what to think. My head's spinning after what Gladys told us.'

'You never know what goes on behind closed doors, that's a fact,' Mary said sadly. 'We think we've got problems, but we're not suffering like Abigail and that poor little child.' She handed Ruby another chunk of bread. 'Here, try this. You've not eaten anything yet.'

Ruby pushed the bread on to the poker and slid it back over the flames.

'Keep your eye on this one,' Mary warned.

Ruby kept watch until the white of the bread turned golden and crisp. Then she pulled it from the fire and laid the poker on the hearth.

'There's some blackcurrant jam in the pantry,' Mary said.

Ruby's eyes lit up. 'Jam?'

'Ann Hutton brought a couple of jars yesterday. She's been picking berries down at High Farm.'

The mention of Ann's name reminded Ruby of her promise to Polly. 'Is Ann's fella still calling on her?'

Mary thought for a moment. 'The whippet man? Elsie hasn't mentioned him in a while. Why do you ask?'

Ruby told her mam about reconciling with Polly the previous night, and about the trouble Polly had in the pub caused by Ann's friend setting the fellas off gambling.

'There's no harm in having a word with her, I suppose,' Mary said. 'Although whether she'll have any influence over him remains to be seen.'

Ruby spread the chunky dark jam on her toast. 'I'll speak to her this morning and talk to Stan this afternoon,' she said, then she bit down into the warm bread, feeling its delicious crunch in her mouth and the sweet berries on her tongue.

Later that morning, Ruby walked down the back lane with Lady at her side, heading for the house where the two Miss Huttons lived. She found Elsie and Ann sitting in the yard, a clippy mat stretched on a frame across their knees. The sisters worked in silence, concentrating hard on pushing coloured scraps of cloth through holes in the tightly stretched hessian. It was slow, laborious work, but the end product would be a thick, colourful mat to keep the chill off their feet in the cold days to come.

'Morning, Ruby, what can we do for you?' Elsie called when Ruby entered the yard.

'I've come to speak to Ann.'

Ann's head shot up. 'Me? What have I done to deserve the honour?' She smiled. 'It's normally Elsie that you and your mam have business with. Speaking of your mam, did she like the jam?'

'We both did,' Ruby said.

Ann laid down her progger, the little tool used for pushing the scraps of cloth through the hessian, and looked at Ruby.

'The Queen's Head . . .' Ruby began, not entirely sure how to frame her request.

'The pub, yes?' Ann said. 'What about it?'

'They're having a few problems. I mean, Polly's having a bit of bother with one of the men who goes in there.'

Elsie rolled her eyes. 'It's nowt *but* trouble, that pub. But what's it got to do with our Ann?'

'Well . . .' Ruby said. She swallowed hard before continuing. 'There've been more fights breaking out lately; the men are getting angry with someone who's started going in there, a fella who encourages them to gamble.' She bit her lip. Had she said enough for Ann to catch the meaning behind her words?

'I knew it,' Elsie said, casting a glance at her sister. 'I told you he was up to no good.'

'Is it my friend the whippet man?' Ann asked.

'Course it's him,' Elsie said.

Ruby nodded.

'Leave it with me,' Ann said matter-of-factly. 'I'll have a word when I see him next.'

Ruby breathed a sigh of relief. Ann returned to her work, head down, fingers working quickly. Elsie, however, sat back in her chair and eyed Ruby keenly.

'How are things with you, Ruby?'

'You don't want to know. If I started to tell you, I wouldn't know where to stop.'

'Everything's all right between you and Stan, though, right?'

'I hope so,' Ruby said, thinking of the conversation about the fight she would have with Stan later that day.

Elsie lifted her end of the frame from her lap, stood from the chair and stretched her arms up in the air.

'You all right if I disappear with Ruby for a while?' she asked Ann.

Ann gave a sharp nod.

Elsie threaded her arm through Ruby's. 'Come on. I'm itching for some fresh air and exercise. I've been cooped up here working on that flaming mat since sunrise.'

Ruby and Elsie headed into the lane with Lady. Elsie asked how Ruby's mam was, and about her dad too. Ruby told her about Michael and his new friend Grace, the nurse at the asylum.

'Did old Sowerby ever pay up over . . .' Elsie paused, reminding herself not to use Gordon's name in Ruby's presence, as Ruby had requested, 'his clothes and whatnot, as she promised?'

Ruby shook her head. 'I've called at the house that many times I've lost count. But each time I go there, Mrs Sowerby isn't in and there's no answer at the door.'

Elsie's face clouded over. 'Come on, let's go for a walk.'

Ruby was confused. 'A walk? Where?'

'Mrs Sowerby's house. I'm going to get you your money back whether Sour Face Sowerby wants to give it to you or not.'

Chapter Forty-Two

Ruby and Elsie headed down the colliery bank with Lady.

'What's up with you and Stan, then?' Elsie asked.

'Oh, nothing,' Ruby sighed.

'That sigh doesn't sound like nothing,' Elsie said. 'Come on, you can tell me. If it's private and you don't want me to mention it to your mam, you know I can keep a secret.'

Ruby was about to tell Elsie about the fight Stan had managed to get himself involved in when they heard the clip of a horse's hooves behind them and a wooden cart slowed to a stop at their side.

'Elsie! Elsie, my little darling!' a man's voice called.

Ruby and Elsie turned to see Bert Collins driving the store's cart with his big black horse Lucky Star.

Elsie winked at Ruby 'Would you just listen to him? *Darling*, he calls me!'

Ruby watched as Elsie and Bert chatted and flirted, the banter flowing easily between them and ending with Elsie inviting Bert to tea on Friday. Bert blew her a kiss, told her his heart would burst without her until he saw her again, and then geed up the horse and continued on his delivery round. Ruby and Elsie walked on and Ruby saw that Elsie's face was flushed.

'I didn't have you down as the type to get embarrassed easily,' she said kindly.

Elsie's hands flew to her face. 'I haven't gone red, have I?' Ruby nodded.

'He always does that to me, that fella.'

'He's clearly besotted with you, Elsie.'

Elsie pushed her hair behind her ears and gazed into the distance, watching Bert and his horse and cart make their way past St Paul's church. 'Trouble is, there's nothing I can do. There's no future for me and Bert. How can there be? I can't leave Ann. It wouldn't be fair.' A troubled look crossed her face. 'Me and Ann, we know each other inside and out. What use would it be if I got married, at my age, and moved out to live with a fella? Why rock the boat when things are going smoothly?'

She waved her hand dismissively, changing the subject.

'Anyway, forget Bert, what's going on with you and Stan?'

Ruby told Elsie about the fight.

'Stan?' Elsie said, shocked. 'Fighting at the Blood Pit?'

'That's what I've heard,' Ruby said. 'I'm going to speak to him this afternoon and find out what's going on. He's up against someone called Ronnie Clarke.'

'The fella who's living with Kate?'

'That's him,' Ruby said.

At the mention of Kate, Ruby wondered about confiding in Elsie about Abigail neglecting her child, and what she'd learned from Gladys. Maybe Elsie could offer advice. However, they were approaching the corner of Burdon Road, Mrs Sowerby's house lay ahead and their conversation changed to what Elsie planned to do.

'Let me do the talking,' she said.

Ruby led the way along Mrs Sowerby's garden path. She noticed that an upstairs window was open to let in the warm air of the late summer day.

'There's someone home, at least,' Elsie said, glancing up.

Ruby knocked hard at the green door, then took a step back and squared her shoulders, ready to take on Mrs Sowerby if she answered. But as always, there was no reply, no sound from within, no movement at the front window. She knocked harder, then again, but still there was no response.

'Here, let me try,' Elsie said. She banged on the door with her fist, four, five times. When there was no reply, she lifted the heavy cast-iron letter box, peered inside, then yelled, 'Come on! We know you're in there, Sowerby! And we're not leaving until you answer the flaming door!'

She stood back. Ruby fully expected the door to be flung open and Mrs Sowerby to answer with a furious look on her face. But still there was nothing. Elsie stepped further back, shielded her eyes from the sun and glared up at the open window. Then she had a thought. 'Follow me. We're going to try the back door.'

Ruby hesitated. It felt wrong to be heading into Mrs Sowerby's back garden. They'd be invading the woman's privacy; besides, there was a fence they would need to climb to get in.

'Well, don't just stand there like a jug of milk!' Elsie cried.

Ruby glanced around, and only when she was certain the coast was clear did she hitch her skirt above her knees and carefully climb over the wooden fence.

'Stay, Lady,' she ordered the dog, then followed Elsie into the garden at the back.

It was a small garden, well tended, with a display of yellow and purple pansies along with pretty red flowers Ruby didn't know the names of. It was a little oasis, with bushes and trees framing the flowers within. How pretty it was, she thought, pausing to look around; how comforting to have such a beautiful space to sit in on a sunny day instead of a dirty back yard like the Dinsdales'.

Elsie, however, marched straight to the back door and banged on it with her fist. 'Come on, Sowerby. I'm not leaving until you show your face.'

Mrs Sowerby appeared at a small kitchen window, peering out anxiously to see who was making so much noise.

'Get out here, you old bat!' Elsie yelled.

Ruby tutted loudly. 'Elsie, that's a bit harsh.'

But Elsie had the bit between her teeth. 'Come on!' she called. 'Open up now or I'll smash your bloody window.'

Ruby stared at her. She'd always known Elsie had a lot of spirit, but she was learning a lot about how determined her mam's best friend could be.

The back door slowly opened, and Mrs Sowerby stood in front of them, one hand gripping the handle, the other planted on her hip. She looked from Elsie to Ruby and her face dropped as realisation set in. She knew there could only be one reason for their call; she'd finally been caught.

Ruby pasted a smile on her face. 'Mrs Sowerby, Elsie's come with me today for support. I'm hoping you've got an answer for me about whether you've sold Gordon Fisher's belongings.'

'She wants more than an answer. She wants the money she's owed,' Elsie said.

'Elsie Hutton.' Mrs Sowerby shook her head. 'You always were a troublemaker.'

'And you always were a mean old goat.'

Ruby stepped forward, positioning herself between the two women, hoping to calm tempers. Mrs Sowerby drew herself up to her full height and sucked air through her teeth. She knew she had no choice now but to do what she should have done eight long months ago.

'Very well. Wait here.'

The door closed in Ruby and Elsie's faces. Elsie let out a long sigh of relief. 'I think we did it,' she breathed.

Ruby crossed her fingers and waited. After a few moments the door opened again abruptly.

'Here,' Mrs Sowerby said. She thrust a small white envelope at Ruby.

Ruby took it, felt the heavy weight of the coins, heard them as they clinked against her fingers.

Mrs Sowerby glared at Elsie. 'Check it, it's all there,' she barked.

Ruby opened the envelope. There was more money inside than she'd expected; a lot more.

'I don't understand . . .' she began, looking into Mrs Sowerby's eyes.

'Is it not enough?' Elsie said.

'It's too much,' Ruby said, confused.

'Your Mr Fisher paid in advance when he started renting his room. I always make my lodgers pay in advance. Two weeks' rent is what I ask when they join me, and two weeks' rent is what I give back to them when they leave. Plus there's a few extra bob in there from the bits and pieces I sold to Meg Sutcliffe's rag-and-bone round.'

Elsie stepped forward and spoke sharply. 'You've had that money for months! Months! And you knew it didn't belong to you. You knew it was money that Ruby should have had at the turn of the year. Shame on you, Sowerby. Shame.'

But Mrs Sowerby wasn't in the least bit intimidated. 'There's no shame in what I do. I'm a businesswoman. I've got to look after my own interests. If I don't do it, no bugger else will.' She scowled, then gave a nod towards Ruby, talking about her as if she wasn't there. 'Anyway, she could have had the money sooner if she'd wanted it. If she'd been desperate enough to catch me in, she would've done what you did today.'

'I tried many times to catch you in, Mrs Sowerby. I came every week,' Ruby said firmly, but Mrs Sowerby ignored her and carried on.

'And if she'd had her wits about her, she would have known her fella had paid me in advance. Makes you wonder how many other secrets he was keeping from her, doesn't it? It seems to me there was a lot she didn't know. From what I've heard, she was a blind fool, didn't even know he was having it away with her best friend!'

Ruby gasped, unable to take any more. 'Mrs Sowerby! There is *no* need for that!'

'You hadn't a clue what went on under your own nose,' Mrs Sowerby said spitefully.

Elsie took Ruby's arm and turned her away from the door. 'Come on, we don't have to stay here and be insulted,' she said over her shoulder, making sure Mrs Sowerby heard.

The landlady put both hands on her hips and cocked her head to one side. 'Why, where do you normally go?'

The comment was too much for Elsie. She dropped Ruby's arm, spun around and was about to lunge at Mrs Sowerby when Ruby pulled her back.

'Leave her, Elsie. She's not worth it.'

Elsie was like a caged animal, her breath coming out of her thick and fast. She shook Ruby off, then walked slowly back to Mrs Sowerby, delivering her final words in a smooth, even voice. 'Rest assured, Mrs Sowerby, we'll be counting every single penny in that envelope. And if we find there's just one ha'penny missing, we'll be back.'

'Think I'm scared of you two?' Mrs Sowerby hissed.

'We'll be back,' Elsie repeated, locking eyes with her. 'And we'll bring fellas with us. Fellas with strong fists and no qualms about who they might hurt.'

'Do that and I'll set the coppers on you.'

'You've been warned, Mrs Sowerby,' Elsie said. 'And if you dare breathe a word of any of this around Ryhope, we'll be back even sooner than planned. And we'll tell everyone about you keeping tight hold of money that wasn't yours.'

The door slammed in her face.

'Come on,' Ruby said. 'Let's go home. I can't believe you did all that for me.'

'I can't believe I did it either,' Elsie smiled. 'Whatever you do, don't tell Ann. She'll never forgive me for saying what I did to old Sour Face.'

'It's our secret, I promise,' Ruby said.

'What'll you do with the money?' Elsie asked.

'Give it to Mam,' Ruby replied quickly. It was unthinkable that she'd do anything else.

Elsie turned to her with a mischievous glint in her eye. 'Does your mam need it all?'

'Of course,' Ruby said. She thought of the food it would buy: fresh beef from the butcher, a fish and chip supper for the whole family. Perhaps there might be enough spare to buy a bar of scented soap instead of the carbolic for their baths. Ruby had seen the advertisements for rose-scented soap in the pages of *The Red Letter*.

But Elsie wasn't ready to give up. As they headed back to Tunstall Street with Lady trotting behind them, she cast a sidelong glance at Ruby.

'That fight you were telling me about . . .'

'What about it?'

'You reckon Stan might stand a chance?'

Ruby shrugged. 'He's a big lad, strong, but I don't know if he can fight.'

'Then ask him,' Elsie said, pulling Ruby close and whispering as they walked. 'When you speak to him this afternoon, find out all you can.'

'But I don't want him to get hurt. I don't want him to fight!' Ruby said.

'He might not have any choice,' Elsie said. 'Fights at the Blood Pit aren't games, love, they're not even sport. They're business. A lot of money is made there.'

'Lost too, I reckon,' Ruby said.

'That's as may be.' Elsie pulled her even closer. 'But you've got a canny little wager in your pocket. Bet it on the right man to win, and you might even double your money.' She raised her eyebrows and looked at Ruby meaningfully.

Ruby's mouth opened in shock. 'You mean . . .' she gulped, 'I should bet on Ronnie Clarke to win?'

Chapter Forty-Three

Ruby and Elsie walked on in silence, Ruby wondering if Elsie had lost her mind and Elsie wondering if she'd gone too far and said the wrong thing. When they reached the store, Ruby told Elsie to walk back to Tunstall Street without her.

'I'm going to have a word with Stan about the fight,' she said.

'Look, love,' Elsie began hesitantly. 'I maybe shouldn't have said what I did. It's just an awful lot of money you've got there in your pocket. Whatever you do with it, use it wisely, that's all I'm saying.' She gave Ruby a peck on the cheek and walked away.

Ruby carried on up the colliery bank, past the Blue Bell pub and the tobacconist and newsagent, until she reached the Queen's Head. The door was locked so early in the day, but she knew that if she banged at it long and hard enough, someone would answer. It was Polly who opened the door. She looked dishevelled, Ruby thought, as if she'd just woken from sleep, and she was scowling. There wasn't anything unusual in that, but Ruby was surprised by the look of tiredness etched on the landlady's face.

'Oh, it's you,' Polly said sullenly. She held the door open to let Ruby enter. 'If you're after Stan, he's in the yard.'

'Is everything all right, Polly? If you don't mind me saying so, you're looking a bit the worse for wear this morning.'

Polly looked at her hard. 'Did *you* know about this fight?'

Ruby shook her head. 'Not until Michael told me when he came home last night.'

'Think you can talk him out of it?' Polly asked. 'Because heaven only knows, me and Jim have tried. We were up all hours last night, but he's that bull-headed and stubborn. Why he's fighting he won't say, but he's determined to go through with it.'

'It's what I've come to speak to him about,' Ruby said.

'Go on through. I'm going back up to bed to see if I can catch up on some sleep.' She ushered Ruby into the bar and indicated the door that led out to the yard.

Ruby had expected Stan to be working out there, moving beer barrels or shifting boxes. But he was standing with his naked back to her, moving his arms in short jerks, left, right, left, right, hitting an imaginary opponent. Ruby had never seen him undressed before. She watched him a moment, saw the muscles in his back and shoulders shimmering with sweat as he worked his body hard.

'Stan?'

He spun around and dropped his arms to his sides. 'Hey! How are you?' he beamed. He held his hands up in mock surrender. 'I won't hug you, I'm a bit sweaty. I've been preparing for the fight, getting myself in shape.'

Ruby could smell the rawness of him, saw the power

in the muscles at the top of his arms. She'd come to talk him out of the fight, but standing in front of him at that moment, she wanted nothing more than to run her hands over his glistening skin. She gave her head a shake and tried to pull herself together.

'Have you been visiting with Abigail and the baby? How's little Emily doing?' he asked.

Ruby's head spun with everything that Gladys had said. Slowly she began to tell Stan what she'd learned about Abigail neglecting her child.

'I'm not sure what to do for the best,' she said.

'If I can help, let me know,' Stan said. 'I could have a word with Mam if it'll help.'

'No,' Ruby said quickly. 'Your mam's only just got her head around the idea of us two courting. I don't think she'd take too kindly to me asking for advice about Abigail's baby.'

'You'd be surprised. Mam's nowhere near as hard-hearted as she appears. And where bairns are concerned, she's got a real soft spot. You should see her with my brothers' little 'uns, her grandbairns. She adores them, wouldn't let anyone hurt a hair on their heads.'

A silence fell over them both for a moment.

'You're still determined to fight, then?' Ruby said. 'I was hoping to be able to talk you out of putting yourself in danger.'

Stan rested his bare back against the brick wall. Ruby studied him, took in the sight of his chest, his arms and his muscled shoulders.

He shook his head. 'I've made my mind up. Mam and Dad've tried to talk me out of it already. But I'm doing it, Ruby. I have to.'

'But why?' she cried. 'Ronnie Clarke'll knock you out to Silksworth and back. Did you know he used to be a boxer when he was young?'

Stan stared at her. He tried to form words, but none would come.

'You didn't know, did you?' Ruby said. 'Oh Stan. Listen to me. Don't do it. Call it off. The whippet man who's arranged it, he's a friend of Ann Hutton's, who lives in our street. I know Ann, she's as good as family; she'll have a word with him to ask him to send a message around Ryhope that the fight's been called off.'

Stan pushed himself off the wall and stood firm in front of her.

'I'm doing it, Ruby. I have to.'

'But why?' Ruby urged again.

Stan looked away from her imploring gaze.

'Your pride, is that it?' she said. 'Your stupid pride? You're willing to get yourself hurt, knocked about by that idiot of a man Ronnie Clarke?'

'How do you know so much about him?' Stan said.

'He lives with Abigail's mam,' Ruby said. 'And he knocks her about.'

'He hits women?' Stan said, visibly shocked.

'He hit Abigail too, when she was pregnant. It's why Abigail can't go home.'

Stan's face dropped. 'What kind of monster is he?'

'The worst kind,' Ruby said. 'You can't take on someone like him, Stan. He'll end up killing you, can't you see?'

Stan was silent for a moment, then he lifted his eyes to meet Ruby's. 'I'm doing it, Ruby. I've got to.'

Ruby sighed. 'And that's your final word on the subject, is it?' she said. 'Even if I begged you?'

'I'd still do it. There's more at stake than you know.'

'I thought I knew you, Stan Hutchinson,' she said sadly. And with that, she began to walk from the yard.

'Ruby!' Stan called, but she kept walking, back into the pub then out to the street.

Alone in the yard, Stan picked up a length of old rope he'd found in the stables and began using it as a skipping rope until his heart was pounding again. He couldn't tell her what Ronnie Clarke had said about her in the pub. No woman deserved to hear lewd words spoken about them, and certainly not his precious Ruby.

Ruby was furious with Stan, and scared for him too. Outside the pub, she turned her face to the sky, closed her eyes and took a deep breath. She was too upset to go home. Her dad would be up out of bed, and she couldn't cope with any questions about Stan and the fight, or about Abigail and Emily. Instead, she decided to head to Gladys's house. She still wasn't sure what she could do to help Abigail, or even what she would say, but she had to at least try to understand what was going on.

When Gladys opened the door of her tiny cottage, she was holding Emily. Ruby's heart sank.

'Morning, Gladys,' she said. 'I was hoping to have a word with Abigail, but I see she's left you with the baby again. Has she been out all night?'

'You'd better come in,' Gladys said.

'Hello, little one,' Ruby greeted the baby, and Emily kicked her legs and smiled in return. Gladys stood to one side and Ruby entered a narrow, dark hallway. Despite the warmth of the day, the cottage held an unwelcome chill.

'We'll talk in the parlour,' Gladys said.

Ruby followed her into a small, square room. There was a window that looked out to the street, and an empty fireplace dominated the room. Two armchairs sat either side of the hearth, and a heavy, dark wooden sideboard ran along one wall. In front of the hearth, between the chairs, was a mat made of green and brown clippings, nowhere near as big or as pretty as the mats the two Miss Huttons made. There was a mothball scent in the air.

'Please, have a seat,' Gladys said, indicating one of the chairs. She settled herself into the chair opposite, cradling Emily.

'Did she go out again with a fella last night?'

Gladys raised her eyes to the ceiling. 'No, she's upstairs in bed. She's not well, love.'

'She still has the cough?'

'And more,' Gladys said. 'She's been coughing up blood.'

An icy chill ran down Ruby's spine. 'Blood?'

'I walked to Dr Anderson's house this morning, took the little 'un with me to ask if he could come, but he was out on his rounds. I left a message with Sylvia, his daughter. She said she'd get him to call as soon as she could.'

'Abigail can't afford the doctor,' Ruby said. Her hand went to her pocket, where the envelope of money lay heavy. She was on the verge of offering to pay, acting on instinct to help her friend.

'But I can,' Gladys said. 'I'll pay.'

Ruby was surprised at the rush of relief that flooded through her. In her heart she knew her money must go to her mam.

'I'm not an ogre, Ruby. When I took your friend in, it was as much for my benefit as it was for hers. Since Freddie died, it's not been easy. A widow woman's life . . .' Gladys shook her head. 'But I never expected her to turn out the way she did. I was hoping – wrongly, I know – for someone a little different, someone without so many problems.' She stroked Emily's tiny face. 'I got more than I bargained for. I'm too old for this.'

'How is she? Can I go and see her?' Ruby asked.

'Up the stairs, first door on the left,' Gladys said.

Ruby left the room and headed into the hall. With each step, the pungent mothball smell became stronger. She put a hand to her pocket to feel for the envelope of coins Mrs Sowerby had given her.

Abigail's bedroom door was closed. Ruby knocked lightly. 'Abigail?'

There was no answer, so she turned the handle and opened the door. The room was dark inside, heavy curtains closed at the window. Ruby's eyes adjusted to the gloom until she could make out the bed where Abigail lay under the blankets.

'Abigail? It's me, Ruby.'

She crept towards the bed, but Abigail didn't turn or wake. Standing close to the bed, she heard Abigail's chest wheeze with torturous breaths. She left the room as silently as she'd entered, closed the door firmly and headed downstairs.

'Will you have a cup of tea while you're here?' Gladys asked once Ruby was back in the parlour.

'No, I shouldn't,' Ruby said. 'I've been out long enough; Mam will be wondering where I've gone, and there's sewing to be done.'

'Please?' Gladys pleaded. 'I wouldn't normally press you, Ruby, but I've got Abigail's sheets to wash that I took off her bed this morning, and bloodstains, well, you know how difficult they are to remove once they're left to dry. I thought you might look after Emily while I get them done.'

Ruby's gaze lingered on Emily's sweet face. Her heart lurched with a mixture of emotions as she struggled to comprehend how on earth Abigail could neglect such a precious little life.

'Of course I'll stay,' she said.

Gladys stood with Emily in her arms and passed her across. 'I'll go and put the kettle on,' she said as she bustled away.

Holding the baby carefully, Ruby sank back into the armchair. There was silence in the room, perfect silence, just the almost imperceptible sound of Emily's breath in the air. Ruby gazed into her face: her tiny mouth, her delicate nose, her clear blue eyes staring up at her.

'Hello, little girl,' she said.

Emily kicked her feet and gurgled with pleasure at the sound of Ruby's voice. And then came a noise from above, from Abigail's room, a great hacking sound as a cough racked Abigail's body. Ruby winced as she listened, but knew there was nothing she could do.

Within a few minutes, Gladys returned with a hot mug of tea, which she set on the hearth at Ruby's feet.

'I don't have sugar, so you'll have to take it as is,' she said.

'She's been coughing again. I've just heard her,' Ruby said.

Gladys looked up to the ceiling. 'Heaven only knows

what time the doctor might arrive. Now if you'll excuse me, I'll go and see to those sheets. Are you sure you don't mind looking after Emily while I'm busy? And if there's a knock at the door, it'll be the doctor; no one else ever calls. Send him upstairs, then come and find me. I'll be in the yard.'

'I'll be fine,' Ruby said, smiling down at Emily. 'The two of us will be just fine.'

Chapter Forty-Four

Gently and softly, Ruby began to sing, letting the notes rise and fall around Emily, who seemed to enjoy the sound, kicking and smiling. Ruby felt joyful in a way she had never done before. She gazed at Emily's face, those clear blue eyes staring up at her, and felt her heart bursting with love.

There was a sharp knock at the front door.

'That'll be the doctor,' she whispered to Emily.

She walked into the hallway and opened the door. Sure enough, it was Dr Anderson.

'Mrs Smith?' he said politely.

'No, I'm a friend. Come in, Doctor. Gladys is in the yard. I'll fetch her. Your patient is in a bedroom upstairs.'

While Gladys and Dr Anderson were with Abigail, Ruby walked around the living room with Emily, chatting to her, enjoying seeing her face break into a smile. Meanwhile, the black iron hands on the mantelpiece clock ticked the minutes away. Some time later, she heard footsteps coming downstairs. She moved towards the parlour door, positioning herself so that she couldn't be seen but could catch the conversation between Gladys and Dr Anderson.

'Does she have family?' the doctor asked.

'A mother, I believe,' Gladys replied.

'Then fetch her,' Dr Anderson said gravely. 'She may not see the end of the week. I'm sure her mother will want to say her goodbyes.'

Ruby gasped with shock. Feeling her legs go weak, and worrying for Emily's safety, she moved from the doorway and sank into a chair.

'Thank you, Doctor, I'll send word immediately. And when she goes?' Gladys asked.

'Let me know,' Dr Anderson said. 'I'll arrange the certificate, and removal of her body.'

Ruby covered her mouth with her free hand to stifle her cry. She could hardly believe what she'd heard. Blood pounded in her ears and her heart sped with fright. She kissed Emily protectively on the top of her head.

She heard the front door open, heard the doctor saying goodbye, and then Gladys was at her side, standing by the chair. Ruby looked up and saw tears in her eyes. Gladys swallowed hard.

'Did you hear any of that?'

Ruby nodded. There was no point in pretending. Gladys sank into the chair opposite, shaking her head.

'I knew she was ill . . . I knew it was serious, but I never expected anything like this. A blockage in her lungs, the doctor says. It must have been there for some time.'

'Do you think she knew?' Ruby began hesitantly. 'Maybe she'd been feeling unwell for some time and that's why she was making the most of the time she had left – you know, with her men.'

'It's possible,' Gladys said. She reached for Emily. 'May I?' she said to Ruby.

Ruby gladly handed the child over, for her arms were aching with the weight of her.

'The poor little mite,' Gladys said. 'What hope is there for her without her mam, even if . . .'

'Even if her mam was someone like Abigail?' Ruby said coldly.

'No child deserves such neglect,' Gladys said, giving Ruby a hard look.

'Just as Abigail deserved a better life too.'

Gladys's stern expression softened. 'Was her mam as bad as I've heard?'

'Worse,' Ruby said, remembering when she and Abigail had been girls. She told Gladys about the times Kate didn't come home for days and Mary had to take Abigail in to feed her and give her a bath. She told her of the nights when she and Abigail shared a bed at the Dinsdales' house because Kate had abandoned her daughter.

'Would you like me to go and tell Kate?' she offered.

'Would you mind?' Gladys said. 'It might be best if the news comes from you.'

Ruby straightened in her chair. 'I don't mind. I'll take Emily with me.'

'You won't leave her there, will you?' Gladys said, worried.

Ruby thought of Ronnie Clarke, of the bruises on Abigail's arms.

'I wouldn't dream of it,' she replied.

It was a sorry scene indeed that Ruby found in the house at the end of Railway Street. As she stood on the pavement, she heard screaming and yelling coming from inside. She banged hard at the door, and it was Ronnie who answered. It was the first time she had come face to face with the beast of a man she'd heard so much about. He was unshaven, and a beer bottle hung loosely from his hand. As Ruby demanded to see Kate, he brought the bottle to his lips and took a long swig. He swayed slightly and put his hand to the door frame, and Ruby knew in an instant that he was drunk.

Under his dirty, stained vest, his fat stomach rolled out over the top of his trousers. He might have been a fighting man in his youth, but he was very much out of shape now. The tops of his arms, where muscles might have bulged when he'd been a lad, hung flabby with loose skin. Ruby had expected to feel slightly afraid of meeting him, his reputation being as fearsome as it was. But the worn, tired drunk who stood in front of her now didn't scare her in the least.

She glared at him and told him she had important news for Kate, but she didn't mention Abigail's name. As far as she was concerned, Abigail was none of his business. Ronnie dragged Kate to the door, flung her out on to the street and slammed the door behind her. Kate was crying, her blouse torn, her hair matted to her head. Ruby's heart broke for her. As soon as Kate saw the pram, though, her face lit up, her arms reached to her granddaughter. And that was when Ruby told her the bad news about Abigail.

'Dr Anderson doesn't think she'll last the week,' she said. 'You've got to come now. It might be your last chance to say goodbye.'

Kate pushed her hair back from her face and looked to

the heavens. 'What have I done to deserve this?' she whispered.

'Come on, we'll go now,' Ruby said.

Kate backed away like a frightened rabbit. 'I can't. He'll want to know where I've gone. You don't understand. I can't go.'

'You can't say goodbye to your own daughter?' Ruby tried to keep her voice as calm as she could while anger built up inside her. 'She's dying, for God's sake! She's been ill for who knows how long.'

'No,' Kate said shaking her head. 'He'll come and find me. He'll punish me. I've got to go back inside.'

She made a move to run back to the house, but Ruby caught her arm. 'Kate, listen to me,' she said more harshly than she'd intended. 'Who are you going to choose? Him in there, a poor excuse of a man, a man who hits you, who hit Abigail when she was pregnant? Or will you choose your own flesh and blood? The girl you brought into this world. Abigail, the strong, strapping lass who played for Ryhope ladies' football club? The girl who was my friend? Is she to slip away alone, without her mam?'

She saw her words hit home, and a flicker of pain crossed Kate's face, but still she tried to pull away from Ruby's grip. Ruby dropped her arm. 'Kate, please, come and see her,' she pleaded. 'I know you've had your problems, but Abigail is dying. You've left her to fend for herself all of her life. I won't let you abandon her now.'

Kate's eyes darted between Ruby and the door of her home, then they rested on the pram with her granddaughter inside.

'Kate?'

She shook her head. 'I can't!' she cried.

The front door was flung open.

'Get in here,' Ronnie snarled.

Kate gave one final look of longing at Emily in the pram.

'Get in now, or else you know what'll happen,' Ronnie said.

Ruby stepped forward. 'I hear you used to be a boxer,' she spat. 'And it's come to this, has it? Hitting innocent women? Shame on you, Ronnie Clarke.'

Ronnie looked stunned. 'Who the hell are you to think you're better than the likes of me? I know your sort. Everyone in Ryhope knows. You're a fool, letting your fella get another lass pregnant. Shame on me?' He threw his head back, opened his mouth wide and laughed. Ruby saw his yellowed teeth, his unshaven face, the dirt in his fingernails. And she couldn't miss the stench that came off him. 'And now you've got mammy's boy Hutchinson wrapped around your little finger. I'll be knocking ten bells out of him soon, as I've no doubt you'll have heard by now.'

Ruby squared her shoulders. Her heart was going nineteen to the dozen, but she kept her feet firmly on the ground as she spoke. 'If you raise a fist to me, I'll go straight to the police and tell them what you're like. It's about time they knew the truth.'

'Get away with you,' Ronnie yelled, then he turned to Kate. 'And you, get yourself in here. Now.'

'Kate?' Ruby said. 'What's it to be?'

Kate stepped back from Ronnie's reach and stood behind Ruby and the pram. 'I'm going to see my daughter,' she said. 'She's not well.'

Ronnie glared at them both, then slammed the door

again. Behind it, they heard him roaring like a demon, cursing and swearing the worst kind of words.

'Let's go, before he comes after us,' Kate said.

The two of them began walking quickly, Ruby pushing the pram, then they broke into a run. Ruby lifted a hand from the pram and pushed the envelope of money further inside her pocket so that she wouldn't lose it. The pram's wheels kept catching in the rutted cobbles, but on Ruby and Kate ran, hearts pounding, until Railway Street was safely out of sight and Ronnie was far behind.

Chapter Forty-Five

'Kate's living with Gladys?' Mary said, trying to make sense of what Ruby had told her.

Ruby and Mary were in their kitchen, enjoying mugs of tea with Elsie Hutton. Elsie had brought some of her home-made crumpets, and her tin of golden syrup was softening on the warm hearth. Lady was sprawled on the floor.

'She's not living with her; she's just moved in for a few days to look after Abigail until she . . . Well, Dr Anderson says she only has a few days left.'

'Poor love,' Mary said. 'I can't imagine what must be going through Kate's mind. I wonder if I should go and ask Gladys if she needs any help.'

'I'd leave them be, Mam. Kate doesn't know whether she's coming or going.'

'And is the baby there too?' Elsie asked.

Ruby nodded. 'Gladys is looking after her.'

'Not Kate?'

'Kate's in no fit state to look after a baby; she can barely look after herself.'

'She never could. Railway Street will be no place for a

child with Ronnie living there, that's for sure,' Mary said. She took a sip of her tea, then glanced at Elsie. 'What do you think about our Ruby, then?' she said, changing the subject. 'She finally got her money out of old Sowerby.'

Elsie and Ruby exchanged a look.

'That's good news,' Elsie said. Her face gave nothing away as Mary carried on.

'She got a full week's rent back from Gordon's account. That'll go a long way to putting food on our table. We might even be able to afford a fish and chip supper for the first time since . . .' Mary paused, trying to remember the last time they'd eaten such a feast, 'since our Michael was in short trousers.'

Elsie raised an eyebrow towards Ruby. 'A full week's rent, eh?'

Ruby glared at her, offering up a silent prayer that Elsie wouldn't say anything more about the money she'd received from Mrs Sowerby. The last thing Ruby wanted was for her mam to find out that she was planning on spending some of the money on a bet at the fight.

'I reckon the syrup will be soft enough now,' Elsie said.

Ruby's shoulders dropped with relief, and her hand went to the envelope in her pocket. After handing over half the money to her mam, she'd stuffed a piece of cloth in her pocket. It helped to stop the coins jangling and giving the game away. She didn't want to alert Mary to the extra cash, not yet. Not when there was a chance to earn more money from it. If she told her her plan, she knew she wouldn't be allowed to carry it through.

Mary lifted the heavy syrup tin and set to spreading the sweet, thick golden syrup on the crumpets. Ruby bit into hers, letting the syrup ooze in her mouth, savouring each bite. Lady looked pleadingly from Mary to Ruby, hoping for a bite of crumpet, but she was to be disappointed.

'I'll have to get the water on for Arthur's bath after I've eaten this,' Mary said. 'He'll be home soon.'

'And I'll have to get back to Ann,' Elsie said. 'I've given her a bit of space. Her fella turned up this morning.'

Ruby shot her a look. 'The whippet man's at your house right now?'

Elsie nodded. 'He might still be there, if Ann hasn't had words with him,' she said. 'She's getting a bit fed up with him, to be honest. She never knows when she'll see him. He turns up out of the blue without a word about where he's been. And now she knows about the trouble he's been causing at the Queen's Head, she's not happy with him at all.'

Ruby stuffed the rest of the crumpet in her mouth and licked the syrup from her fingers.

'Mam? Could I go and have a quick word with . . . with Ann?'

'Shouldn't you leave them, love, if Ann and her fella are having words?'

'She's fine, let her go,' Elsie said, guessing correctly that it wasn't Ann Ruby was so desperate to see.

The tall, gangly man with the red neckerchief was coming out of the yard when Ruby reached the house where the two Miss Huttons lived. She was about to call out to him before she realised she didn't know his name. He was simply the whippet man; everyone on the pit lanes knew him that way.

'Mister!' she shouted.

The man turned instantly and flashed her a smile. 'What can I do for you?'

'I'm a friend of Ann's,' Ruby began, nodding towards the yard he'd just left.

'Ah, if only I could count myself as one of Ann's friends too,' he said sadly. Ruby saw him glance at the house and shake his head.

'But I thought you two were close?' she said.

'We were,' he said gently. 'And we might be again one day. But for now, little lady, what can I do for you?'

Ruby took a deep breath. 'I hear you're taking bets on the fight?'

Elsie walked home carrying her tin of golden syrup and the plate on which she'd brought the crumpets to Mary's house. As she neared her yard, she could see Ruby talking to the whippet man. She was too far away to hear what was being said, but she guessed what Ruby was up to. She felt torn. Mary was her best friend. But she'd promised Ruby she would keep the money received on their visit to Mrs Sowerby a secret. She saw Ruby dig into her pocket, then saw the flash of white envelope as she handed over her coins. The whippet man took out a small notepad and pencil from his pocket, scribbled something on it, tore a sheet from the book and handed it to Ruby. Then, without another word, he went on his way.

Ruby turned to walk back up the lane, but when she caught sight of Elsie coming towards her, she stood stock still.

'I see you took my advice after all,' Elsie said. 'Don't

worry, I won't breathe a word. I'm assuming you'll be at the fight?'

Ruby glanced at the signed piece of paper in her hand. 'I wouldn't miss it for the world.'

When Saturday came, Ruby woke with an awful churning in her stomach. Earlier that week, Michael had told her that Stan had taken to running, and when he wasn't working in the pub, he was out in the yard throwing punches, skipping with a length of rope or doing press-ups. Now the fight was just hours away. Stan had asked Ruby not to come and see him before the fight. He said he'd be too busy, too nervous.

The day wore slowly on. Arthur came home from work at midday and Ruby helped her mam prepare his bath. While Mary scrubbed Arthur's back, Ruby took Lady for a walk past the Queen's Head. She wanted to be near Stan, and this was the closest she knew she could get. She saw a handwritten note nailed to the door. It was an announcement to say the pub would be closed that night. She wondered if it had been Polly's decision to close the pub, to keep Stan away from the men who would be eyeing him up and wondering how much to bet on Ronnie after closing time at the Toll Bar.

Back home, Ruby sat with her dad by the fire while Mary visited Elsie and Ann.

'Will you be at the fight, Dad?'

'Course I will, pet,' Arthur replied. 'But it won't be pretty, I'll tell you that now. Get rid of any fancy notions from your head. It's going to be brutal and raw. It's not called the Blood Pit for nothing. And Stan could well come out of it much the worse for wear.'

'I hear Ronnie used to be a boxer, is that right?'

'It was a long time ago, but he could throw a decent punch.'

'And now?' Ruby asked.

Arthur laughed. 'Now? Ronnie Clarke's a waste of space, everyone in Ryhope knows it. You saw what he did to Abigail, what he does to Kate. Only a coward hits women.'

As the night drew in, the fire roared high in the Dinsdales' kitchen. Mary served a dinner of potatoes, leeks and bacon. Not for the first time, Ruby felt guilt stab her heart. She closed her eyes, forcing the tears back. If her mam ever found out what she'd done with the remainder of Gordon's rent money, she'd never forgive her. What had she been thinking? There were bills to be paid, boots to be bought for Michael, trousers to fit his growing frame. She opened her eyes, looked at her mam's worn, lined face, her sad expression. How could she have done it to them? How could she have deprived them and been so selfish? She ate in silence, forcing each mouthful down.

The clock on the mantelpiece ticked the minutes and hours away until it was time to set off to the fight. Lady was forced to stay in the yard. Ruby, Michael, Arthur and Mary headed into the night for the walk to the Blood Pit. Elsie and Ann joined them in the back lane and the small group walked together. Others from Ryhope were heading in the same direction. At a quarter to midnight, Ruby and her family reached the Toll Bar hotel. Oil lamps flickered in the windows; the place was open for business, serving drink at the bar.

'They know the police won't come, not on the night

of a fight; it's too dangerous for them,' Arthur told Mary.

Mary looked at the pub, inviting, cosy and warm. The thought of cold beer trickling down her throat sent a shiver running through her. How easy it would be, how delicious, she thought, to give in to temptation again.

'Will we take a drink before the fight?' she asked. But as she licked her lips in anticipation, an almighty roar went up behind the pub. Arthur laid his arm protectively around her shoulders and pulled her to him, all mention of drink forgotten.

Ruby and Michael walked ahead, and Ruby gasped when she saw the Blood Pit. It was a square marked out roughly by sticks, logs and stones on the ground. In each corner, a low fire burned, throwing shadows around and sending sparks shooting into the night. She saw the whippet man first, his face twisted with excitement as he called for silence. Ruby and Michael pushed their way forward. Ruby scanned the crowd for Stan and finally found him standing with his mam and dad behind the whippet man. A small group of men were gathered beside the Hutchinsons, and Ruby guessed these were Stan's older brothers. She hadn't yet met them, but there was no denying their resemblance to Stan.

'Ronnie Clarke!' the whippet man yelled, and the crowd roared again as Ronnie stepped forward into the burning square.

'Stan Hutchinson!' the whippet man yelled. This time there was a more muted response.

Both men were naked from the waist up. Ronnie Clarke's muscles were soft, his stomach bulging. Ruby looked at Stan, hoping he would catch her eye and acknowledge that he'd seen her, but he was staring straight ahead, concentrating, his body tense.

'He'll be all right,' Michael said to Ruby, sensing her unease.

Ruby looked at her beautiful Stan, her gentle, calm, good-natured Stan. His muscles were lit by the light of the flames as they flickered over his body. He looked scared, she thought, scared and out of place. Her glance flicked to Polly and Jim behind him, and she saw Polly make the sign of the cross, saw Jim with his pipe hanging from his mouth.

Jim slapped Stan on the back. 'Good luck, son.'

Ruby crossed her fingers. She could feel the heat on the side of her face from the fire at the nearest corner. There was silence as the two men faced each other. The whippet man said something to them both that the crowd couldn't hear, then stood to one side. He untied his red neckerchief and held it high above his head. Then he brought it down sharply, the signal for the fight to begin.

An almighty roar went up, a bloodthirsty roar, a feral sound that made Ruby's heart pound. She reached for Michael's hand as the crowd behind and around them pushed this way and that, shouting and yelling. She heard Ronnie's name being called.

'Get him, Ronnie!'

'Come on, Ronnie, do your stuff!'

Stan was hesitant, holding back, defending himself against Ronnie's blows rather than attacking his opponent. Yet Ronnie's swings and punches seemed even to Ruby's untrained eye clumsy and random, and Stan easily batted his fists away.

'Get into him, Ronnie! What are you waiting for?'

'Lost his touch.'

'Bloody useless.'

'Too much ale, that's Ronnie's trouble.'

Ruby looked around her, saw men shaking their heads, despairing. She saw one man tear his betting slip in two and throw the pieces to the ground before walking off in disgust.

The fight continued. Ronnie swayed from side to side, muscle memory from his days as a boxer coming back to him now. He began jabbing at Stan, hitting him harder, faster, dancing from foot to foot. Stan easily stepped up to match Ronnie's more eager strategy. All those days he had spent in the yard at the Queen's Head doing press-ups and sit-ups, all those hours running and skipping and getting his body in shape for the fight, all those years of heavy manual work, moving beer barrels in the pub, throwing out unruly customers – all of it had prepared him for this moment. He might not have a good fighting technique, but he had strength and youth on his side.

As Ronnie continued attacking, Stan kept defending until it was almost too much for Polly to bear.

'Hit him, Stan!' she yelled. 'For God's sake, just hit him!'

'Couldn't hit the skin off a rice pudding, that one,' a fella called.

Stan's right arm shot out and caught Ronnie Clarke hard on the shoulder. Ronnie's body twisted, the force of the blow knocking him off his feet, and he fell to the ground like a wounded animal. Stan waited, moving from foot to foot, fists up, teeth bared. Ruby had never seen him so angry. Ronnie tried to get up, but the pain in his shoulder kept him pinned to the ground. The whippet man stepped forward and looked down at him. Then he took his red neckerchief from his pocket and raised it high.

'No! I'm not done yet!' Ronnie cried.

'Then get up, Clarke,' the whippet man said. 'Or this flag comes down.'

Ronnie struggled, but it was no use, and he sank back to the ground, arms splayed, exhausted. The red neckerchief was thrown down. A murmur rippled through the crowd. This wasn't the fight they'd wanted, the fight that had been promised, the fight they had bet on. The whippet man took Stan's hand and held it high.

'Stan Hutchinson wins!' he called. 'Stan Hutchinson wins! All bets on Stan Hutchinson will be paid inside the Toll Bar hotel!'

'Anyone daft enough to have bet on him, you mean,' a fella called.

'I wish I had now,' another one yelled, throwing his ticket to the ground.

The crowd thinned out, disappointed that no blood had been spilled and that the fight had ended so soon. As they made their way home, Polly and Jim huddled around Stan, Polly checking his face for wounds.

Ruby let go of Michael's hand. 'Tell Mam and Dad I'll meet them at the Queen's Head.'

'It's a result we thought we'd never see,' Michael said. 'I'm shocked that Stan won.'

'You're not the only one,' said Ruby, and she walked around the burning corners of the Blood Pit towards Stan.

Polly and Jim were saying their goodbyes to Stan's brothers as the lads walked into the night back to their wives and bairns. As soon as Stan saw Ruby, he opened his arms. He was sweating and dirty, and blood was running from a wound on his face where Ronnie had caught him. Ruby fell into his arms. She felt the heat from his body surround her.

'I love you, Ruby,' he whispered.

'I love you too,' she replied.

'Come on, you two,' Jim said. 'Let's get back to the pub, get Stan cleaned up and have a drink. We've got some celebrating to do.'

Polly cast a nervous glance at the lights inside the Toll Bar hotel. Jim slid his arm around her shoulders. 'Don't worry, the coppers won't come to the Queen's Head tonight, just as they'll avoid the Toll Bar. They'll not come anywhere near Ryhope after a Blood Pit fight,' he said.

Polly handed Stan his shirt.

'Are you coming to the pub for a drink?' Stan asked Ruby.

'Of course,' she said. 'But I'll follow on in a moment. There's something I need to do first.'

She watched Stan and his parents walk away, then headed to the Toll Bar hotel. Elsie was standing by the door, talking to Bert Collins. When Ruby reached them, she stepped to one side to let her in. As she passed, Elsie whispered in her ear.

'How much did you lose?'

Chapter Forty-Six

'You won?' Stan was stunned. 'You actually bet money? On me? Where did it come from?'

'I'll tell you everything when I can,' Ruby said. 'It's a long story, but yes, I put money on you. I knew you could knock Ronnie out once I'd seen the state of him at Railway Street. I had every faith in you after I saw you training in the pub yard.' She ran her fingers along his upper arm. 'Nice muscles, too,' she teased. 'But I'm still troubled over why you agreed to the fight.'

Stan and Ruby were sitting in the Queen's Head as drinks were taken in celebration of Stan's win. There was a small group in the pub: Polly and Jim, Mary and Arthur, Elsie and Bert and Ann. Michael was working the bar. Stan nodded towards Ann, who was sipping a small glass of stout.

'Where's the whippet man gone?'

Ruby looked around the pub. 'Isn't he here?'

'There's no sign of him,' Stan said, turning his head from Ann so she couldn't hear his words. 'I heard he did a runner with the money, without paying up the bets placed on me. It's lucky you caught him in the Toll Bar and he paid you your winnings before he skipped town.'

Ruby glanced at Ann and sighed. 'Never mind the whippet man. I want to know why you took the fight on in the first place.'

Stan took a long drink from his pint and set it slowly on the table in front of him. Then he put his arm around Ruby's shoulders and looked deep into her eyes. 'I did it for you,' he said.

Ruby was startled. 'Me?'

'I didn't want to fight,' Stan said. 'And I wasn't going to. I was determined not to let Ronnie provoke me. But that night in the pub, he went too far. He said things he shouldn't have.'

'About what?'

'I didn't want to tell you this, Ruby, but he said things, bad things, about you and . . . and the miner,' he said, remembering not to use Gordon's name in front of Ruby. 'I couldn't let him get away with it, so now do you understand?'

Ruby felt tears prick her eyes, and she swallowed hard. 'You defended my honour, Stan, and I'll never forget it. But please, promise me one thing.'

'I'd promise you the moon if I could,' he said.

She smiled and snuggled in close. 'Promise me you'll never fight again.'

A cheeky smile played over his lips. 'We could make a pretty penny if I did.'

Ruby playfully nudged him with her elbow, then Stan turned towards her and brought his lips close to hers. 'Ruby?'

'Yes, Stan?'

'Will you marry me?'

Ruby felt as if her heart would burst. 'Yes,' she breathed as Stan's lips brushed hers.

They kissed, lost in their embrace. When they finally released each other, Stan called for everyone's attention. Ruby looked towards her mam, caught her eye and beamed.

'Everyone, I'd like to propose a toast,' Stan said.

'To Stan!' Polly called.

'No, Mam,' Stan said. 'To Stan and Ruby. I've just asked Ruby to be my wife, and she's agreed.'

Polly's mouth dropped open. Jim stepped forward.

'Raise your glasses, please,' he called. 'To my son and the best thing that's ever happened to him, Ruby Dinsdale! To Stan and Ruby!'

'Stan and Ruby!' everyone cried.

Mary and Arthur jumped up, hugging Ruby, wiping away tears of joy, shaking hands with Stan.

'Mikey!' Jim called. 'Drinks all round, on the house.'

Michael beamed from ear to ear at Ruby's news and began pulling pints for the men and half-pints for the women.

Arthur turned to Mary. 'I don't think you should have a beer, love. You know how you are once you've got a taste for ale. Maybe celebrate with another glass of lemonade?'

'I don't need anything more than lemonade to raise my spirits tonight,' Mary smiled.

Mary was lost in the joy of the moment, in the happiness of Ruby and Stan's news. 'I'll take a glass of cordial,' she said. 'That's how it'll be from now on.'

Arthur pulled her to him and hugged her tight.

As drinks were being poured and Elsie and Bert were

congratulating Stan and Ruby, a noise outside caught everyone's attention. Laughter and chat in the pub quietened as everyone listened.

'Is it the coppers?' Polly whispered.

Again the noise came, and this time it was clear what it was. Someone was knocking at the pub door, but it wasn't the hard knock of a policeman coming to find out what the pub was doing open in the early hours of Sunday. Everyone looked at Polly as she walked towards the door and shot the bolt. 'Gladys?' she said when she saw who it was. 'Come in.'

Gladys looked nervous and tired, and Ruby's heart dropped the minute she saw her. There could be only one reason for her to call at such an hour.

'I've come with news for Ruby,' she announced.

All eyes turned towards Ruby, who stepped forward and took her hands. 'Is it Abigail?'

Gladys bit her lip and nodded. 'I'm sorry, pet. She's gone.'

Ruby took the news stoically. She'd been expecting it for days. She'd been determined to be strong when it finally happened. She breathed deeply, trying to calm her racing heart. 'And Emily? Where's the baby?'

'The doctor's taken her to his house. She'll be safe there. She'll be looked after until . . .'

'Until Kate takes her? No, she can't live at Railway Street, not with Ronnie Clarke,' Ruby said. She felt shaky, her legs turned weak as the news of Abigail's death made itself felt.

'No.' Gladys squeezed Ruby's hands. 'Until other arrangements are made.'

'What other arrangements?' Ruby said.

'I hope they're not talking about giving the child away?' Stan said, concerned. He slid his arm around Ruby's shoulder. 'As if the poor little thing hasn't suffered enough.'

Gladys reached into her pocket and pulled out a small, folded piece of blue paper. 'Abigail asked me to give you this, but only after she'd passed. She was very clear on that; made me promise not to let you see it before she'd gone.'

Ruby stared at the notepaper, then slowly took it and sank into a chair.

'Michael, pour a brandy for your sister,' Arthur called.

Michael quickly placed a glass of amber liquid in front of Ruby, but she was too stunned to touch it. The note was still folded in her hands. Stan stood behind her and laid a hand on her shoulder.

Ruby unfolded the note. She recognised Abigail's handwriting. Her heart pounded as she read, her eyes racing over the words, her mind unable to take in the enormity of what was written there. Everyone in the pub stayed silent. Elsie and Bert snuggled close. Arthur reached for Mary's hand. Jim chewed ferociously on his pipe. Polly lifted her glass of stout and downed it in one.

At last Ruby raised her eyes to meet Stan's. 'She wants me to take Emily in.'

She heard a gasp. Whether it came from Polly or her mam, she couldn't tell.

'What about Kate?' Polly asked. 'She's the child's grandma. She's family. She should take her, surely? You can't possibly take the bairn on. There are places it can go – the hospital, surely? Or there are women who'll buy orphaned babies.'

'Mam, this is for me and Ruby to decide,' Stan said firmly.

Polly marched to the bar and refilled her glass.

Stan sat beside Ruby. 'May I?' he said, reaching for the note.

Ruby handed it over. Stan read each word, just as Ruby had done. When he reached the end, he looked at his mam, who was now standing behind the bar. 'Abigail's instructions are clear. The child is to see her grandma and know of her, but she's not to live with her or be left in her care.'

Elsie lifted her glass and locked eyes with her sister. 'She was always a bad 'un, that Kate,' she muttered darkly.

'Shocking,' Ann agreed.

'Dr Anderson and his wife will keep Emily for a few days, until something is decided,' Gladys said. 'Now if you'll excuse me, I must head home. Kate's . . . well, I'm sure you can imagine what kind of a state she's in. She's fragile enough as it is. I've told her she can stay with me as long as she needs to. I won't send her back to that vicious man.'

'Yes, of course,' Ruby said. 'Thank you, Gladys, for everything.'

'I'll keep you informed about funeral arrangements, once things are worked out,' Gladys said. And with that, she walked from the pub.

Ruby turned to Stan. 'Do you realise what this means?'

'Yes,' Stan said. 'And I still want to marry you, I still want to spend my life with you.'

'And Emily?'

'We need time to think it all through. But if we don't take her on, the only other option will be the hospital, where she could be taken by anyone. And neither of us would wish that for the child. I know how close you feel to her; you've told me many times. We'll talk it through while Emily is at Dr Anderson's house. And when we decide . . .' He squeezed Ruby's hand.

'When or if?' Ruby said. 'I adore Emily, you know that, but this has come out of the blue. We need time to think.'

'We'll help as much as we can,' Mary said.

'Can we take her in at our house, Mam, until Stan and I decide what to do?' Ruby asked.

She saw the worried look that passed between her parents. She knew the last thing her dad needed was a crying baby in the house while he was sleeping off his shift at the pit. With the money Ruby had won on the fight, there'd be a little extra cash to spare, but how long it would last with a baby to care for remained to be seen. It might not stretch as far as she'd hoped.

'We could set up a cot for her at the end of your bed,' Mary said, as encouragingly as she could. 'I'm sure we can work something out.'

'You'll do no such thing!' Polly called.

All eyes turned towards the bar, Polly's domain. She stood with her hands firmly on the bar top and her gaze fixed on Ruby and Stan.

'We've got rooms upstairs that don't get used. The baby can live with us, and Ruby can move in too,' she said.

Ruby saw Jim remove his pipe from his mouth. 'Poll, love, are you sure?' he said.

'I'm sure,' Polly replied. 'If it's what our Stan wants, then I'm certain.'

'It's what we both want, Mam,' Stan replied. Then he quickly glanced at Ruby. 'Isn't it?'

Ruby choked back her tears and nodded, speechless.

'Are you sure you've got room to take Ruby in?' Mary asked Polly.

Polly nodded. 'We used to be an inn many years ago, taking guests. There's room for the bairn, and for Ruby.'

'But . . . before Ruby and Stan are wed?' Mary said, shaking her head. 'It's not right.'

'They'll have separate rooms, Mary. There's a spare room for Ruby. Me and Jim will keep an eye on them, don't worry about that.' Stan and Ruby shared a smile as Polly continued. 'And when little Emma is—'

'Emily,' Stan said.

'When Emily's bigger, she'll have a room of her own, overlooking fields at the back.'

Ruby stood and walked towards the bar. She took Polly's hand where it lay on the bar top, then leaned across and kissed her on the cheek. 'Thank you,' she said.

Polly kept hold of Ruby's hand a few seconds longer than necessary as she whispered in her ear. 'But if you hurt our Stan or put one foot wrong, you and that miner's bairn will be out on the streets faster than your feet can carry you. You hear me, little Miss Ruby?'

'I hear you,' Ruby replied.

Polly forced a smile on her face and let go of Ruby's hand. 'Good,' she said. 'And now that we understand each other, there's a chance we might become friends.'

Chapter Forty-Seven

Ruby and Stan's wedding took place on Ruby's twentieth birthday, a cold day in late October. Stan waited with Reverend Daye at the front of the church. He was nervous, and kept looking around, wondering where Ruby was and what could be holding her up. Reverend Daye cleared his throat and looked into the congregation. On the bride's side of the church sat Mary, done up in her best dress and hat. Her mam's red sea-glass brooch was pinned to her jacket lapel. Michael sat next to her, wearing one of Arthur's clean shirts. Mary had unpicked the hems of his trousers to make them fit his long legs. Next to Michael sat Grace, the nurse he'd met in the asylum grounds. The two of them held hands and smiled shyly at each other.

In the pew behind sat the two Miss Huttons, still dressed in their usual black, though Ann wore a red scarf around her neck. The whippet man hadn't been seen since the night of the fight, but his neckerchief had been found at the Blood Pit and handed over to her. Bert Collins sat between the sisters. He slid his hand on to Elsie's knee and she let it rest there as she and Bert exchanged a smile. In the next row sat Jean's boyfriend Ted alongside Jean's brothers and their wives and her parents. Gladys Smith sat alone behind Jean's family. She had her head bowed and her eyes closed, offering a silent prayer.

On the groom's side of the church, Polly and Jim sat with Stan's brothers, their wives and bairns. Polly was dressed in a violet dress with a matching stole around her shoulders. Jim was smart in a black suit and tie. He held his pipe in his hand, ready to stick it into his mouth the minute he left church. He was looking forward to the celebrations afterwards at the Queen's Head, where a party was planned for family, friends and their most loyal customers. Ronnie Clarke had been barred from the pub.

Right at the back of the church, two women sat together, apart from everyone else. They were Mrs Sowerby and local gossip Lil Mahone, who was never one to miss a Ryhope social event, whether she'd been invited or not.

'I don't know how she's got the nerve to get married in church after what happened with her miner and all,' Lil Mahone whispered.

'Her friend getting pregnant right under her nose,' Mrs Sowerby hissed. 'It's all wrong, if you ask me. I blame the football. She was too strident, that Abigail. And I notice her mam's not here. I thought she was a friend of the Dinsdales?'

'She's probably drunk somewhere, or out with that fella who knocks her about,' Lil said. She leaned closer. 'Not much of a turnout for Abigail's funeral, was there?'

Mrs Sowerby shook her head. 'Very disappointing, if you ask me.'

'Ruby Dinsdale's taken the miner's baby on as her own, you know,' Lil whispered.

'She never has!' Mrs Sowerby replied.

Lil nodded, a knowing look on her face. 'She's got the church booked for the christening next week. Course, she won't be Ruby Dinsdale after today, she'll be Ruby Hutchinson. And I heard that Stan Hutchinson not only allowed her to take the baby on, but was all for it, apparently.'

'No!' Mrs Sowerby was aghast. 'I can't wait to tell Renee Watson in the grocer's!'

At the front of the church, Reverend Daye faced the congregation. He kept glancing at the church door, ready to receive the signal from his curate that the bride was on her way. Finally the curate waved and the vicar breathed a sigh of relief. He nodded towards the organist, and as the unmistakable opening bars of the wedding march rang out, the vicar indicated for the congregation to stand.

'Oh, here she is. Just look at her,' Lil Mahone said.

But Mrs Sowerby didn't need to be told. Everyone was looking at Ruby. She floated into the church in a plain white gown that fell straight to the floor. She wore a white veil topped with a twist of white and yellow freesias. The same flowers were in her bouquet, which fell in a teardrop in front of her gown. Arthur was at her side, holding her arm, walking his daughter down the aisle on the most important day of her life. He felt like his heart was in danger of bursting with pride. Bridesmaid Jean walked slowly behind, carrying a small bouquet. When she reached the pew where Ted and her brothers were sitting, she winked at Ted and he smiled in return.

'It's getting chilly, they ought to close that door,' Lil Mahone moaned.

'I told you we should have sat closer to the front. We

wouldn't have felt the chill down there,' Mrs Sowerby replied.

And then the reason for the open door became clear.

It was the battered old pram that appeared first, trundling into the church after Ruby and Arthur. Lil Mahone gasped with shock. She nudged Mrs Sowerby with her elbow.

'Well, would you just look at that.'

'Some people have no shame,' Mrs Sowerby tutted.

Kate's hair was sleek and shiny, her face painted with rouge and powder. She was looking better than she'd done in months. And in the pram, baby Emily was sitting upright, smiling and gurgling for all the world to see. Kate brought the pram to a stop, then, as Ruby had asked, she turned it so that Emily faced the front of the church. She took her seat at the end of a pew and brought the pram alongside. At the church door, the curate was shooing away a large, skinny black dog. It had followed the wedding party all the way from Tunstall Street.

'Get away!' he called. Lady slunk away to a spot under a tree.

At the front of the church, Ruby reached the vicar and held her bouquet tight. She looked at Stan and smiled through her veil. Stan returned her smile and took a deep breath. Arthur straightened his shoulders. The organist lifted his fingers from the keys as the final notes floated up to the high ceiling. The vicar looked from Ruby to Stan.

'Ready?' he whispered

Stan nodded, Ruby too.

'Ladies and gentlemen,' Reverend Daye announced. 'Please be seated, and then we'll begin.'

The Miner's Lass

Bonus Material

Behind the Scenes of *The Miner's Lass*

Readers always ask how I dream up ideas for my books. It's a difficult question to answer, because as a writer, my mind is always making up stories, and it's often hard to know where ideas come from. Sometimes ideas come from overhearing a snippet of conversation on a bus. Sometimes I get ideas for stories from a picture I come across while researching the village of Ryhope at the end of World War One. It could be a picture of an old woman, say, with her arms crossed under her stout bosom, glaring at what would have been an unfamiliar camera, as if challenging it to a fight. I love pictures like this, the woman's face stern and suspicious, as if she's ready to give the photographer a harsh word the minute the photograph is taken.

But the idea for *The Miner's Lass* didn't come from photographs or dialogue, it came from three words on an old map.

When researching my books set in old Ryhope, I always use the Ordnance Survey map of the village in 1919. And as I write these words to you now, I am sitting at my desk underneath that map; it's pinned to the wall of my writing room. The map shows streets and shops that are now long gone but I bring back to life in my books. The map includes names of pubs, many of which still exist in Ryhope.

However, one pub on the map is called The Toll Bar. It was demolished some years ago and, in its place, now stands a small apartment complex. However, on the 1919 map of Ryhope, The Toll Bar is not only situated in a prominent spot on the road between Ryhope and Sunderland, but there's an interesting addition at the back of the pub. It's those three words I mentioned, and they read 'Old Sand Pit'.

Glenda Young

Research at Sunderland Antiquarian Society showed me that the 'Old Sand Pit' was a piece of rough ground at the back of the pub. Unremarkable, and not enough to inspire a novel, I'm sure you'll agree. However, when I learned that the sand pit was nicknamed 'The Blood Pit' by locals, I was intrigued and a shiver ran down my spine. What was a blood pit? Why was blood mentioned? And why was it near a pub? I had to find out, of course!

It turned out that The Blood Pit was where bareknuckle fighting took place. It sounds a gruesome place, where blood was spilled, and even lives were lost. Once I knew what The Blood Pit was, my imagination went wild. I could see two men fighting, shirts off, angry, sweating, but why were they fighting? Was money involved? Were they fighting over a woman?

That was when I created Ruby Dinsdale, a miner's daughter, who I decided would be the reason for the fight. Once I had that germ of an idea, I created Ruby's family – her coalmining dad and brother, her loving mam and their nosy but supportive neighbours. Then I brought to life Ruby's friends, and a whole community sprung up around her. More characters made their way into the story as I plotted, and yes, that woman with the stern face and her arms crossed, the one who was glaring into the camera, helped to inspire me too.

I've been as true to miners' lives and families in 1919 as I could be in this book. I've done a lot of research which underpins the main story points while allowing my imagination to fly and drama to ensue. I hope you've enjoyed reading it and that you've enjoyed finding out how the book came into being, inspired by three words on an old map. You can view the map online here: http://bit.ly/TheBloodPit.

Glenda Young

All About Ryhope

Ryhope is a village on the northeastern coast, south of the city of Sunderland in Tyne and Wear. The first mention of Ryhope was in 930AD when the Saxon King Athelstan gave the parish of South Wearmouth to the See of Durham. King Athelstan's name lives on in Ryhope with a street named after him – Athelstan Rigg.

The name Ryhope is an Old English name which means 'rugged valley'. Originally Ryhope is recorded as being called *Rive hope* and has also been recorded as *Refhoppa*, *Reshop* and *Riopp*.

Ryhope developed as a farming community and was popular as a sea bathing resort. However, in 1856 sinking operations reached coal seams deep beneath the magnesian limestone and Ryhope grew as a coal mining village. Ryhope had two separate railways with their own train stations, putting Ryhope within easy commuting distance of Sunderland. By 1905 electric trams also reached Ryhope from Sunderland. The coal mine closed in 1966, marking the end of an era for Ryhope.

For more on Ryhope's past, present and future, Sunderland City Council have a very interesting planning document showing historic pictures. You can find it at http://bit.ly/RyhopeHistory.

And if you'd like to know more about the village of Ryhope, here are some good websites you might like to explore for historic maps, guided walks and a visit to the ever-popular Pumping Station at Ryhope Engines Museum.

Glenda Young

A guided walk around Ryhope – From agriculture to coal
http://bit.ly/RyhopeWalks

Historic map of Ryhope
http://bit.ly/RyhopeMap

Ryhope Engines Museum
http://www.ryhopeengines.org.uk/

Chapter 1

Helen Dexter was sitting on the window seat at the Seaview Hotel, looking out over the sea. The Seaview was her home, a three-storey, ten-room hotel on Scarborough's North Bay. She'd been sitting there all night, gazing out of the window, a bottle of whisky by her side.

It wasn't something she made a habit of, sitting up all night drinking. But then it wasn't every day that she held a memorial service for her late husband, who'd been the love of her life. Helen and Tom had known each other for over thirty years: attended the same schools, gone to the same youth clubs, hung around with the same friends. But it wasn't until their late teens that they finally started dating and became inseparable. Everyone said they were made for each other. They married on a warm July day when she was twenty-one and Tom twenty-three. On their wedding day, Helen pledged her love for Tom in front of their families and friends, vowing to love him and cherish him 'till death us do part'.

How the years had flown by since. Helen was forty-eight now and Tom would have been celebrating his fiftieth birthday in April, a milestone that would now go unmarked.

After Tom's memorial, Helen had invited close friends and family to the Seaview for a bite to eat as a way to say a final farewell to the man they'd all adored. Around her now lay the detritus of half-eaten sausage rolls and glasses stained by wine and beer. Her best friend, Marie, had offered to clean up before she left, but Helen wouldn't hear of it. As the afternoon had dissolved into evening, she had tried hard to disguise how relieved she was when everyone started to leave. She wanted to be on her own, for she had a lot on her mind.

She slid her legs along the window seat and noticed a ladder in her stockings above her right knee. Her calves shone in sheer black nylon seven-denier, smooth as silk and now ruined. She pushed her bobbed hair behind her ears and caught a reflection of herself in the window. Her big brown eyes stared back at her; she was surprised that she didn't look as tired as she felt. Her black jacket hung on a chair and her black shoes lay at the end of the window seat. She'd kicked them off after everyone had left, but when Suki had padded into the lounge, she'd had to lift them from the floor. Suki had a thing about shoes; she liked to chew them and Helen had to be careful about what she left lying around. Suki was sprawled on the floor like a pool of liquid caramel. She was a retired racing greyhound, all long limbs and soulful eyes.

Helen turned back to look out of the window. The sun was beginning to rise now, turning the sky milky blue.

Tom had been ill for months, cancer eating away at him at a cruel, relentless pace. When Helen could no longer manage his pain and care, he'd been moved to St Paul's Hospice. She'd visited daily, sometimes taking Suki so that Tom could see the dog through the floor-to-ceiling window by his bed. Suki would stand outside, cocking her head, staring in at him. As he'd neared the end of his life, Helen had promised him she'd carry on running the

Seaview, but he'd been too ill to notice her cross her fingers when the words slipped from her lips.

The small, family-only funeral at St Mary's Church that had marked the end of Tom's life had done him proud. Afterwards, at the crematorium, his favourite hymn had been sung, hugs given and tears wiped away. When his coffin had disappeared behind the curtains, the first soulful notes of his favourite Elvis ballad had played, his only request. He had been an Elvis fan all his life. On the wall of the lounge in the Seaview was a jukebox filled entirely with Elvis songs, but it hadn't been touched since the day Tom was moved to the hospice. Now, more than three months after the funeral, Helen still couldn't bring herself to play it for fear of the emotions that would overwhelm her if she did.

She took a sip of whisky. After the funeral, she had felt unable to cope with her grief. So when Tom's sister Tina had invited her to stay with her and her family on their farm in a remote part of Scotland, she had jumped at the chance. The farm was in the middle of nowhere, far from Scarborough, far from the sea, far from everything that reminded her of Tom. She'd locked up the hotel, bundled Suki into her car, packed a suitcase, put her foot to the accelerator and driven like a woman possessed. She couldn't get away quickly enough.

She'd told Tina she'd only stay a few days, but those days became weeks and ended up turning into three months. Tina had insisted she stay for Christmas, and Helen gratefully accepted her invitation; she couldn't face returning home to spend Christmas on her own. Being on the farm proved restorative for her. She'd helped feed the chickens, and walked the dogs through fields and along streams each morning. Being around Tina's teenage sons, with their energy and vitality, had helped bring her out of herself.

When she'd finally felt strong enough to return to Scarborough, she'd decided to hold a memorial service for her beloved husband, a chance to fully celebrate his life now that she was about to face her future alone. However, something at the back of her mind was troubling her now as she remembered the guests arriving at the Seaview for drinks. It took her a few moments to remember what it was. Two of her best friends, Sue and Bev, had seemed distant with each other and she couldn't figure out why. Had she imagined it, or did Sue make a deliberate show of walking out of the lounge each time Bev walked in? She shook her head to dismiss the thought. She had more pressing things on her mind.

She set her glass on the table and ran her hands over her face. She still had her make-up on, her mask from the day before. But there was no one here to see how crumpled she knew she must look, no matter what her reflection in the window said. In front of a mirror in the harsh light of day, she knew her soft, round face would be pale, and the skin under her eyes dark from lack of sleep. Her plan was to take Suki for a walk, then head to bed to sleep. The Seaview had no guests booked in. Once Tom had taken ill, Helen hadn't the heart or the energy to run the place; it became too difficult even with the help of her staff. She had cancelled all the bookings, emailing the news that due to a family situation the Seaview was taking a break.

Now it was early March, the Easter holidays were around the corner and the holiday season was about to begin, but for the first time in decades, the Seaview was quiet. When asked by disappointed guests, whose holidays she'd had to cancel, if she could recommend somewhere else for them to stay, she gave them the number of the hotel next door. This was the four-star Vista del Mar, run by Miriam Jones, a woman who thought herself and her hotel a cut above Helen and Tom's three-star Seaview. But it wasn't Helen and Tom's now; it was just Helen's, and that scared her more than she dared admit. Because despite the promise she'd given Tom on his deathbed, she wasn't sure she wanted to keep it. What kind of life waited for her on her own in a hotel that catered for families and fun?

She glanced out of the window again. The tide was rolling in, frothy waves breaking. Early-morning surfers, clad head to toe in black to keep out the worst of the North Sea's icy chill, were making their way to the beach.

Helen often felt as if her heart would never recover from losing Tom. He'd been her husband, lover, soulmate and best friend. He had been her life, her everything, for decades. In the early days of their marriage, she'd fallen pregnant twice, but hadn't been able to carry her babies, first a daughter and then a son, to full term. The raw pain never left her, and she and Tom agreed they wouldn't put themselves through more agony by trying again. That was when they'd bought the Seaview. Now, with Tom gone, could she carry on running it alone? Did she even want to?

Don't miss Glenda Young's page-turning Helen Dexter cosy mystery series!

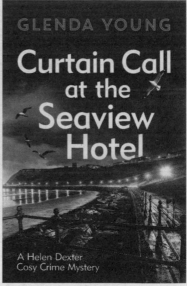

'I loved this warm, humorous and involving whodunnit with its host of engaging characters and atmospheric Scarborough setting' Clare Chase

HEADLINE

Don't miss the other enthralling sagas from Glenda Young!

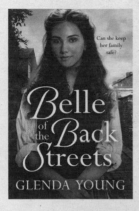
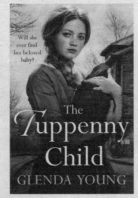
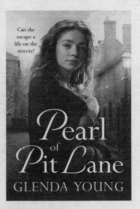

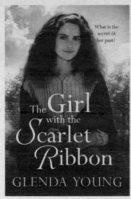

'Real sagas with female characters right at the heart'
Jane Garvey, *Woman's Hour*

© Les Mann

Glenda Young credits her local library in the village of Ryhope, where she grew up, for giving her a love of books. She still lives close by in Sunderland and often gets her ideas for her stories on long bike rides along the coast. A life-long fan of *Coronation Street*, she runs two hugely popular fan websites.

For updates on what Glenda is working on, visit her website **glendayoungbooks.com** and to find out more find her on Facebook/**GlendaYoungAuthor** and Twitter **@flaming_nora**.